THE STONE
LOVES THE
WORLD

ALSO BY BRIAN HALL

FICTION

The Saskiad

The Dreamers

*I Should Be Extremely Happy
in Your Company*

Fall of Frost

NONFICTION

*Stealing from a Deep Place:
Travels in Southeastern Europe*

*The Impossible Country: A Journey
Through the Last Days of Yugoslavia*

*Madeleine's World: A Biography
of a Three-Year-Old*

THE STONE LOVES THE WORLD

Brian Hall

VIKING

VIKING
An imprint of Penguin Random House LLC
penguinrandomhouse.com

Library of Congress Cataloging-in-Publication Data
Names: Hall, Brian, 1959– author.
Title: The stone loves the world / a novel by Brian Hall.
Description: New York: Viking, [2021]
Identifiers: LCCN 2020046556 (print) | LCCN 2020046557 (ebook) | ISBN
9780593297223 (hardcover) | ISBN 9780593297230 (ebook)
Classification: LCC PS3558.A363 S76 2021 (print) | LCC PS3558.A363
(ebook) | DDC 813/.54—dc23
LC record available at https://lccn.loc.gov/2020046556
LC ebook record available at https://lccn.loc.gov/2020046557

Printed in the United States of America
1st Printing

DESIGNED BY MEIGHAN CAVANAUGH

For Elizabeth,
who grew up two miles from the
Holmdel Horn Antenna

운명이 아닐까 싶어

사랑해

The thrushes sing as the sun is going,
And the finches whistle in ones and pairs,
And as it gets dark loud nightingales
        In bushes
Pipe, as they can when April wears,
    As if all Time were theirs.

These are brand new birds of twelve-months' growing,
Which a year ago, or less than twain,
No finches were, nor nightingales,
        Nor thrushes,
But only particles of grain,
    And earth, and air, and rain.

—THOMAS HARDY

PART
ONE

Tuesday, February 16, 2016

Feeling like a freak, she almost ran out of the office, rode the B62 home to pack her bare minimum shit, hopped the G and the E, and here she is under the sign of the dog.

"Where to?"

The lean animal devours miles on the wall behind the bored woman's head. Ten customer service windows, two open. Possible combinations of two from a set of ten is forty-five, four times five is twenty, largest prime number less than twenty is nineteen, nineteenth letter is S.

"Seattle."

"Seattle, Washington?"

"Is there another one?"

"I meant, that's a long trip."

Woman is smiling. Probably pointless friendliness.

"Depends what you're comparing it to. Can I get a ticket to Saturn?"

Now a puzzled look.

"Never mind."

The woman, like a Skee-Ball machine, produces a chain of tickets, z-folds and hands them over. Liquid scarlet inch-long artificial nails, gold ring on fourth finger with bulky ruby or rhodolite garnet or chromium paste. The gleam of it is terribly distracting.

She takes the ticket, finds the gate. There's no such thing as luck, but the next departure is only seventy minutes away. First stop, Baltimore. The narrow sprung device bolted to the wall is deliberately designed to be uncomfortable (this fucking world), so she unrolls her pad and settles on the floor. The tiled wall is white, with a black border cutting in at the corners to isolate white squares, very common, there must be a name for it. She googles, finds nothing.

She would take out her Newman, but can't concentrate. Well she certainly fucked up everything, didn't she? Instead of escaping on the bus, she could escape under it. They're everywhere in the city, just wait at a corner and launch yourself so that the two vectors of motion intersect. She envisions the shining wall of white steel and glass humping up and over, then gulping as the driver hits the brakes too late. Windshield wipers like praying hands. Brainless bystanders screaming, fainting. Most people call this ideation. Mathematicians call it "doing a Ramanujan."

So why doesn't she? Cowardice?

A man waiting in line at the next gate keeps looking at her. Twenties, scruffy beard, skinny jeans, dun winter jacket. She wants to inform him, the reason you have skin is so that you will always know where you end and the rest of the world begins. Nature provides this service free of charge. He should read Wishner (everyone should read Wishner): "From the Eastern chipmunk we have learned the lesson of how an animal survives and prospers by minding its own business."

Ambling to the corner, minding her own business. The city where no one notices you. The bus approaching, forearm across her eyes, goodbye, cruel world! Maybe it's not cowardice that's stopping her, but a modicum of dignity. Too dramatic, too public. Calling attention to herself, the way her mother likes to do. She has never needed anyone, witnesses included. A concealing cornfield and a combine harvester. A long-abandoned vat of acid in a crumbling factory in the Rust Belt. A turn-out in the Cascades with a spectacular view.

What she needs is a little time to think.

1965–1976

When Mark was five years old, his parents took him and his older sister to the New York World's Fair. They stayed in a dark house that belonged to some lady his mother knew. The front yard sloped down to a busy street. During the boring evenings when they talked, his parents seemed to think he would play in this yard. But *he* could see: the smallest stumble and he'd roll, roll faster, fall flailing and die under screeching tires.

On the way to the fair, subway doors opened and closed automatically. A family entering a car could be sliced in two, parents and older sister in the accelerating train looking back at the orphaned five-year-old on the platform.

The fair was bright and hot. His mother called it "sweltering," which made him think uneasily of swimming in sweat. There was a big metal Earth called the Unisphere. It had three rings that his dad said represented satellites named Echo, Telstar 1, and Telstar 2. His dad said the theme of the fair was "Peace Through Understanding," and both of his parents laughed. Mark sat with his mother in a boat that floated through the Disney pavilion, while puppets twirled, clacked, and sang "It's a Small, Small World." When they sang, their faces split in half. Mark liked the igloos.

Everyone was eating Belgian Waffles. They were big fluffy seat cushions with pits to hold all the strawberries in syrup and whipped cream Mark wanted. He flapped his arms. His father told him to pipe down.

In the sweltering heat, on a stretch of bright sidewalk, he vomited up a Belgian Waffle.

The Ferris wheel was a like a big automobile tire. Susan rocked the gondola, but Mark was scared and Dad told her to stop. There was a time capsule that would be opened in five thousand years. There were long lines in the glare. He held his mother's hand while Susan fidgeted in and out of the line and he worried that a man in uniform would appear and announce that she had lost her place, and they would all have to go to the end of the line and it would be her fault but she would never admit it.

Mark loved the ramps, which rose in curvy sweeps and sweepy curves, like flight paths of Whisperjets taking off. There were escalators, monorails, elevators, cable cars, floating seats, rising stands. "Man conquers gravity!" Susan read from a sign. "Pretty corny." Mark fought with her over who could be first to pretend to drive the luxury convertible on the Magic Skyway. He cried and got his way because he was younger. Susan was ten and should know better. The car floated up a ramp and went through the time barrier. Animatronic Triceratops babies broke out of shells; a Brontosaurus in a swamp lifted its head, chewing weeds. Then came the dawn of man. Cavemen invented the wheel and fought a mammoth. To Mark's disbelieving delight, one father caveman was rubbing his butt in front of a campfire.

Even better was Futurama. Mark climbed on the conveyor belt and drank in the dioramas, while the chair he sat in whispered in his ear about the wonders to come. Transports on balloon wheels served lunar mining colonies. Submarine trains carried riches from the ocean floor. The best came at the end: the City of Tomorrow! Streamlined cars moved soundlessly down automated highways. Elevated disks of parkland and arcades led to clean skyscrapers that glowed with yellow squares of rooms and offices.

Mark's whole being ached.

IN FIRST GRADE, he felt serious and adult. The desks were arranged in a grid. The teacher, Miss Peabody, showed the class how to write the full heading that went on top of your schoolwork, if you already knew how to write, which Mark did: Mark Fuller, 1st Grade, Miss Peabody, September 8, 1965.

Writing the year on an official document made him think about it for the first time. He had been born in 1959. He'd just turned six. By the end of this grade, he would be writing "1966" on the heading. 1959 and 1965 would never come back. When he got to Susan's age, it would be 1970.

How strange.

Then it occurred to him that he would probably still be alive, and not even very old, in the year 2000. Which meant that, one day, he would live in the City of Tomorrow. Happiness flooded him. It was a long way off, but he was content to wait. Waiting, in and of itself, had always made him happy.

THERE WAS A NEW SHOW on TV that Mom thought he might like called *Lost in Space*. It started at 7:30 and was over by 8:00, so he would have time to get ready for bed afterward and have his light out by his bedtime at 8:30. At eight, Mom called downstairs, where he was kneeling on the living room floor with his elbows on the hassock, his face near the screen. Since the show was over, he should come up and brush his teeth.

But the show wasn't over. There had been a mistake in the *TV Guide*. The show was an hour long. And at some point during the previous half hour, Mark had had a revelation: *Lost in Space* was the most important thing in the world.

Mark had always obeyed his bedtime, but he howled upstairs to his mother: he couldn't!

Maybe she heard the true note of anguish in his voice. For the first— and it would prove to be the last—time of his childhood, she relaxed the bedtime rule. He rushed upstairs at 8:30, ready to perform speedy, grateful miracles, and his light was out by 8:40. For the rest of *Lost in Space*'s three-year run, he watched it (elbows on the living room hassock, face inches from the screen) in his pajamas with his teeth brushed.

FOR CHRISTMAS THAT YEAR, he got *The Giant Golden Book of Dinosaurs and Other Prehistoric Reptiles*. He loved the biggest ones, the sauropods— Brachiosaurus and Diplodocus and Brontosaurus—the ones that stood in swamps and chewed weeds. He loved their long necks and tails and their plump strong legs and circular flat-bottomed feet that looked like the hassock. He loved their smooth gray skin. His favorite was Brontosaurus, Thunder Lizard. "Like the two other giants, she is a peace-loving plant-eater," the *Golden Book* said. The drawing showed her being attacked by Allosaurus. "He likes meat—great chunks of fresh meat!" In the drawing, she was up to her shoulders in water. Her long neck was stretched back in a sweeping curve, her long tail curled around her, trying to protect. You couldn't see her eyes, but the straight line of her jaw made her look sad. Allosaurus was biting her neck, and his clawed foot was digging into her back. Blood was dripping down the smooth skin. "What a battle this is!" But Brontosaurus only wanted to chew weeds. "Brontosaurus cannot save herself now. But as she sinks, she throws her great weight upon the killer. Allosaurus, with his jaws still locked about Bronto's neck, is pushed beneath the water. Thirty tons pin him, helpless, in the sand."

So they both died. But only one of them deserved it.

When Mark took the book out, he usually turned to this page. He stared. He read the text again and looked again at the picture. The rain clouds were dark and mottled. The weeds were bright green. The Allosaurus had evil yellow eyes. You couldn't see *her* eyes. Sometimes it made Mark cry. "But soon the water rolls peacefully over the hidden forms. Slowly a layer of shifting sand blankets killer and victim alike . . . And so the years roll on." This made Mark sadder. Did her pain matter? She was there, and then not there. The years rolled on. Her suffering, like 1965, would never come back.

That winter his parents gave him and Susan a talk about fire safety. If they smelled smoke or saw a fire, they shouldn't stop to put on clothes or get anything, *anything*, they should run straight out of the house.

Mark nodded. He had earned their trust. They grilled Susan, whom they suspected of inattention and disobedience. Susan gave Dad the runaround about what if she was in the bathtub, she wasn't going outside bare naked. Susan was close to getting popped. Mark, meanwhile, was surprised to find himself making a mental reservation. He even seemed to be feeling a sly pleasure from the thought that he knew something his parents didn't know, and that the reward of earning their trust was that they would never suspect he would harbor such a thought. Yes, of course he would run straight out of the house—except for a lightning-fast secret diversion to the toy closet, where (he knew exactly where it was, he always put it in the same place) he would grab the *Golden Book of Dinosaurs* and carry her out of the fire.

Was the luxury convertible that he'd driven on the Magic Skyway a Chevy or a Ford? Dad said Fords had better bodies, but Chevys had better engines, and that was why he always bought a Chevy.

"It was neither, dumbass," Susan said. "It was a Lincoln."

. . .

IN SECOND GRADE, the superintendent's son came in talking about a Vulcan nerve pinch and started tossing other kids around. He spent the day trying to draw what he said was the coolest spaceship ever, but couldn't get it right, so he got frustrated and scary.

Later, Mark learned that *Star Trek* came on at 8:30 on Thursdays, which was past his bedtime. One night he woke up with a stomachache and came downstairs and found his father watching the show. He was allowed to lie on the couch for a few minutes. A man wearing those futuristic clothes like pajamas was running through the woods and then a piece of metal like a TV antenna popped up from behind a rock. Mark thought, "This is the kind of show grown-ups watch," thus absolving himself from having to spend any time worrying about it, and fell asleep.

MOM BROUGHT MARK to an optometrist. He picked nice frames with dark plastic on the top and clear gray plastic on the bottom, because they looked like what scientists on TV wore. The optometrist called them "classic."

He thought glasses would bring everything closer, but instead they made things slightly smaller and clearer. It was astonishing. He wondered how it worked.

He started taking piano lessons. He practiced on his mother's Cable & Sons upright.

There were eighty-eight keys on the piano, and there were also eighty-eight constellations, which was pretty interesting. Mom had wanted to be an astronomer, but she also wanted children. "I made the right choice," she said. He practiced in the dining room while Mom cooked in the kitchen. "That's a wrong note!" she called out, whenever necessary.

.   .   .

"I LOVED SUMMER CAMP," Mom said, and showed him the brochure. Up until this moment, Mark had assumed he would also love summer camp, but when he looked at the pictures he saw gangs of smirking, confident boys holding balls of various kinds, and he got a dreadful sinking suspicion that camp would be like two straight weeks of gym class.

He was eight. Mom sewed his name tag into all his clothes. She gave him a white cotton laundry bag with a drawstring. She bought him a forest-green sleeping bag with ducks and hunters printed on the flannel inside.

He went.

He had never before experienced the fear and misery of the next two weeks. The kids were bullies. The counselors were inattentive and unjust. One of the latter, refusing to listen to an elementary fact regarding the cause of a disagreement, grabbed the back of Mark's neck and pinched it so hard that Mark was sore for two days afterward. One of the meanest boys could hawk up and send flying gobs of spit so voluminous and solid they looked like milkweed pods. Mark dreamed long afterward of those floating, saggy, soggy hammocks of mean-spirited spit.

WHEN MARK WAS TEN, his father bought a TV that fit on the kitchen table. Now they had two black-and-whites. Dad scoffed at color TVs, with their red and green ghosts. "They haven't figured out the technology yet," he said, chuckling.

The new TV had a second dial that you turned to reach strange new channels called UHF, which stood for Ultra High Frequency. It turned out the old familiar channels had always been VHF, which meant Very High Frequency, though no one had had to call them that before UHF showed up. The existence of this second dial bothered Mark. It hinted at future additional complications. Also, the two UHF channels had weirdly high numbers: 38 and 56. Why were they so far apart? You could click the dial to dozens of other numbers and you got only static. It seemed like a wasteful system.

But Mark reconciled himself to it because Channel 56 was showing reruns of *Lost in Space.* They cut off the credits and music at the end, which was extremely annoying.

When he had watched the show at age six, in the living room, Susan would stand behind him sometimes and sneer. "That just wouldn't happen." Or, "For chrissake, they don't even know the difference between a galaxy and a solar system." Or a final verdict, when the pretty melody came on during the warm family moments: "Vomitous." But now, passing through the kitchen, age fifteen, she was no longer mean. She'd say, "That's Zachary Smith, right? He's an amazing asshole, right?" Or, "Have you noticed the guy playing the dad has this one little spot of gray hair on one side? I wonder why they don't dye that?"

When she lingered like this, Mark felt proud that the show was holding her attention. He hoped she would sit down after a minute and get absorbed, and then they could watch it together and he could fill her in. If a stupid bit happened to come along—he had begun to notice these—he mentally winced, even though she didn't pounce. But she always walked out after a little while, and it pained him to think that the show had failed her, and at the same time he wanted to protect the show from her indifference. He wished there were a version of the show with all the great parts and none of the stupid bits.

Now it was his mother who sneered. "That family deserves everything they get," she'd say, passing through the room. "Smith betrays them over and over, and they still save him." The boy in the show, Will Robinson, was Mark's favorite character. He had dreamed many times that Will and he were friends. He'd even had a couple of dreams about Will that were kind of weird and intimate. Will was Zachary Smith's friend, and always championed the idea of forgiving him after one of his betrayals. "That kid is as soft as a peeled grape," his mother said. Regarding Zachary Smith, she always proposed the same solution: "I'd kick him in the balls and shove him out the airlock." Mark didn't mind these comments, the way he would if Susan or Dad said them. Mom hated all TV.

Around this time, he got a Frisbee for his birthday. He loved it because it looked sort of like the *Jupiter 2*. Mark couldn't think of a more evocative name for a spaceship than "*Jupiter 2*." Sometimes he said the words under his breath and was filled with an unnameable emotion, like a key fitting a keyhole in his mind. He liked drawing the *Jupiter 2*. If you drew it right, it was wonderfully plump and yet pointy at the rim, sleekly curved yet also paneled in an indescribably pleasing way.

On the show, the ship always crash-landed at an angle behind a rocky ridge, so you never saw the impact itself. Mark practiced in the side yard and got pretty good at throwing the Frisbee in a tilted arc. If he got the range right, the Frisbee flew high, then hesitated, slid off the curve and came angling down behind the bushes near the house. When that happened, it looked almost exactly like the crashing ship in the show. Mark would investigate the site: suspended in twigs (the Robinsons clambering down, John helping Maureen, Don helping Judy), or cushioned in moss, or resting half on a little stone that looked exactly like the huge boulder it was supposed be. He would evaluate the site for its potential as a makeshift settlement. Then he'd throw the Frisbee again.

HIS FATHER WAS a physicist. When Mark asked him what that meant, he said, "A physicist is someone who figures out why some things stand up and other things fall down."

Mark was bothered by what he suspected was condescension in that answer.

.   .   .

FOR CHRISTMAS Mark got a book called *The World of Tomorrow*. He recognized the cover—it was a photograph of the City of Tomorrow that he'd seen at the World's Fair five years ago. Most of the book was about other things; he never read those parts. Instead, he looked at the photos of the City, reading and rereading the accompanying text. "Vacations are very popular in our World of Tomorrow, for every worker has almost five months off each year. Some people do not work, but prefer to get along on the government's guaranteed annual income of more than $10,000 a year."

Scrutinized at length and up close, the City was as clean and inviting as he remembered. Little trees and clipped grass and little people and futuristic bubble cars sitting in circular white parking garages. Rosy evening light. People promenading on plazas. Circular buildings, circular fountains. Mark kept gazing at the skyscrapers with their sides that curved out toward the bottom, their random pattern of lit and unlit windows. He gazed at the windows, those translucent squares of uniform yellow light, and became filled with that same unnameable emotion.

THAT SUMMER CAMP two years ago, his mother told him, had just been the wrong one. This new camp was recommended by the parents of one of Mark's friends at school. Doug had gone there last year and loved it, and he would be going again. Mark was going for a month this time and it would be great. Mom's favorite memories of childhood were all from her times at summer camp.

When he arrived, Mark learned that he and Doug were assigned to different cabins, but he was assured this would make little difference. He waved goodbye to his parents.

For the next four weeks, Mark hardly ever saw Doug. Doug was good at baseball and it turned out he had sports buddies from last year. Mark couldn't throw, bat, or field. Doug distanced himself. Mark was also terrible at volleyball, basketball, soccer, tennis, and archery. He had the further disadvantage of crying when kids made fun of his tendency to cry whenever they made fun of him.

His cabin of ten was ruled by Kenny, a small boy with a pale face and dark curls who had dirty magazines in his footlocker, and who lay in bed wriggling under his blanket and cooing in a baby voice about the enormous boner he'd just gotten. Like bullies in books, he had two big cabinmates who served as his enforcers. Kenny was kind of a genius. He got all the kids in the cabin to do what he wanted by continually holding out the slight possibility of being accepted by him, and thus of his calling off his two goons, who did whatever he wanted with an unquestioning devotion that puzzled Mark. Between them, they could have torn Kenny in half, so why didn't they? There came the day when Steve, the only other kid who had consistently been at the bottom of the pecking order along with Mark, and who Mark had occasionally looked to for a spark of compassion, offering Steve the same—there came the day, about two weeks in, when Steve also begged excitedly to see Kenny's latest boner, and Mark was alone.

One day, Mark came into the cabin to find it empty except for one of the goons. He hesitated at the door, but the goon waved him in. This one was Jeff. He was looking through the other goon's footlocker. That one was Russell. "You're not such a bad kid," Jeff said. "Kenny's a little prick, isn't he?" Relief and hope warmed Mark. Might this be the wished-for rebellion of the goons? He didn't say anything. He stood in the glow of Jeff's humanity. Jeff was still rummaging in Russell's locker. He pulled out some candy bars from Russell's care package. He unwrapped one and took a bite. "You want one?"

"No thanks."

"Come on. No one will know."

"No, that's OK."

"Russell's taken some from your care package, you know. And from mine, too, that asshole. That's why I'm getting back at him. Don't be a wuss. Take it."

Mark didn't want to jeopardize this fragile new bond. "OK." He reached out his hand.

There was a hoot of glee from the platform above where the tents were stored, and down hopped Russell. "You fuckin' stealing from me, fag?" He came scooting over the intervening cots and footlockers with simian agility, arms already pinwheeling for the pummeling. As Mark went down, terrified and despairing, a part of his mind considered the possibility that the goons were smarter than he'd given them credit for.

HE COLLECTED MATCHBOX CARS. His parents gave him two or three every birthday and Christmas, and he also bought them with his allowance at Woolworth's. One car cost fifty cents. They were made in England, by the Lesney company. His mother always said (he was beginning to realize that whatever Mom said, she *always* said) that Matchbox cars were better than Hot Wheels. "Look at that detailing on the front grill. Whereas, look at this flakey chrome crap. Leave it to the Great American Businessman to make a shitty toy car."

Mark's favorites were a copper-colored 1950 Vauxhall Cresta, a gold Opel Diplomat, a cherry Rolls-Royce Silver Shadow, a green Ferrari Berlinetta, and a royal blue Iso Grifo. There was something about the vibrant color of the Iso Grifo that particularly entranced him. It glowed like a deep pond inviting him to jump in.

One of his blankets was made of a lightweight artificial material that, when you lifted it at its midpoint and let go, would settle into perfect mounds and curvy channels. Bowl-shaped depressions became home sites, whereas channels were roads working their way over the hills. He drove the cars along the channels, admiring the way they handled the curves, which demonstrated their precision engineering.

On his eleventh birthday he got an electric train, along with a signal tower his father had preliminarily made from a kit. The tower was beautiful, with a red brick storage room on the first floor and a green clapboard office above. There were window-shade decals in the upper windows and a tiny broom and lantern glued immaculately next to the door. Over the following months Mark used his allowance to buy other model buildings and tried to construct them as heartbreakingly neatly as his father had done, never quite succeeding. His father had chosen HO gauge, which fit the Matchbox cars pretty well, and now Mark had a train and buildings and cars and crossings and crossing gates, and he set them up in different configurations. The train circled, the cars waited at the crossings, then crossed. The Vauxhall Cresta turned right, accelerating. The Iso Grifo parked by the old mill. It all gave him that unnameable emotion. He could almost believe it was real, and the closer he got to that fugitive belief, the more he felt that feeling.

He added buildings and cars. Now he had a Mercedes-Benz ambulance and a Ford Galaxie police car. He had a cattle truck with a cow and three calves. One of the calves sometimes wandered onto the track and got hit by the train. Sometimes that made the train derail, which looked realistic. He was eleven, twelve. Susan sometimes joined him on the rare occasions when she was in the house, or not heavily asleep and more or less unwakeable in her bedroom. She asked him who lived where, where did they work, who was having affairs with whom, what was the name of the town. Mark was so thrilled at her interest that he would never have admitted that he had never thought about any of this, and so had to make up answers on the spot. "That's the Feebersons' house. He's a dentist."

"That's a strange name."

"Is it?"

"But that's OK."

Susan was the one who pointed out that his town had hardly any homes in it. He had two different log cabins and one modern house that Susan called a fifties tract house (that was where the dentist now lived), and the rest were train stations, lumber mills, granaries, warehouses, and factories. He had five train stations (he loved the long platforms with the variously distributed barrels and trolleys) and three big factories (he loved the complicated chutes and stacks and conveyor belts). "But that's OK," Susan said. "It's kind of cool. It looks like a Siberian labor camp." She sometimes even drove one of the cars from one place to another. She put two cars in front of a factory with a space between them, then took the Rolls-Royce ("The cigar-chomping factory owner," she explained) and parallel parked it, with a confident flourish, ending with it beautifully snug against the imaginary curb. Mark worried a little at first, but he was never able to detect mockery in anything she said. After a few minutes she would disappear, and Mark would go back to executing left and right turns, speeding and getting stopped by the police car. Whatever cars Susan had touched, he always left where they were.

How had Dad painted so perfectly, so bubble- and streak-free, so gleaming and uniformly smoothly red the 1962 Ford Thunderbird that sat on the shelf above the desk in his basement study?

How did his mother cut Christmas wrapping paper with one steady thrust of the scissors, not even opening and closing them, simply parting the paper against the sharp inner edge, making a line as straight as a yardstick?

How did she wrap Christmas boxes so that, on the ends, when she folded the last perfect triangle against the other perfect triangles, she didn't get that little wave of extra wrapping paper at the top that (after Mark applied the last piece of tape on *his* box) deflated and lifted the paper off the box a little, making the edges frustratingly uncrisp?

How could Dad tell that Mark had missed a patch in the lawn when the uncut grass was barely a quarter inch longer than the cut grass? "Stand in the sunlight. See? No, bend down. Come on, don't be dumb, look *along* the row, surely you see the shadow."

Why did they have to argue about how to hang the toilet paper? Mom: "It's supposed to hang off the inside, so when you pull the paper toward you, you tear it off against the roll."

Dad, pretending patience (but you could tell he was angry because the outside corners of his eyelids were turned down): "If you hang it that way, the flowers are upside down."

"Why should I give a fuck which way the flowers go?"

"I'm only pointing out that the manufacturer, who might be expected to know, designs it to hang with the flap forward—"

"Why should I give a flying fuck what the fucking manufacturer thinks?"

CLEMENTI WAS CHARMING, Mom said, but Kuhlau was a no-talent bum. The last good composer was Brahms. Scarlatti's music was fascinatingly different from Bach's, you could hear it from the first measure. Schubert had beautiful melodies, but he worked them to death. Schumann was underrated.

The Hardy Boys books were insipid pieces of shit, Mom said. Mark read Enid Blyton, whose books Mom brought home from the library. Blyton was famous in England, but none of Mark's Hardy Boy–worshipping friends at school had ever heard of her.

Mark drank Ovaltine, while his friends drank Nestlé's. Nestlé's was sweeter, so of course they liked it.

Drake's was first, with Yodels and Ring Dings. They were covered in dark chocolate and were good. Hostess shamelessly ripped Drake's off with Ho Hos and Ding Dongs, which looked exactly like Yodels and Ring Dings except they were covered in pandering milk chocolate. When Mark's friends brought out their Ho Hos at lunch (no one else seemed to eat Yodels anymore) he couldn't resist telling them the disgraceful corporate history.

All Mark's friends' families had multicolored lights on their Christmas trees, which looked gaudy and cheap. The Fuller Christmas tree had only blue lights, and only blue and silver metallic balls, and the old heavy lead icicles that hung down properly but you couldn't buy them anymore because of stupid safety concerns, and white paper snowflakes made beautifully and variously by Mark's mother (how did she six-part fold the paper so exactly, how did she cut with the X-Acto knife so neatly?) and ironed by her to perfect planar flatness (which, when Mark said it once, Dad said was a redundancy). When you turned off the room lights and plugged in the tree, it glowed ghostly blue, like a tree from the fourth dimension, signaling to you with its finger-spread arms.

The best candy bar any company had ever made was Goldenberg's Peanut Chews, but you could never find them in the Boston area, and as far as Mom knew, maybe they weren't even made anymore, which would be typical.

FOR FUN, Mark assigned a constellation to each key on the piano, going up alphabetically, so that Andromeda was the lowest note, and Vulpecula the highest. "Golden" notes—a term he made up—were the ones where the note name corresponded to the first letter of the constellation name. Only the white keys counted for this test, because if you allowed, say, G sharp, then why couldn't you also call it A flat, and once you opened that can of worms then why couldn't F be E sharp any time it

suited your purposes, and for that matter why couldn't G be A double
flat, and so on?

There were only three golden notes on the piano: the lowest A, Andromeda; the C two octaves below middle C, Capricorn; and the C above
that, Corvus. Middle C, the fulcrum, was Hercules, and A 440, the
tuning note, was Libra, the scales. Mark knew these were just coincidences, but still, there was something magical about it, wasn't there?

ON THE SECOND DAY of junior high school, Mark was crossing the
street in front of the building when a kid came up behind him, hooked
a finger into the notebooks under his arm, yanked them to the asphalt,
and kicked them. The bookstrap snapped and the binders disintegrated,
fanning pocket folders across two lanes of traffic. "I'm in serious school
now," Mark thought.

He was in the Advanced Program, and on Thursday in the first week,
his seventh-grade English teacher assigned *The Yearling*, which they
were supposed to read in its entirety by Monday. Mark accepted the
challenge. It rained all weekend, and he spent both days lying in bed
with the book. This was the first novel he had read that didn't involve a
mystery (when he'd outgrown Enid Blyton, his mother gave him Dick
Francis and Andrew Garve) and for a while he didn't see the point. Where
was the puzzle you were supposed to figure out if you were smart enough?
Jody's life was just a boy's life, and Mark had his own life, so why read
about Jody's?

But as the hours wore on, he started to get interested. He started to
like Jody's small, kindhearted father, Penny. The rough, big Forresters
were scary. The hunt for Ol' Slewfoot was exciting. By Sunday afternoon, Mark was 90 percent done, cruising along with all these people he
knew pretty well, and thinking, "This is literature; this is serious reading," and suddenly Penny got badly hurt hauling on a tree stump, and

he didn't recover in the next chapter. In fact, he seemed to be kind of permanently damaged. Which was a little shocking. And then there was Flag, the motherless fawn Jody had found 200 pages back and had been taking care of. Ma hadn't liked him, but she was grumpy in general, and Penny had always supported Jody—but now, with only forty pages to go, Mark started to feel unease. Flag trampled the tobacco crop, then ate the corn seedlings, and the family couldn't afford to lose the food. Jody emphatically proved he deserved to keep Flag by working hard for a week planting a new corn crop and building a higher fence, winning the respect of stern Ma, but Flag—and this was really shocking—jumped over the higher fence as though it were nothing, as though all Jody's work and all Jody's deserving counted for nothing, and ate the second corn crop.

Flag had no idea what a huge problem this was.

When Penny told Jody to shoot Flag, Mark couldn't believe what he was reading. Jody walked into the woods with Flag and Penny's shotgun, but he wasn't able do it, of course, some other solution would appear, and he snuck back home after dark. Mark turned the page to find the solution to the puzzle, but Ma discovered Flag alive, eating the peas, and she shot and wounded him, and Penny handed Jody the shotgun again, and he had to follow Flag, who ran from him in terror, not understanding, bleeding and floundering, to where he collapsed by a pool and looked up at Jody with "great liquid eyes glazed with wonder" and Jody had to put the gun against his neck and kill him, and Mark put the book down and stared at the bedroom ceiling for a long time.

Why? Why would Marjorie Kinnan Rawlings want to do this to him, to anyone? Some old lady he'd never met who'd lured him into this place by himself, who made it inviting, then blew out the lights and locked the door.

He struggled on toward the end, trying to get over it. Characters offered hard-earned wisdom. He half bought it, only because not buying it made him feel terrible. Jody ran away, and almost starved, and had to come home, where Penny was still bedridden and showed no sign of ever getting better, not "scarcely wuth shootin'," as he said, which if you thought about it, was a tactless thing to say to Jody. "Boy, life goes back on you," he said.

So was that the comfort?

"You've seed how things goes in the world o' men."

So growing up was the consolation?

Mark reached the last page: "He did not believe he should ever again love anything, man or woman or his own child, as he had loved the yearling. He would be lonely all his life. But a man took it for his share and went on. In the beginning of his sleep, he cried out, 'Flag!' It was not his own voice that called. It was a boy's voice. Somewhere beyond the sink-hole, past the magnolia, under the live oaks, a boy and a yearling ran side by side, and were gone forever."

Mark burst into tears. She'd tricked him again! She'd held out a little scrap, and in the last line she'd stabbed him in the heart. *Gone forever.* In the dank gray September light, Mark lay in bed, outraged at Rawlings and the irreversibility of time.

SERIOUS SCHOOL: NOW there were psychopaths to contend with. There was one enormous kid in particular who was coming down the stairs one day just as Mark was opening the fire door in the first-floor hallway. "Hey!" he barked, his voice low and gravelly. Mark whirled, alarmed. "You don't—*ehv-ver*—go through a door before me." He tossed Mark sideways and proceeded. Mark was happy to oblige him, and to hang far enough back that their paths might diverge forever.

No such luck. In the following weeks, the mere sight of Mark seemed to frenzy the kid. He would fight upstream through a dense hallway crowd, pummeling innocent bystanders, in order to reach Mark and punch him. When he was in too much of an apeshit hurry to divert his course, he would turn as he flashed past, his face contorted, groaning with rage, helplessly shaking his fist.

Mark pondered this. He also pondered, come winter, the snowballs that hit him in the back of the head. There were other kids who would intentionally attract his eye, then make exaggerated expressions of imbecility and moan, "Fag!" The injured hatred they managed to pack into that one syllable was hair-raising. It was lucky that Mark was big for his age. They didn't ever try to really beat him up. No doubt they could have—Mark hadn't the tiniest conception how to fight—but they didn't know that, and just as episodes of *My Three Sons* had it, bullies seemed, beneath all the bravado, to be cowards. Mark was grateful. But he never stopped feeling a plunge into sick dread at the sound, behind him, of that furious, indignant "Fag!"

What was it? Maybe his glasses? Different lenses, but the same sturdy frames he'd picked when he was seven. It was possible they were out of style, but so what? He liked familiar things. His trumpet case? The thick wedge of books under his arm? The bookstrap holding them together?

Everyone had had bookstraps when Mark was eight. Maybe they were popular only among eight-year-olds. Mark neither knew nor cared. They worked. Mark liked how strong the rubber was. He liked drawing patterns with his Bic pen on the strap when it was stretched and watching how the shapes contracted and solidified when he let the rubber relax. Hand-drawn serif fonts compressed themselves into convincing professional type. Stretched again, waiting on his desk in a boring class (math, puerile; history, pointless), the strap tempted him to poke holes in it, using the same pen, and he'd watch the pinholes deform into ellipses that lengthened day by day until finally, after he'd grouped several in a Pleiades-like cluster, the strap would break and he'd have to stop at Woolworth's on his way home to buy another. In the aisle with the eight-year-olds.

.   .   .

OR MAYBE (thinking of keyboards and constellations) it was the coincidence itself that was magical. If it were actually *magic*—some wizard's intentional scheme—it wouldn't be magical, but kind of dumb. How cheaply symbolic to decide that middle C should be Hercules, and make it so. But how wonderful that it was random.

IN THE SUMMER OF 1972, when he was almost thirteen, Mark had strange dreams. Some of them involved human bodies that fell apart or changed into bloody pot roast on the kitchen table. Sometimes there were terrible bodily smells. One night a grown woman in sheer black leggings climbed on his shoulders and pressed her undulating crotch against his face and he had his first "nocturnal emission," as they called it in Health class.

One night he dreamed that Susan was helping him set up his electric train. He was arranging the buildings, and he turned to say something to her just as she was aligning two pieces of track, holding one in each fist, and as he looked on helplessly she shoved them together and her eyes flew open and her face lit up red as a buzzing filled the room and she was electrocuted. He woke to the buzz of his alarm clock, his heart thudding.

He frequently had a dream that was much different, that filled him with peaceful euphoria. It varied in detail, but always began with him walking along an unfamiliar path through a darkened landscape. It might be in the woods, or it was twilight—"penumbral," a word he'd recently learned. Coming to the bottom of a hill, he looked up and saw, at the crown, his own house. The path wound up to the front door. The house was always exactly like his real house, except that, as he came closer, he saw that it hadn't been lived in for many years. The front door was ajar. He went in, and all the rooms were the same, all the furniture was the same, but there were cobwebs and dust and small items scattered on the floor, as though wind had blown them there, or some animal had come in at night. Mark was never surprised that the house was empty. He had already known somehow, in the dream, that his family had gone away, or were all dead. That part didn't matter. It had happened in the normal course of things and Mark didn't mourn; instead he felt an overpowering love for the house that had stood empty all these years, waiting for someone to come and take care of the things inside. Now Mark was here, and all his family's things were here: letters, bills, toys, games, his dad's LP collection, his mother's mysteries, his sister's secrets. Mark now had all the time in the world to go through it, bit by bit, drawer by drawer, lavishing his attention on every detail, with no one to interrupt him. And although the specifics of the dream varied, the words that occurred to him as he stood in one of the silent rooms contemplating the soul-satisfying job before him, those words were always the same: *It's all over now.*

THAT SUMMER HIS mother tried a music camp. "Maybe the kids won't be so mean," she said. It was on the shore of a lake in Maine. On the first day, as Mark and his parents parked on the grounds and walked toward registration, boys were running around boisterously, catcalls were flying. Mark cringed, waiting for the first ball accidentally thrown straight at his head. But in the registration office he met short, round Rudy, a fellow camper, who said, "Everyone has to take a swim test; you want to take it with me?" A pulse of relief and gratitude shot through Mark that was so strong, Rudy would become his best friend for the remainder of his adolescence, even though Rudy lived in the Bronx and Mark lived in a Boston suburb.

It turned out that Mark's mother, at last, was right. There were a few rough kids but hardly any mean ones, and having girls on the sports teams in the afternoons seemed to restrain the cheerful thoughtless violence, and everyone sang a hymn before each meal and a girl told Mark that he had a beautiful voice, and the counselor in his cabin wasn't a neck-pinching moron but a French horn player who marveled at Mark's hospital corners before Sunday inspections and bounced a quarter on his blanket, and although it was beginning to be clear that Mark was a lousy trumpet player, his piano was coming along, and he performed Debussy's *The Sunken Cathedral* at one of the evening recitals and was praised for it by his fellow campers rather than pummeled and ostracized, and he even turned out to be good at one sport—not a sport, really, but at least it was physical—namely tetherball, where his height allowed him, once he got the ball, to keep pounding it around the pole past the outstretched arms of his opponent more or less indefinitely.

Most momentously, Rudy introduced Mark to science fiction. It might seem strange that, after *Lost in Space*, he hadn't found sci-fi on his own, but he had always read what his mother gave him. From now on, Mark read whatever Rudy recommended—Asimov's *Foundation* series, Heinlein's *The Moon Is a Harsh Mistress*, Herbert's *Dune*, Brunner's *Stand on Zanzibar*.

Mark returned to the same music camp every summer for the next five years. It constituted the happiest part of his life. He paid for the second month in the last three of those years from money he'd earned on a paper route years ago and had never spent. He quit the trumpet, took up bassoon, continued with piano. He sang at meals and in the chorus. He became infatuated with a series of girls—Mendelssohn Violin Concerto; Poulenc Flute Sonata; Brahms E-minor Cello Sonata—but never told them (could they hear his applause?). After concerts, before curfew, he sometimes lay out in the big field, looking for shooting stars, imagining heartfelt conversations. Rudy recommended Niven's *Ringworld*, Clarke's *Childhood's End*. Mark performed the Beethoven Opus 10 number 3. Most days he could hold the tetherball court against all comers, and he thought of Susan, eighteen, nineteen, twenty, who could hold a pool table all night at the various bars she hung out in, getting free drinks. Mark got nothing, but who cared, he liked it, the rhythm, the mesmerizing orbit of the ball. At the ends of the summers, in the camp yearbook, *Sharps and Flats*, girls wrote that he was sweet and funny and should never change. One girl he had a suffocating crush on (Mozart Bassoon Concerto) wrote, "It's been really great playing next to someone who wasn't boring." Actual love notes he had to write himself, and did so, in the margins of his own yearbook, thinking he was being lighthearted: "I'll miss you so, dearest Mark, please come back, I cannot live without you. Rachel." (Rachel had been the Poulenc.)

In other seasons he lay on his bed on the weekends and read about time travel, galactic empires, teleportation, aliens benign and malign. He visited Rudy in the Bronx and half-conquered his fear of the subway. Whenever he smelled fresh-cut grass on a hot day the unbidden mental image was so strong it was almost like teleportation, back to the big field in Maine between the dining hall and the concert hall. On many nights when the moon was down, he lay out in the side yard and star-gazed. (When he came out early, the twilit sky was the deep melting blue of his Matchbox Iso Grifo.) Boston's light pollution was worse than Maine's, but it was on these suburban nights that he learned how to recognize the constellations as they appeared in the sky, rather than on a chart. Of all of them, Cygnus aroused most powerfully the emotion he now thought of, complete with quotation marks, as "the nameless feel-ing" or, when he was in the mood to wryly self-dramatize, "wordless longing." Of course he was aware that he had thus named the nameless feeling and found words for the wordless longing. Susan called this "eff-ing the ineffable."

Why Cygnus? Mark pondered this, lying out in the yard in the alu-minum lounge chair with the hollow rubber straps that thunked like bullfrogs when you plucked them. Cygnus was the Swan, but it was also called the Northern Cross, and maybe he liked the balance, or maybe the rivalry, with the Aussies' Southern Cross. (Theirs was flashier, but ours was more beautiful.) He liked the fact that the Northern Cross was almost but not quite regular: a form flexed as though by motion. Motion implied migration, and many species of *Cygnus* migrated. Unlike most constellations, Cygnus actually *looked* like what it was supposed to represent, a long-necked bird with a bright tail, its two wings curving slightly backward. There was something poignant about that long neck, Mark couldn't put his finger on it, but you could see how it was stretched forward, reaching toward its destination, maybe with "wordless longing," which reminded him of that other migration he still dreamed of, namely his own to a lunar colony, or to a domed city on Mars. Or one that science fiction novels had taught him to yearn for: when a good boy's lonely contemplation of the night sky was rewarded with one of the stars brightening, lowering, proving to be an alien spaceship, landing, opening, welcoming.

THINKING OF THE MAGIC of randomness—how amazing it was that as soon as you got twenty-three people together in a room, the probability that two of them shared a birthday was over 50 percent. But maybe the really interesting question was, why did the 50.73 percent probability, which was provable, strike everyone, including Mark, as counterintuitive? Why would our intuition, evolved over millions of years, be wrong about the incidence of coincidences?

SUSAN WAS LIVING with friends but occasionally came by to see him, mainly to slaughter him at pool down in the basement. He understood the math of her bank shots, the accumulated spins, the transferable momentum of rigid objects colliding. What he couldn't quite believe, no matter how many times he witnessed it, was how she could communicate so much mathematical information in the tiny fraction of a second during which her stick was in contact with the cue ball.

He didn't mind losing. (One reason he was not good at any sport was that, in fact, he preferred losing. Like waiting, losing gave him the pleasurable sense that somebody else had to worry.) He particularly loved a certain shot that even Susan could get right only about half the time. When a ball intervened between the cue and object balls, she would raise the back of the stick and punch down on the side of the cue. The ball would spurt sideways, spinning, and would describe an arc around the intervening ball.

Sometimes his father came out of his study to watch. Sometimes he even played. It was the only time he and Susan got along. He played better than Mark, but not as well as his daughter. Mark—fourteen, fifteen, sixteen—had become dimly aware that his father was depressed, maybe had been depressed for years. Mark could count on two fingers the times he'd seen his father happy. The first had been after a snowstorm. His father hated snowstorms. He hated clearing the driveway, he hated ice on the paths, he hated the chance of a power outage, he hated making a fire in the fireplace when there *was* an outage because it heated the house unevenly. When Susan had lived at home, he hated the runaround she gave him when he asked her to help shovel. But on this one day, for some inexplicable reason, after the shoveling was finished, he made a snowball and threw it at Mark. Mark, nonplussed, threw one back. Susan joined in and peppered the old man up and down his long winter coat with snowballs until he begged for a ceasefire. She granted it, and when she turned around he snuck up behind her and dropped a chunk of plowdrift over her head. He laughed so hard he wheezed.

The second time happened at pool. Dad and Susan were playing Rotation, and it was usually a case of watching Susan run the table, but

Dad had a couple of good early turns, and then Susan flubbed two shots in a row, and suddenly he found the zone, he sank the eight, the nine, the ten, and now he was on the downward slope picking up speed as the table cleared, and the next three shots were not that hard, and he really lucked out on a bank shot for number fourteen, and Susan called him Minnesota Fats, and the last was a straight shot down the whole table, and he banged it home. The part that Mark couldn't believe, but would always remember, was the utterly uncharacteristic (although if he did it, didn't that mean it was some buried part of his character?) silly dance that his father broke into, pointing to various corners of the room as he jived over to his workbench, picked up a stick of chalk, and scribbled the final score on the basement wall:

Susan—4

me—116

Tuesday, February 16, 2016

Baltimore in the dark. The bus is late, throbbing into the station at 6:18. She has two minutes for the transfer, makes it in one. People everywhere, in chairs, in lines, on the new bus. No matter where you go, what rise you top, what cape you round.

She grabs one of the last empty pairs of seats, sits at the window with her knapsack on her lap, watches the subsequent boarders. Eyes slide over her without a snag. Coats find overhead compartments, asses find cushions. The bus pulls out of the station with four empty seats, one of them next to her. On the bus out of New York there were three empty seats, one of them next to her. Twenty-seven pairs of seats on a Greyhound bus, therefore random odds of this happening to her on the two buses so far are three twenty-sevenths times four twenty-sevenths, or about 1 in 61. Couples prevent seat selection from being truly random, but she can't determine couples with any confidence, so fuck that, fuck them.

She places her knapsack on the seat next to her. Pulls out her notebook.

Her greasy hair? Her thick glasses? Her bomber jacket, her black lipstick, her scarlet pants, her shitkickers, her jug ears, her fat lips, her horse teeth?

She gazes out the window. Her manner, her gaze, her affect, her smell? Maybe people can tell she hates having anyone sit next to her. Even the single women shy away.

Broad lazy river of taillights drifting with the bus, inexhaustible torrent of headlights rushing against. High-rises with brilliant windows in their thousands. Higher, blinking winglights of jampacked planes. Seven and a half billion chimps, rubbing noses, dominating, submitting. Since yesterday, another 220,000. This one has never belonged. She opens her notebook, writes, *Here is a Miss who here is amiss.*

Sunday was Valentine's Day. She always thought it was the stupidest of all the holidays, and that's saying something. Glancing through the steamed-up windows of full restaurants as she walked home, flowers on tables, couples leaning into each other, *I love you*, meaning, *You must remain exactly this way for me, otherwise I'll hate you.* Yet she wondered, this past Sunday, every minute of the day, where Alex was, what they were thinking, who they might be talking to, who they might be talking about.

She's not blind, she's known all her life that people look at her funny. Why doesn't she speak up? Why doesn't she smile? Why doesn't she wash her hair? Why doesn't she stand up straight? Why doesn't she ask me how I'm doing?

Their ignorant second-guessing: *I recognize her type. I know what she needs.*

Don't understand me too quickly, somebody said. (She googles it: some writer named Gide.) How about, Don't understand me at all? How about, Get your grubby thoughts off me. She didn't just want to be left alone, she wanted to float free of their stupid judgment, their stupid categories. Don't have the foggiest fucking notion what to say about me.

Then she met Alex. A new hire at Qualternion, the imaging software company she worked at. A little older than her, she'd guess. Or maybe just more easy in the world. It shows how solitary her life had been, how out of touch, that there it was, October 2015, and Alex was the first person she knew who floated free of that most grubby-finger-smeared category of all, gender. Alex was a "they." She had to learn what AFAB and AMAB meant, and she had no idea which Alex was. Breasts or no? She couldn't tell. Then she realized she was smearing her own grubby thoughts all over Alex, and to her intrigue was added sympathy. Not to mention self-disgust. Then she started noticing everything about Alex: their programming skill, their hilarious sly comments, their generosity, their abundant freckles, their gleaming white straight teeth, their ten different-colored baseball caps. When they looked at her. When they asked, when going out on an errand, whether she wanted something. When they remembered the way she liked her coffee. She still doesn't know if Alex is AFAB or AMAB, or cis or trans, or if those labels apply in this case, they've defeated that deepest of all chimp-reflexes, *Do my genes pass through you or do yours pass through me*, they've rendered the question as stupid as it should be, and there's something pretty fucking awesome about that.

She had never had a boyfriend or a girlfriend or a nonbinary-romantic-friend or a Platonic friend and had never wanted one, and then she found herself thinking about Alex, knowing where they were in the office, wondering what they might say to her, and did they ever think about her and what did they think. Being alone suddenly seemed undesirable, and that terrified her, and she hated herself for thinking about Alex, *You must remain exactly this way for me*, all ten baseball caps and each tooth and freckle in place, but argued with herself, that wasn't true, Alex could be anything, it was their floating-free that she loved, but wasn't that bullshit, what if Alex stopped floating free? Not just her self-respect, but her self-possession, her control, were gone. She was all she'd ever had or wanted, and suddenly she wasn't enough. Alex, save me, Alex, I love you, by which I mean, give me exactly what I want. So, just at the time she started to give a shit about whether a person liked her, she was convinced even more than usual that no one could, because she had turned into exactly the kind of presumptuous needy private-space-invader that she detested.

She composes a snowball sentence:

I am all done, folks, really (raucous applause, gradually increasing).

Sunday, February 14, 2016

Mark wanders through the emptied house at dusk, switching on lights as he goes. He contemplates each room for a long time.

Of course this is like his old dream. Which makes sense. Even as a kid he must have known that he would be the one to clear out the house after his parents died. Susan would have had neither the desire nor the patience. He's driven the six hours from Ithaca one last time for the closing tomorrow. He'll spend the night in his old bedroom, in a sleeping bag on the newly polished floor.

He is fifty-six years old, a professor of astronomy. His expertise is in two subjects of little interest to the public, astrometry and galaxy formation. He prefers it that way. Let people in the spotlight worry. Strangely, perhaps, for a recluse, he's a good teacher. He has always been excited by the implications of the big view, and he loves explaining things. (Someone once told him he loved it too much.) He has won teaching awards.

He never married, but has a daughter who is now twenty. She was raised by her mother.

The house is in excellent shape. The realtor told him that the easiest houses to sell were those owned by engineers, because they were the best maintained. Mark was tempted to remind him that his father had been a physicist, but the other man, in a way, had intuited a deeper truth.

So . . . Does Mark feel a peaceful euphoria? In fact, yes. And when he recalls the numinous words from that dream, *It's all over now*, they flow through him with their old comforting power. For twenty years his father suffered terribly from Parkinson's disease and its associated Lewy body dementia. When he died, Mark thought his mother would feel liberated, maybe rejuvenated, but instead she fell into a steady mental decline. It reminded him of something he had read years ago, comparing long-married couples to plants with interpenetrating roots. He wondered if, in fact, a shared biome was indicated. Perhaps regardless of the conscious feelings involved—the presence or absence of love, for example—long cohabitation adapts two bodies to mutually interacting pheromones, skin and mouth bacteria, intestinal flora, etcetera, on which the couple gradually grows dependent. Remove one partner, and the surviving organism weakens.

Whatever the reason, the moment his father died, his mother started dying. For six years she blurred and shrank and drifted backward into the past. She returned to the period when she loved dogs and hated cats. She forgot that Mark was an astronomer. She forgot that Susan was dead. When she was diagnosed with pancreatic cancer, she couldn't retain the news, so she spent her last weeks contentedly smoking her cigarettes and watching her beloved horse movies on DVD. (Severe dementia had finally enabled her to enjoy TV.) Pain only came in the last week, and was alleviated by generous applications of morphine in the hospice facility to which Mark had moved her. To the very end, whenever she was awake, she was peaceful.

"What are you reading, Markie?" she would ask when she woke up and saw him sitting with a book in her hospice room.

"*Berlin Diaries*, by Marie Vassiltchikov."

"Is it good?"

"It's interesting."

"Oh, good!" Maternal relief in her voice. Marky-lark was happy. She would open a book of her own, *Ruffian*, the true story of a racing horse with a big heart who died young. She had been staring at random pages off and on for the past two years. Like a small child, she would gaze at the text for a few seconds, then fall asleep with her finger in the book.

Mark contemplates the kitchen. Her domain. "I hate this fucking kitchen," she would spit out every few days, when the appliances were from the fifties and there was too little countertop space. One Christmas Susan gave her, as a joke, a poster that read FUCK HOUSEWORK in huge fluorescent letters and Mom surprised everyone by putting it up on the wall next to the refrigerator. It stayed there for ten years, only coming down when she finally had the kitchen remodeled. She liked the amenities better after that, but she still announced regularly that she hated cooking. Yet every night she made dinner.

She never allowed anyone in the kitchen while she was cooking. It took Mark years to figure out (when *did* he figure it out? he can hear Susan calling him a dumbass, and later, when she was kinder, referring to his "healthy obliviousness") that his mother had arranged her day so that she would spend as little time as possible with his father. Dad got home from work at 5:30, at which point Mom was already in the kitchen cooking. Dinner was at 6:30. At 7:00, Mom would go upstairs with a gin and tonic and a mystery, and read in bed until she fell asleep at around 8:00. She would sleep through the evening as heavily as Susan did all those afternoons when she was fifteen, sixteen, seventeen, doing drugs (about which Mark was equally clueless). When Dad climbed into the marriage bed toward midnight, Mom would pop out to walk the dogs, then sit downstairs in the living room with another gin and tonic, reading more in her mystery until—well, Mark doesn't know. Susan probably knew.

Maybe his father was as blind as he was. Hard to believe, but evidence

suggested it. When Mark was in graduate school, his mother moved
into his old bedroom, informing his father of the new state of affairs,
and Dad seemed thunderstruck. As far as Mark knew, Mom never re-
lented, and Dad never got over it. Through all Mark's childhood, his
father had not uttered a word to him about his marriage, but now he
broke down regularly in Mark's presence. "She says she's not sure she
ever loved me. I asked her, 'Were the children, at least, conceived in love?'"
Mark noticed that his father—who had never talked about emotions,
either his or other people's, or their existence as a human attribute—
drew on an almost Victorian vocabulary now that he was forced to.
Mark, heartsick and helpless, would tentatively pat his broad back as he
crumpled over the nearest tabletop.

For years Mark heard the same anguish every few weeks, virtually
word for word, the story frozen, the pain ever fresh. He began to wonder
himself if his mother had ever loved his father, and his old nighttime
dream of visiting the house in the future morphed into a daydream
about traveling into the past. It was like an answer to that silly hypo-
thetical question people sometimes ask, as far as Mark can tell, just to
keep a conversation going—if you could go back in time only once,
when and where would you choose? For Mark, there was no contest. He
would return to some weekend in 1965. He would ring the doorbell of
this house, and when his parents answered (not recognizing him), he'd
convince them to let him come in, a friend of a friend (though his parents had no friends), a third cousin, a census taker, an anthropologist,
and he'd spend the day observing. What did the young couple talk about?
Or if they didn't talk, were the silences companionable? Seething? Who
was the genius loci, the serene boy in his bubble of hobbies, or the smarter,
haunted girl?

He eventually came to believe it was Susan, because his mother said
such bitter things before and after his father died. But then one day he

was sitting with her at the kitchen table, looking at some photos of the old man she'd unearthed during one of her unremembered rambles through the rooms and drawers, and she murmured in an unsteady voice, "He was such a good man." She began to weep. "I miss him so much."

Mark was gobsmacked. Time-traveling, his mother had arrived at the station where Mark's boyhood lived. "Mom," he wanted to say. "What year is it? Look around, do you see a newspaper?"

He leaves the kitchen and enters the dining room. The ceiling light is reflected in blurry stars on the newly polyurethaned floor. Probably a consequence of the circular polishing. The walls are a beige cream that the realtor chose, and earlier today apologized for. "Against the white trim, there's too much green in it."

"Looks all right to me," Mark said truthfully.

His family never ate dinner here. That's what the kitchen was for. Instead, the dining room table was where he did his schoolwork. During his high school years it was covered a foot deep in his books and papers. In his busiest period, the winter of eleventh grade, he would come downstairs at four in the morning to finish an essay and sometimes he'd fall asleep huddled next to the radiator. He would dream that he still had his paper route, but had somehow forgotten to do it for years, and all his trusting, loyal customers had been wondering where their newspapers were. Their wounded patience was the most painful part of the dream.

The upright piano used to be here, too. Every time the piano tuner came, his mother would push him into playing a piece for the man. He'd pick something short, since the poor guy must have had other work to get to. When he was sixteen, he considered applying to Oberlin to do a double major in physics and piano performance, and his father volunteered to fly with him to visit the campus. This was surprising. Mark knew how much his father hated to travel. Only later did it occur to him that perhaps his father was hoping he'd become a professional pianist. He would never have expressed this directly to Mark. He had always said he believed that every child had the right to find their own way. (Susan would pipe up here, "Just so long as that child's name is Mark.")

Mark steps into the living room. He looks at the spot where the TV always stood. Where are the hassocks of yesteryear?

The original broadcast of *Lost in Space* is an expanding shell of electromagnetic radiation now 51 light-years in radius, a volume of space containing approximately 1400 star systems. How many little alien boys are now having weird dreams about Billy Mumy? But the signal is likely far too weak to be picked up by extrasolar receivers, even if they were monitoring the correct frequency. To Mark's six-year-old self, John Robinson seemed the perfect dad, and Maureen, he half believed, was based on his mother. The two women had the same wavy hair, pointy nose, chirpy voice. Years later he could see that John Robinson looked like JFK, and a sad fact he'd picked up somewhere was that *Lost in Space* was John F. Kennedy Jr.'s favorite show in 1965.

When Mark visited during his mother's decline, every morning she would wake up and say, "Markie, I'm worried about the TV. I don't think it's working."

"Let's check. It was working last night." He would accompany her downstairs, where she would settle on the couch and he'd hit the remote. She never tried to turn on the TV herself, convinced as she was that it was far too complicated.

"It seems to be working, Mom."

"Oh, good."

"What would you like to watch?"

"Can we watch *Miracle of the White Stallions?*"

"Sure thing."

"But we need to get cigarettes. Aren't we out of cigarettes?" Mark and the daytime aides he employed hid the cigarettes every evening and told his mother she had run out, so she wouldn't get up during the night and burn the house down.

"Let me check. Gee, it turns out we do have some."

"Oh, good. Can I have a cigarette?"

Mark watched *Miracle of the White Stallions* and *National Velvet* each approximately 120 times. He was fascinated to notice that, each time he saw them, they seemed more perfectly executed—perfectly acted, perfectly written, perfectly edited—and consequently their emotive power grew and grew. When the good Nazi General Tellheim lit his cigarette and said, "After such a terrible winter, I think we're going to have quite a nice spring," and walked off into the dark to his suicide, it felt like the most profound expression ever voiced by man of nature's dreadful and wonderful indifference to human suffering and death.

Mark handed his mother her cigarettes. He brought from the kitchen her bottle of Ensure and a packet of animal crackers, the only things she would consume. He listened about 200 times to a tape recording of a voice recital he'd done with Susan during a brief period, fifteen to sixteen, when she was taking singing lessons. His father had made three backup copies, easy to find within his enormous music collection by consulting his handwritten card catalog, and each copy in succession warbled more as it deteriorated. Every time they listened, his mother would cry. "What a beautiful voice! Who's playing piano?"

"That's me."

"Is Susan still singing?"

"Yes."

"Where?"

"There's an ecumenical church. It has a big choir. She solos sometimes. She really enjoys it."

"That's you playing piano."

"Right."

"Is that a mistake there?"

"Not right there."

Mark goes up the stairs. The floor refinishers filled the holes left behind when the chairlift was taken out. Dad rode the lift in his last years, a big man ascending slowly, whirring, his face the impassive mask of Parkinsonism. He had once scoured the newspapers of the English-speaking world to find the hardest crossword puzzles, the ones with clues built around puns and anagrams. He and an equally avid co-worker eventually determined that the ones in *The Guardian* were the most diabolical. The co-worker would go to a university library once a month and photocopy back issues, then he and Dad would race to see who could complete them first.

More than degrading memory, Lewy body dementia disrupts the ability to organize information. (His father explained this to Mark, as it was happening.) The dozen pieces of observed data in any moment are slippery uniform balls. The need to tie your shoelace and the need to escape a burning house have the same weight. Midway in the long decline, Mark watched his father struggle to write down (handwriting shrinks, freezes) a daily schedule for his meds: sixteen hours awake, pills spaced evenly throughout the day, four of this medication, three of that, two of that. Mark looked at the wavering lines of the chart his father had drawn, the microscopic names of the drugs, the empty spaces awaiting checkmarks, the pencil in hand returning again and again to the parameters noted above: sixteen hours, four of this, three of that. His father would become agitated, his memory good enough to know that this was not his brain, not anymore.

Susan's old bedroom is at the top of the stairs. Mark doesn't go in. The deaths of his parents he accepts, but he was only thirty-three when Susan was killed, and the moment he heard the news it seemed to him that he had entered an alternate universe, where everything was the same, from the disposition of galactic superclusters to the jiggle of air molecules in his lungs, except for this one detail. Susan was alive in uncountable other universes, including the correct one, the one he had been kicked out of. Those are the words that have always accompanied the feeling: he had been *kicked out.*

He has wondered ever since if it was this persistent, illogical conviction of unreality that allowed him—it was an alternative him, wasn't it? a quasi-unreal him—to do something that he would like to believe the real him would not have done. But then again, if he hadn't done it, he wouldn't have a daughter. Who is dear to him, even if he rarely sees her.

An uncomfortable subject.

Mark heads down the hall, in search of more of that peaceful euphoria. Here is his own old bedroom, overlooking the backyard. Bright and bare, his sleeping bag on the floor. When Mark was nine or ten he picked up from some book the phrase "bathed in moonlight," and when the moon was in the right position relative to either of his two bedroom windows— one facing southeast, the other southwest—to cast its light across his blanket, he would say to himself, "I'm bathed in moonlight," and a little bit of that feeling would come. Immanence. Epiphany. The oceanic feeling. What epileptics are said to feel right before a grand mal seizure. What schizophrenics experience in its nightmare form.

He still prefers to call it "the nameless feeling." He suspects everyone means something different when they refer to it. My own private nameless feeling. Which is ironic, since a common element of it is a sense of expansion and connection. My own private self-serving confusion of my ego with the cosmos.

All his adult life he's experienced the feeling when he sees a certain style of line drawings in young adult books. N. C. Wyeth and his imitators. Say, a sketch of a farmhouse under a tree. There's the shapely abundant crown, with the two small rogue branches that poke out toward the bottom to keep it from looking too perfect; the house with its roof shaded in parallel lines, smoke undulating up from the stone chimney. There are the tufts here and there in the foreground representing the meadow-like turf, the one small squarish boulder half sunk in soil, flanked by a tall grass stalk, the fence of stripped saplings. Most stirring of all, there's the trodden path that starts at the bottom of the picture and curves over the brow of the hill, dipping out of sight, reappearing smaller and farther away on a distant hill, and beyond that hill the mountains, and behind the mountains, towering cumulus clouds, suggesting that out *there*, far distant *there*, beyond those cloud-ramparts lies Aslan's country, the Land of Faerie, Amber, Alpha Centauri—in other words, Heaven— and that the pebbly, homely footpath is the way to get there.

He wondered why that style of drawing meant so much to him. Then he cleared out the family attic five months ago and came across an edition of *The Yearling*, with illustrations by N. C. Wyeth, and there they were: sapling fences, chimneys capped with sinuous smoke, paths curving off toward hills and clouds. And he remembered (he hadn't thought about this for a long time) his ambitious, lively, slightly crazy seventh-grade English teacher, whom he came to adore, and her tag phrase to her students, these favored sons and daughters of professors and scientists, launched on a Titan rocket of public money in pursuit of Sputnik: "To whom much is given, much is expected." And he remembered that dark rainy weekend, rather strangely dark, "penumbral," when he'd lain in bed curled around *The Yearling* with his back to the door and had his conversion experience, the discovery of a more-real world beyond and behind this one. That idea could lead to dangerous falsehoods—e.g., Platonism, Christianity—but it was also, in a way, the root of science, particularly mathematics and physics. No accident that Plato was a mathematician; that Christianity was Neo-Platonism. An illusion powerful enough to break his heart. Dreaminess hardwired in the human brain. A necessary concomitant, perhaps, to creative intelligence.

He also found in the attic *The World of Tomorrow*. (He's gone up there now, he's staring at the patch of subflooring where the box used to be.)

It must have been his father who packed it away, since his mother never saved anything. As an adult he could see, in the photographs of the City of Tomorrow, the obvious artificiality of the model: wayward grit looking like hazardous rocks on the superhighway; dried-moss "trees" that he recognized from his days constructing model railroad towns. Yet the old ghostly yearning possessed him all the same, the longing to live in the ordered City. And at last he thought he could see why the skyscrapers' featureless glowing windows had called to him so powerfully. It was precisely because he couldn't see through them. Radiant behind one of them (*where is Carol Merrill standing?*) was his future life, so wonderful no photograph could depict it. His longing wasn't for the future per se, but for his unimaginable adulthood. Maybe he would have a theremin, but that wasn't the point, the point was that his unimaginable wife would play theremin sonatas with him. Sure, he'd have a Rocket Academy yearbook, but the part he would read over Martian brandy in the evenings would be the love notes his wife had written to him in the margins when they were cadets. And his hovercar out on the telepad was merely the outward sign of something far more wonderful: the unimaginable job, at which he was an acknowledged whiz, awaiting him at the rainbow-end of his ballistic commute.

Mark was *forty-three* years old before he realized he had never quite stopped believing that one day he would take a spaceliner to visit the lunar colony, or to Mars to advise on some thorny problem of terraforming. He had sealed the dream in a suspended-animation pod in the back of his mind. He remembers exactly where he was when the pod popped open and the dream proved to be as dead as the fourth astronaut in *Planet of the Apes*. He was in his office at the university, putting on his coat to go home on a wintry March afternoon. The lining of his coat had started to detach at several points simultaneously, and he was intrigued by the fact that the threads of the various seams had a roughly equivalent longevity regardless of the amount of friction or tension to which they were subjected (shoulder seams, for example, enduring more daily wear and stress than bottom-hem seams). This led him to ponder the inevitable degradation of cotton at the molecular level, from oxidation, dust mites, bacteria, etc. This led to a general thought-bromide about entropy, energy loss, the eventual end of the universe, and so on, and that in turn led to the daunting problem of fuel requirements, and therefore the necessity of additional mass, in spaceflight, an issue he was familiar with, lecturing on it annually in his Introduction to Astronomy course. But for some reason, this time—was it because the coat had belonged to his father, who was sixteen years into Parkinson's, now wheelchair bound, laid out at night in his bed like a stone effigy?—this time, out popped genuine shock, a stab of loss. He stopped shrugging on the coat. *He would die, never having left Earth.*

Not just him. Sure, a few cocky test pilots and politically savvy scientists will probably set foot on Mars someday. But a colony? Given human shortsightedness and folly, he doubts it. And beyond? When he was a kid, not just science fiction writers but real scientists, in the main, confidently predicted that man would one day "reach the stars." How, exactly? Faster-than-light travel is almost certainly impossible. And given the enormous time and energy required to reach even the nearest star at sublight speeds, plus the highly debatable benefit of doing so, Mark suspects that humanity will never leave the solar system.

He is gazing out the attic window, down at the eighty-year-old one-car detached garage that's slowly falling apart. The new owners will have to figure out what to do about that. Zoning, bringing up to code, grandfathered footprint, blah blah. Good luck to them.

As for a visit or phone call from the neighbors—after forty years of SETI, we've heard nothing. Which, granted, also means little. We've monitored only a tiny fraction of the stars in our neighborhood, forty years is nothing on the cosmic timescale, and who says civilizations reliably produce radio emissions? The one civilization we know of, with the advent of fiber optics, may go radio silent in the next few decades. But Mark is one of those who finds Enrico Fermi's question unsettling: *Where is everybody?* Fermi reasoned that, if intelligence were not vanishingly rare in the galaxy, then given the fact that planetary formation likely began eight to ten billion years ago, there would almost certainly have been civilizations that formed billions of years in the past. Some fraction of them, with thousands of years of technological development at their disposal, would surely have devoted energy to exploring the galaxy. Even we puny humans, with a mere two centuries of industrialization, can glimpse the technological feasibility of von Neumann probes that would multiply and spread from star system to star system. With nothing more than our present-day rocket technology for transport, such a scheme could fill the entire galaxy in less than 300 million years.

All right, then: Where are they?

Maybe intelligence is common, but equally common are catastrophic climate change, resource depletion, technological self-destruction. In 5,000 years, when serene bubble-boy imagined opening the time capsule of the 1965 New York World's Fair and mulling over the contents in euphoric peace, it probably really will be all over, at least in Flushing Meadows, under a mile of ice, or 200 feet of water, or two inches of radioactive ash. Humans will still exist somewhere, but will they be theorizing about von Neumann probes or trapping rats for dinner?

Intelligence that's out there, but of which we will never be aware, is scientifically equivalent to intelligence that's not out there.

Mark comes down the attic stairs. He imagines a poster for a movie they'll never make, showing a radio telescope and a dejected scientist, with the tag line, *Turns Out We're Alone After All.*

He stops for a moment in the bedroom his parents shared while he was growing up. One could make an unpleasant joke. *Move along, folks, nothing to see here.*

He continues down. The only part of the house he hasn't contemplated yet is the basement. Through the living room, off the kitchen, down again; rough wooden steps, exposed joists, bare lightbulbs. If the kitchen was Mom's domain, this was Dad's. In addition to his study, he had his workbench, his storage boxes, his tinkering notebooks. As soon as he went into the nursing home, Mom asked Mark if he could, at long last, clear out all Dad's "crap down there." It was so neatly stored, there was more than Mark realized. Boxes of rescued vacuum tubes, sash weights, pipe collars, doorknobs, lamp sockets, transistors, porch balusters, old-style fuses, circuit breakers, brakelight bulbs. There was a box filled with electric cords his father had cut from every house appliance he'd finally thrown away after Mom complained long enough about deteriorating performance. One box was marked "TV speakers," and there they all were, from five generations of living room consoles and four of kitchen-table portables. Mark recognized the twin speakers from the 1959 black-and-white Motorola on which he had first watched *Lost in Space*. There were the ingenious, simple tools his father had made to help him in his tinkering. Artful stands to hold a tool or component at the right height and angle, so that he could accomplish a three-handed job. Hooks of various lengths and shapes set in homely carved wooden handles. Even the simplest things had a marvelous, seemingly effortless precision: pieces of boxboard cut to function as dividers in drawers of sized screws that perfectly slid in and out of their channels, that looked machine-made until you noticed the fragment of breakfast-cereal logo on one side.

Mark would throw stuff out, then drive in his father's eighteen-year-old Toyota station wagon to visit him at the nursing home. He'd be sitting in his wheelchair in his double room, with his tray of half-eaten food, his juice or coffee mixed with a gellifier so that he wouldn't aspirate it, looking with emptied wonder at the air in front of his frozen face. "Hey," he'd say to Mark. Was he trying to smile? Mark would sit with him, utter comments on the fleeting images on the TV that was always on, pull the child's crossword out from under the lunch tray. "How's this one going, Dad? Let's see, five across, man's best friend, three letters, what do you think?"

His lower lip would work, his pale gray eyes hold fast on Mark's face. "Damned if I know." He'd try to laugh. "My mind is going; I don't remember things the way I used to."

When Mark got up to leave, his father's face, in spite of the Parkinsonian mask, would somehow express, it would positively radiate, a look of bleak abandonment. The last time Mark saw him conscious, there was something (he would swear in retrospect) especially horrified in that parting look, as though his father were seeing deeper than ever before into the abyss. Not seeming to see Mark, nor anything in the room, he said slowly and distinctly, like a blind oracle, "What a way to go."

Mark drove back to the house, to clear out more of his crap. In the glove compartment of the old Toyota he found a notebook his father had started when he first bought the car, to check how the mileage claimed by the dealer compared to the actual mileage. Other people might do this, with one column recording odometer readings and another the number of gallons of gasoline consumed, but what made his father unusual was that once he'd started it, he couldn't stop. The list went on for fifteen years. In the back of the notebook he'd created scatter plots with lines of best fit: fuel consumption by car's age, mileage by year.

More than the rest of the house, the basement, now empty, looks different. The concrete walls and floor are shoddy and cold. Hard to imagine that a man lived most of his real life down here, perhaps found his only happiness down here. Mark slips through the narrow door into the windowless box where his father listened to his music, paid his bills, thought his thoughts. He was in high school before he finally noticed that it must have been originally designed as a fallout shelter. (His sister's voice: *Dumbass*!) There is no ceiling light, so the room is almost pitch dark.

When Mark cleared out the desk in here he found, beneath road maps and instruction manuals going back forty years, every birthday and Father's Day card his father had ever received from his children and his wife. He also found, folded, a sheet of paper with lines in his father's handwriting from a poem by Robert Frost called "Revelation."

> We make ourselves a place apart
>> Behind light words that tease and flout,
> But oh, the agitated heart
>> Till someone find us really out.

Mark stands motionless for a long minute. The room surrounds him with that uncanny silent hum of small enclosed spaces. The Holy of Holies. Maybe once a year he could ritually purify himself, enter this darkness, and query, "Dad?"

Heading back through the main basement to the stairs, he notices still chalked on the wall:

Susan—4

me—116

He turns out the lights as he ascends, floor to floor. Brushes his teeth in the upstairs bathroom, crawls into his sleeping bag on his old bedroom floor. He's not bathed in moonlight. The moon is low in the west, hidden by the house next door.

Sleep won't come.

His memories of this room from his childhood are overlaid with those of the years after his mother took it over. (*I lost my sweetheart*, his father cried. The same words, every time.) Scores of his mother's mystery novels filled bookcases along every wall. One entire case was devoted to mysteries involving cats, including ones purporting to have been written by a cat. Mark noted that other than Dick Francis, all the authors were women.

Here he helped his mother dress, while she apologized for subjecting his eyes to her "disgusting body." Here he sneakily deposited deodorant on the inside armpits of her shirts when she was refusing to bathe. Here she told him that the next-door neighbor, Jim, was coming into the house at night to steal her cigarettes, and to sabotage the coffee machine so that she wouldn't know how to operate it.

On one visit he discovered a framed photo on her dresser that he'd never seen before, the head and shoulders of an attractive dark-haired woman in a tweed coat from (perhaps) the 1950s. It was the only photo in the room.

"Mom, who's this?"

"That's someone I used to be pen pals with, I can't remember her name. Isn't she pretty?"

"Yes, where'd you find it?"

"It's always been there."

A few months later he asked, "Mom, who's this woman, again?"

"That's no one. I just like the picture."

When he moved her into the hospice, he brought along the photo, and set it up on her bedside table next to photos of Susan, himself, his father. He sat near her and read about the Allied bombing of Germany, watched her drift in and out of sleep with her finger in *Ruffian*. During the long hours he would often gaze at the woman in the photograph and wonder who she was. His parents had never talked much about their pasts, and now he realized there were many things he would never know.

His mother's last day was in mid-May. A saucer magnolia was in full spectacular bloom outside her window. He tried to direct her attention to it, but she seemed uninterested. The day shifted between sun and clouds, and in the late afternoon a sudden shower blew through. His mother had been unconscious most of the day, but as the rain spattered against the screen she perked up and said to Mark in a clear, strong voice, "Someone better close that window." Which he did. She slipped back asleep, and that night she died.

Back in Ithaca, when he was in the midst of trying to figure out what to do with all the stuff in the house, he got a call from Frank, a cousin of his mother's, who in the last few years had been phoning the family house every six months or so to see how she was doing. Mark had met him once decades ago, when he was in the Boston area for a relative's wedding, but barely remembered him. Frank had lived all his life in Alabama, where Mark's mother's family came from, and he spoke with a wonderfully slow and thick Southern accent.

"Mark, I'm so sorry. Your mother was a real live wire."

"Yes she was."

"When I was six or seven and she was nine or so she dared me to peek into the girls' changing rooms at the beach. She taught me all sorts of things my momma would have whipped me for, if she'd known."

Mark turns over in his sleeping bag. He should have brought a thicker pad. He doesn't want to be tired tomorrow for the closing and the long drive home.

On the drive here, he stopped at a McDonald's along I-90. He ordered a special, an Angus burger with swiss cheese and mushrooms, and he asked that they add a slice of raw onion. The gawky, acned teenager who brought him his order said something as he handed over the bag that Mark didn't catch. "What was that?" he asked.

"I said, I always eat it with a slice of onion, too. My friends say I'm crazy."

Mark thought about this for a couple of seconds. He knew he should say something friendly in return, maybe something witty, but he couldn't think of anything. Finally, he just said, "They're wrong."

The kid beamed, and as he turned away he said happily, "They *are!*"

Back in the car, Mark wondered why the exchange pleased him so much. The warmth of it lasted all the way to Boston.

This reminds him of a larger bubble of happiness, equally mysterious, that formed around him a couple of weeks ago. He was driving to the county recycling center to renew his trash disposal license. He stopped at a light. A blue car turned right off the intersecting road, and as it passed Mark's car in the opposite lane, euphoria blossomed in his chest. It kept expanding, filling the passenger compartment. After a moment of puzzlement, Mark realized that the color of the vehicle that had passed him was the exact blue of his Iso Grifo Matchbox car.

Suddenly, he noticed everything. Or perhaps more accurately, the fact that he was capable of noticing things suddenly seemed miraculous. A teenage girl was standing on the corner. Her dog had lifted its foreleg, looking up at her with ears canted forward in expressive dog-worry, to show her the leash was tangled, but she wasn't paying attention, she was texting a friend. A semi-trailer was making a left-hand turn into Mark's street, and the minivan in front of him wasn't backing up, even though there was space for it, to give the truck more room, and Mark wondered if it was sexist of him to have the impression that women were more likely than men not to notice that backing up in such situations was helpful. The truck driver inched along, eyes on his side mirror, stone-faced, barely making it, and the bubble of happiness kept expanding, taking in the small truck with the slat-walled flatbed that now zipped through on the late yellow light, carrying discarded Christmas trees that had been picked up along the city sidewalks and were shipped to barrier islands for burial, where they helped stabilize sand dunes.

It kept expanding, and there was no open cattle truck with cow and careless calf, no panel van with fifties script reading TV REPAIR, but everywhere there were people turning right and left, crossing railroad tracks, accomplishing errands, living their lives on a speck of space grit, and he thought of the list written by every first-grade nerd who ever lived since the invention of writing and cosmology, only now with adult completeness: Mark Fuller, Room 3, Munroe Elementary School, 1403 Massachusetts Avenue, Lexington, Massachusetts, United States of America, Earth, Solar System, Orion Arm, Milky Way Galaxy, The Local Group, Laniakea Supercluster, Universe, Brane-verse—and behind it all, Leibniz's question: Why is there something, rather than nothing?

The light turned green. The minivan in front turned left. It was a woman. Mark followed her, and the words that flowed around and through him, lifting him higher and higher, were, *We're all in this together.*

Wednesday, February 17, 2016

The bus was scheduled to arrive in Cleveland at 2:55 a.m., but it was 50 minutes late. It was supposed to depart at 3:55, but now it's 4:02, with no sign of the driver. She's been trying to sleep. The bus is overheated. Except for the terminal, there's nothing but parking lots in every direction. Correction, behind the bus, across a derelict street, there's a featureless brick warehouse. Correction, there's a louvered steel vent in the otherwise featureless brick warehouse, obscenely gummed up with gray glistening foamy material that appears to have boiled out and frozen. She imagines the warehouse filling with toxic waffle batter, some military-industrial process spiraling out of control, fleeing workers pressed into the corners, suffocating, creating negative molds of themselves like Pompeiians.

In Pittsburgh, 33 passengers got off, 18 got on, leaving 19 empty seats, five of them in pairs and nine single—one of them next to her—meaning presumably the other 13 pairs were all occupied by couples. Such a high percentage of lovebirds would indicate that her probability figures regarding her pariah status have been worthless from the start, since seat selection isn't close to being random. Fuck that, fuck them. Here in Cleveland 15 passengers got off and four got on, making 24 passengers, each of whom could have a pair of seats to themselves, yet seven pairs are full. Ratio of lovers to loners in the last bus was 26 to 9, making lovers about 74 percent of the total; ratio in this one is 14 to 10, or about 58 percent, suggesting that as night hours deepen, more loners crawl out from caves and climb on long-distance buses. If she adopts 74 percent as likely closer to a daytime average, then, of her first two buses, both had approximately 38 lovebirds in 19 pairs, leaving only eight additional seat pairs for determining pariah status, thus 3/8 times 4/8, or 12/64, or 1 in 5.3, instead of the self-dramatizing 1 in 61 she originally came up with. She's perfectly aware she's calculating rotely to reduce stress, she's not stupid.

Here comes the driver. 4:16. He's got a thermos in one hand, papers tucked negligently under the other arm (maybe it's the schedule). A graying trapezoidal moustache, bloodshot hazel eyes above puddled pouches. If he falls asleep, it will turn out that escaping on the bus equals escaping under it, a fine irony. He slewfoots down the aisle wheezing, checking tickets. Looks at hers, grunts. "Seattle."

A theme, apparently. "You are correct."

"Long way."

"So I've been informed."

"Family out there?"

She stares at him. He likely means no harm. Blathering in the wee hours, one loner to another. "No."

He moves on.

They leave the station at 4:23. Ten blocks of unloved Cleveland shudder by, then they hit the ramp for I-90. 423 is not a prime number, but 421 is. If he hadn't indulged his curiosity about her family life, they could have left two minutes earlier.

She closes her eyes, hoping sleep will come.

She spent half an hour Saturday night trying to figure out how to look. Black lipstick or white, bomber jacket or army anorak, shitkickers or sneakers, red pants or black. She has never worn earrings or nose rings or anything like that. Her hair is bottle-black because, shit, she doesn't know, because it's been that way for years, because otherwise it's her mother's color, because when it's greasy it's glossy, because in the dark you can't see it. She looked in her mother's mirror and didn't know if she should be feeling satisfaction or self-loathing. All that female body dysmorphia, she hates that shit. Who cares what you look like, stop obsessing over yourself.

Alex had said to her on Wednesday in the glass cube and exposed brick playspace Miles (CEO, brilliant weirdo, dick) called their office, "Hey, dark lady, you free Saturday? Let's go on a date."

Alex talks to everyone that way. "Listing tower of manflesh blocking the aisle." "Want me to get you a latte while I'm out, winsome tidbit?" They say it all deadpan, as though these are the names everyone uses.

She froze. Her brain drowned in stupid scenarios. Alex and her walking in a park, sunlight gamboling. Lying with a bottle of blushing wine on a checkered picnic blanket. The two of them programming together, maybe even rubbing each other's shoulders.

"You can just nod, turtle bean," Alex said.

She nodded.

"Seven p.m. I know the perfect place."

It was in Williamsburg, 1.2 miles from the apartment where she lived with her mother. She walked down in the deepening cold, anorak and shitkickers having won out, plus a mud-green scarf, her only one. The restaurant was Japanese, looked expensive. She had plenty of money, but she never ate out. Alex arrived unhurriedly, twenty minutes late. They came right up to her and kissed her on the cheek, flustering her. "Why are you waiting outside? I made a reservation." They intertwined their arm with hers. "Let's scurry."

The seating was in little booths with bamboo screens that rolled down for privacy. She and Alex took off their coats. Alex gestured her forward and she sat, and instead of sitting opposite, Alex sat next to her.

They did the thing with the arm again. "How could anyone come here and not feel romantic?" they said.

She basically couldn't believe that any of this was happening. Her, on a date! And with the only person in her entire life she'd ever wanted to go on a date with. What were the odds? She had no idea how to behave, so she let Alex do everything, which Alex seemed comfortable doing. The restaurant recommended a variety of eight-course tasting menus, with sake pairings. "Food restrictions?" Alex asked.

"None."

"Alcohol?"

"Anything."

"You're perfect, aren't you?"

Alex ordered the most expensive course. "This is on me."

"I have a ton of money—"

"So do I, and you're my date. Let's start with a sake tasting, I've always wanted to. You're my excuse."

On the bus, wishing like death she could sleep, she doesn't remember much of the talk. It wasn't a dialogue, Alex talked and she floated in a dreamlike state. Alex touched her hand, stroked her thigh, nuzzled her ear. Little cubes of food came on lanceolate leaves, or in lacquered bowls with wooden spoons. There were miso broths and grilled fishes and curly herbage; jellied rounds, red roe in a cobalt dish, jewel-green snow peas arranged like a fan. The sake came in clear glass bowls that glittered in the candlelight.

"You're putting me in a mood," Alex said, and she didn't know what Alex meant, but liked the sound of their voice when they said it. She liked, disbelieving, the brush of Alex's lips against her cheek. She liked the way Alex leaned into her at the climax of something they were say-ing, the press of their shoulder, like a conspiratorial nudge, like saying, *Just you and me, and nobody knows.*

Alex took pictures of the food, and of the two of them, their arm around her, cheek pressed to cheek so that the two near-side eyes, one hers and one theirs, were pulled into tadpole shapes. She kind of liked this, as proof she had a social life, and kind of didn't, because who knew what strangers might pore over these, tag her, post her, caption her, look at those jug ears, look at those horse teeth. She only ever took pictures of things she wanted to model on the computer, such as self-ordering or emergent phenomena in nature, motions of constrained objects subjected to forces, complicated lighting effects.

Alex told her that "Alex" was not the name they were born with. "I'm only admitting this because I'm kinda drunk, but I picked 'Alex' because 'a-lex' means 'outside the law.' That's the sort of thing that impresses you when you're fifteen."

This was one of the few times she was inspired to say something. "What a coincidence. People never know how to pronounce my name, so I tell them, just think 'meta,' like metadata. So, you know, 'beyond,' or 'transcending.'" A-lex and Meta, lovers who transcend the world and its categories, a couple of nerds chuckling over language games.

"I'm falling in love with you," Alex said, which was ridiculous, but she hummed with ridiculous happiness, she wanted to hear them say it again. Her conch-pink agar dessert was nestled in a transverse cut of a large bamboo. The polished edge of the bowl was stippled with vascular bundles, umber dots on amber, decreasing in size and increasing in density toward the outer edge in a distribution that was partly random but kept tending toward Fibonacci spirals. She marveled at how beautiful it was. She longed to program a model that would mimic just that level of randomness.

By the time she and Alex left the restaurant it was nine degrees outside and windy. Alex held her close and said their apartment was just around the corner. They gave her a long kiss on the lips. She felt panic, which maybe Alex could sense, because they said, "Are you okay?"

She found she couldn't speak. She nodded.

"Why don't we get out of this cold?"

She and they turned into the wind, and she shivered, and Alex held her closer. When they reached the corner Alex turned her to the right, but she wished the two of them could just keep going, hugging, matching strides, red frosty cheeks braving the wind, reaching the park along the East River where there were too many BBQ pits and tables and too few trees, but where there was at least a small chance that she might glimpse a chipmunk sprinting away with its tail up, and she would point it out to Alex, who would express sincere interest and want to know more, and she is dimly aware (on the bus) that she must be dozing because of course there would be no chipmunks to see in the middle of winter, they would all be asleep in their burrows.

Tuesday, February 16, 2016

Saskia is a slave girl in the mumbojumbium mines of Altair VI. "Please, would you untie me?" No doubt she has a skimpy torn scrap of shirt, great abs and firm full breasts, deliciously grimy. Wouldn't you love to lick them clean, boy-wanderer. Ooh my hardening nipples seem to have burst my shirt straight off me! She does a more urgent take: "*Please* would you untie me?!" On second thought, don't touch those knots. Surely a pasty-faced fourteen-year-old such as yourself knows how to take a hogtied woman to heaven. A helpless take: "Please . . . w-would you untie me?" That one for the sados. Only if you suck my cock, bitch. Oh no, please, I've never . . . gobble gobble. Hey, Mikey, she likes it!

Now the responses. First fork: "My god! *Thank* you! You've restored my faith in humanity. I haven't much, but please, take this." Second fork—if he accepts the offered item, a charmed doodad or a note leading to a hidden cache, whatever—"You deserve it. I wish I had more." If he doesn't take it: "Well, thank you for that, too. I could use this myself." Back to the first fork, if he doesn't free her: "Thanks for nothing, ass-hole." Way to show some sass, girl. Maybe they could have a cutscene of the slave girl kicking him in the balls, the boy-wanderer collapsing in his own vomit. If he clicks on her again: "Unless you're willing to free me, I've got nothing more to say to you."

Then a series of utterances randomly generated when the wanderer navigates close to her. "Is someone there?" "My family has no idea what happened to me." "At least I'm not on sublevel six. I've heard . . . terrible things." Then four different sounds of distress. Four more of fear. Huffing, for running. Mild pain grunt. Sharp pain shriek. Mortal wound gasp followed by *morendo* moan.

On it goes, four hours in the gray box at two hundred dollars an hour. There's nothing else she's doing these days that pays so well. If she manages sixteen hours a month, minus her agent's commission and taxes, it covers her rent. If she can get a second four-hour session on the same day, she always takes it. There's a lot of yelling ("Fire the laser cannon!" "You miserable worm, I almost feel sorry for you!") and some actors worry about blowing their voices. But she has steel cords, maybe because she grew up screaming at a clutch of under-supervised younger stepsiblings.

Bye-bye, slave girl. (Good luck! Write!) Now she's Countess Rhaelga Irtassa of Wherethefuck V, who—she glances ahead through her lines— appears to be a corruptible member of the Imperial Council. "How dare you approach me in my chamber! Explain yourself at once or I shall have my bodyguard slit your throat!"

She asks the team in the engineering booth, "Is this woman young, old, attractive, what?"

Phil's voice in her ear: "Middle-aged. Heavy face. Enormous headdress."

She goes for asperity, attempting clumsily to be silken, undercurrent of self-deluding over-the-hill coquetry. "Well that depends, my rash young friend, on whether you're willing to do me a favor. It's not an easy task I demand. It will require patience, stealth, and a complete lack of . . . shall we say? . . . moral squeamishness. Not to mention the other kind of squeamishness." Oh dear. Surely there's a better way to write that.

The countess fills the rest of the session, at the end of which Phil asks how she's holding up.

"Bring it on."

"Great. Come back in an hour, we'll do two to six?"

She pops out into the cold glare of Avenue C. The recording studio is just below the Con Ed power plant. She heads south, through two blocks of linoleum eateries, then three blocks of chichi that seem to have sprouted since the last rain. Not many people out in the frigid wind. The sky is bright blue, the sunlight on the brick walls a pale flesh color. She passes a trio of young men, tattoos and earrings, an old woman tottering behind a dog, an underdressed man hunched in his jacket, *Daily News* under his arm. She loves the shortness of so many New Yorkers. "These are my people," she announces, polishing her Polish accent. The nearly equal distribution of skin tones—does any other American city come close? English as a second or third language. Maria can't decide if her café is Maria's Cafe (awning) or Maria Cafe (window sign). The deli is Deli Corp on the front, Deli Corb on the side. Do they mean Deli Corpse? Deli Carbs? Everyone riding the subway together. Take that, heartless heartland Christians and Taliban crazies! She's lived here for fourteen years, and she still can't get past the gratitude, after growing up in a rural warren upstate where everyone was cottontail-white and scared of the world, and nothing ever happened, and nobody could distinguish, for their very lives, between shit and shinola.

She decides on Happy Wok, orders the chicken and broccoli. She was raised on vegetarianism, but her father used it as a sword to separate the saved from the damned, and her mother literally prayed to plants and trusted herbal supplements to defeat, via satyagraha, her wholly operable breast cancer, dying like a blighted ash tree at fifty-one. Saskia still prefers vegetables, but the occasional meat tastes like freedom to her, a once-a-week feast of fuck you.

She checks her messages while she eats. There's a text from Quentin confirming he can meet her for dinner near his office at 6:30. Nothing from Mette, though Saskia texted her this morning, asking if she would pick up a few things on her way home. She tries again. eggs fruit bread? confirm or deny. There are two other customers in the Wok, both heads deep in the cybersand, thumbs wrestling. She closes her eyes and listens to the ghostly castanets. If she had read a scene like this ten years ago in a sci-fi novel, she'd have scoffed at the implausibility. Why would anyone who could leave a voice message prefer to laboriously *type* one?

Back in the gray box at two, she's an ace pilot (galaxy-class fighting skills, musky allure you could cut with a chainsaw), then a nihilistic laser weapons merchant (eyes full of dead, mouth full of shit), then the supercilious computerized doors of the Presidium Headquarters (refusing to open: "I . . . don't think so," or deigning to open: "*Do* wipe your feet, there's a good supplicant"). Another four hours, another eight hundred dollars, yeah! She never perches on the stools, they'll creak on your best take, and they're always too high for her anyway. She moves the script stand out of striking range, plants her sneakers shoulder-width apart, speaks her lines with her eyes closed. It's like being in an isolation tank. In her stage work, she has never liked elaborate sets. The more realistic they are, the faker they look. Hey, Vanya, have you noticed that every room in this crazy dacha is missing a fourth wall? Give her a dark stage, spotlights, props descending on wires. Hello, audience, it's time to use our (jazz hands) *imagination*.

This game, *Dhark Rebellion*, is the third installment of a franchise, so she's seen the artwork in the previous iterations. It tends toward your standard sci-fi argon blue and spotless white gleam on the fascistic Torkan Alliance ships. The Dhark rebel bases vary, but they all trade on adolescent boys' article of faith that the narrow way to coolness leads through the pigsty: gadgety junk shops, germy brothels brimming with attitude (*still* no male prostitutes), windblown alleys with abused trash-cans and pouty denizens. The desert planet is out of *Dune*, the forest planet is *Return of the Jedi* minus the Ewok plus the whirling-dervish razory beasties from *Edge of Tomorrow*. The rebel spaceships look on the outside like arthropods and on the inside like decommissioned WWII battleships, with wires dangling from the ceilings and steel plates bolted randomly across walls and floors. There is always something not work-ing, *Millennium Falcon* style, which is what drives a good fraction of the game, because the player needs a part, which sends him (82 percent are "him," according to company research) into the junk shop, where he has to do a favor for the comic-relief android who runs it, which leads him down an alley, where he pulverizes a pouty denizen to get the key, which opens up the back room of the brothel, where the tong kingpin manages his empire, and no matter how the boy-wanderer plays this scene, a sumptuous feast of gunplay ensues.

She knows this because four or five years ago, out of curiosity, she asked Mette to help her play the original *Dhark Rebellion*. She withstood it for three hours, while her daughter critiqued the graphics and occasion-ally emitted impatient comments such as, "You're turned around again, you've tried to go out that door three times already," or "Strafe left, you're about to die; no, *hold* the button."

It was fascinating but kind of awful. After the first hour they ran into one of the characters she'd voiced, and for every line, of course, only one of her takes was used, and depending on how you navigated the dia-logue, her readings sometimes didn't mesh. A side creek, say, touching on reconciliation would feed back into a river of dismissive scorn. And the limitations of the programming were obvious. Plot choices were mainly illusory, since real deviations had to be extensively scripted. The small genuine freedom the game engine allowed was restricted to killing some-one the game didn't expect you to kill, which often resulted in nonsen-sical dialogue. "You'll have to talk to Taggart about that." Well, Idaho, since he's lying at your feet with his head blown off, that's gonna be a tough one.

Yeah, she loves the voice work, but it's not the game, it's the dream in the gray box. With her eyes closed, the sets are not merely realistic, they're real. The spaceship smells of ozone, and the artificial gravity varies nauseatingly from AG node to node. When the Alliance troops come around the corner, her body explodes with tingles of dread. So what if the line is cheesy? Cheesy lines are video verité when you're a mite mining through a block of bleu. In her first-ever session, years ago, in a game called *Infymy*, she sent the script stand flying (she still remembers the line: "Let me . . . *go*!"). Phil tells her she claws, kneads, pummels the air. She has learned to wear a sleeveless cotton t-shirt that makes no noise no matter how she moves.

End of the fourth hour. She's getting punchy. Her last line of the day, prompted if the boy-wanderer opts to abandon the Hispanic cutie with the howitzer who's helpful in a firefight, but will use up oxygen in the escape shuttle and thus reduce its range: "You . . . bastard." Her cheap tricks are creeping in on little shit feet. That pause in the middle, that hitch of unbelief, timed so predictably you could schedule a train by it. Let's face it, it's all tricks. But keeping the tricks fresh, that's the trick. Tricking yourself into believing they aren't tricks.

Six o'clock. "Thanks, Saskia," Phil says. "Great day's work. Tomorrow and Wednesday Tom's in to do the Commander. How's Thursday for you?"

"I'll have to check my busy—hey, lucky you, I'm free."

She drums down the stairs and out into the dhark, heading west toward Third Avenue. That CGI hottie was a younger Hispanic version of herself: short, hippy, breasty, kind of a Babylonian-fertility-figurine look, although the hottie had thicker hair, fuck her.

So the boy-wanderer is abandoning her? She's long suspected he was a weasel. She feels righteous rage. *"You bastard!"*

She's been wondering when he would grow a pair and betray her. She's amused, contemptuous. "Youuu . . . bastard . . ."

She taunts him with a bounce of her astonishing mammaries, accompanied by a *noli me tangere* smirk. "*You* . . . bas-tard!"

She's exultant, gleeful, at the chance to paint the walls of the launching bay with his teaspoon of brains. "Youuuu *bastaard*!!"

She's never suspected a thing. She loves him. She's so stunned she can't process what he's saying. "You—bastard—"

All men are snakes. Trusting them is a fool's game. "You bastard."

There's no morality. The universe is a hilarious playground for superbeings such as herself. "*Youu! Bastaaard!*"

She's arrived at a corner. She looks around. Broadway. Damn! Too far. She backtracks.

Interesting that a lot of the fans seem to feel the same unhappiness at the limitations of gameplay that she does. She's poked around on the Dhark wiki, where the characters are described as real people, complete with speculations about their pasts and their motives. The entry for a greedy brothel madam she voiced in *Dhark Rebellion II* said something like, "Angela Quikcustard runs the brothel in Iron City on Smilin' Jack's Moon. She came to Iron City in 2256. Some say she ran away from an abusive home on the Torkan home planet, others say she gained her cynical attitude toward life during a stint in the rebel army, in the disastrous Keyhole Nebula campaign of 2254." Saskia remembered the character, but where did the abusive home come from, the experiences in the army?

She's also read some Dhark fanfiction. Most of it doesn't involve any of her characters, which tend to be minor, but she did voice a ditzy blonde volcano-rim shack dweller in the first installment (she assumed the intended humor was the juxtaposition of her fetid quarters with her bubbleheaded lines, which she voiced in a Valley Girl drawl) who has turned out to be surprisingly popular in fan porn with a fuck-the-brainless-bitch-every-last-way theme, and inspired at least one actually not-bad story, in which the girl-wanderer (go 18 percent!) realized the blonde was speaking in code because her shack was bugged by the Presidium, and the code eventually led the two of them, now power sisters, to discover something or other, but what Saskia mainly remembers is the clever elaboration of the blonde's lines so that they sounded both hilariously vacuous and pregnant with meaning.

She finds it kind of marvelous, this fan love. Like most love—let's not say "all," shall we?—it's a heroic effort of the imagination to turn a pedestrian object into something worthy of one's . . . well, imagination. Thousands of fans gather around this inert mountain of clay, this crude giant's form with *Dhark* incised on its forehead, and with a great collaborative heave they stand it on its feet, and with a great collaborative shout they awaken it, and then they bow down before it as though it had awakened *them*, its creatures.

Corner again. Third Avenue, damn straight. Who says she's got no sense of direction? She's at 11th, the restaurant is just past 12th, a Thai place.

Quentin's not there yet. The room is pretty empty. They give her a window table so passersby will say, "Hey this place can't suck too bad, there's a really short woman in there." It's drafty near the door, but she's worked on and off as a waitress for years, and customers who ask to be moved are a pain in the ass. She keeps her coat on.

"Would you like anything while you wait?" Gorgeous slim girl with glossy raven tresses in a wine-red tunic with lotuses stitched in black. Actress, model, locked-away daughter of quaintly traditional owner?

"Tea, please, thank you."

        Houston to Mette. Do we have
        a problem?

She looks up to see Quentin coming through the door.

It's ridiculous, but sometimes she's still surprised to see him all grown up, in a dapper black wool coat with a leather satchel over his shoulder and black-framed glasses shaped like CD slots over his adorable blue eyes. He's thirty-nine, for chrissake, but family myths are as hard to dislodge as ticks, maybe there are a few sugary drops of big-sis self-satisfaction she can still squeeze out of picturing him at seven, stumbling around pigeon-toed and clueless, letting drool gather on his chin, occasionally still wetting his bed. Maybe she misses having a boy who so nakedly needed her, so openly loved her. (I see our time is up, Saskia. See you next week.)

"Pretty frigid out there, huh?"

He comes over, glances at her coat and tea. "Aren't you cold here?"

"I'm fine; I like being by the window."

He shrugs off the satchel, unwinds a scarf, dips bilaterally out of his coat. He's got a charcoal cardigan on over his olive buttondown. The lime tie is either intentionally bold, endearingly boy-blind, or ironic. He's six feet tall, shaven, fit. He couldn't look more adult if he tried.

"How's Annabelle?" she asks.

"Sleeping better now. The walking tires her out, I think."

Annabelle is fourteen months. "And Marly?" Quentin's wife, a social worker.

Small talk, luscious waitress, apologies!, menu scan, luscious waitress redux. Quentin comically can't keep his eyeballs from rolling all over her sleek surface.

He works for a small architecture firm, finds most of what he does boring, but the partners count on him, will probably offer him a partnership in three more years, though he says he doubts he'll accept. He's tempted to launch out on his own with a friend from graduate school. He's more settled and responsible than she's ever managed to be.

When did she stop calling him Quinnie? He started requesting it in his teens, never insisting, and it took her three or four years, she's chagrined to recall, before she took the idea seriously. None of the rest of the family ever made the switch. To them, he was still the foggy, weepy boy, coming home with notes from school about homework he'd never done, which he seemed not to know he'd ever been assigned. The 1580 he got on his SATs at sixteen didn't make so much as a golfball ding on the shiny bumper of the Quinnie Slowmobile the family loved driving around in.

Half an hour of Annabelle news, for which Quentin keeps apologizing, but Saskia loves babies, misses the hell out of the seeming thirty-six hours during which Mette was a member of the tribe. In the old days, Quentin would have had snapshots to rock out of his wallet, but now he passes her his phone, and she tosses the glowing photos around like Tom Cruise conducting (literally!) an investigation in *Minority Report*. (The fact that she even notices this marks her, she's pretty sure, as over-the-hill.) She hasn't seen Annabelle in several weeks. "Oh my god, she's adorable." Embarrassed by the foam-mouthed avidity that Quentin can no doubt see in her glowing blue face, she retreats into self-mockery via Valley Girl channeling: "Ohmygawwd! Like—tcha!—I mean—ohmygawwd!"

She hands the phone back. "Just send me the entire contents, OK?"

The food arrived a while ago. Quentin is half done, she has hardly started. Her portions are too big, she'll let Quentin vacuum. She's switched from tea to hot water, something she discovered years ago. Great for the cords.

"How's Mette?" Quentin asks.

"Oh, the usual."

"Yeah?"

"Doing her own thing."

"She's a fascinating young woman."

"That she is."

"I really like her."

She wishes Quentin wouldn't say that. She wants Quentin to be special, and this is what Saskia's friends always say. No, really, I *do* like her!

"Well, she likes you." She tries to remember if Mette has said word one about Quentin or anything remotely connected with Quentin in the past few weeks or, hell, ever. "She's interested in that building that's going up on whatever, you know—near Union Square, is it Fourth Avenue and something? With the copper panels."

"I know the one. Why's she interested?"

"She mostly doesn't articulate to me her reasons for being interested in something." Three or thirty months ago she emailed Saskia some photos she'd taken. Mostly close-ups of the panels, with streaks of reflected light, little dimples harboring distorted images, pools of darker color. Her caption said: get a load of these.

As usual, Saskia didn't know precisely what load she was supposed to get, but nurtured a small hope that her daughter might help her out. She opted for generic encouragement. Wow. They're beautiful.

Mette answered immediately, meaning this really was the object on her radar at the moment. you think so?

Saskia hated it when she did that. Did she *mean* it to be a test, or was she just being oblivious? Backtracking, hedging your bet, wimping out with a don't you? was never wise, Mette hated opinions that weren't sincere. Well it was perfectly plausible to see them as beautiful, so fuck her. Yes I do.

Mette didn't answer.

Was that a conversation?

"I want to hear more about what *you're* doing," she says to Quentin.

"Futzing with windows on an ugly apartment building."

"But I'm actually interested. What's the futzing you're doing?"

So they spend the rest of the meal on that, on bathroom placement, on which way doors open and why, concrete strength, cautious engineers, crazy clients, squabbling partners, with detours into Marly's fatigue, her own boss troubles, her encouragement that Quentin start his own business before his soul gets crushed, their fixer-upper off Cortelyou in Brooklyn that is turning out to need work costing the equivalent of two brand-new houses of equal size, plus several long sudsy baths in everything Annabelle.

Quentin vacuums. Saskia's heart warms. She's Ma on the prairie, rough reddened hands on hips, watching her strapping son tuck into his second helping of apple pie. "Don't forget to drink all your buttermilk," she says.

He doesn't miss a beat. "Shore thang, Maw."

Quentin grabs the check.

"No, you did that last time."

"I'm an architect, you're an actor."

"I'm doing fine."

"Next time."

"Quentin, I'm serious. It doesn't make me feel good." She doesn't add, You're being Male.

He gazes at her for a second, then hands her the check. "OK."

When they hug goodbye out on the sidewalk, he says, "I'm just trying to repay you for taking care of me for so many years."

"Oh, Quentin." She squeezes him. "You're the only reason I survived adolescence."

He lets go, smiles questioningly.

"I have to go," she says. "Mette . . ."

"Of course."

She heads up the avenue, toward the L.

She regrets that last exchange. Mette is almost twenty-one, but the mere mention of her name is accepted as a reason that Saskia must get home. She didn't mean it that way, she was thinking only that she hadn't heard from her, wanted to check in, leave time to go out for the groceries in case Mette had forgotten. Did other people, even Quentin, think that her daughter needed, what?—supervision?

A score of human bundles are scattered along the subway platform. Freezing, drafty, damp. Saskia hugs herself.

The family . . . Seeing Quentin always brings it back. Her "child-hood." From the age of ten, wasn't she the only adult in the house? Well, no, that isn't fair. She was no more adult than her mother. The two of them tried to raise the Lost Kids like a pair of Lost Girls who kept pointing at each other: You be Wendy! No, *you* be Wendy!

Saskia detests movies that culminate in the idea that, hey, we're un-traditional, but we're a *family*. (She was even in one once, as a harried receptionist at a Planned Parenthood clinic. The totality of her lines, post–cutting room: "Next!") They hide the hard issue behind the easy one. The question isn't whether Dad is married to another Dad, or if Sis has accomplished a virgin birth, or if the contra-colored urchin from down alleyway is always at the dinner table. The pesky question in most families is, Does anyone *really* care about anyone else?

Whenever Saskia starts a new relationship, she dreads this topic. The supposedly innocent icebreaker, "So what about your family?" Every an-swer she gives leads to another question. "Wait—*what*?" The men pursue it because it's a puzzle; the women, because they mainline this stuff.

When she was four, her Danish father tried to commit hara-kiri and subsequently disappeared in an ambulance. Being dead would have been an adequate excuse for never coming back, but he healed up just fine and went on to wander the world, pursuing a series of interests that absorbed him way more than Saskia ever did. Meanwhile, her mother, Lauren, climbed into Space Shuttle *Denial* and lifted off into orbit (don't worry, Earth lovers, it ran on vegetable oil). There were five kids on the property, a former whacked-out commune drowning in wild grape along Cayuga Lake north of Ithaca, New York. (Mr. Gets-a-D-in-Suicide had been the guru.) Saskia, Lauren, and the other children lived in the old house. Lauren's series of pot-smoking boyfriends lived successively in one of the two trailers until ineffectual Bill moved in and stayed. In the other trailer was thin, raspy Jo, devotée of that older sacred American drug, tobacco, and abandoned mother of the four kids who weren't Saskia. This is where Hallmark can clap the clapstick: all eight human bundles gathered nightly 'round the groaning board. Jo's four children were cuddly Melanie (one year younger than Saskia), the proto-delinquent twins Austin and Shannon (three years younger), and the underwatered houseplant known as Quinnie (five years younger). Of the many family secrets Lauren never got around to telling Saskia, one of them was that Quinnie's facial resemblance to Saskia's wasn't a Lamarckian consequence of her years of singlehandedly nurturing him, but because Dad had fucked Jo shortly before decamping.

Saskia's pillow talk with new partners was terse on this dialogue thread, no matter what options the player chose. She wasn't trying to be enigmatic, she was just sick of the subject. Also, aware of her propensity for fanciful elaboration—not to mention occasional substitution of entirely different narratives of ad hoc inspiration—she did not want to start a new relationship dishonestly.

Back to the Afternoon TV Special: yes, they passed the string beans to each other, and even laughed on occasion—where's the freeze frame when you need it?—but who would be in the sequel? She had grown to like boyfriend Bill, his hopeless writer's dreams, his decent loyalty to Lauren, but when Lauren died he wandered off and stopped answering Saskia's emails after a year. It's possible he was heartbroken, but weren't he and Saskia "family" by then? How many fucking string beans does it take? Jo died of throat cancer five years ago, so she gets a pass. Melanie, a stay-at-home mom in San Jose, sends Saskia Christmas greetings, but that's it. When they were children, Saskia adored the younger girl, but when Melanie was eighteen, the thirty-four-year-old minister of a local evangelical church led her to Jesus, his bed, and the altar in an order Saskia would be very curious to know, and since then Saskia's bisexuality has been a bit of a sore subject. Austin and Shannon grew up most like Jo, a couple of wisecracking, school-skipping, drug-loving troublemakers. They're both somewhere in northern Maine, and don't return calls.

And then there's Thomas. (That would be "Dad.") He will live forever. Failing to kill himself with a ceremonial Japanese tantō was the fairy-tale proof of his immortality. The last Saskia heard, he's been incarnating a holy hermit perched atop a windmill on some remote Danish island. She kids not. Anyway, the point is, when this flamboyant three-masted schooner with its tangled rigging went gurgling to the bottom, the only thing that bobbed to the surface in Saskia's vicinity was Quentin. I'll be flotsam, you be jetsam.

Speaking of which, she's emerging from the depths at the north end of the Greenpoint Avenue Station, into arctic winds. Jumping Jehosaphat! She shrivels, turns her shoulder upwind, hobbles homeward. She got a tiny bit inured to the cold during the past two winters when all that polar-vortex shit was going on, but this winter has been mostly milder. *I may be some time*, she says to her tentmate and fellow explorer, heading out to her plucky British death. *God save the Queen, and damn the torpedoes!* Her apartment is only a block away, but the wind is against her. She turns around and leans backward into it, pushing with her feet against the peanut-brittle ice on the sidewalk. She fumbles with her keys through her mittens at the door, shoulders in, mashes it shut behind her. On through the inner door, past the door to the ground floor apartment, which belongs to the family she rents the second floor from. Sounds of television. True to Greenpoint's Wikipedia paragraph on demographics, they're Polish American, an old woman and her middle-aged bachelor son. His divorced sister and her two young children lived upstairs until they all died from carbon monoxide poisoning in a snug little cabin in the Poconos eight years ago. The old woman, Aniela, used to be talkative in her grief, and Saskia sat with her on a number of afternoons in the early months of her rental. Aniela lived in Krakow until she was twenty-six, and Saskia's generic Polish accent is a shameless full-bore imitation of her.

She unlocks the door at the top of the stairs. "Mette?"

She walks through the sitting room, glances in the kitchen. Knocks on her daughter's bedroom door. "Mette?" Cracks the door. (Mette would prefer to lock it, but the fire escape is through her window, and Saskia vowed to never under any circumstance step across the threshold when Mette wasn't there, unless a roaring inferno convincingly blocked the stairway.) "Mette?" Swings the door open.

Damn that girl. (Woman.) Nothing for breakfast tomorrow, and Saskia's not going back out into that cold. Why can't she answer her texts?

Saskia makes tea, grabs the remote, settles on the couch under a chenille bedspread she rescued from the attic of the old house upstate. Something from her mother's childhood (which Saskia knows nothing about, beyond rumors of family wealth, six older brothers, and Grand Guignol). It's coming up on nine-thirty. She'll wait up. She sips the tea and listens to the wind against the window.

There was a line today, toward the end of the session. If the player decides to bring the Hispanic cutie along in the escape pod, apparently the oxygen runs out and they have to make an emergency crash landing on an uncharted planet (these people have faster-than-light travel, but pre-Columbian mapping technology). Phil explained there'd be a cutscene, so Saskia imagined a descent through atmosphere, red haze of heat-shield burn, clouds parting, jungly riverine valley, looming treetops, kaboom! Compressed-air sound effect as hatch opens. Player stumbles out. Cue the cutie, bloodied and dazed (tits, thank God, intact): "Wh—where are we? What is this place?"

She did the usual three takes on the line, then asked Phil if she could do them over.

"Um, sure," he said, sounding surprised. "Those were good."

"I can do it better."

"Go for it."

In the previous takes she'd been distracted trying to fight the shivers running up and down her body, but now she cracked open the door to the memory, which lent to her voice an authentic thrill of awe. She asked to hear the playback. She was delighted. No, it isn't all tricks. (In other words, tricked herself again!)

Years ago, she acted in a Shakespeare company in Ithaca. It's how she caught the bug. She'd dropped out of college and popped out Mette, was living with Lauren on the old commune. Brainless besotted baby worship was just giving way to the willies: she would end up like her mother, waiting tables in Ithaca and selling produce at the Farmer's Market, wrapping her lonely self in a New Age crazy quilt. She'd disliked college, so going back wasn't the solution. It never occurred to her that acting might be, she just had to do *something* to get her sorry ass off the property. She saw a notice about auditions, went into town and read, and they gave her Ursula in *Much Ado*.

She didn't get paid, of course. This was a bunch of amateurs, for whom friends donated five dollars at the door. They used the money to rent a space in a small defunct movie theater. Costumes were pieced together from the Salvation Army store. Sets were minimal, and therefore pretty good: ships were ropes hanging in swags, thrones were tall chairs, woods were shadows of paper leaves hung in a mesh over the stage lights. Looking back, Saskia has no idea whether she could act, but she could tell right away that some of her fellow actors couldn't. The younger ones weren't bad, because most of them hailed from the Ithaca College theater department. Additionally, there were two former Equity actors who had fetched up on the town's shores ("Wh—where are we? What is this place?") and decided to stay. But there was a coterie of old codgers with only three ways of delivering any line given to them: angry (incomprehensible shouting), neutral (rotely cadenced, deaf to meaning), and distressed (like angry, only scrunch-faced). There was also the occasional smug young jerk with one or two tricks up his sleeve (95 percent were "he"), such as a naturally rich voice or the ability to produce tears on cue, that sufficed so well for his self-esteem that he could otherwise sleepwalk through his part.

Observing all this, Saskia discovered a mission—she could dedicate herself to not sucking as an actor.

They gave her scraps: Third Servant in *Henry IV*, Second Murderer in *Macbeth*, Mariana in *Measure for Measure*. Progress toward bigger parts was slow, because Dorothy, one of the founding members of the company, took the best roles for herself, and there were always one or two fresh Ithaca College faces to snap up the secondary female roles. Finally, though, at the end of Saskia's second year, they gave her Thaisa in *Pericles*, partly because the June performances came too late in the spring for the students and partly because, even though Dorothy wanted to play both Thaisa and her daughter Marina, she was vetoed by her husband (the director) who didn't want to use a double in the final reunion scene, in which the two characters appear together. There was a lovely childish fight about this, in front of everyone. Actors are fun that way.

Could Saskia act? Impossible to know. But something happened to her in that play. At its midpoint, Thaisa gives birth to Marina on a ship at sea during a storm and, seeming to have died, is tossed overboard in a sealed casket. This washes up in Ephesus, near the home of a doctor named Cerimon, whose servants discover it, carry it into his house, pop the lid, and marvel at the beautiful corpse. Recognizing all the signs of a Shakespearean resurrection scene, Cerimon calls for his medicines, bids the viol play, and lo! Thaisa wakens and speaks. If you're playing Thaisa and you're a bad actor, it's an easy scene, because you've only got thirteen words. If you have hopes of someday being a good actor, it's terrifying—you've got only thirteen words in which to blaze forth a miracle, make the audience gasp, swoon, and then wake, as you, reborn.

Rehearsals of the scene had focused on practical issues. Since she had to be in the casket when they carried it in, much time was devoted to figuring out how to bang her around less. Also, if the platform they put her on was too low, Cerimon had to crouch, which didn't look solemn, but if it was too high, it called to mind an operating table, thus Frankenstein. Should they position the casket so that the audience could see her while she was still lying in it? Should Cerimon touch her in some way, as part of the wakening process? As a result, the only time they played the scene straight through was at the dress rehearsal.

On opening night, twenty-five indulgent souls showed up and the imaginary curtain rose. Thaisa's first scene is undramatic and kind of dumb—a pageant of knights crosses the stage, each bearing a shield that Thaisa describes at length to her father, King Simonides. The king was being played by one of the talentless duffers, whom Saskia wanted to poleax. The audience was a lump of clay and all her lines seemed inert and abject. Then she had her brief bit with Pericles in which he wins a tournament and dances with her and steals her heart. Then there's the sea-storm, Thaisa dies without a word, and lies on stage like an obedient dead woman while Pericles eloquently mourns her. After that, it's into the old box with her and over the side, heave-ho. (Which would make her jetsam, rather than flotsam.)

So—although this was Saskia's largest role to date, she was beginning to realize, as it flew by in performance, that there wasn't much to it. Well, of course, that's why they gave it to her. Virtually all she had left for the night were those thirteen words. She was in tears in the half-gutted, junk-filled side room they called "backstage." But she had only ninety seconds between getting carted off on a bier and carted back in in a box, so she blew her nose and thumbed her eyes, while First Servant patted her shoulder and said, "Hey, hey," but wasn't experienced enough to add, "You're doing great!" She threw on the Salvation Army moth-eaten magnificent "cloth of state" and lay down. First and Second Servant put in the bags of dried leaves that were the spices, the gilded plastic crap that was the treasure, then dropped the lid onto the Velcro strips and lifted her. She was swayed and bumped up the stairs.

"So; lift there!" she heard through the plywood. (That would be First Servant.)

"What's that?" (Cerimon.)

"Sir, even now did the sea toss up upon our shore this chest. 'Tis of some wrack."

"Set't down, let's look upon't."

With a final pitch and a yaw she came to rest. She closed her eyes.

"How close 'tis caulked and bitumed! Did the sea cast it up?"

"I never saw so huge a billow, sir, as tossed it upon shore."

"Wrench it open: soft! It smells most sweetly in my sense."

"A delicate odor."

"As ever hit my nostril. So; up with it!" The lid was removed. "O you most potent gods! What's here, a corpse!"

The audience couldn't see her (Blocking Decision #2), but she kept her eyes closed so as not to distract the players. (If she'd been an old hand during a long run, especially if British—those blokes play rough— she'd have crossed her eyes and stuck out her tongue just as Cerimon bent over her.) Maybe her disappointment in her performance so far made it easier for her to believe that she was someplace far away from upstate New York, so why not on Ephesus's shore? She had been an actor on a troupe ship, and they'd hanged her for incompetence. But the currents had been merciful, directing her shoreward, and a handsome young serving lad (long naked tanned torso, loincloth, hint of pubic hair peeking out, hello!) pulled her casket out of the surge. She was being given a second chance.

Cerimon had lifted her right hand out of the box, and was massaging it (Blocking Decision #5). "Death may usurp on nature many hours, and yet the fire of life kindle again the o'erpressed spirits."

Charles was one of the former Equity actors, having trod the boards in minor roles in New York and a couple of major ones in Philadelphia. When he was sixty, he'd moved to Ithaca with his partner—now husband, yay!—to enjoy a quiet life gardening and occasionally directing plays in the summer. He had a magnificent voice, but had somehow managed not to fall in love with it, so it remained his servant. He also had a wonderfully large craggy face with bright black eyes. If Saskia ever needed resurrection for real, he would be on her short list of mages to do it.

"The fire and cloths," Charles went on. "The rough and woeful music that we have, cause it to sound, beseech you."

Brandon was an Ithaca College performance major in viola who'd grown up in the area and was staying home for the summer because his mother was ill. He had taken it upon himself to compose the moonlit air that he now began to play. Saskia lay in the coffin and listened to the music—for every performance Brandon was on stage for only three minutes, and like everyone else, he worked for free—and felt her hand being warmed by Charles as he knocked Shakespeare's words out of the park: "She is alive! Behold, her eyelids, cases to those heavenly jewels which Pericles hath lost, begin to part their fringes of bright gold; the diamonds of a most praisèd water doth appear to make the world twice rich. Live, and make us weep to hear your fate, fair creature, rare as you seem to be."

She opened her eyes and saw the edges of the casket like a frame, within it Charles's rapt, wondering face looking down at her, Brandon still playing softly, and she was suddenly swamped by a wave of emotion as she realized how insanely lucky they were, this small-town gang of enthusiasts, to have Charles and Brandon, and how lucky that humans have such a thing as a viola, and the whole crazy series of episodes in *Pericles*, in which Fate seemed to count for everything and individual merit nothing, suddenly seemed right and true, we're all lost and helpless and continually washing up on a shore somewhere, and we can only hope that someone will find us and pry open our lid and say that we smell good.

She sat up, wanting to throw her arms around Charles and kiss him and wrestle him to the ground and sit on him, but restrained herself, and in rehearsal she had worried about technique, about keeping clarity while conveying emotion, but all that was forgotten in a blaze of ecstasy and idiocy so complete it could only be holy. "Oh dear Diana, where am I? Where's my lord? What world is this?"

None of which is to say that she necessarily delivered the line well. Private spasms are dangerous. But this story is about *her*, not about whoever had nothing better to do that evening than fork over forty bits, expecting not much and getting it. What *she* got was her first heroine (heroin!) glimpse of what acting might mean for her, if she could get it under control, learn to ride that breaking wave.

Where am I? Where's my lord? What world is this?

Okay, sure, "where's my lord," patriarchal horseshit. What Shakespeare meant—or anyway, what *she* meant—is, Where's my guidance? What is my purpose on this earth?

She sips her tea, gazes on the familiar objects of her sitting room. She's a single mother, an unknown actor barely making ends meet. The world is overheating. Gays can marry in every state, while a third of Americans seem to have been driven literally insane by the election of a Black president. Her ambition when she was young was to know everything, to read all the great books, including the Zulus' Tolstoy, to know French history and the human genome, theories of consciousness and artificial intelligence, the complete works of Bach and the multiple authors of the Bible. Now she thinks she'd be satisfied with understanding her daughter.

She hits the remote, streams an episode of a show with an actress she had a fling with years ago. Then a different show, and a third. She tries to enjoy the solid work she's seeing without dwelling on how her oppor-tunities have mostly dried up. This business has taught her that the human sin underlying all others is not pride, but envy. Pride is merely an injury to the patriarchal god she doesn't believe in, whereas envy is an injury to one's fellow human beings. She finishes with an episode of the old *Twilight Zone*. That gorgeous look of black-and-white film.

Then it's midnight. She picks up her phone.

don't torture your mother

Goes to bed.

When she startles awake at 6:00 a.m., she checks Mette's room. The bed is neat as a pin, unslept in.

Wednesday, February 17, 2016

"Hello, what's up?"

"Mette's missing."

"What do you mean, missing?"

"What do people usually mean when they say 'missing'?"

"How long?"

"Since yesterday."

"Maybe she pulled an all-nighter at Qualternion, some programming problem."

"Of course I called. Someone there said she showed up yesterday morning and a few minutes later she walked out. Didn't say a thing. She's not answering my texts. Some of her clothes are gone."

"So she hasn't been kidnapped."

"Don't joke, for chrissake."

"I'm not joking. If she went somewhere on her own volition she's probably fine."

"So why worry? How convenient."

"I'm just—"

"I think she's run away."

"Run away? I don't think—"

"She's been withdrawn lately."

"I don't think you can—"

"I mean more than usual."

"I don't think you can run away when you're twenty."

"Mark—*fuck*! Could you please pass the test? I'm worried because there's a good reason to be worried. Can you just accept that?"

"Okay."

"I'm telling you because you should know."

"Okay."

"I might need to reach you, you're not about to run off to a conference?"

"No, I'm teaching."

"Good."

1993–1994

Numerous studies have shown that visual memories are untrustworthy, but for what it's worth, he remembers seeing her for the first time. He was in his second year teaching Intro to Astronomy, and back then he talked too much about his own work in the opening lecture, imagining that students would find it helpful to keep in mind his particular perspective as he guided them through the field. Also, looking back, he thinks he was nervous, and talking about his areas of expertise has always calmed him.

He was in Taft Auditorium, looking out at a hundred and fifty young strangers in varied warm-weather dress, bored or studious or on the tiresome mating prowl, a few of them actually interested in astronomy, the rest satisfying the college's science distribution requirement with a course light on math. He nattered on about himself (it's embarrassing to remember this), telling them more than they wanted to know about astrometry, and why—although measuring the positions and relative velocities of stars as accurately as possible certainly sounds dull, doesn't it?—it was a necessary foundation for all of the other branches of astronomy, because how could any theory be evaluated without firm data etc etc.

A hand went up (he still sees it, for what it's worth, about halfway up the rows on the left-hand side), which surprised him, since questions were supposed to be reserved for after lectures or during sectionals, but he said, "Question?"

"So you're like a modern-day Tycho Brahe."

He was so startled, he said, "Excuse me?"

"You're like Brahe, making Kepler's fancy-pants theories possible."

He must have just stared at her for a second or two. She was petite, swallowed up in a sweater that looked too warm for the room. She had curly hair and complicated dangling earrings. She was smiling. It was a show-off question—or strictly speaking, a comment—but he was impressed that she knew enough to make it, and had the temerity to do so on the first day of class. It almost felt like she was teasing him. Finally he said, "Exactly." Then he went on, but feeling self-conscious, he cut his description short. (Was it possible, he wondered much later, that that was her intention all along?)

She came up to him at the end of the lecture and he thought she was going to flaunt some more knowledge. He wanted to tell her that grading was done by the section leaders. But instead she apologized. "I have a tendency to show off."

"Not at all. You're interested in the subject. That's great." She really was quite small, perhaps not even five feet. She had a narrow asymmetrical face, glistening dark eyes, and a rather large nose, also asymmetrical. "Were you in the astronomy club in your high school?"

"Ha! God, no."

"But you're thinking about majoring in astronomy?"

"Not really."

"But you know something about Tycho Brahe."

"That's only because I had a—" She stopped, shook her head, snorted. "I had a strange childhood."

He couldn't read her expression. Embarrassed? Proud? Could it possibly be flirtatious? Surely not. His students never flirted with him. In any case, he had no idea what to say, so he said nothing. After a moment she walked off.

In the following weeks, against his will, he always noted where she was sitting. She never missed a lecture, usually arriving at the last second, barreling through the door in the back on the left—though small, she really did kind of "barrel," other students stepping and even jumping out of her way—and running down the left-hand steps, slipping into the first open aisle seat. She'd pull out a fat spiralbound notebook (few students had laptops then) and spend the hour writing furiously, pausing to chew on her pen, cupping her high forehead with her left palm. She didn't raise her hand again, or speak to him after the lecture, and it bothered him that he even noticed this.

Against his will—of course that phrase makes no sense in this context—he asked her section leader, Paul, how she was doing. He'd briefly considered inventing an excuse for his interest, but he hated lying.

"I think she's a couple years older than her classmates," Paul said. "Talks a lot, is always wandering off topic into stuff like I'm not kidding medieval philosophy or eighteenth-century mapmaking. The other students roll their eyes. But she's bright as hell and seems actually interested, which of course puts her in the minority."

Sometime after that, he had a dream about her. He was lecturing in his underwear, and hoping that if he could just keep talking about Barnard's Star, no one would notice. He was running out of things to say, and since there was a new university policy, adopted with great fanfare, that legally proscribed repeating yourself in a lecture, he was beginning to panic. She raised her hand. He was trying not to look at her, but she came down the aisle with her hand still in the air and sent him a challenge with her eyes across the lectern. He knew for a certainty that she was going to ask him something arcane about Barnard's Star, but phrase it in such a way that it would sound like it was really about his underwear.

He kept leaning right and left, trying to see past her, but she kept floating in front to block his vision. That's when he woke up, wondering at
himself.

Could it have to do with Susan? She had died in the spring, and he'd
had a terrible summer, sleeping badly and having trouble concentrating.
He had just turned thirty-four, and apart from a couple of relationships
in his twenties that had lasted a few months, then seemed to fade away
of their own accord (he worked too much, was one refrain), he'd been
alone and never minded it. Or in any case, he'd never felt the desire to
initiate a relationship. Both Stephanie and Janice had approached him.
Yet it was true, now that he thought about it, that his distress after
Susan's death felt not unlike loneliness. Which in a way was odd, because he'd hardly seen his sister for years, and only rarely traded a letter
with her. Of course there had never been a time when she wasn't part of
his world. He'd always looked up to her, not only as the smarter one, but
the more honest, or . . . He didn't know what word he was looking for.
She was the delver, the unearther. She was like his emissary to the realm
of meaning. She made the world feel more real. She even made his own
feelings feel more real. He couldn't articulate it any better than that.

And then someone killed her.

He actually saw her just before she flew out of New York, because he
happened to be in the city for a conference. He watched the back of her
head as she went down the subway steps, her short unkempt hair, the
worn leather knapsack on her much-traveled shoulder.

He'd spent the summer doing nothing but trying to work and trying
to sleep, mostly failing at both. A mass of data from some telescope time
the previous summer on molecular clouds had looked promising, but he
just couldn't get excited. Which was kind of terrifying. He'd always been
puzzled by the large fraction of people who didn't seem to love learning
new things. Now he was just another sleepwalker.

He would get over it. Research indicated that people have emotional set points to which they return, following both good and bad events. But it didn't feel like he'd get over it. Of course that feeling was a predictable aspect of not yet being over it, but still . . . Anyway, he wasn't himself. And now he'd just had a dream about a student and he'd woken with an erection. REM sleep in men induces erections regardless of the content of the dream, but the chance contiguity of her presence in his dream with his waking in a tumescent state had now added to his thoughts of her a spurious erotic tone.

Her name was Saskia White. He went that far, bothering to learn it from the class list. And the fact that she was a local. But no further. After two or three more lectures he realized he was addressing his remarks to the right side of the room to avoid looking at her. How ridiculous.

Then one day she approached him again at the lectern. This was after the midterms, because he remembers that by this time he'd perused her test booklet and been impressed—ridiculous that he'd looked—and as she came up to him he addressed her by name, forgetting that there was no good reason why he would know it.

If she was surprised, she didn't indicate it. But she surprised him all over again. He had been lecturing on the outer planets of the solar system and she had a question about Triton. He must have mentioned that Triton's retrograde motion around Neptune showed that it could not have formed in the same part of the solar nebula as its host planet, but was probably a captured Kuiper Belt object. She wondered to him how likely that hypothesis was, given that Triton's orbit was almost perfectly circular. "I mean, what are the chances that Triton would collide with another Kuiper Belt object and end up with exactly the right trajectory for that to happen? Isn't that like the orbital dynamics version of a hole-in-one from, I don't know, thousands of miles away?"

For a sophomore in an intro course who wasn't already an amateur astronomer, this was a remarkably sophisticated question. "Good for you," he has a feeling he might have said. "The initial orbit would have been eccentric, but tidal forces tend to circularize orbits, because a circular orbit is in a lower energy state, tidally, than a noncircular one."

"But why is Triton's orbit *more* circular than most of the other moons and planets?"

"The orbital influence of tidal forces depends on a number of factors, so there's no standard timetable for circularization. Triton almost certainly interacted with other Neptunian moons, which had the effect of ejecting them entirely from the local system while reducing Triton's eccentricity. This would help explain why Neptune has so few moons compared to the other gas giants. But as it happens, you've hit on a question that still is a bit of a puzzle since, despite what I've just said, the solar system isn't old enough to entirely account for the near-total absence of eccentricity in Triton's orbit. There's a theory involving gas drag from a planetary debris disk—" and off he went (probably, he doesn't remember exactly), chattering and nattering, backing and filling, restating and elaborating. He starts to use his hands a lot.

Finally, he noticed her looking bemused. Or maybe bored. "Sorry," he said.

"What? Why?"

"I can go on too long." (This part he remembers exactly. For what it's worth.)

"Shit— Oh, sorry, I mean damn, or . . . darn. Or maybe even fudge"— and here she laughed—"don't apologize, I'll bet I could talk you under the table, most people talk about nothing but themselves, it's adorable."

Again he thinks a few seconds probably went by during which he just stood there like an ox. Even when he's alone, his mind works deliberately. In social interactions he's always three steps behind everyone else. Did she just call him adorable? Or did she mean the people who only talk about themselves? And if she meant him, wasn't that kind of condescending and presumptuous? But if so, why did it fill him with delight? And if it was about him, and it delighted him, where were the warning bells that ought to be going off in his head? Or was wondering about warning bells in fact the warning bell?

He must have said something in response, but he can't remember what it was. He suspects that even just seconds later he wouldn't have been able to recall it. At moments of emotional confrontation he has no short-term memory of anything he says. Not so, his visual memory. He can call up now, twenty-two and a half years later, exactly what she looked like at that moment. She had applied a coral lip balm against the November weather, and her mouth was narrow and shapely beneath a well-defined philtrum; her smile was what people would probably call "roguish"; when she tensed her cheeks, as now, she had a dimple beneath her left eye; her earrings were lily-of-the-valley bells made out of misty blue-gray glass; her eyebrows were sparse; her irises, which he had thought nearly black because of her eyes' gleaming quality, were in fact a milky brown.

That was the moment he— What would be the right phrase? "Fell in love with her" is ridiculous. It was the moment after which he found himself thinking about her much of the time. He no longer had to wonder where the warning bells were. He was fixated on one of his students! How pathetic!

Ah, maybe "fixated on her" is the right phrase.

For the rest of the semester he forced himself to address both sides of the lecture hall, and yes, he always noted when she arrived and where she sat, and when she chewed on her pen, and when she stopped taking notes. (Was he nattering on?) He hoped she wouldn't ask him any more questions and he also hoped she would. (She didn't.) He had two more dreams involving her, neither of them erotic, but unusually vivid. In one of them he and she were in a hot-air balloon under a lurid sky, and he wanted to descend while she wanted to rise. In the other he was stretching a carpet while she was sitting on it, but for some reason that was helping rather than hindering him. He woke up from both dreams with an erection but, to repeat, all REM sleep induces erections.

He read her final exam, and was again impressed by her intelligence. More than that, she displayed an imaginative engagement with the material that suggested she might make a good astronomer. He worried that she would take the companion course in the spring, then was disappointed when she didn't. He went so far as to inquire with the registrar and was informed she had taken a leave of absence. He wondered what that implied, but restrained himself from looking further. He did not want to make a complete fool of himself.

Sometime in March he found a note from her in his faculty mailbox.

Hi Prof Fuller,

I don't know if you remember me, I was in your intro course last semester, I'm the one who paraded my soupçon of knowledge about Tycho Brahe in front of the class at your first lecture. I'm taking a break this semester and frankly contemplating not coming back, I liked a couple of my courses but I'm not sure I can bear to jump through all those hoops just for that piece of paper, most of my life I've been mostly self-educated and I also have issues with authority figures that probably don't serve me well, but there you go. Anyway, I wanted to say that your course was my favorite, and I also liked the way you taught it, you seemed unpompous and kind for a professor, though I'm probably breaking protocol here. But now that I've broken it, I'm wondering if you'd ever like to get together for coffee or tea, I don't know anyone else who's interested in astronomy the way I've been for as long as I can remember. You can see from my address that I live in the area, and I can come into town most days. Let me know. Or not!

Saskia (White)

Two or three weeks went by during which he pretended to have qualms. Then he called the number she'd written below her name. They met at a coffee shop and talked for three hours. Some of the thoughts he remembers going through his head on that bright cold April afternoon in the booth by the streaky picture window:

Her mind worked much faster than his.

It reminded him of Susan.

She wasn't his student now.

She was twenty-two.

Twenty-two is way more than half of thirty-four.

When they parted outside she said, "That was a lot of fun."

He said, "For me, too."

She said, "You're sweet."

He stood like an ox, saying nothing.

She turned abruptly. "Call me again." This was over her shoulder, as she walked away. "Or not!"

He watched her recede down the long sidewalk, moving faster than everybody else, including people with longer legs, which was everybody else.

2006

Back in the sixties, when Mark was a boy, his family rarely ate out. However, occasionally they would go to the Pacific Hut at the Burlington Mall. Compared to the brightly lit concourse, the restaurant was murky. Photographs of thatched huts were framed in bamboo stalks the size of bass flutes, and similarly large bamboo halves covered the panels dividing the booths. His sister would sing under her breath, "Just sit right back and you'll hear a tale, a tale of a fateful trip . . ."

Whenever his family went anywhere, they always did exactly what they did the last time they were there. At the Pacific Hut, he and Susan would share a Pu Pu Platter. His mother would get the Tahitian lobster and say that it wasn't as good as the lobster at the Willow Pond Kitchen, but it wasn't bad. His father would order the Sweet and Sour Chicken, and Mark would be struck anew by the velvety DayGlo-orange sauce draped over the golden puffs of batter.

That was his entire childhood experience with the kind of food his family referred to as Chinese, though he later supposed it was Americo-Sino-Hawaiian. It wasn't until freshman year of college that he was taken by worldly classmates to a Cantonese restaurant in Boston's Chinatown, where he looked on agog as they wielded chopsticks with the skill of his father wrangling a slide rule. According to some prior agreement he wasn't party to, they shared all the dishes, and the platters quickly emptied to the sound of clacking pincers while he chased a slippery snow pea pod around his plate. He pocketed a pair of the disposable chopsticks and over the next few days practiced in the freshman dining hall until he was adept at picking up single grains of rice.

He sometimes remembered this when he was busy in his university office in the evening and decided to order takeout. The Wok Inn was a mile from campus, tucked away in a small plaza oddly removed from foot and vehicular traffic, down an access road that curved behind a hotel. At night it was badly lit and forlorn. When he entered the Wok Inn to pick up his order, no one was ever sitting at any of the tables. A woman would come out from the kitchen and hand him his food and ring up the amount. After stepping out, he would sometimes stand for a minute under the flat concrete awning that ran part of the way around the square. The plaza was so isolated, you couldn't hear the traffic along the road on the far side of the hotel. With a step forward he could look up and see Vega or Sirius or Rigel, depending on the season, and those stars seemed less isolated than this parking lot. No one else ever arrived while he stood there. Yet the bag of food was warm in his hand. If he looked back at the Wok Inn, the lights were on, but no one was visible, not even the woman who'd served him.

It led to fanciful thoughts. It felt as though the Wok Inn had sprung into existence a moment before he'd arrived, and would disappear as soon as he left. Or maybe what gave him such a happy thrill was the opposite notion: that the Wok Inn existed without any need for him, or apparently for anyone else; that it was always there, whether anyone visited it or not, like prokaryotic life on exoplanets, which probably existed in some form, but which humans might never discover. Like virtually everything in the universe, for that matter, galaxies and radiation and cubic kiloparsecs of expanding space, the whole shebang—out there for certain, but just as certainly not there for us.

One night after he'd returned to his office with his order, he sat in front of his computer and contemplated for the umpteenth time that nameless feeling—the mystery of ordinary moments that seemed "pregnant with meaning," as some people liked to say. This was poetry's domain, as he understood it. He had never much cared for poetry. Most of it seemed unnecessarily obscure. Yet life did offer up moments of intensity, whose precise meaning was ambiguous. He wondered if it might be possible to convey the phenomenon in words, but without using all that annoying poetic language. Since the feeling was engendered by simple real-world facts, why not simply list those facts? Mightn't such a list engender in the reader the same or a similar feeling?

He opened a new document on his computer and wrote down the sort of list he had in mind. He read it over, discarded it, tried again, read again, rewrote, and eventually had something that roused in him a feeling not dissimilar to the one he often had outside the Wok Inn. Of course a better test would be to find out if it had such an effect on a reader who hadn't experienced the antecedent moment. However, he felt abashed at the thought of letting anyone else see it. Probably it would mean nothing to them. Probably it would seem simple-minded.

He decided to send the list to his daughter, who was eleven years old and precocious. She didn't live with him, so he and she mainly communicated by email.

11:49 p.m., April 30, 2006

Dear Mette,

I hope you are well, and that you're still having fun with algebra. Please say hello to your mother for me. Here's an amusing proof that all numbers are equal:

Let x and y be any real numbers.

Let $z = (x + y)/2$

Multiply both sides of the above equation by 2, to get: $2z = x + y$

Now multiply both sides by $(x-y)$: $2z(x-y) = (x + y)(x-y)$, or $2zx-2zy = x^2-y^2$.

Rearrange: $y^2-2zy = x^2-2zx$.

Add z^2 to both sides: $y^2-2zy + z^2 = x^2-2zx + z^2$.

Factor both sides: $(y-z)^2 = (x-z)^2$

Take the square root of both sides: $y-z = x-z$

Add z to both sides, and voilà: $y = x$!

Can you figure out where I cheated?

Also, I wrote a "poem." Or something, anyway. I'm not sure what to call it. It reminds me a little bit of a data set, except here each datum is a descriptive sentence. Anyway, here it is:

Walk In, Take Out

The parking lot is at the end of an access road that curves behind the hotel.

You would never find it if you didn't already know it was there.

At night the lot is always dark and empty.

There are six other shops that appear to still be in business, but they're always dark.

The Wok Inn has a dining area that is narrow and deep.

There are eight tables and twenty-eight chairs.

The fluorescent lights in the drop ceiling are always on.

The plastic red lanterns on the tables are never lit.

The room is always empty.

No one is ever at the cash register.

In front of the cash register is a bowl of after-dinner mints.

When I call to order take-out, the phone is always answered promptly.

When I park in the dark lot and come into the empty room, I always call out, "Hello?"

A woman always comes immediately out of the kitchen at the back with my order.

She never asks for the name on the order.

The order is always correct.

She rings me up at the cash register.

She always offers me a mint.
I sometimes glimpse a child at the back of the kitchen in the
    back of the room.
I'm never sure if it's the same child or the same woman.

love,
Your Father

2006

Secrets of her solitary life:

Her age is the smallest nontrivial palindromic number. Her nest is behind her computer, between two bookcases, against the window. She crawls into it through a foot-wide gap. Wishner waits on the windowsill. Her school is P.S. 17Q. Q stands for Queens, 17 is a prime number, and Q is the 17th letter of the alphabet. The windowsill is 14 inches above her mattress. Her apartment is on the third floor, which is also the top floor. When she lies in her nest no one but birds and stars can see her. She reads Wishner by daylight filtered through grimy glass. At night she contorts the gooseneck of her desk lamp, casting a cone on her pillow.

On the book cover, Pickwick sits on the flat end of an upturned log, his striped back toward the viewer, his bright-eyed face in profile. Sunflower seed casings are scattered around his rump and tail. Wishner's caption: "The nobility of character and elegance of independence: Pickwick looks at the world over his shoulder."

Her mother sleeps on a futon in the other room. That's also where she and her mother eat. The open floor space in the kitchen is only eighteen square feet.

Her address is 30-51 33rd Street. The buildings on her block are connected in a right-angle back-and-forth pattern like what you sometimes see on Greek friezes, or like cogs on a wheel, if you were to cut the wheel and straighten it out. The buildings are red brick on the first floor, beige brick on the upper two floors. On some signs and maps the street numbers don't have dashes (3051) and on other signs and maps they do (30-51). She did research and discovered the dash is the older form. The first two digits indicate the lower of the two avenues flanking the street in question. The historic use of the dash is disappearing. She is fighting this.

There is an endearing photograph of Gutrune on page 47. She is standing on the same upturned log with her hands to her mouth and her cheeks stuffed with sunflower seeds. Wishner's caption informs us she is twenty-seven days pregnant.

She and her mother have been living in New York City for four years. Her mother wants to find an apartment that's either bigger or cheaper or both. She dreads this. She has made her nest perfect. Why do people have to move so much?

To get to school, she walks northeast on 33rd Street and turns left at 30th Avenue. At 31st Street she walks under the N and R, an elevated railway fallaciously called a subway. At 30th Street she crosses 30th Avenue via a crosswalk that's diagonal because 30th Street makes a jog right there.

At P.S. 17Q other children insist on speaking to her. Their motives are unfathomable.

Here is how young chipmunks mature. When they are one day old and weigh five grams, they squeal. When they are five to seven days old and weigh ten grams, their lower teeth, stripes, and hair begin to show. When they are ten days old and weigh fifteen grams, they move about. When they are thirty days old and weigh thirty grams, their eyes open, and they are weaned. When they are forty days old and weigh sixty grams, they emerge from their burrow. When they are sixty days old and weigh eighty grams, they are fully grown. When they are one hundred days old, the females are sexually mature. Repeat cycle.

In the autumn of 1974, Lawrence Wishner installed lights over a
woodpile on his back porch. The porch stood thirty feet from the woods.
He mounted a camera inside one of his house windows that looked out
on the porch. In front of the woodpile he stood two logs on end at pre-
calculated exposure distances from the lights.

She glimpsed a chipmunk for half a second in Astoria Park before it
put its tail straight up like the antenna of the transistor radio she's been
taking apart in her room and zipped under a bush.

She and her mother used to live with her grandmother in a house
next to the lake north of Ithaca. Then her grandmother got cancer and
died. They moved to New York City because her mother wanted to find
more acting jobs. She didn't want to make that move, either.

On the back flap, there's a photograph of Wishner. He has dark hair
falling across his forehead and squarish glasses with dark frames. He has
dark lines under his eyes, maybe from rising early every day for six years.
He's sitting at a picnic table and behind him stretches worn and weedy
ground that presumably is his backyard. He's wearing a plaid workshirt.
Around his neck he has a black strap attached to a camera with a tele-
photo lens. A fine caption for this photo would be, "The nobility of
character and elegance of independence: Lawrence Wishner looks at the
world."

She emails back and forth with her father. He sends her mathematical
puzzles and word games. Her last message to him was a cryptogram of
the Epimenides paradox: *Iyhcimhoip bri Agibem peho, "Euu Agibemp egi
uhegp."*

P.S. 17Q is also called the Henry David Thoreau school. She found a
Riverside Edition of *Walden* in the natural history section of the Strand
bookstore and read it in two days. On days after school when it isn't
raining she looks for squirrels in the trees of Athens Square, which is
next to P.S. 17Q. She never sees a chipmunk, nor expects to, since Athens Square is small and chipmunks are shy. Athens Square has a sunken

plaza and a peristyle of three Doric columns with an entablature. Entablatures traditionally consist of an architrave, a frieze, and a cornice, but the entablature of Athens Square is lacking a frieze. The entablature is broken to make the peristyle look like a ruin. There is a bronze statue of Athena and a bronze statue of Socrates. Socrates is sitting on a smooth piece of granite that slopes downward so he looks like he's going down a slide. As far as she can tell, no one in the square ever pays attention to any of this.

Wishner is not a wildlife biologist, but a biochemist. He used to teach at Mary Washington College in Fredericksburg, Virginia. He specializes in the metabolism of Vitamin E and antioxidants. He is an accomplished photographer. One day he saw two chipmunks playing in his woodpile. He spent the next six years observing and photographing them every day. He learned to individually recognize fifty-nine resident chipmunks and forty-nine transients. He made maps of burrow entrances and charts of family relationships over several generations. He noted the start and end of every individual's hibernation period. His book is respected by experts.

Thoreau called chipmunks "striped squirrels," and although he wrote several times in *Walden* about seeing regular squirrels, he mentioned a striped squirrel only once, and that wasn't about seeing one, only hearing it, which tells you how shy they are.

People like to go down slides. Socrates was a person. Ergo—

On the back cover is Wishner's photograph of Lady Cheltenham. She is down in the grass, at the edge of protective vegetation, perched on a piece of quartzite slightly larger than herself. She is looking straight into the camera. One front paw is raised. Wishner's caption is, "Lady Cheltenham alone."

She reads a couple of pages to her mother every night, trying to make her see how wonderful it is. Her mother swears she's fascinated, then falls asleep.

It was in the Strand bookstore that she found it. She wasn't even looking. She spotted the spine: *Eastern Chipmunks*. It raised its tail and tried
to zip away, but she grabbed it. The subtitle was maybe the most beautiful phrase she had ever read: *Secrets of Their Solitary Lives*. It was a hard-
cover book published by the Smithsonian Institution, but the Strand was
selling it used for only seven dollars.

"No one can say when the appropriate genes appeared that led the
first solitary chipmunk on its road to independence, but that those genes
have been serviceable is obvious." The book was published in 1982.
There's very little online about Wishner, but Mary Washington College,
which is now called the University of Mary Washington, lists him as a
professor emeritus. He's probably in his seventies.

For a few days she took notes and photographed the pigeons that
congregated outside her window and on the sills of the apartment building next door. But she couldn't learn to tell them apart, and they never
did anything interesting. Wishner says that when he was a child he noticed chipmunks but was "too young and preoccupied to enjoy a system-
atic curiosity about their lives." Maybe that's her problem. She's thought
about writing him a letter, but doesn't want to intrude on his solitary
life. "A chipmunk with social tendencies appearing in a present-day population is sure to get clobbered."

One of her father's word games is snowball sentences, in which each
word has one more letter than the word preceding it. She is proud of the
one she sent him in her last message: *I am one who's quite liking Wishner,
Lawrence—nominally biochemist, nonetheless impressively multitalented.*

How to become less young is obvious, if slow. But how to become less
preoccupied—this is the mystery.

The scientific name for the chipmunk is *Tamias striatus*, which means
"striped steward." Steward of seeds, maybe. She likes that. "Gutrune was
able to carry an average of thirty-five whole sunflower seeds at a time."
This is in her cheeks. The photograph is adorable. "There can be no doubt

that chipmunks do not store food to satisfy their immediate needs, but rather because they are genetically programmed to do so, and that this instinctive characteristic has enabled them to remain independent for 25 million or so years."

She wishes her mother wouldn't fall asleep when she gets read to. She says she's interested, but she's an actor.

She lies in her nest where only the birds can see her and turns again to the back flap. Wishner sits at his picnic table in black and white, his beloved domain behind him. He looks patient and thoughtful. He could be called *Tamias tamias striatus*, steward of chipmunks.

2006

11:56 p.m., May 9, 2006

Dear Mette,

I hope you are well. Please say hello to your mother for me.

I'm glad you're finding the algebra puzzle interesting. Here's a hint: when we multiply both sides by $(x-y)$, what do we have to be careful about?

I enjoyed your substitution cipher. I noticed you used letter-frequency ranking as your encoder. Maybe that was an unstated puzzle within the puzzle? By the way, I wonder if you've noticed that the Epimenides paradox is not logically complete. There is no necessary contradiction if we assume his statement to be false, because he is claiming that *all* Cretans are liars. There could of course be truth-telling Cretans that just don't happen to be him. A sounder version of this paradox is the one ascribed to Eubulides: T ntf stds, "Zktv B tn stdbfc fxz bs t wbu." (You'll be able to solve this immediately if you guess what encoder I used as a quick and lazy way of ensuring I was including all possible letters.)

I was also quite impressed by your snowball sentence! Here is a variant form I just thought of that perhaps could be called a snowball palindrome:

I do not like dense people wrongly saying words thus: for "me," "I."

There aren't many options for beginning and ending this form, but once you have a frame such as the one above, the challenge is to expand the middle:

I do not like dense people wrongly subbing always words thus: for "me," "I."

One could classify snowball palindromes into two groups, peaked and truncated. The first above is peaked, with one seven-letter word at the center, whereas the second is truncated, with two seven-letter words next to each other. Can you add a peak to the second sentence?

By the way, I've written another one of those whatevers. It probably won't mean much to you, but anyway, here it is:

Data Set: Haunted House

In an attic box, I found a memorandum book my father kept
    when he was in graduate school.
He wrote simultaneously from the front and back, so that
    entries converge toward the middle.
I fill notebooks the same way.
On the last page is written:
    Dates to remember:
    September 6: Margaret's birthday
    October 26: Engagement
    April 29: Ring
These lines are crossed out, and immediately below them is
    written:
    May 2: Imogen's birthday
    June 12: Engagement and Ring
I wonder if it was the same ring.
In the middle pages of the book my father drew a floor plan
    of the house he and my mother were planning to rent in
    Santa Monica.
He has measured every wall, door, and window.
He has measured the height and horizontal placement of
    every light switch and electrical outlet.
He has measured the height of the kitchen counters and the
    height of the living room mantelpiece.

On a following page he has made a chart of all the furniture
he and my mother owned, with length, depth, and height
listed for each.
Three blank pages follow.
Then he wrote:
The way your smile just beams
The way you sing off key
The way you haunt my dreams

Love,
Your Father

1:14 a.m., May 10, 2006

You tried to be a fox, but I worked like a dog, and I solved your
cipher in approximately one minute. As for putting a peak on your
ziggurat:
    I do not like dense people wrongly, stupidly subbing always
words thus: for "me," "I."
    That took me another minute.
    Re: multiplying by (x–y), if x = y that screws it all up, right? Is
that relevant?

7:47 p.m., May 11, 2006

Dear Mette,

It does more than that, it introduces a second solution, because
0 = 0.
    I do not like dense people forever stupidly employing incorrect
pronouns, subbing always words thus: for "me," "I."
    Now another peak is needed, and since you're so good at it . . .

Love,
Your Father

7:51 p.m., May 11, 2006

Oh, yeah, duh! It introduces the solution that x = y, which is the whole trick. That's pretty neat.

I do not like dense people forever stupidly employing farcically incorrect pronouns, subbing always words thus: for "me," "I."

That was too easy.

2:03 a.m., May 13, 2006

Dear Smarty-Pants,

I do not like dense people forever stupidly employing farcically, moronically (alternatives: ludicrously, retardedly) incorrect pronouns, subbing always words thus: for "me," "I."

Love,
Your Father

11:10 a.m., May 13, 2006

I was asleep when you sent this, otherwise I would have answered sooner.

I do not like dense people forever stupidly employing farcically, moronically, pathetically (alternatively: ridiculously, cretinously, hopelessly) incorrect pronouns, subbing always words thus: for "me," "I."

I'll admit, even with the thesaurus this took me an hour, mainly because I didn't see at first that I could change "alternatives" to "alternatively." And by the way, "retard" is an offensive term these days, old man.

10:38 p.m., May 13, 2006

Dear Captain of the Language Rangers,

And "cretin" isn't?
    I do not like dense people forever stupidly employing farcically, moronically (alternatives overextending sesquipedalian possibilities, respectively: "ludicrously," "retardedly") incorrect pronouns, subbing always words thus: for "me," "I."

Love,
Your Offensively Superannuated Father

10:43 p.m., May 13, 2006

"cretin" isn't offensive because most non-ancient people today are cretinously ignorant of its meaning. I'll figure out how to add to the snowball later tonight

11:09 a.m., May 15, 2006

Dear Mysteriously Silent Snowballer,

Epimenides the Cretin said, "What I am saying now is a lie, but I'm too stupid to know it."
    Question: Is that a logically complete paradox?

Love,
Your Father

3:51 p.m., May 15, 2006

I've been busy doing other things. I guess I have to admit it's a little harder to add something at this point. Don't send any suggestions. I'll figure it out.

Your Epimenides statement isn't a paradox at all. Epimenides is lying.

7:19 p.m., May 15, 2006

Dear Mette,

Good for you!
    While I wait for you to fire a snowball back at me, here's another data set. (You haven't told me to stop, so you only have yourself to blame.)

Data Set: Old Guy

Guy Williams played John Robinson on *Lost in Space*.
I wished he were my father.
John Robinson was handsome and wise and could swordfight.
He looked like JFK in futuristic polyester pants and black
    zippered booties.
My father was smart, but dismissive and irritable and less
    handsome.
Plus, he couldn't swordfight.
After *Lost in Space*, Guy Williams wasn't offered any
    television or film roles and most people forgot him.
In 1973 he visited Argentina and was mobbed by thousands
    of fans.
It turned out everyone in Argentina loved *Zorro*, which Guy
    Williams had starred in before *Lost in Space*.
In 1979, he moved to Argentina.
I felt strongly that this was too far away.
He lived alone in an apartment in Buenos Aires.
In later years he went around doing swordfighting in a
    circus act.
It was all choreographed ahead of time.
For some reason this made me sad.
When he was sixty-five, Guy Williams died in his apartment
    of a brain aneurysm.
His body wasn't discovered for a week.

Love,
Your Father

p.s. My father died earlier this year, so I guess he's been on my mind.

8:17 p.m., May 16, 2006

Duck!

I do not like dense people forever stupidly employing farcically, moronically (alternatives shambolically hyper-extending quasi-exhaustive sesquipedalian possibilities, respectively: "cretinously," "hopelessly") incorrect pronouns, subbing always words thus: for "me," "I."

I don't really understand your data sets, but I don't mind reading them, so you can keep sending them. I'm sorry to hear about your father. Who's JFK?

Wednesday, February 17, 2016

Chicago, 10:53 a.m. Twenty-three minutes late. Greyhound buses are always late and all they would have to do is change the published schedule to reflect actual travel times, yet they don't. She has sixty-eight minutes. She washes up in the restroom, confers with the cloud, walks two blocks north toward an Indian restaurant. She packed inadequate clothing. Monday it was in the 60s, but yesterday it turned frigid again. Wild swings this month. More energy in the system, greater amplitude. Anyone who thinks for a second that humans are going to deal with climate change should consider the immovable object that is the Greyhound bus schedule.

She opens the steamed-up glass door, ducks into the warmth. (*Scurries.*) That cumin smell, like stale sweat. Some people don't make the connection, probably a genetic thing, a difference in olfactory receptors.

"I'll have the aloo saag and an order of poori."

"Here or to go?"

"Here."

The place is empty. Worker bees still hiving. She takes a table in a corner, pulls out her notebook, writes simple snowball sentences.

I am not good today, father dearest.

I do not feel smart, mother anxious.

I do not want other people judging anybody's qualities, absolutely forevermore.

Wishner's Law: Mind your own fucking business!

She googles cumin and sweat, scans comments on various forums, people expressing puzzlement at each other. Nothing scientific.

The lights in the restaurant are buzzing at the usual 60 hz, between B-flat and B-natural. The tires of the last bus at cruising speed on asphalt were mostly A-flat, while the concrete of the bridges brought out the harmonic at E-flat. Household timers and alarms all use a chip that emits a high B-natural, about 2000 hz, which is curiously close to, but not exactly, a multiple of 60. For some reason most trucks back up beeping either C-sharp or D-sharp. She tries not to notice these things, because once she does, she can't get the pitch out of her head. She might start humming, and then people will side-eye her instead of minding their own business, and anyway it's so fucking classic, isn't it?

She eats her saag and poori, rotely writing down doublings of 60.

Is she humming?

She stops.

She, she, she! Hey everybody, I'm a girl! You can't see what I have between my legs, but you know it's there!

Hungarian, Finnish, and Turkish use gender-neutral pronouns. Truth be told, she kind of dislikes the use of "they," since it gets confused with the plural. She likes the Turkish terms, *o* and *ona*. O goes on a date with ona. O runs screaming from ona.

There's a sentence in Wishner that has stuck in her head ever since she read it a decade ago. "Pumpkinseed excavated a simple burrow and failed to reappear from it in the spring."

She returns to the station, gets early in line for the new bus, boards. Witching hours are over, the bus is nearly full. After everyone has settled, four empty seats remain, one of them next to her.

To excavate a simple burrow and simply—

The bus takes off, a mere five minutes late. It retraces her path to the

Indian restaurant—a small man and bundled child entering through the door at this very moment—then turns west toward I-90. Ramp, river of humanity.

In the cold night she let Alex turn her to the right, and it turned out that Alex lives in a spacious upscale apartment, filled with things that are probably beautiful and probably expensive. Alex probably makes good money, but Alex's family must have money, too. She had just enough time to register this, sitting on the ample couch and taking her first sip of the cognac Alex poured, before they came at her, kissing and fondling. She tried to fight down her panic and Alex seemed to want to help, repeating, "Relax." She had previously been coaxed into removing her sweater along with her anorak (the apartment was warm) and now they were unbuttoning her shirt while kissing her neck. They still were wearing one of their baseball caps, the purple one, the bill reversed so that their mouth could get at her, and a phrase came to her, *Alex is batting a thousand.* An image also came—her naked and supine on the couch, Alex still clothed on top of her, her gender obscenely revealed while Alex's was still mysterious. Was she supposed to think in those terms? Was it only mysterious if one was still stuck on binary ideas? She doubted herself in every way. Maybe all dates went like this. How else could sex happen, unless clothing was removed? Was agreeing to have a date the same as agreeing to have sex? Her shirt was open now and Alex was murmuring approval of her unshaved armpits as they nosed there.

"I'm . . . um . . ." she said.

"It's all right," Alex said, their nose zigzagging down her stomach, something tugging at her pants' zipper, which must be their fingers, though she couldn't see past the purple cap, so maybe it was their teeth. *Alex is swinging for the fences.*

She found strength in logic. It couldn't be *all* right, because one of them was distressed. "No, please." She sat up, closing her shirt around her.

"Am I going too fast?" Alex asked. Their adorable freckles, their snub

nose, their large wondering gray eyes. Her unshaved armpits, her unshaved legs. Was that weird? Why else would Alex comment? How
clean was she supposed to be? What was she supposed to want?

"I'm sorry," Alex said. "I'm just so attracted to you."

She put Alex *in a mood*.

Alex got up to get more cognac. They lit a candle on the coffee table.
Alex sat crosslegged on the couch facing her. They talked about conser-
vative parents in Chicago, a dyke sister. They asked about her family. She
mentioned the mother at home, the father in cyberspace.

"And?"

"And what?"

"What about them? What's their deal?"

"They're fine."

"That's all?"

"I have no complaints."

"You're a woman of mystery."

Alex went back to talking about their family. Father, banker, mother,
homemaker. Christian. Heartbrokenly loving the sinners they'd birthed,
praying for them. Then Alex talked about work colleagues, and she
added a comment, and the two of them laughed about a couple of things,
and she gradually relaxed, as Alex had suggested all along that she do.
Alex stroked her hand and that was nice, then kissed her gently and that
was okay, and then their hands were everywhere again and buttons were
back to springing open. *Spring season.*

She popped off the couch.

"What's the matter?" Alex asked, as she retrieved her sweater and
anorak, pulled on her shitkickers. "I'm sorry," they repeated. "I've been
misreading."

"No, I'm sorry," she said. "It's my fault."

She fled down the stairs, she scurried north through dark streets.

Was she a freak?

Alex's single-mindedness—was it right to call it that? The direction. The goal. The whole point. So then, the humor the two of them shared, the programming issues discussed, the talents admired, the considerateness, the coffee, the expressed interest in past and family and feelings— was all of that a ruse?

Was she wrong?

Don't understand me too quickly. Did Alex want to understand her at all? Did nothing matter but a momentary paroxysm? As though the only reason they were interested in programming was to make the computer explode. Or the only reason she studied chipmunks is so she could find them easily and hit them with a rock.

Was she a freak?

Was wanting to love someone the same as wanting to have sex? Was being lonely the same thing as wanting to share bodies?

Every human and animal on Earth was alive today only because of a two-billion-year unbroken chain of sex, sex, sex. No wonder the world ran on it, look at advertising, look at clickbait, look at jokes. People are robots run by their genes, scraps of code that exist only to keep existing, instructing everyone to care about nothing but seed-spraying, seed-growing, copy-making, or failing that, sublimations like flirting, tonguing, tussling, writhing. One line of code for all life on Earth: if fuckable, then fuck.

Okay, she was a freak, she didn't want to be reduced to a stand-in for a transport vehicle of soulless monomaniacal fragments of DNA, she was a person, she had thoughts and feelings and a personality, and maybe no one was interested in her, but that didn't mean she wasn't interesting. Right? Facts are only facts if someone knows them. If no one knew *her*, did she exist? Being alone used to be enough, but Alex changed that. She wanted to communicate with a special person, she wanted to teach and learn.

On Monday at Qualternion she forced herself to go to Alex. They had said they'd been misreading, so it was no doubt her fault. Forgive her, she had no experience with dates, she must have suggested something in her body language, her eyes. If she could just explain her point of view to Alex, the way the world looked to her, it all made sense in its own way, in her way. Then the two of them could still be friends, maybe better than before, maybe someday Alex would look at things the way she did, and the two of them could hold hands and walk in the park and program together and sleep next to each other and know each other fully and love each other.

Alex cut her off. "No need to apologize, Morticia. It's okay. I wanted a fling, you didn't." They gave what might have been a rueful little laugh. "I can be too much for some people." She stood there for a second or two, the eloquent thesis she'd rehearsed in her head for two days spinning tractionless. "It really is okay," they repeated. "Let's just get back to work." And they turned away.

She spent the next twenty-four hours refining and rehearsing a slightly different thesis. When she came to work on Tuesday morning she headed for Alex's workspace, but Alex wasn't there. They were perched on the edge of Seo-yeon's desk, deep in conversation. She stood to one side, waiting her turn, until it gradually became clear that Alex was flirting with Seo-yeon. Jokes and inferences pattered back and forth between them. Their eyes sparkled. It was like watching two Ping-Pong players enjoying a nimble game. Neither of them noticed her, probably, when she walked away.

Yes, she was a freak.

She becomes aware again of the world outside the bus window. The huge concrete plain of O'Hare is rotating slowly around the spindle of its control tower as they pass. She can see planes in the air, descending in orderly lines. People hurrying home to partners, beds waiting.

She texts her mother, who's been pestering her: Don't worry about me I'm just dandy.

Wednesday, February 17, 2016

"Any news?"

"I got a text from her a minute ago."

"What did it say?"

"It made me more worried."

"Noted. What did it say?"

"Hold on a sec. I know you'll want it word for word."

"Yes, why not?"

"Need to make sure I'm giving it to you precisely correctly."

"Our discussion will be more apropos. You must see that."

"Must I? Apparently, I must. Here it is—'Don't worry about me I'm just dandy.'"

". . ."

"Yes, Professor?"

"That doesn't sound like her."

"Good. Even you see it."

"That's not fair."

"You're clueless, you've said it yourself."

"Not so much about her. Anyway, I like to think. You've spent nearly all the time with her. I wish you had let me—I've said all that before."

"Yes, you have."

"She didn't say where she was?"

"I just read you the complete text."

"Did you—"

"To enable apropos discussion."

"Did you text her back?"

"I wanted to check with you first."

". . ."

"To see if you'd heard anything from her."

"I would have told you."

"Would you have?"

"Of course. I knew you were worried."

"Whereas you're not."

"Not really."

"Not even now."

"No, not really."

"You just said it doesn't sound like her."

"It sounds sarcastic, and she's not usually sarcastic, that's all. How many times did you text her?"

"You haven't tried to get in touch with her at all, have you? That's why she texted me instead of you."

"I've been working—"

"Christ!"

"—and I figured if she wanted to communicate with me, she would."

"So you've never entertained the idea that someone might need reassurance, might need someone else to take the first step. A child needing that from her parent."

"That's the subject you've made it clear you don't want to talk about."

"What's that?"

"Whose child she is."

"For Christ's sake, Mark, she thinks exactly like you."

"You know I'm not talking about that—"

"Like you squared."

"You're wasting time. And by the way, her mind is quite different from mine. She has a temperamental need to be an autodidact. That could help or hurt her, foster originality or make her a crank. I think—"

"Who's wasting time now?"

"I'm just trying to be accurate."

"Unlike sloppy me."

"I'm not saying that."

"What are you saying?"

"I'm—I'm— Look, could we just talk about this calmly?"

"So you're telling me to calm down."

"Yes."

" . . . "

"Hello?"

" . . . "

"Hello?"

1993–1994

Looking back, trying to calm down, she reminds herself that she's always had a thing for tall, older men. Maybe because her father is short, and she had an allergic reaction to that asshole when she was thirteen. Or maybe because her father *seemed* tall to her when he mysteriously vanished when she was four years old, and she spent her formative years fantasizing about his whereabouts and activities in nauseatingly romantic terms, until he reappeared when she was thirteen and proved himself to be a short asshole.

She'd hated high school, thought college would be different. Believe it or not, she imagined a community of scholars who would stimulate each other intellectually. The faculty would be no more than facilitators, wise mentors; in her imagination, mostly male—see absent father, above. Of course the mostly male part turned out be true. She was actually surprised that college had grades. She lived in her own world, she sees now. By her third semester she had one foot out the door. She saw the desirability of studying a broad range of subjects, but thought the distribution requirements were insultingly rigid. (Insulting, because it assumed students would seek to evade becoming "well-rounded" if not hemmed in by rules.) At the same time she wasn't blind to the fact that many of her fellow students were neither self-motivated nor intellectually stimulating nor discernibly interested in learning anything. In other words, college really *wasn't* much different from high school.

She thought, well fuck this rodeo. (Man, she must have been insufferable. No wonder she didn't have any friends.) For her third semester she ignored her adviser's suggestion about getting certain requirements out of the way and just took what she wanted: Woolf and Auden, Beginning Arabic, Principles of Limnology, The French Revolution, Astronomy. It was a heavy load, but she already suspected she was going to save her mother and herself a ton of money by not continuing, and she didn't have any friends, nor at that time wanted any (you know—you can't fire me, I quit), and she liked the idea of going out in a blaze, or at least a wan glow, of scholarly lucubration. (Using words nobody else knows: see having no friends, above.)

So she was exhausted a lot of the time, but really kind of having fun, haunting the libraries and hauling around piles of books and being the butt of jokes and ignoring people. The limnology class was drier than she'd expected (cheap irony!) but it overlapped with marshland ecology, which she'd always been interested in because the plot of land she'd grown up on was next door to a swampy little delta. Woolf and Auden was a blast, not least because the professor, a small hirsute male chordate *d'un certain age,* was so egotistical he might have been clinically insane, which condition she found so absurd she grew fond of him, in a semi-horrified way. He, in his turn, took a shine to her because she was just the sort of woman he liked: interested in a subject he knew ten times as well, and half his diminutive size. Arabic was a lot of work, but she loved learning how to read that gorgeous script and try to make those amazing sounds with her throat, and as for the French Revolution, a blood-soaked object lesson about societal collapse appealed to her sense of alienation.

And astronomy? Well . . . That one's a tad embarrassing. One of her adolescent fantasy father-lover figures was Tycho Brahe, the sixteenth-century astronomer who built an observatory on an island a brief pirate's sail south of Hamlet's castle and compiled the most accurate star catalog to date. Why Brahe? Suffice it to say that he was Danish and tyrannical and forever out of reach, just like her dad.

She has an uneasy feeling she may have done something cringeworthy at an early astronomy lecture, something to get the professor's attention and simultaneously maybe take him down a peg. (Shower me with approval, aren't I the smart daughter, and by the way, fuck you.) Whatever it was, she remembers she felt embarrassed, and reined herself in after that. Then a few weeks later there was a post-lecture exchange on god knows what when she practically made a pass at him. (Bathe me in lust, aren't I the sexy daughter, and by the way, aren't you ashamed of yourself?) For the rest of the semester, she forbade herself further antics.

But she had to admit she was attracted to him. And it didn't have to be for solely unhealthy reasons, right? Because, yes, he was older and accomplished, but really the person he most reminded her of was her younger brother. He displayed an oblivious absorption in his subject that called to mind six-year-old Quinnie regaling her with the nutritional preferences of dinosaur species she'd never heard of. She remembered an early lecture when he was explaining emission spectra, and he'd brought in a step stool and colored Ping-Pong balls, and he stood on various steps and stepped down one or two or three levels and tossed away different colored balls to represent the emission of photons of different wavelengths when electrons jumped from higher to lower states. The whole idea was so corny, and made downright comical by the fact that he couldn't seem to keep himself from demonstrating every possible energy shift, long after the point had been made. He was exhausting the permutations because, for the zillionth time, they were fascinating *him*.

He was a beanpole, almost a marsh-wiggle. She thought when she first talked to him he must be 6'2", then found out later he was 6'4", only he slumped. He had narrow shoulders and large hands, a beaky nose with a fluorescent gleam along the flat bridge, gray eyes and sandy hair in an awful cut, and the kind of pale pink skin that turns papery in middle age. When she spoke to him the second time (what *was* it about? she seems to remember Saturn) her main impression was one of helpless honesty. He was simply too obtuse socially to be anything but straightforward. (Maybe another relevant thing to know about her dad is that he is a sociopath and an adept reader of character and consequently an extremely good liar.)

So there you have it: a man with the rough physical outline of a father to replace the one who charmed and abandoned her, but temperamentally like the younger brother she raised and protected and loved. What girl could resist? She teased out from the department secretary the information that he wasn't married, and sometime after she left school she sent him a brazen note, something on the order of, Hey, you alluring gormless telephone pole, how about you and me?

He didn't respond for a while, which she resented but also respected (after all, she had once been his student), but then he called her, which thrilled her and also made her think less of him (for god's sake, she was his student just yesterday!). They met for coffee, or maybe lunch, no, probably just coffee, and she remembers that she warmed to his kindness, lusted after his hands, wished he'd let her cut his hair and powder his nose, and wondered how quickly his total absorption in his subject would drive her crazy. She also wondered if he was a virgin. She liked the idea, anyway. ("Who's the professor *now?*") But it turned out he'd had a couple of girlfriends in his twenties. Still, maybe they only held hands and shopped together for Rubik's Cubes.

He worked a lot, so it took three or four weeks to accomplish, but she thinks they had a lunch date, and definitely a dinner date. He was considerate of the waitstaff, which earned him brownie points. Unlike many men, he asked her questions about herself and her opinions and seemed actually to find her answers interesting. On the other hand, it was a lucky thing she was already into astronomy, because he did talk an awful lot about it, and she could more or less tell when his mind fell into a rut in his brain and proceeded to rattle down it like a driverless stagecoach. She dislikes labels, because what's most interesting about people are the things that make them unique, but she supposes this could be called perseverating.

In April he asked her if she wanted to see the Lyrids with him and she thought, Ahh, this is how astronomers get up the nerve to kiss a gal.

Because not the tiniest whiff of that had occurred in their three dates thus far. When he said good night, he stepped back, tucked his elbow, and executed a vibrating little-boy wave. It occurred to her that he might be unconsciously invoking childishness to hide from himself what he really wanted and perhaps felt ambivalent about (she had been his student, etc). Sure, she could have grabbed his lapels and done a chin-up, but for chrissake, he was thirty-four years old. It was time to grow up. If he liked it, he should put a smooch on it.

She had never let him drive to the old commune to pick her up because that felt way too old-school, too *Ozzie and Harriet* (and besides, she didn't like people seeing the conditions she lived in), so on the night in question she borrowed Jo's clapped-out Honda and fetched him from his cute little Arts and Crafts house in a less palatial part of Cayuga Heights. He piled in with blankets and a thermos of hot chocolate and the little-boy wave. It was 35 degrees Fahrenheit, 1:30 a.m., April 20, 1994.

He'd explained at a length that would have been absurd even if she'd been an ignoramus on matters lunar, which she was far from being, but she'd let him do it (see condition that will remain unlabeled, above): the peak of the meteor shower would occur on the night of April 22–23, but by then the moon would be only three days away from full, which would make viewing harder because it would be up for most of the night and, you know, when there's a bright light like the near-full moon in the sky, then seeing fainter meteors is harder because, you know, your eyes adjust

to the brighter light, that is, your pupils contract, and your retina re-
ceives less light, which it needs if you want to clearly perceive fainter
signals, such as—

She drove them to the top of Mount Pleasant, where there was a 360-
degree view and the grounds around the small university observatory
made a comfortable place to lie down. The pesky moon was just setting.
They spread out one blanket and piled the others at its foot for use as
needed, shared hot chocolate while waiting for their eyes to adjust to the
dark, then lay down side by side. After a moment he sat up again to take
one of the spare blankets and cover himself. He was careful to keep the
blanket from touching her also, because who knows, that might suggest
something. After another minute she grabbed another blanket to cover
herself.

They lay in silence. After several minutes of meteor-free viewing, he
said, "We might see only five or six an hour. They'll radiate out of the
constellation Lyra."

"That's why they're called the Lyrids," she confirmed.

"You can find Lyra by—"

"It's there." She pointed. "It's easy to find because of Vega."

He didn't speak for several seconds. Then he said, "I'm sorry."

"That's OK," she said. "You're a professor, you can't help it. And since
I'm sure there's a ton of stuff about the Lyrids you know and I don't, why
don't you tell me, while we lie here and wait for—" you to get up the
fucking courage to lay one on me "—some celestial fireworks?"

So he rattled on, and it turned out that the comet responsible for the
Lyrids has an orbital period of 415 years, and they're more spectacular
once every sixty years, but this year wasn't one of those years, and it used
to be thought that there was a cloud of debris that had shifted into a
60-year orbit, but now they know that it's a consequence of gravitational
mechanics that steer into the path of the Earth the one-revolution dust
trail, by which term is meant the material shed during the revolution

prior to the last return, which was in one, two, buckle my shoe, near, far in our motor car, what a happy time we'll spend, bang bang chitty chitty bang bang.

In the meantime, she would say every once and a while, "Oh! There's one!" and he'd stop talking for a moment to say, "Where?" and she'd point and say, "It's gone now," and he'd say, "Was it a good one?"

He reached the end of the *Encyclopedia Galactica* entry on the Lyrids, and the night got colder and they sat up to have more hot chocolate.

"There's one," she said.

"Where?"

"Have you seen a single one tonight?"

"I've seen three. But you're right, I seem to be missing a lot of them."

They sipped for a while in silence. Then she said, "I had glow-in-the-dark stars on my bedroom ceiling when I was a kid. I actually used a star chart to place them."

"Is that what got you interested in astronomy?"

"No. Maybe. Well . . . I was already interested. Anything related to wandering appealed to me. I'd read that seafarers used to navigate by the stars, so I'd lie in bed and pretend I was steering my boat to some far island or undiscovered continent. Anywhere but here, that sort of thing." She hadn't yet told him anything about her childhood.

"You weren't happy?" he asked after a few moments.

She felt a surprising stab. "I don't know. Not miserable. I sometimes felt lonely, that's all. Like a lot of kids."

He seemed to be waiting for her to go on. No fucking way was she going to talk about her family right now. "How about you?" she asked. "Happy childhood?"

"I was lucky. My parents loved me. I mean—not to suggest that your—"

"That *is* lucky. There's one!"

"Where?"

"Jesus, you're terrible at this."

"I'm usually better."

"I'll bet."

He flopped onto his back. "I'll be the first to see another."

She lay down again, closer to him. "No way."

Then, of course, several minutes went by during which neither of them saw anything. Touch me, kiss me, tell me I'm lovable.

Finally he said, "So yes, I was a happy kid. But there's something about nighttime and stars, isn't there? I used to lie out in my parents' yard at night and wish that one of the stars would turn out to be a spaceship, and it would come down and land in the yard, and a door would pop open and this bright light would spill out, and a friendly alien would say hello and they'd whisk me away and I'd learn everything about the universe. No matter how good we have it, we always want more. At least, I think so. Don't you think?"

She thought, Of course, you dolt. Is that a new idea for you?

Suddenly, she was fed up with waiting. And besides, if she thought it was too old-school to let him pick her up in his car, why the fuck was she lying here with expectant doe eyes like mermaid Ariel waiting for Prince Eric to kiss de girl? "Well by golly, Mark, now that you mention it, I think you're right!" And she grabbed his hand and rolled over on top of him.

IT TOOK HIM another two weeks before they had sex, and right after that it started to go south. Not that the sex was bad. She'd give the first time a five. He did seem to understand that heterosexual congress wasn't all about the human male's temperamental—a girl is *tempted* to call it hysterical—plumbing, so good for him. And he was teachable. They had sex half a dozen times and by the end the judges were awarding solid 6.5s.

But she had imagined that once they became physically intimate, some species of emotional intimacy would also appear, or at least poke its topgallants over the horizon and crave parley. She kind of thought that all the opaque logician needed was to have his ashes skillfully hauled and he'd turn into something like her best girlfriend with balls. ("Oh, oh! Doctor! Now I can *see!*")

Well, no, she's being hard on herself. But her expectations were unreasonable. Of course, if he was in some way a father-substitute, then in some way she wanted to convert him from the absent hero into the available homebody. And naturally, that didn't happen. Who knows, there might have been progress after a few years, but they dated for only two months. (Six dates in nine weeks: yes, he worked all the fucking time.)

He had a blank way of staring at her just after she said something that looked an awful lot like he was trying to decide whether or not she was spouting nonsense. His expressions in general were hard to read. She thought at first she'd be able to see more in his eyes when he took his glasses off, but instead that somehow made them look even emptier. Not always—they grew animated when he was talking about ideas or facts. At those times he looked to the side, or down, and his eyes darted and sometimes filled with joy. But when he looked at *her*, they seemed to go dead. She looked for, and could never find . . . what? Affection, maybe; appreciation, fellow feeling. Just the tiniest hint of, you know, Hey, nice to have you around, whatever your name is.

Her response was to storm the Bastille. She jumped on him, tickled him, teased him, poked him. None of it offended him, and some of it he even seemed to like. But he had no physical playfulness of his own. The moment she stopped, he retreated into his fortress. On the last couple of dates, she admits, she resorted to trying to piss him off. She criticized some habit of his (she can't remember what it was, something trivial, a weapon to hand) and later made a mean comment about his hair. But that didn't work, either. He only looked surprised, and a touch disappointed in her. The only way she could get a rise out of him was by putting forward an idea he disagreed with. She said once, toward the end, that he lived only in his head. He *was* provoked, but not in response to her transparent emotional reasons for saying it. No, it was the fucking conceptual framework of the argument that irritated him.

"The head-heart dichotomy is bogus," he said. "Feelings originate in the head, too."

"Well *of course.* I'm referring to thoughts versus feelings."

"The thought-feeling dichotomy is so simplistic it's functionally useless. Feelings are also thoughts, they're just unexamined. I like to analyze my feelings before I dump them on other people."

Obviously, she had hit a nerve. And equally obviously, he wasn't going to admit it. Maybe he didn't even realize it.

The end came on the summer solstice, under a romantic full moon. They'd had a late dinner downtown and then walked to the lake and picked their way out along the crumbling concrete breakwater to the little lighthouse that marked the entrance to the flood control channel. The sun had set an hour previously. No one was around. The moon had just cleared East Hill and was lighting up the lake in a way that was totally predictable in a thirteen-times-a-year kind of way, yet miraculous and unspeakably beautiful. They sat dangling their legs off the breakwater and as usual she had to make the move to hold his hand. A pity—those beautiful big hands, and he had no idea what to do with them.

"No matter how many times I've seen the full moon, it thrills me," she said.

"It always surprises me how convincing the optical illusion is, that it looks bigger near the horizon," he said.

She played with his fingers. This little piggy went to the weekend conference. This little piggy stayed home and caught up on a shitload of work. During dinner she'd talked about some writers she liked, and he'd mentioned that he didn't read much fiction anymore. He said novelists often wrote about things they were ignorant of—the job their protagonist supposedly had, for example—and got basic facts wrong, and it killed his enjoyment because it reminded him that it was all made up. She said something about it being a pity that a little detail like that kept him from reading good fiction since there was no better way to broaden your understanding of other people. He hadn't responded.

But now he said, "I read a novel by a Pulitzer Prize winner which began with a scene in the evening. The people described in the scene were believable—no one had three arms, for example—and the sentences I'm sure were very pretty. But in the sky there was a rising crescent moon. And I thought to myself, why should I have any confidence in this writer's ability to observe *anything*, if she's never noticed that crescent moons in the evening can only sink? Does she not understand why the moon is a crescent? Does she think the moon's motion is retrograde?"

"But a lot of smart people don't know that. Modern people spend most of their lives indoors, especially at night."

"I think there's an arrogance among literary folk. 'I understand people better than you scientists do, so I don't have to bother my head with simple facts.'"

Ah, so her comment during dinner *had* wounded him. Did he even understand why this bee was buzzing in his bonnet right now? She took pity on him. "That's a good point. I can see how that would irritate you."

"I tried to read another 'acclaimed' novel, and in *that* one a full moon rose at midnight. If the idiot had written that the sun set at noon I think even his literary readers would have realized something was wrong."

"You're right, you're right." You poor thing, you feel attacked. The good news: you do seem to care about my opinion.

They sat in silence for a couple of minutes, during which the full moon correctly kept rising. You couldn't see Polaris for the glare, but you could trust with all your heart (that is, the one in your head) that it was 42 degrees above the north horizon, standing as still as a soldier guarding the tomb of the Unknown Murdered Novelist.

She said, "When I was a kid, I don't know, maybe eight, I first read about Newton and the apple and I didn't get it at all. Everyone knows apples fall to the ground, so why would seeing that tell him anything about gravity? It wasn't until I read a book for older kids, which explained his insight was that the same force might govern both the apple and the Moon—then I understood. And ever since, when I see the full moon, I think of it as a big ghostly apple."

"The same force governs the apple, the Moon, *and* the Earth. Part of Newton's insight was that the Earth also falls toward the apple."

"Sure."

"Strangely enough, that detail about the apple is true. It sounds like the storybook nonsense people love to make up later. But Newton mentioned the apple in his journal."

"So anyway, with this apple and Moon thing, and of course the Earth, too, you're right, being governed by the same force, and the fact that at first I didn't understand the Newton story—I ended up with this vivid sense of how all things everywhere are tied together by gravity. I mean, that's obvious—but the *idea* of it just stuck in my head and really appealed to me. Maybe because my family was pretty disconnected. My father was for all practical purposes as far away as the Moon. I don't know, that's kind of pop-psych. Anyway, then I read somewhere this medieval idea that gravity was a manifestation of love, you know, God's love working in nature. I thought it was something Aquinas said, but then later I couldn't find it. Maybe it was Boethius. But this idea that gravity is love, that it makes everything in the universe want to get closer to everything else, that you could say, in a way, that the apple loves the Earth that it falls toward—I thought that was just wonderful."

He was silent. Then he said, "That's silly."

Stung, she glanced at him. He was looking straight ahead, so she only saw his profile—his cow-catcher nose, his out-of-style glasses. "What do you mean?"

"What's the point of having two different words, 'gravity' and 'love,' if you're going to use them to mean the same thing?"

"It's called a metaphor."

He made a dismissive gesture. "Metaphors are attractive falsehoods. They only confuse people's thinking. Most people are too confused already."

At that moment one of the washed-out pitiless stars above them brightened and descended, roiled the water with its retro-rockets and landed on the crumbling jetty. The door hissed open, and out of the blinding light stepped a couples counselor who approached Saskia and took her gently by the hand and said, "Get out now, and don't look back."

Did she and Mark talk more that evening? Did she go home with him? She can't remember. She remembers writing him a day or two later and telling him it wasn't working.

He didn't even call. He wrote a note, starting with something like "If that's the way you feel then of course—" He expressed no regret. It confirmed all her doubts.

Then, as in an annoying indie rom-com, she discovered she was pregnant. (She used a diaphragm, but there was that one evening a couple of days after her period ended when she had accidentally left her bag in the car, and how could she have been so stupid, and how fucking *Leave It to Beaver* was it—ha!—that she was blaming only herself, as though pregnancies were parthenogenetic.) Angry at him, she didn't tell him for six months, during which he didn't call or write or hire a single plane to fly over her house with an apologetic banner, and then she wrote him another letter in which she said she was a few weeks away from giving birth and he was the father, and he deserved to know, but she wanted to raise the child on her own, because he wasn't around even when he was around, and because, to be fair, she had left him no say in the matter, whatever small say a man should get in such a case.

If this was a final test, he either failed it spectacularly or aced it, responding with the same passive acceptance. Under a surface of generosity and understanding that probably made him feel good about himself, she sensed an ocean of indifference. His own child! It was appalling.

In retrospect, she can see that in those years, still so close to her traumatic adolescence, the most wounded part of her wanted to rip a man's heart out and hand it to him on a silver platter. But he didn't have a heart. And by the way, Tin Man, everyone knows what they mean when they say that.

Thursday, February 18, 2016

She has to admit, this is kind of interesting—Newman's volume 3, page 1936, "Paradox Lost and Paradox Regained," by Edward Kasner and the man himself. There's a tricky little cheat that could be applied to the bus she's riding on. Consider the tires. When a tire makes one revolution, it travels a linear distance along the road, assuming no slippage, equal to the circumference of the tire. That much is obvious. But now consider the smaller circle formed by the wheel hub. During the same interval, that circle also makes exactly one revolution and travels the same linear distance. Doesn't that therefore prove that the circumference of the hub and the circumference of the tire are equal?

Of course not. Kasner and Newman's elucidation, involving cycloids and curtate cycloids, leaves something to be desired. The more fundamental point is that here we have one of those conceptual sleights-of-hand whereby a particular case is falsely generalized. Obviously, every point throughout the volume of the wheel is displaced the same horizontal distance, regardless of what cycloid it inscribes—or straight line, if we consider the center of the wheel. At the same time, none of these points travel the same curved distance, because the parameters of their cycloids vary. It is only at the point of contact with the road that we can infer the circumference of the wheel, precisely because that is the point of contact. But that measurement is not the same as the actual distance traversed by a point on the circumference, because that, too, is a cycloid.

Amazing, how easily you can fool people with simple ideas.

She remembers one from third-grade math class: Three friends (of course men) arrive at a hotel and rent three rooms for ten dollars each. They pay the thirty dollars and go upstairs. Then the manager (male) remembers that the hotel is running a discount: three rooms for twenty-five dollars. He gives five dollars to the bellboy (boy) and tells him to return it to the guests. (The boy passes one woman mopping the stairs and another sponging toilets, but neither woman appears in the puzzle.) The bellboy, being dishonest, returns one dollar to each man and pockets the other two. Each of the three men has now paid nine dollars. Nine times three equals twenty-seven, plus the two dollars that the bellboy kept makes twenty-nine. So what happened to the thirtieth dollar?

It turned out that the kid sitting next to her in class had already heard the puzzle from his father, and he said to her in awe, apparently quoting his pre-arithmetical progenitor, "And you know what? No one has ever figured out where that dollar went."

She turns off her overhead light and stares out the window into the blackness and thinks about human stupidity.

Oh—hers, too, for sure.

Here's a simple idea that a simple mind believes, despite itself, to be true: Mette loves Alex, therefore Alex loves Mette. There's something compelling, conceptually, about symmetry. Look at physics, Newton's third law. Look at physicists, searching for supersymmetry. Look at a number line. Look at your face in the mirror. There's something DNA-ish in our attraction to it. Yet DNA itself is right-handed. And for some reason matter slightly predominated over antimatter just after the Big Bang. And time has a direction, since entropy never decreases. But still, her anguish that Alex gave up on her, despite what she told herself she expected—that must come from some deep feeling that Alex *should* love her. Why? Symmetry!

Really, it's only one step beyond sympathetic magic. Ingesting this mushroom shaped like an erect phallus will make my dick hard. This plant with red sap must be good for my circulation. If I eat low-fat foods, I will have less fat in my body. Fooling ourselves with simple ideas.

She keeps staring out the window. Nothing out there. Flat, empty, lightless. She wants more of it.

The bus left Fargo at 2:30 a.m. Not even a station there, just a parking area between a pair of one-story windowless buildings and an unmarked side door into which the driver disappeared for forty minutes. Coffee, cigarettes, NoDoz, cocaine? Now it's 3:45. Crawling across the flattest and coldest state in the continental US. Outside it's minus fifteen degrees. Due in Bismarck at 5:30 a.m. Eight others on the bus at the moment, spread up and down, all asleep except possibly the inert human in the penultimate row with headphones on, leaking 120 pulses of white noise each minute.

She turns her light back on, reopens Newman. *In rubber-sheet geometry, curves are defined in such a way as to eliminate every naive appeal to intuition and experience.*

Our theme for today: naiveté.

She keeps reading, trying to concentrate. She has always been able to lose herself in Newman, but not so much now. If she has lost her ability to focus, that would clinch the argument. What is she waiting for?

She glances out the window again. With the overhead light on all she sees is her unlovable face.

Where is she going?

(She's going to Seattle.)

What is she doing?

(She's sitting on a bus going to Seattle.)

What's in Seattle?

(Seattle.)

She plows through four more pages and comes to this: *A proof that 1 is equal to 2 is familiar to most of us. Such a proof may be extended to show that any two numbers or expressions are equal. The error common to all such frauds lies in dividing by zero, an operation strictly forbidden.*

This reminds her of something. Years ago someone sent her one of those fallacious proofs. It must have been her father. Thinking of him, her eyes burn. If she finds the courage, of course her mother would be upset. But for some reason it hits her harder, thinking about her father. Who would he have to share snowball sentences with, goofy math puzzles, those weird things he writes? Who would he have at all?

Thursday, February 18, 2016

He's talking with Beth Davis, a colleague in his department, in the hallway outside his office. She's holding a sheaf of printouts in one hand and a Styrofoam cup in the other, describing to him some new data on supernova neutrinos. She pauses to take a sip of her coffee, ducking her head and pursing her lips, and suddenly a memory floats up from years ago, dim, barely recoverable, but it strengthens as he focuses on it. One night he and Beth had the most amazing sex. Images and sensations flood his mind. He can't believe he hasn't thought about this since then. They had sex all night. It was *perfect sex*. Where were they? At a conference? And when was it, and how is it possible that he's never thought about it since then, and why did they do it only once?

He wakes.

Cancels his alarm, which is set to go off in thirty seconds. Lies in bed, pointing an erection at the ceiling. Did it really happen? It did! He still remembers it, how wonderful it was. Beth was— Beth is— He can't believe he hasn't—

He gets out of bed, puts on his bathrobe, and goes to piss, pushing his boner down. With the pressure from his bladder reduced he starts to detumesce. More awake now, he knows that of course it never happened. He often has dreams similar to this one, involving various women of his acquaintance. The memory of sex is always evanescent at first, then over-powering and euphoric. He's known Beth slightly for two years. They haven't even sat down to coffee together. She's married. But now when he sees her he will feel an inappropriate attraction. His subjective im-pression is that the dream engenders the attraction, but he acknowl-edges it's more likely that he's unconsciously attracted to unavailable women and therefore dreams about them.

He goes down to the kitchen to start coffee, comes back up, shaves, clothes himself, redescends. Boils three eggs, two for breakfast, one for lunch. When the eggs are done, he puts the pot lid facedown on the counter and drains the water. He turns back from the sink to see the lid creeping stepwise across the Formica. The steam trapped under the hot lid is condensing against the cool surface, forming a vacuum and a water seal around the rim. When the vacuum gets strong enough to break the seal at its weakest point, the air flowing in under the rim pulls it, hy-droplaning, in the contrary direction. The pressure equalizes and the lid stops moving until more condensation causes the phenomenon to recur. It's a steam engine powered by condensation rather than vaporization. This is the sort of thing that makes scientifically illiterate people believe in poltergeists.

He eats standing at the counter, forcing himself to listen to a few minutes of NPR news. Stupidity appears to be on a relentless rise. This sociopathic moron Trump just won the New Hampshire primary. Of course there's little chance he'll survive the primaries, but the other Re-publicans aren't much better. Such a lineup of ignoramuses and poltroons, it's scarcely to be believed.

He washes his plate and cup, puts his papers and laptop in his shoul-der bag, shrugs on his coat. 7:20 a.m. Sun just coming up. Lecture at nine.

People forget to turn off a light, then remember distinctly that they did turn it off, so they say a ghost turned it on. Studies have shown that habitual actions generate spurious specific memories. People hear a distant sound, incorrectly register it as a nearby sound, and think a ghost is in the next room. This especially happens to older people because the human brain, as it ages, has more difficulty identifying the direction and range of sounds. People sense low-frequency vibrations, which often occur in enclosed underground spaces, and ascribe the physical unease engendered by such vibrations to a malign "presence." People with no mathematical ability and consequently no notion of the prevalence of coincidence see providential intention in every random correlation of their lives.

He looks at the five dials on the stove, says "off" five times. Goes out and locks the door, thinking, "I'm locking the door."

He doesn't like taking the time to put on his seat belt before he gets the car moving, so he attaches it while he's rolling down the driveway and turning onto the street. His Toyota Corolla complains more about this than his old Ford Escort did. If he delays his seat belt long enough, the Corolla will beep eight times, once per second, then fifty times, twice per second. The first eight beeps group themselves naturally into twos, and thus the following faster beeps seem to come in groups of four. But since there are fifty beeps instead of forty-eight, the final two sound like a mistake.

It fascinates him, how convincing the illusion is that the first of every four beeps is louder than the others. But it *is* an illusion. If he blocks out several beeps and then "resets" his attention, the following beeps always fall into groups of four with convincing first-beat emphasis, regardless of where they actually are in the sequence. Might this stem from the fact that most Western music is in 2/4 or 4/4, so his brain is conditioned to hearing repetitive sounds in those groupings? Might that also be the reason people hear a "tick-tock" in clocks and a "ping-pong" in a Ping-Pong game? Older pendulum clocks really did sound "tick-tock," since the escapement mechanism had two distinct stages. Maybe people hear "tick-tock" in electric clocks because the old phrase "tick-tock" conditions them to hear it. An interesting example, if true, of language influencing apprehension.

The weather has warmed again, almost up to the freezing point, with patches of pale blue sky and pinpricks of snow in the air. On the way to campus, he passes a spot in the steep terrain of his neighborhood where the downhill side of the road began to slump a year ago. The town set up three Jersey barriers to keep cars away from the edge, then seemed to forget about the problem. Of course the barriers are ugly: blotchy gray concrete, crumbled here and there at the edges, a nub of rusted rebar showing. Some of his neighbors complained. About a month ago, someone used pink spray paint to write in cursive along the three scorned objects: "Tell me/I'm/Pretty." Yes, he's a ridiculous person; he finds this touching.

It also fascinates him that most people have no idea how many beeps their own cars make. (He was curious, so he started asking.) It's not an utterly trivial question, because it is, after all, an engineering decision stemming from a social-science judgment. Manufacturers want to annoy people enough to get them to attach their seat belts, but can't annoy them so much that they'll buy a different car. Toyota is willing to harass him more than Ford. Could that be because Japanese are more comfortable than Americans in using social pressure to enforce norms?

He once asked all his acquaintances to sing for him, on the spot, the chimes produced by the university clock tower. The full sequence, on the hour, is sol-mi-sol-do-sol-mi-do-mi. They had heard parts or all of this melody four times every hour, every day, for years. Of the ones who didn't merely shrug and admit they hadn't the foggiest, about two-thirds responded by singing the chimes of Big Ben. A fine example of pattern dependence. One study has shown that if you display to people on a screen, even for several seconds, an ace of hearts falsely colored black, they will perceive it as an ace of spades. Much of what we "see" is not actually data acquired through our retinas. Our brains economize processing power by looking for patterns, then relying on them as shortcuts. If you project on a screen a regular grid with dots placed randomly near the edges, then stare at the center of the grid, the dots will disappear from your peripheral vision.

He parks near his building, checks to confirm the doors are locked, makes a circuit of the car to ensure the headlights and taillights are off. Takes the stairs two at a time up three flights.

Departmental hallway (right *there* is where beautiful Beth stood, endearingly sipping her coffee), office, desk. He likes to start each morning by seeing what the Astrophysics Science Division at NASA has chosen to post as their Astronomy Picture of the Day. Today's is a photo of yesterday's launch of the Hitomi satellite by the Japanese Aerospace Exploration Agency. A beautiful image—the H-IIA rocket is riding a dazzling fan of fire up out of a cloud of water vapor, about 15 degrees off vertical. It's interesting how the tilt makes the flight seem more "dynamic" than a purely vertical rise, and he wonders if the photographer manipulated the frame. But the orientation of the cloud argues against it.

He loves the look of rockets. In his early boyhood, that's what all the "spaceships" on the covers of sci-fi paperbacks actually were—sleek convex cylinders with fins, a wonderfully alluring design that he had no idea at the time was a copy of Hitler's V-2. So those vehicles "reaching for the stars," paeans to human idealism, were actually Nazi terror weapons. Which is kind of a fun fact. The enormous Saturn rockets of his adolescence were much less appealing, looking like Empire State Buildings lumbering aloft. But Atlas I through V got gorgeous again, satin-sheen white pencils with enlarged pointed heads evoking futuristic arrows, and delicate articulated boosters like flanking organ pipes. The H-IIA in today's photo is a slim cone-topped cylinder, the exact shape of a Crayola crayon.

Rockets make Mark think of his father, whose feelings about them, one could fairly say, were mixed. He liked to watch clips of failed launches: the rocket rising a few meters, hesitating, schlumping back, exploding. Or rising farther, fishtailing, turning upside down, now using its thrust to drill itself into the ground. He found these clips hilarious. The poor guy got more and more reclusive as he grew older. The inability of Mark's parents to communicate with each other in the smallest helpful way in their last twenty years pained Mark a great deal. They were each locked in their own world, comforted by mutually antagonistic interpretations of every event of their lives. Ah, well.

Time to get to class. He grabs his laptop and heads down the hall. (Right *there*, exactly there.)

Should he be worried about Mette? Her mother often berates him for not "passing the test," by which she means the Turing test. He wonders occasionally if she has a point. Whereas, as far as he can tell, she never questions her own emotional responses, which is somewhat annoying. He's not blind to the evidence that he's slow to notice certain things. And really, it's not that he's not a tad concerned. But he's never gotten the impression that Mette relies on him for emotional support. His impression is that when her mother tries to interfere, she bristles. He and his daughter sometimes go months without communicating, and it has never bothered either of them.

"Hi, Professor!" Students are entering the lecture hall.

"Hello," he says to their collective heads. Follows them in, glances at the clock. Six minutes to go. The only way to never be late is to usually be early.

Shortly after his father died, Mark found among his papers a file containing testimonial letters from his colleagues, solicited and compiled on the occasion of his retirement by his long-term publication collaborator, a younger female colleague who seemed to have a soft spot for the old man. Mark can't remember her name. One of the notes, from a much younger male colleague, was arranged like a poem on the computer printout, that dear old z-fold paper with the printer track-holes along the side:

> I usually think I know the answer
> Then there's a UV question
> I haven't a clue
> I turn to you for help
> You know exactly how to explain
> A light dawns
> You are a guide
> With a kind heart.

Of all the testimonials, this one was the most moving, and Mark has wondered if his attempts to write those data set things stem from having read it.

He's never been good at remembering names, and he seems to be getting worse as he ages. He has also begun to experience mild anomic aphasia. For some reason, "table" gives him particular trouble. "Put that on the—on the—on that—" Whereas he's always had, and still has, an excellent memory for numbers. So much so that he never bothers to enter phone numbers in a contact list. Through all these recent months during which he was packing up his childhood home and preparing it for sale, he had nostalgic thoughts, but was never close to tears. Then yesterday he called the relevant telecommunications giant to cancel the telephone number he'd grown up with. The woman on the other end of the line said, "Our records indicate that you've had this number for a long time. Would you like to transfer it to your new location?" Mark said no, because he already had a number. And discovered that his eyes were smarting.

He remembers when his home exchange was called Volunteer 2. His dad's workplace was Volunteer 1. Then came All-Number Calling, when he was six. When he was eleven, his dad's lab reorganized and his office number changed, which bothered Mark. He still remembers both numbers, plus all four of his college telephone numbers and all three from his graduate years. He pulls out his phone, keys Mette's number, composes a text.

Your mother is concerned.

He stares at that for a moment. Doesn't seem quite right. Deletes it.

Are you okay?

Presumes too much, maybe. Might be offensive. Deletes it.

Hope you're doing well?

Sounds like something from a business acquaintance. Deletes it.

Time's up. He mutes his phone and pockets it.

"Hello everyone. Let's get started." He opens the file on his laptop, throws the lecture title up on the screen behind him. "This is the eighth lecture of our course, entitled 'Planets are Everywhere, but Where is Everybody?' You all should have read chapter 24 in the textbook and the two excerpts I posted on the portal, from Kasting's *How to Find a Habitable Planet* and Ward and Brownlee's *Rare Earth*.

"To recap from the previous lecture: the first confirmed detection of an extrasolar planet did not occur until 1992, yet today, thanks in large part to HARPS and the Kepler space telescope, we have identified more than two thousand. And when we get the first data release from the Gaia astrometry spacecraft later this year, that number will increase dramatically. Who among professional astronomers would have predicted, twenty years ago, the existence of hot Jupiters? Today we know that, not only do they exist, they are quite common. It turns out that planetary

systems are far more varied than we had previously assumed, and this realization presents fascinating challenges to our theories of stellar-system
formation. Astronomers today are lucky to be living at a time in which,
in so many areas, we are discovering just how wrong we have been. To a
scientist, being right might be good for the ego, but being wrong is good
for the brain. Or to put it another way, being wrong is much more interesting."

This is his favorite lecture of the course. He changes it every year to
accommodate new information, and since he doesn't write his lectures
out but works instead from notes, he has to be especially careful on this
one not to rattle on feverishly, figuring out five different ways of making
the same point, only to realize his time is up when he's halfway through.
He used to give this lecture at the end of the semester, since it's about
the Ultimate Question—does extraterrestrial life exist?—but by late
April most of the students are dismaying sacks of apathy, partied-out or
spring-fevered, sick to death of using their brains. It gets worse every
year—all his colleagues have noticed this—and five years ago he moved
this lecture up into the first half, right after the February break, figuring maybe they've caught up on their sleep, or have just watched 96
hours of their eight favorite TV shows, and are feeling refreshed.

"—so now that we've established that planets are abundant in the
galaxy, the next question is how many of them might be habitable. But
since we can't land a shuttle on any of these planets and open the door
and sniff the air, like in *Galaxy Quest*, we need to devise a series of questions that we can apply to the data we collect from these incredibly
distant objects. I want to elaborate a little on some of the excellent points
Kasting makes on this subject—"

While he talks, he glances at the box in the corner of his laptop
screen which shows him how many students have clicked in: 96 today,
out of a total enrollment of 109, so 13 absent. He allows students to miss
three of the semester's twenty-seven lectures without penalty, which

means if no student exceeded the limit, an average of 12 students would be missing every class. Of course some students do exceed the limit—on average, about 9 percent—and their grades suffer. He announces at the first lecture that laptops cannot be used in the first eight rows because there are still about a quarter of the students who take notes by hand— these also tend to be the more studious ones—and having someone else's laptop screen in your field of view can be distracting, especially when that person is chatting on Facebook. Mark isn't naive, some healthy fraction of the approximately seventy students with open laptops are not paying attention. He doesn't let himself worry about it. Anyone who can spend all that money on college tuition, or have someone else do it for them, and then ignore what's taught in their classes is a lost soul, as far as he's concerned. Merely to satisfy his own curiosity, he sometimes asks a multiple-choice question based on something he has said in the past ten minutes, and after the students hit their iClickers, he throws the results up on the screen as a bar graph. Occasionally there might be a genuine misunderstanding, but usually the 15 percent or so who are laughably off-base—for example, the ones guessing today that the current estimate for the number of planets in the Milky Way is around one million—are right now shopping for spring sweaters or playing *Angry Birds* or hoping to learn what happened between Audrey and Brendan at the rad party last night. (He is under no illusion that his lingo is up to date. "Rad" probably went out years ago. Maybe *Angry Birds*, too. And come to think of it, these kids were probably ten when *Galaxy Quest* was made.)

"—Ward and Brownlee caution us that there may be reasons why Earth is not 'average' at all. And what we're learning right now about other stellar systems suggests that the arrangement of our solar system may also be unusual, perhaps even quite rare. We have to be careful about overusing the Copernican Principle, which assumes that we, as observers, are not in some privileged position. For example, it's often said, even by astronomers, that our Sun is an average star, but that's not true. Most stars are part of binary or trinary systems, in which stable planetary orbits are either extremely unlikely or impossible. Sol is more massive than 95 percent of the stars in the Milky Way. Planets in the habitable zones around smaller stars, such as red dwarfs, are tidally locked, which is likely unconducive to life. Stars more massive than Sol, because of the luminosity-mass relationship, have exponentially shorter lifetimes, and also emit a larger fraction of their light as ultraviolet and x-ray radiation. Both of these facts probably make the development of complex life unlikely."

And on he goes—or maybe, on and on and on he goes—tossing up images on the screen, tossing out iClicker questions, checking his timer against his place in the outline. Sure enough, he falls behind and has to skip over a fascinating bit about the dinosaurs, and another about interstellar travel and planetary resource depletion, which he very much regrets. In the last ten minutes he hurriedly dismantles the Drake Equation, invokes the Fermi paradox and ends with a foreboding speculation about the Great Filter.

If he can find the idea moving that three Jersey barriers might hope to be pretty, it's probably no surprise that he struggles against being audibly emotional in the lecture's last minute, which concerns whether humans are alone in the universe, and the chances of their survival as a species. Like his aphasia, this troublesome excess emotionalism plagues him more each year. It is profoundly embarrassing to think that he can move himself to tears with his own words. He steadies himself by focusing on the faces in front of him, many of which seem bored or distracted. Is he being unfair to them? Just as he doesn't want to become a weepy old man, he doesn't want to become an old fart, continually comparing the younger generations invidiously to his own.

"—I'm sorry, I see that I've gone over five minutes, so I'll stop there. Remember my office hours are tomorrow, four to six, and Monday, three to five. See you next Tuesday." They instantly come alive, chatting and bustling toward the doors. Detention's over, thinks the old fart. He closes his laptop, hits the button to raise the screen.

"Professor?"

Two students with decent questions. One of them he's talked with before, clearly bright. He *is* being unfair. Who knows how blank-faced he looked when he was twenty and underslept and absorbed in his own thoughts? Who knows how blank-faced he looks *now?*

Back in his office, he does what he always does after a lecture, typing up notes on ways he might make it better, maybe reach a greater percentage of those faces. Life in the universe! The fate of humankind! Why can't he get them as excited as he is? He googles *Galaxy Quest* and sees it's much older than he realized: most of his students were only two when it came out, no one has any idea what he's talking about, it's a lame attempt at humor anyway—the old man trying to be "with it"—so he cuts it from his notes. (Does anyone say "with it" anymore?)

He often wonders what percentage of his colleagues were first drawn to astronomy when they were kids because they were dying to know if there were aliens on other planets. Scientists are people, too, they pass the Turing test every day, and on the subject of extraterrestrial life, more than any other in astronomy, Mark thinks his colleagues' speculations are distorted by wishful thinking. Sometimes even serious astronomers, if they're speaking to the general public, will invoke the enormity of the observable universe and say something like, "There must be life out there, because otherwise think of all that wasted space." What a foolish thing to say! It would make as much sense to contrast the 100 trillion neutrinos passing unscathed through our bodies each second with the approximately one neutrino during our lifetime that will hit something, and say, "But that can't be. Think of all those wasted neutrinos." Or when some astronomers get duped by poetry, and say something along the lines of human intelligence being "a way for the cosmos to know itself."

So, just because we happen to be intelligent, the cosmos somehow wants to be intelligent? Just call the cosmos your personal God and be done with it.

It's probably hardwired in the human brain, this tendency to see life everywhere. Mark read somewhere that babies see a "face" in anything that's round and has a couple of buttons on it, like smoke alarms. Humans' instinctive belief that consciousness exists in other humans is probably an evolutionary advantage, helping the species survive through empathetic cooperation. Mark doubts there would be much selective pressure to limit that instinct merely to other humans, and so people evolved to see gods in the sky and spirits in trees. So Percival Lowell saw canals on Mars. So scientists in the 1940s saw Venus's eternal cloud cover and imagined a warm, wet world conducive to life. So now we detect subsurface oceans on Europa and Enceladus and envision sea creatures.

Kasting, to his credit, is unusual in openly admitting his bias. In the excerpt Mark had his students read, Kasting writes somewhere—Mark searches the file, finds it—"I am one of those people who, like Carl Sagan, would like to believe that life is widespread in the universe." Mark flags this, adds a note: *Life tends to see life.* Maybe he should include a few sentences on this. But where to fit them in? He already doesn't have enough time to say everything he wants to about the Drake Equation. Sometimes he toys with the notion of devoting an entire lecture to the Drake Equation.

He hates the Drake Equation.

The textbook Mark uses presents a modified version of the equation, which he finds useful for an introductory course:

$$N_{civ} = N_{hp} \times f_{life} \times f_{civ} \times f_{now}$$

To put it in words, the number of civilizations extant in the galaxy today equals the number of habitable planets in the galaxy, times the fraction of those planets on which life has arisen, times the fraction of *those* planets on which life has progressed to civilization, times the fraction of *those* planets whose civilization is extant right now. (As opposed to, say, a billion years ago.)

The Drake Equation is the one bit of "math" regarding the search for extraterrestrial intelligence that most people know, if they know anything. And since it's "math," they have the feeling it tells them something quantitative. But this would be true only if we had a likely range of values for the various terms, which we don't. Mark thinks that even a few of his colleagues fall into the trap. They plug in numbers that they know are wild guesses, they acknowledge that the resulting number is also a wild guess, and yet that result is a specific number, and numbers are alluring. To be fair to Frank Drake, a fine astronomer, he intended none of this. He was merely formulating a way to think about the problem.

Just in the last few years astronomers have gotten to the point where they can replace the first term to the right of the equal sign with a number that's not pure garbage. He's seen a rough calculation based on data from Kepler, HARPS, et al. that suggests there are around ten billion habitable planets orbiting Sun-like stars in the galaxy. Maybe the true figure is a billion, maybe it's fifty billion. But at least we now have a range based on real data.

But if you move on to the next term in the equation—the fraction of habitable planets on which life does in fact arise: right here is the trap. We have an equation in front of us, our undergraduate students are listening, or the TED talk audience is waiting, and let's face it, this is the only thing non-astronomers care about, and we're the experts, we have our expensive PhDs to prove it, so we feel the need to say something. But we should resist! We should shrug our shoulders and look sheepish and put down the chalk. Because any number we put in the equation, no matter what disclaimer we utter as we do so, will seem to have more weight than all the numbers we didn't put there.

Mark makes a note: *Specific numbers have weight, mislead—optimism 100%, pessimism 1%??!*

Two weeks ago he read an article—written for a general audience, but by genuine astronomers—in which the authors established a range for f_{life} by suggesting "optimistic" and "pessimistic" bounds. Of course, everyone can agree that the optimistic bound is 1—that is, 100 percent of habitable planets will go on to develop life. For their "pessimistic" bound, these two professional astronomers chose .01. Mark could hardly believe his eyes. Given the enormous range of numbers the universe throws at us for our daily perplexity and amazement, 1 and .01 are practically the same number. Scientists have no emotional difficulty in believing the calculation that out of approximately 10^{23} neutrinos that pass through a human body during a normal lifespan, only one hits something on the way through.

Mark notes down, *Remember the neutrinos.*

Or the Sun! Maybe that's a better example. (He notes down: *Proton-proton chain.*) The chance that any particular proton-proton collision in the interior of the Sun will result in the formation of deuterium is roughly 1 in 10^{29}. That means that the average proton, experiencing approximately one trillion collisions per second, will successfully produce deuterium only once in about three billion years. And yet the Sun indubitably shines—because the particle density in the Sun's core is about 10^{26} per cubic centimeter. Thus, every second, for each cubic centimeter, there are approximately 10^{9} successful reactions. And how many cubic centimeters are there in the Sun's core? The solar core has a radius of about 150,000 kilometers, and there are 100,000 centimeters in a kilometer, and the volume of the sphere is approximately the cube of that times four, so the number of cubic centimeters is approximately 1.4 x 10^{31}. Multiply that by the number of reactions per cc per second, and you get 1.4 x 10^{40}. The real number is somewhat less, because reaction rate decreases as density decreases with greater distance from the Sun's center: about 4×10^{38} reactions per second. Or to write it out (since un-scientific people don't have any decent sense of orders of magnitude), 400,000,000,000,000,000,000,000,000,000,000,000,000. The point is, mathematical measurements of the universe are flooded with numbers like this. To declare that any number is "big" or that any probability is "small" is to get fooled by human-scale assumptions. Ten billion habit-able planets in the Milky Way galaxy sure sounds like a lot, but if the chance of life developing on a habitable planet is one in 10^{10}, then voilà, Earth is unique.

There's a knock on the door. Mark looks at the time. Yikes, one of his graduate students, an appointment, the Centaurus A project. "Come in."

Super bright young woman, new this year, parents Bolivian, grew up in Michigan, undergrad at Michigan State, did work on molecular clouds, is new to TRGB measurements, a night owl, always drinking coffee, smokes out on the quad, likes scarves, what's her name, shit, he knows it, did he write it on his appointment calendar, no, damn it, she told him it meant "sky," which is kind of neat for an astronomer, not Adriana, not An-tonella, not Alexa, Ar-something, not Ariana—

"Hi, Professor, this is the right time, isn't it?"

"Yes, please, sit." Ara-something. If he gets the last name, he'll get it all. Ma—something like macho, macha—Machado! Aracely Machado! "So tell me, Aracely. How's the work going?"

And they talk. Aracely is one of two graduate students (the other is Gerhardt, easy to remember *his* name because he's not in the room) who are helping Mark crunch reams of Hubble Telescope and ground imag-ing data on the Centaurus A galaxy group. Last year they published a paper showing that 29 of the 31 dwarf galaxies of Cen A lie in two planes. The ongoing project is to get increasingly precise information on the positions and motions of the Centaurus A dwarf galaxies, and in particular to determine how many of them are rotating in the same di-rection. If nearly all of them do, it will suggest there is something wrong with the CDM model of galaxy formation, which in turn would raise questions about the behavior of gravity on the largest scales. Imagine if the theory of gravitation had to be revised. That would be super exciting.

After Aracely takes off, Mark emails colleagues for an hour, eats his lunch at his desk, reads some of the day's online science articles written for the general public. Since he deals so often with undergrads, he likes to keep up with popular conceptions and misconceptions. He avoids poisoned clickbait relating to anything political. He's intrigued by the algorithms that search engines use to determine, from his browsing history, what links to tempt him with. Since language is tricky for computers, they often make comical mistakes. He just read a piece on supermassive black holes, and embedded in it was a link to an article the computer determined might be related: *Don't miss: Can women really have 100 orgasms in a row?* He notes this down. Alas, he could never use it in a lecture. Writes next to it, "Gravity = bliss."

He spends the rest of the afternoon happily (blissfully, in fact) engaged in Centaurus A work, stopping now and then to lope down and up the three floors of stairs to keep his mind fresh. Gerhardt comes by for an anxious consult. He's capable, but high-strung, not needing direction so much as reassurance. It took Mark forever to figure this out. Actually, a colleague had to point it out to him. Beth walks by his open door, innocent of coffee and printouts.

At 7:00 p.m. he knocks off. A thin film of snow coats his car. As often happens with snowfall on a cold and windless day, many of the crystals are undamaged. In the light of the parking lot sodium lamps they glint like minuscule silver coins lying flat, several sheets deep. Or maybe, being hexagonal, they're more like tiny parquet tiles. He takes off his glasses and leans close (the great thing about being nearsighted is this ability to focus on something an inch from your nose) and examines their varied shapes. He blows lightly and watches them swirl aloft like kites, then float back down to lie flat again. He remembers a scene in some movie, a man—was he a rabbi?—talking about holding on to a sense of the miraculous in the ordinary, and the man gestures out the window of his office and says something like, "Will you just look at that parking lot!"

He sweeps the flakes gently with his gloved hands from the car windows, trying not to damage them. They fall, tumbling and twinkling. He's never learned to like the light from sodium lamps, partly because their color rendering index sucks, but maybe more because the powdery orange color reminds him of Bayer Children's Chewable Aspirin, whose taste he hated when his mother made him take it. He can still visualize with a pang the teal-white glow of the mercury vapor street lamp that stood across the street from his house when he was growing up. It looked so lunar and lovely and lonely in the rain at night. His town started changing over to sodium when he was in high school, and since he couldn't believe anyone would do it for aesthetic reasons, he went to the library to research the motive. Subsequently he went around saying to his classmates, intending it as a parody of a fatuous conversation opener, "Say, did you know that sodium lamps give off 12 percent more light than mercury lamps for half the energy cost?" He thought it was funny. God help him, he even did it at school dances. No wonder the girls ran from him.

He liked that scene in the movie about the parking lot, but his beef with popular culture is that it's always religious or spiritual people who say things like that, things about transcendence. Whereas in his experience, scientists are more likely than anyone else to feel wonder in the contemplation of mundane phenomena.

He heads downhill into town. The city hasn't salted the street yet, so he creeps along at fifteen miles per hour. Three years ago a truck lost control on this very hill and smashed into the porch of the church at the bottom of the slope. The nose of the truck knocked out both pillars holding up the gable, substituting as support its own cab roof, and the fit was so perfect,

the porch superstructure didn't tilt an inch. Mark found himself hoping
they'd leave the truck where it was, as a bold new design element. It would
be no quirkier than one or two of the newest buildings on campus.

He drives west across town. He's lived here for almost thirty years.
Since the downtown streets form a rectilinear grid, there are dozens of
alternate routes of identical length to many destinations, and he's staved
off the boredom attendant on trivial errands by clocking different options. Thus he's ended up knowing, without even trying, the timing of
all the downtown traffic lights. It has given him insight into how traffic
planners work. For example, the north-south street that runs directly
from the high school and just misses the bolus of the pedestrian zone to
connect with the east-west state route at the south end of town becomes
predictably congested every day at 4:30 p.m., when the late-schedule school
buses and the early commuting traffic coincide. As the problem wors-
ened over several years, growing numbers of drivers, like Mark, shifted
west one block. This alternate street was more residential, and had fewer
traffic lights than the streets on either side of it. Suddenly, one of its
lights was shifted from a 30-second red to a 75-second red. The street
residents had probably complained to the city about the increased traffic, and the engineers had responded. With the longer red, the heavier
flow on the street abated. But Mark waited, figuring that even the residents didn't want a 75-second red at the end of their block. Sure enough,
after three months, the light was reprogrammed to 45 seconds, and it
has stayed there ever since.

Driving west, as he's doing now, is easier because the lake starts at the
north edge of town and three of the four state routes cross town laterally
in order to reach the opposite shore. Mark flows along with the one-way
traffic through the timed lights, marveling as always at the large fraction of people who run reds, and the 100 percent of cops who witness it
and do nothing.

Tonight he's eating at Leslie's Cafe. He crosses the tracks and the inlet, parks on the small street paralleling the state route. Locks the car, circumambulates to note the inarguably unlit head- and taillights.

He's never been inside Leslie's Cafe, though it has been in business since before his arrival in town. It occurred to him about three years ago that he was always returning to the same few restaurants, and all of a sudden it seemed ridiculous that after living here for so long there were still so many places he had never tried. He decided that once a week he would make a point of eating in a new place. His choice would have nothing to do with expectations that the food might be good, he would just work his way exhaustively through every establishment, including all the chains he'd never eaten in, like Applebee's and Chili's.

"Just one? Sit wherever you'd like." The waitress swings past him with four bottles of beer on a round black tray. The place is nearly empty. He goes to a table in the far corner next to the sliding glass doors that look out on a deck, closed for the winter. He examines the room. A dozen tables with wood-grain Formica tops and scarred rims. Wooden chairs with turned legs, worn pale at the tops of the backs where people have grabbed them to pull them in or out, or upend them on the tables for shift-end cleaning. The floor is yellow linoleum tile over an uneven substrate. A gleaming bar, untended, backed by shelves sparsely populated with bottles, and a cluttered counter near the door with an old-style cash register, also untended. Only one waitress that he can see, five other customers, four at one table, all men, drinking rather than eating, the fifth a woman working through a platter of french fries with a large hairy dog at her feet. A drop ceiling of fire-resistant fiber tiling, stained brown here and there, as custom seems to require. A stale smell of standing water coming from the kitchen, which he can glimpse through a swinging door next to the bar.

He is happy. He's probably doing what they call "drinking in."

The waitress brings him water and a menu. "Anything to drink for a start?"

She's a slender middle-aged woman with an oval face, teaspoon chin, long straight nose, corded neck with a deep hollow just above the clavicle. Her blond hair is pulled back in a ponytail, but a number of wisps have worked free to curl like smoke around her ears and peek up from her crown. Her forehead and the hollow of her neck glow with perspiration. She's wearing jeans that bunch at her knees, sneakers, a blue polo shirt with a collar faded to aqua.

"No, thank you, water is fine."

"I'll be back for your order in a minute."

He watches her retreating back and tries to discount his feelings of attraction. He's read somewhere that many men are attracted to waitresses, the hypothesis being that it stems from male desire to have females serve them unquestioningly, even constrainedly. He finds it disturbingly plausible.

The menu lists clam chowder, cream of tomato soup, baked haddock, meat loaf, N.Y. strip streak, etc. It could be from his childhood. He has a feeling that in a place like this the fish would not be good. Maybe not the meat, either. When the waitress comes back, he orders eggplant parmesan, chooses salad for the side. Can't resist watching her walk away again, tucking the pencil behind her come-hither right ear.

At some point during his elementary school years, his class was shown a travel film about the island of Corsica. All Mark later remembered was an aerial shot of a car on a narrow road rounding the flanks of a vertiginous coastline. That one image remained in his mind, and for years afterward whenever he or his equally studious, unadventuresome friends idly speculated about traveling in the far future, he invariably said he wanted to go to Corsica. The world was a big place, so he liked having a specific plan. The last thing he wanted to do was investigate other options, still less find out more about Corsica, as either of those things might undercut his decision. (Only much later did it occur to him that the film clip in his head looked very much like a Matchbox car negotiating curves in a mountainous blanketscape.) So when, after four years of hard study intercalated by working summers, he finished college and saw that he had enough time before graduate school to carve out three weeks, he bought panniers, a tent, and a camp stove, packed up his ten-speed, and flew to Nice, where he caught a ferry to the fabled isle.

He still knew nothing about Corsica beyond the fact that it had mountains, a coastline, and roads (plus Napoleon). Using his terrible high-school French, he bought food and a map in the port town, then biked into the hills. With the aid of his map he chose the narrowest and wiggliest roads, biked over mountain ridges and down valleys filled with maquis, through small stone villages that seemed largely abandoned. The landscape was arid, but for the first week it rained every day. His tent was too small and his sleeping bag got wet and free-range cattle wandered into his unofficial campsites at dusk. The palms of his hands went numb from the handlebars and his ass hurt. He wasn't unhappy, but he pondered his inexplicable foolishness at expecting some sort of magical encounter or revelation based on nothing but a decade-old image in his mind from a travelogue.

There came a day halfway through the tour that he spent battling headwinds, fixing a broken spoke, and getting run off a dirt road by an old priest in a battered station wagon. He stopped in a town to buy food and gauze bandages, waited out an afternoon shower under an awning, then biked higher into the hills. The clouds in the west were breaking up. As he looked for a possible campsite on either side of the rural road, he felt tired, out of sorts, bored. He came to a smaller dirt road that diverged to the right. He had learned by now that the best campsites in this steep and stony landscape were to be found along unused byways that once led to fields or hamlets now abandoned. He leaned his bicycle against a rock and walked up the side road, trying to determine if it was indeed unused. After about fifty meters he found a flat grassy patch that would make a fine sleeping spot. He turned around. He had a view all the way down the craggy mountain-slope to the sea in the west. Just above the horizon, the sun had broken free of clouds. He looked at the burning orange orb, the bruised purple clouds flanking it, the glittering sea, the rosy broken rocks of the Corsican mountains, the dark green vegetation glowing in the light, the one-lane rough mountain road curving along the contour line leading toward his bicycle, which also glowed, looking trustworthy and workaday with its loaded panniers, its bungee-corded sleeping bag and festooning water canisters. He was "hit between the eyes," as they say, by the unaccountable beauty of everything.

He had to sit down for a minute to sort out what he was experiencing.

He realized that if he had seen this exact scene on a poster in a travel agency over the caption "Bike through an ancient land," he would have been overwhelmed with desire, he would have yearned for that bicycle to be his, for that trip to be his. And what struck him now was that his principal feeling was still yearning. The paradoxical thought underlying his appreciation of how beautiful it all was, was still *I wish I could be there*. It occurred to him that beauty, maybe, is always a thing you can only see from the outside. And he has wondered ever since if the key to a happy life is to learn ever more deeply to be satisfied with standing off to the side, perceiving the beauty that is separate from you, but nearly everywhere.

His eggplant arrives, along with one of those metallic-green canisters of grated parmesan cheese (Kraft) and a smaller red-capped vial of pepper flakes (McCormick). It's not particularly good, with the usual watery "red sauce" of cheap restaurants, devoid of discernible herbs, but it's edible, and it would be unfair to condemn Leslie's Cafe for serving him indifferent food when its cuisine had nothing to do with the reason he chose it. When the waitress returns to refill his water glass and asks him how he's finding everything, he says, "Fine," and means it.

As he eats, he studies the outdoor wooden deck on the other side of the sliding glass doors. It sags so much in the far left corner he wonders if it's structurally stable. Judging from the arrayed tables and chairs under winter tarps, he assumes it's still open in the warmer weather. Since it abuts the inlet, it's probably the only tourist draw this shabby place has. He remembers reading in the local paper that the five-mile waterfront recreation trail, which the city has been piecing together from municipal and private land for years, was complete except for these few feet right here. The owner of Leslie's Cafe (Leslie, presumably) adamantly refused to sell, or to allow a public right of way, saying the business wouldn't survive the loss of the inlet frontage. Mark has seen letters in the paper decrying the owner, citing the rundown nature of the property and calling for the city to take the land through eminent domain. Mark gazes at the quasi-wreck of the deck, glances around the near-empty room. He disagrees with the letter writers. It has been the woman's (the man's?) property for many years. Leslie, he assumes, pays taxes, and has every right to serve soggy eggplant and mountainous platters of french fries to eccentric lone diners, with or without dogs.

The waitress pops through the swinging kitchen door and Mark glimpses behind her a perspiring man in a white shirt with a big belly, darkly grizzled. Perhaps the stubborn citizen himself. Good luck to him.

"Can I get you anything for dessert?"

"No, thank you."

She scribbles on her pad, rips, smacks the slip down. "You can pay at the register." Her name tag says "Fiona." She smells like vanilla and frying oil. Her hands and forearms are long and sinewy. Her nails are unpainted, well cared for. She trots back into the kitchen, tray under arm.

He puts the tip on the table, threads through the room's empty chairs. Two of the four beer drinkers—men in their forties, reddened by sun

and maybe drink—follow him with impassive eyes. (Who's *that* loon?)
He stands at the empty register for a minute until one of the men behind him yells, "Fiona!" and she comes back out of the kitchen to ring
him up. "Thank you," he murmurs over his shoulder. They rumble a
chuckle at him.

Outside, warmer air has blown in in gusts, scattering small branches
on the pavement. He returns to his car, thinking about the tilting deck,
and thus gravity again. Almost all the covers of the science fiction paperbacks of his youth had as their implicit theme the conquering of
gravity. Their artwork depicted impossibly high and fragile towers, can-
tilevered platforms that would collapse without some anti-gravity field,
ramps that rose and curved for glorious miles without supports. From
glimpses he's had of more recent movies, he'd say the impulse is still
strong. He saw part of a movie that seemed to want to be taken as serious science—a sequence about time dilation in a strong gravity field
was at least minimally plausible—but then the hero went to a planet
where huge rafts of rock hung in the sky like clouds. Nearly everyone,
it's said, has dreams in which they can fly. Does some large fraction of
all sci-fi stem simply from this? Those finned rockets taking off hourly
from spaceports as easily as ships sailing from harbor, as though Earth's
gravity well were some piddling thing. In reality, the enormous energy
expense of countering Earth's gravity is at least as much of a limitation
on space travel as the enormous distance between stars. Do people like
to climb mountains because, when they look from the summits, they
see what birds see? Or thrill looking into the Grand Canyon because the
sheer rock walls seem to defy gravity? Mark read somewhere that in
fancy restaurants the plating is all about getting the food to stand up
improbably high.

Of course, Earth would not have an atmosphere without gravity. Earth
would not *exist*. Without gravity, the universe would be an expanding

formless region of hydrogen and helium atoms, salted with lithium. Mark wonders if defying gravity feels to humans like defying aging, defying death. (His increasingly saggy butt, his greater difficulty loping up three flights of stairs.) Maybe it's no coincidence that angels are imagined to float in the clouds. In Mark's dreams, in fact, he floats more often than he flies. He takes a deep breath, makes a delicate lifting gesture with his arms and rises an inch. Then with gentle undulating motions that have to be timed just right, he ascends another five or six feet. This usually takes place in his department offices, and he gets comfy just under the ceiling while his colleagues look up at him and marvel.

He drives home, zigging and zagging through the grid. He often likes to take the first left, then the first right, then the first left, doing it as long as the grid allows, and see where he ends up. Though by now he generally knows. His choice is constrained once he reaches the bottom of East Hill, so at that point he finds his street and ascends. People think gravity = death, when in fact gravity = life. The exorbitant demands of gravity may well defeat space exploration, but then, space = death. Life was made for planets.

He pulls into his driveway, cuts the engine. Gets out, circles the car. His house has once again not burned down in his absence. Enters through the kitchen door, disposes of keys and laptop in their proper places, keeps on his coat and shoes, grabs a beer and two towels, goes out onto his back deck (unsagging and, like the house, not in flames). When the trees are bare, as now, he has a good view of the sky. The temperature has risen into the forties and the clouds have been blown east. The gibbous moon is just past the zenith. Mark has always thought, for some reason he can't articulate, that when the moon is like this, about 85 percent illuminated, it looks most like a face. A mother's face, to be specific, looking in the direction of its shadowed edge. No discernible features, just something about the shape of the "head," maybe the shadowed hint of an offside cheek. Actually, and he wouldn't want to admit this to anyone, it seems so terribly sentimental, but he always thinks of a mother looking down into a crib. With love, actually. God knows why.

He spreads one towel over the metal-mesh chair and the other over the patio table, sits with his legs up, drinks his beer. 9:05 p.m. No spring birds yet, no crickets; the sound of water trickling downhill. He finds himself thinking again about the day's lecture, all the things he wishes he could add. The only piece of evidence astronomers and exobiologists have to support the hypothesis that life arises easily on a habitable planet is that it seems to have arisen on Earth shortly after the planet's surface cooled enough to make life possible, perhaps within 200 million years. But how robust is this argument? If you take the four billion years between the beginning of habitability and the present time and divide them into 200-million-year intervals, you only get twenty. Therefore there's a 1 in 20 likelihood, which is not insignificant, that life arose purely by chance in the first interval. And the argument is even weaker than that. Because the Sun is getting hotter, the Earth will be habitable for only about another billion years. It's reasonable to assume that what we call habitable planets—Earth-like planets orbiting Sun-like stars—have a similar window of approximately five billion years in which life might develop. On Earth, it took 3.5 billion years for prokaryotic life to figure out how to become eukaryotic and then multicelled. Then it took another 600 million to 800 million years for multicelled life to figure out how to develop enough intelligence to sit on back decks, drink beer, and mull over these questions. If those time frames are typical, then any planet that's going to eventually host intelligent life has to get started somewhere within the first billion years of its habitable window. There's a one in five probability that it will accomplish this within the first 200 million years.

He drains his beer, goes in, checks his email, talks Gerhardt off a ledge. Watches Fox News for an hour. Then sits at the piano and plays the middle ten variations of *Goldberg.*

Almost midnight. He meticulously brushes and flosses his teeth (his dentist heaps praise on him twice yearly), crawls into bed. This room, like his childhood bedroom, occasionally admits moonlight when the trees are bare. A rhomboid of light creeps just perceptibly across the floor. *My discarded socks are bathed in moonlight . . .*

Since there does exist one small piece of evidence suggesting that broadcasting and/or exploring civilizations are not common in the universe (i.e., *Where is everybody?*), then somewhere along the developmental line from habitable world to bustling spaceports lies what astronomers like to call the Great Filter. Of course he has gut feelings. Even he is human. (He blames Mette's mother for the fact that this phrase intrudes on his thoughts once or twice a week.) Despite his reasoning earlier, if he were forced to guess he would say that analogs of prokaryotic life are probably common in the universe. He finds it compelling that bacterial life is so resourceful and tenacious, thriving at extreme temperatures, surviving for millions of years within rocks and meteoroids. Not that tenaciousness once alive really says anything about the probability of coming alive in the first place—but hey, that's what gut feelings are for.

He remembers a charming anecdote—he thinks it was about the physicist Freeman Dyson, or maybe Niels Bohr, he's not sure. Anyway, a visitor to (let's say) Dyson's office, noticing that he had a horseshoe mounted on the wall, exclaimed, "Surely, Mr. Dyson, you don't believe that a horseshoe brings good luck." Whereupon Dyson replied, "Of course not. But they tell me it brings good luck whether you believe in it or not."

As for the Great Filter, there are two periods of time on Earth that give Mark "pause," as they say. The first is that 3.5 billion years during which the prokaryotes seem to have invaded every conceivable niche on Earth, yet failed to figure out how to become eukaryotic and multicellular.

Three and a half billion years is an awfully long time. The second is the 600 or so million years during which multicellular life speciated into a plethora of forms, was forced to redo it from the ground up at least five times after mass extinctions, yet did not develop the intelligence necessary for brewing beer and building back decks. In particular, Mark regards the 170-million-year reign of the dinosaurs with unease. Earth's climate was stable, usable energy was abundant, and thousands of species of dinosaurs ruled. Yet all they did was drool.

Of course, the Great Filter might be in front of us. It's possible that the rise of intelligence is common, but that technological civilizations don't last long. When Mark was younger, people usually thought of nuclear war in this connection, but today most scientists would probably bet on resource depletion and environmental degradation. Intelligence is probably not a smart evolutionary strategy. While the dinosaurs drooled for 170 million years, the conditions in which they thrived remained relatively unchanged. Does anyone think that Earth's ecosystem will survive the onslaught of human industrial ingenuity for a fraction of that time in some recognizable form? Forget a million years, forget a hundred thousand. Mark wouldn't bet on one thousand. In cosmic terms, that's less than a blink of the eye.

Here's Mark's bet: human ingenuity, rather soon, will cause a mass extinction event. Intelligence might survive the initial collapse, but won't endure afterward longer than a few thousand years. Ecosystems will evolve and species will speciate and hundreds more millions of years will go by, with more extinction events, caused by this and that (volcanism, asteroid impact, cosmic ray burst, supercontinent desertification, snowball Earth events), after each of which life will recover and again diversify. There's no reason to think it inevitable, or even likely, that intelligence will rise again, but if it does, it will bring on another environmental collapse in short order. The Sun will continue to get hotter. The seas will boil away. The atmosphere will be stripped off by the solar wind. Eventually, only underground bacterial life will remain. Then the Sun will bloat, burp, make a small fuss, and Earth will be incinerated. What will be left is a white dwarf inside a cloud of expanding gases whose constituent atoms are excited by solar radiation and emit photons as they calm down, resulting in the celestial object misnamed a "planetary nebula." Some of these are extraordinarily beautiful, as the clouds nested within clouds glow at different parts of the spectrum. When Mark was an undergraduate he knew a professor who would end his lecture on planetary nebulae by expressing the hope that, five billion years from now, when Earth is gone, an intelligent creature on some distant planet in the Milky Way might train its telescope on our former Sun and say, "Wow, will you look at that one! That's a real pretty one."

He's falling asleep.

Mette.

His eyes fly open. He hears her mother's voice, "Mark—*fuck*! Pass the test!"

He fumbles for his phone on the bedside table, is dazzled by the awakened screen, types without forethought, I guess I'm a little worried. Could you send me a note? Sends it.

PART
TWO

1935–1951

"Your first word, sweetheart, was 'kitty.'"

Genny is looking at a photo of her tiny self, reaching out a dimpled hand to a calico cat. Calico cats are always girls, isn't that funny? Genny is six.

"I want a cat," she says.

But her mother has told her a hundred times.

"I want a little brother," Genny says.

"Don't be fresh."

She wants to be fresh. "Why can't I?"

"Aren't we a happy family, you and me and Daddy?"

"I want one!"

This gets her a smack on the bottom. "You've hurt Mommy's feelings. Go to your room."

She goes, failing not to cry, furious, bereft.

GENNY LIVES IN WASHINGTON, DC, on Harrison Street, in a square brick house painted white in a line with other houses that look kind of different but are all the same size and shape. Every house has a narrow back yard and there are no trees or bushes, so you can stand there looking through the wire to the other yards and keep hoping to see other children.

.   .   .

GENNY AND HER MOTHER are visiting her grandparents on the farm in Alabama. Daddy has to keep working at his office in DC. He works for the Bureau of Public Roads.

Grampa Stoakes has chickens in the back yard. Genny wants to hold one. She chases them, but would never hurt one. Grammie Eula showed her how to twist the neck for dinner, but she refused to do it. Grammie told her it hardly mattered to a chicken.

For the family photo, cousin Bob is holding a hen, and Genny makes a fuss until she can hold it.

Grampa Stoakes has been losing chickens at night, and he declares he's sure a nigger is stealing them.

"More likely a fox," says Grammie Eula.

Grampa sits up two nights straight with a shotgun. "I always wanted to shoot me a nigger," he says. He talks whiffly because he doesn't have any teeth.

Nothing happens except he gets tired. "Looks like the fox is too smart for you," Grammie Eula says.

Genny thinks Grammie Eula is smart and Grampa Stoakes is stupid.

"You wouldn't take your eyes off that stupid chicken," her mother says when they look at the photos later. "Everyone else is looking nicely into the camera."

"YOU WOULDN'T EVEN nap right until you were six months old. I kept putting you on your stomach and you'd roll onto your back. Then you'd wake up and fuss when I put you the right way down again."

Her mother talks a lot about regularity. "Did you do your business this morning?" If Genny has a stomachache it's because she hasn't had enough B.M.s. She sits on the toilet, waiting.

Every April she gets the dose of strychnine. This is her spring cleaning and it sure does work. It also makes her heart race.

Once a week her mother makes her drink hot lemon juice. "Constipa-
tion is a bad habit," she says. "We're teaching the bowels a new habit."

"But I'm not constipated."

"You can thank your mother."

IN SUMMER ON THE ALABAMA farm she sees her cousins. Her mother
has seven siblings. Aunt Jillie is smart. Aunt Iris is stupid. Uncle Tor-
rance is smart. Uncle Milton is stupid. Aunt Eugenie is *really* stupid.

Frank is one of Aunt Iris's boys. He's two years younger than Genny,
and he follows her around, marveling at everything she does. His mother
is extra religious and she won't let her boys cuss or tell jokes or do anything. Genny takes Frank aside and teaches him a joke:

What did the brassiere say to the hat?

"You go on ahead, and I'll give these two a lift."

GENNY IS GOOD at everything in school—math, reading, science, spelling, civics. She skips third grade.

She's advancing quickly on piano. She practices every day before and
after school. She plays in a recital and earns a bust of Schumann. It looks
like marble, but it's made of salt. Her mother starts a music scrapbook,
and frames Genny's achievement certificate to put on the wall.

Genny's favorite aunt is Jillie, the youngest one, who never married
and is always helping her parents and siblings. In Genny's baby book, it
says Genny's first smile was for Aunt Jillie, who was living with them
back then and doing the cooking and cleaning. It says Genny's first
complete sentence was, "Poor Mama tired!"

For Christmas when Genny is nine, Aunt Jillie sends her a dress for

Shirley, one of her dolls. She draws a picture of Shirley in her new dress and sends it to Aunt Jillie. Aunt Jillie writes that her cat had four kittens, and Genny writes that she hopes the kittens will still be little when she visits in the summer.

She earns a bust of Handel.

She earns a bust of Bach.

One of her certificates has a mistake on it, so her mother gets right on the phone.

For Christmas when Genny is ten her father builds her a marionette stage. She has Snow White and three dwarves and Hansel and Gretel and a Prince and a Solicitor and a horse in pajamas.

In sixth grade she takes the test to join the School Patrol. They used to call them Patrol Boys, but now girls are allowed, too, and the girls wear the same uniform as the boys, white ducks and a white shirt and a white sailor cap and a white Sam Browne belt and a purple necktie. Genny looks like Butch, the ceramic sailor boy on the parlor mantelpiece. She stands on the corner of Lowell and 34th and crosses the children. The little ones are adorable.

There's a patrol parade in May and she stands in her uniform in the back yard. Her father holds the camera. Face left, her mother says. No, *my* left. Put your left foot back so it looks like you're marching. Bend your elbow like you're swinging your arm. Stop being silly. Mother worked hard to wash everything and the smallest stain will show.

She wants a puppy.

GENNY IS TWELVE. On top of her piano Bach, Handel, Beethoven, Mendelssohn, Schumann, Chopin, Schubert, Verdi, and Tchaikovsky are all lined up.

It's Mother's Day. She gets up early and walks to the florist on Wisconsin Avenue to buy a dozen roses she's saved for. She puts them in a vase and arranges them better than last year. She makes breakfast and brings it on a tray to her mother, who's waiting upstairs pretending to be asleep.

"How sweet! Thank you, darling!"

She goes back down and brings up the roses and a card she made.

"How lovely! The card is precious!"

She dresses up and takes her mother to afternoon tea at a café in Friendship Heights. Other girls are there with their mothers, and there's a little argument about how she's dressed compared to the other girls, but it's over quickly and they make up. Daddy takes them both out to dinner and afterward Genny gives her mother a locket, very nicely wrapped. There's one more tiny argument in the evening about some backtalk Genny gave during dinner, Genny can't even remember what started it. But the day ends like last year, her mother crying, "Other girls appreciate their mothers, I don't understand . . ."

Daddy stands there looking useless.

GENNY HAS WRITTEN a marionette play and enlisted two other girls from school to help her. It's called "There Will Always Be an England," and the girls perform it at their junior high school to benefit Bundles for Britain. For the play, Hansel and Gretel stand in for two English school-children, and Snow White is their plucky, inspiring teacher. The Solicitor is Churchill. The three dwarves are Hitler, Goebbels, and Goering. Genny wrote in a bit about delivering a message so they could use the horse, too. They sell thirty-five tickets and make five dollars. The following weekend they perform the play again, this time for free—which is called doing your part—for some servicemen at the Roads Service Club. The men give them a standing ovation. They receive a thank-you letter from the vice chairman of Bundles for Britain and they get their picture in the paper. The other girls are looking at the camera, whereas

Genny—she always does this, why can't she listen, how old is she now, when will she ever—is looking at Gretel, whom she is holding.

IN THE SUMMER of 1942, while visiting the farm in Alabama, Gen gets a chance to ride a neighbor's horse for five minutes around a dirt track while the neighbor walks along holding the bridle and her life is changed forever.

HER MOTHER LETS her have a Jack Russell terrier, no doubt in hopes it will distract her from horses. Gen loves Stubby fiercely. He has a dog-house in the back yard, but sleeps at night with her. (Arguments about that, which Gen won.) He's squirmy and cuddly and lively and causes all sorts of mischief. He digs under the wire fence in the back yard. He skids and scrabbles around the house chasing balls. He waits by the parlor window for Gen to come home from school. He's sad on Wednesday and Saturday afternoons when Daddy drives Gen to Pegasus Stables near Silver Spring where she takes riding lessons. (More arguments about that, which Gen also won.)

AT HER ANNUAL DENTIST checkup Gen learns she has eight new cavities. Her dentist says her enamel has been stripped away. He asks questions. Turns out it was all that hot lemon juice. While she's at it, Gen mentions the strychnine and gets the reaction she wants. "I'm surprised it didn't kill you," the dentist says.

IMOGEN BROWN, five foot five and fifteen years old, hot and dusty, fit and freckled, canters on Margie down the bridle path along Rock Creek, under Beach Drive Bridge, up the slope into a clearing bordering 16th Street and down again into the woods. It's June 1944. She pounds across Riley Spring Bridge, veers left to continue downstream and opens out into a gallop. Jesus, it's just so gloriously fun. Paths fork off into denser woods and steeper slopes, and Imogen knows them well, but today's assignment is to time a direct route through the park all the way to the Tidal Basin.

Because . . . *Meadowbrook Has Gone to War!*

That's a joke she shares with Fran and Dot. Imogen started riding lessons at a public stable, but from the beginning her mother had her beady eyes on Meadowbrook. If she couldn't get her daughter off the brutes, she could at least get her into the equine version of a finishing school. Meadowbrook was where the ambassadors' daughters boarded their horses, and it taught the pure English style. It hosted foxhunts. But it was full up, and Imogen, anyway, was too much a beginner. Then an influential matron of Meadowbrook had the heaven-sent idea of founding an equestrian chapter of the American Women's Voluntary Services, which was aiding the war effort. Meadowbrook constructed additional stables and put out the call, and Imogen signed up so fast it made her mother's head swim.

She barrels under another bridge, then slows Margie to a trot. The route is eleven miles; about half of it has to be trotted or she'll exhaust the mare. She passes Miller Cabin on the other bank, then the picnic area for civilians, whom she's sworn to protect.

Here, by the way, is how fine she looks: creased and worn leather boots, white canvas gaiters, denim jodhpurs, buttondown shirt with a navy blue tie tucked between second and third button, rakish Motor Transport cap. On her left shoulder is a blue diamond patch with a brown horse's head, above which reads the banner, "A.W.V.S." Imogen cut and sewed the patch and banner herself, following the regulation patterns in the training manual.

Now she passes the police lodge—greetings, fellow guardians!—and parallels Ross Drive. She can make out through the trees the hoods of cars, which on this sunny Saturday are backed up in traffic. She skims past them, up a small rise—at the top she sees a complete car, a little girl at the back window who flashes a startled wave—then back down. There's a fallen branch toward the bottom, and Margie shortens up and scampers over it like a happy cat.

Here's the idea: if Washington, DC, gets Blitzed or invaded and all communications are cut (lines down! telegraph operators held hostage!), the brave teenage horsegirls of the A.W.V.S. Junior Auxiliary Rock Creek Patrol will carry messages from temporary command centers in Maryland down through the park to the Lincoln Memorial, where crisp-saluting operatives will wait to further the missives (extracted from dusty leather satchels) on to bunkered leaders in the basements of the White House and the Capitol. Imogen and her fellow express riders are like the Norwegian children in *Snow Treasure* who sledded their country's gold reserves past the Nazis. Who would suspect these youngsters of such grit and valor?

In other words, what a crock of shit! What a wonderful boondoggle!

On past Peirce Mill and the National Zoo, the stolid backs of embassies, down to where the park gets narrow, Margie tiring, now entirely trotting, and finally out along the shore of the basin—fresh breeze off the water, bright clouds in blue sky—around Easby's Point toward the Memorial. She reaches the designated handoff marker—a stick pounded into the grass with a red ribbon tied to it—no real operative in sight, of course, just stern Mrs. Brody in her wool suit and overseas cap, who nods to her while recording the time—68 minutes—then communes longer and more tenderly with Margie.

Imogen waters the mare, gives her hay from the trailer and a carrot from her pocket, brushes her down, feels her legs, throws on a blanket, talks in her velvet ear. Two following riders show up—one is Fran—and their times recorded (71 and 77 minutes, ha!). All three horses and their girls ride back to Meadowbrook in the trailer.

D-day happened two weeks ago.

"Meadowbrook stands alone!" Fran intones in her best radio voice.

All the girls laugh, even the driver, mannish Miss Evans.

Imogen is having a wonderful war.

Mount Holyoke College! Massachusetts! Many miles away!

Imogen is in the class of 1950, whose symbol is Pegasus, which is perfect, as she spends her four years on horses flying over jumps. Technically she's a chemistry major, but who cares about that? She lives in the stables with the other horsewomen, her best friends Mac, Birch, Smitty, Delph. They call her Imp. She's the most fearless jumper of the lot, surpassed only by Mr. Nichols, Master of Equitation, who loves flying so much he levitates above the saddle at the top of every magnificent arc. (Look at the photographs.)

The wonderful, valiant, liquid-eyed horses, so strong, so dear. Early mornings in the outdoor ring, afternoons on the hunt course, evenings with the warm electric light in the stables, the sweet hanging dust, the smell of horse and hay and muck and oats and leather, the currying and feeding, inspecting of hoofs, nuzzling, feeling the warmth rising from flank and neck.

In jumping exhibitions, Imogen takes spills and pops right back up, undaunted. The crowd approves her spirit. She breaks a finger and rides with it splinted. Her wrists ache. She chews aspirin and ignores it.

Her mother thinks she'll spend the summers at home in DC, maybe working as a salesgirl in a clothing store, but she's got another think coming. Imogen finds a position as riding coach and counselor at an all-girl camp in the Poconos. The girls are young and soft, the horses old and for the most part mild, with one or two malicious tricksters. It's like her old school patrol days, shepherding her little sisters across fields and creeks, down wooded paths. Her parents visit, querulous and tired from the long drive, and Imogen can finally see that they were old when they married, old when they gave birth to her. That perhaps the reason her mother never gave her a baby brother or sister was because she couldn't.

Her mother does her yeoman job of making Imogen feel guilty. *The house is so quiet . . . Poor Stubby doesn't understand . . . It must be very exciting and free to get away from your parents . . .*

Her dad, holding the camera, escapes long enough to snap the big barn and the bridge over the creek (gladdening his engineer's heart) before being corralled by her mother to do what he came for. She orders Imogen to stand here and there, hold this and that, try not to be so . . . maybe that hair is the style today, but honestly, who could . . . ? Imogen stands alone, because her mother no longer tolerates having her own picture taken. "I used to be the beauty of the family," she says, sighing. Old photos prove it. Grammie Eula always chirpily conceded she was the prettiest of her daughters. "She got the beauty fairy, so the brains fairy looked elsewhere."

"Oh, the men were always—" and off her mother goes, reminiscing about balls and wintry wagon rides under compendious buffalo robes (but there was decorum and proper manners).

Then why'd it take you so damn long to marry? Imogen wants to ask.

"You're still beautiful," her husband avers, gesturing futilely for her to move into the frame. He means it. "How did I manage to catch such a beauty?" he's often said. He's a small man, five-five, bald at twenty-five, married at forty-four.

Because she saw you'd put up with her.

She looks at him standing there with the camera like a shield, the man her fellow counselors thought at first was her grandfather. *You never defend me.* He may marvel at her mother's beauty, but on vacations he goes off on fishing trips with his buddies, never taking Imogen with him.

She gets back on her horse, returns to college. Her hands hurt like hell, the doctor says she has congenital arthritis, exacerbated by the demanding exercise in cold weather. She keeps chewing aspirin, keeps jumping, stops playing piano. Her mother complains, Imogen tunes her out.

Graduation Day. Of course her parents are there, and maybe there's a bit of her mother in her, the foolish vain part, because she doesn't wear her glasses for the procession, although she's blind as a bat, and her dad snaps furiously as she marches by. Somehow she was off a horse long enough to get good grades and win an academic prize. She's been accepted for the physics program at the University of Chicago, the first female physics graduate student in its history. (She switched to physics in her senior year to get away from her chemistry professor, Miss Edwards, who praised her and encouraged her and it turned out was in love with her and wanted to control her.) She's proud and excited and secretly worried and in mourning for the loss of her horses, her stable, her fellow riders, irreplaceable every one.

Why graduate school? She wonders this herself. It seemed either that, or go back to live with her parents, or get married. Imogen assumes she will be married someday because she wants children, sweet little ones, like the younger siblings she never had. And goddamnit she'll have more than one, she won't do to any child what her mother did to her. But that's off in the future, on the far side of more achievement and more horses and years of freedom and traveling.

On the last day in the dorm, her best friend of all, Mac, gives her a framed keepsake, a photo of Mac on rearing Baker Man. The stallion is nearly vertical, Mac poised and calmly smiling into the camera, heroic and in command. She has signed it, "To Imp, with love," and scrawled across Baker Man's chest a catchphrase from the *Rubaiyat* popular among the sisters working in the stables late into the night: "The idols I have loved so long . . ."

SIX MONTHS LATER MAC MARRIES, with Imogen as her maid of honor. A year after that, Imogen marries and Mac returns the favor.

1926–1996

When Vernon worked at the Hanscom Field lab years later, Don and Mike would joke about the accident that burned his fingers. "I can see it perfectly," Don would say, while Mike started laughing, and Don would put on a shit-eating grin, hide his eyes with one hand and stick the fingers of the other into an imaginary wall socket. Vernon would laugh, too. Don, Mike, and he were always popping into each other's offices with a good joke they'd just heard. It kept the tedium of lab work and the inanities of dealing with the Air Force brass from killing them. The fingers haven't hurt much for decades, but he has reduced sensitivity, especially in the middle finger, which lost its nail and half an inch of length. Women like to claim that nature spares them from remembering labor pain so they'll go on to have more children, but that sounds like female mystification to Vernon. He considers it more likely that all pain is difficult to re-experience through recollection. He "remembers" it hurt like nothing else, but that's just a word.

He was in the Secondary Radio School at Navy Pier in Chicago, working to earn his EMT rating so he could ship out to the Pacific and get killed. In late May 1945 he was a week away from finishing the program, and they were conducting the umpteenth speed trial. He and three other seamen were lined up in front of identical units. When they started the timer you were supposed to switch off the power, take out the drawer, replace the faulty tube, put the drawer back in and switch the power back on. Vernon did all that, then noticed he'd slid the drawer in cock-eyed, so he pulled it out to feed it in straight, only he'd forgotten to turn off the power again. These were your typical electronics racks with no bottom. His right-hand fingers slipped up inside the frame, the juice hit him, and as he convulsed, the heavy drawer settled farther down, frying the holy crap out of index, middle, and ring finger while maybe he screamed or maybe he just vibrated and grinned until someone thought to switch the power off.

His hand was the biggest mess you ever saw, and for six weeks the Navy doctors pulled surviving skin around flesh and bone, dressed and undressed, cleaned and repeated, and during that time his unit shipped out. Some of his classmates saw action, a few were killed in his place. Once his fingers had more or less healed, it took the Navy the usual dog's age to reassign him. All that time he stayed in the hospital up at Great Lakes, playing gin rummy with other grateful malingerers. They had just issued his new orders when the war ended.

JOHN VERNON FULLER—J. V. to his family and few acquaintances, Vernon to his wife and self—grew up in Durham, North Carolina. His mother was an agoraphobe, his older sister a dim bulb, and his younger brother fancied himself an artist whom the world unaccountably failed to appreciate. He loved his father, who endured the weight of them all in their underbuilt little house on First Avenue, just inside the city lim-its. Their front porch looked across scrubby fields and farmland. There were no other numbered avenues, as though, after taking the measure of this one, the planners had thought better of it.

Dad sold life insurance from an oak desk in an office downtown for thirty years. Vernon and he shared a sense of humor, an interest in base-ball teams and a love of playing catch, all of which his brother, Julian, lacked. Julian decided he was superior to that, and everything else be-sides. Dad didn't understand him and maybe Julian felt rejected. He was closer to their mother, whose mind was vacant enough that she could wander in it freely, fearing accidents, decisions, ideas, plans, and changes of plans. She'd grown up as the assigned companion of a disabled sister who couldn't even attend to her own toilet. She had never spent a mo-ment alone, never gone to a dance or movie, never dated a man until she met Dad. Some of his mother's neuroses young Vernon managed to for-give, but one of the many things she would not allow her children to do, on grounds of intolerable risk, was ride a bicycle. To this day, Vernon resents that. His father seemed never to lose patience with the old ninny, but would occasionally trade a glance and a wink with his older son.

One night when Julian was in his late twenties—this must have been the summer of '55—he telephoned their father from jail. He'd been caught in Wilmington soliciting sex from a sailor. Vernon rode buses all night down from the University of Chicago, where he was a graduate student, and witnessed how devastated his father was. Julian, out on Dad's bail, stood shaving in the bathroom in the old house and had the gall to say to Vernon that the discovery was a relief. He even smirked, "You wouldn't believe who else we know—"

Vernon recoiled. Their father had aged a decade and here Julian was gloating, floating free, as always. "Julian," he said, "what on earth makes you think I want to hear who you've fucked or been fucked by?"

Vernon had to hurry again down from Chicago less than a year later, when his father died of a heart attack. Vernon has always wondered if Julian's disgrace helped to kill him. He has also wondered if his father might have survived the attack if there had been someone around other than his worthless mother and his dimwitted sister to get the poor man to the hospital faster.

.   .   .

GROWING UP, Vernon was at the top of all his classes. Later he said to his own son, Mark, when Mark was burning through high school, "I was always being told by one teacher or another, 'You're good at this, you ought to make a career of it.' You can't let that influence you. You can't say to them, even if it's true, 'Hey, I'm an ace—I'm good at everything.'"

Mark is even good at music, which Vernon isn't. Mark must have gotten that from his mother. Vernon played sax in a high school jazz band, honking through big band numbers written out in simplified form. Improvising was way out of their league. He has a photo somewhere of his band playing at the senior prom. He's sweating, sporting a pompadour that looks like a possum, leaning into his sax as though engaged in unrewarding work with a shovel.

The mood at the prom was somber. It was June 1944, and most of the boys had an idea they might die soon. All those "best of lucks" written to him in his yearbook took on a deeper meaning. Only one classmate made a direct reference: "I hope you sink the entire Jap navy. Remember the fun we had in Itchy's class?"

Vernon had taken the Eddy Test in electronics that spring and received notice of passing in May. That allowed him, upon induction, to choose the Navy. His military strategy was to maximize the likelihood of his survival, and the Army looked like cannon fodder on the ground and clay pigeons in the air. He'd prefer to take his chances being a sitting duck. The Navy needed thousands of radio and radar technicians, but the technology was so new that few people had been trained in it. The course of instruction was long. After six weeks of boot camp at Great Lakes, there were four weeks of pre-radio school in Chicago, twelve of primary materiel school in Gulfport, and twenty-eight of secondary back in Chicago at Navy Pier. Vernon did the math. In fifty weeks the war just might be over. He accepted that it had to be fought, he understood society required him to be part of it. He would not shoot himself in the foot or—fuck you, Don and Mike!—deliberately stick his fingers in a high-voltage socket, but he assumed he was like most other people in preferring, on the whole, that somebody else die.

As for his two years in the military, if you'd asked him pretty much at any point during it, he would have sworn he hated it. Obeying people who were by and large dumber than he was came hard. But his memories in later years have had a certain warmth. Maybe, as with physical pain, one remembers only the intensity of unpleasantness, and maybe intensity in retrospect just looks like being fully alive.

At Navy Pier, Vernon and his classmates slept in triple-tiered bunks in a warehouse as large as an airplane hangar, with seagulls in the rafters that shat on the men in the top bunks. They would line up after breakfast and be marched in formation to class, marched back to lunch, marched back to class, marched to dinner. He had always been heavy, like his father, but now he slimmed down. A street photographer snapped a candid shot of him one Saturday night on a Chicago sidewalk, and he's kept it for fifty years tucked into the glass door of his secretary at home. He's in uniform, complete with Dixie cup hat, his ears sticking out like Andy Griffith, counting change in his palm. A person looking at the photo might think this lanky lantern-jawed sailor is heading off to a bar or a cat house. In fact, he was on his way to a sheet music store. He was a small-town boy, high school president of the Baptist Student Union, glad to be away from his mother. It was enough that Chicago was big and bustling, he didn't need it to be sinful, too.

In later years, when Susan or Mark asked for a song at bedtime, he would either give them "Asleep in the Deep" or the ditty he'd learned at the Pier to the tune of Mess Call:

Soupee, soupee, soupee,
without any bean!

Bacon, bacon, bacon,
without any lean!
Coffee, coffee, coffee,
without any cream!

He hated every minute of it, but he kept his watch cap, his Dixie cup, his duffel bag; he kept his *Bluejacket's Manual* and his *Radar Fundamentals*. In the Navy hospital, he read Faulkner and Flannery O'Connor, traded jokes, played gin rummy, practiced the faro shuffle. His fingers healed and the Navy made him hurry up and wait. By that point it was clear the Japs weren't going to give up until every square foot of their country was a smoking ruin. The fact that they wouldn't face reality, that instead of surrendering now, they were going to make hundreds of thousands of people die, including his one and only self, and *then* surrender, made it pretty easy to hate their guts. His reassignment came through on August 5, so the banner headline across the front page of the *Chicago Tribune* on August 7 might as well have read PHYSICS MIRACLE SAVES J. V. FULLER.

Retired and ill, listening to Beethoven in his study, looking back, he wonders if his gratitude at being thus gratuitously handed his future explains his choice of career and, later, his stint at RAND. After the Navy discharged him in July of '46, he heeded the urgings of his father and enrolled at Wake Forest College, near home, where he could be for a while longer the tender chick his clucking mother wanted. (He supposed that, as a woman who'd lost her son in the nation's service every night for two years, she deserved it.) He majored in physics, then did graduate work in nuclear physics back in Chicago. Several members of the U of C faculty, like Fermi, had been part of the Manhattan Project, and they talked of Los Alamos like the Garden of Eden. Sure, at the end, they'd had to drop a couple of apple cores on a couple of Japanese cities, but bliss it was in that atomic dawn to be alive, and to be scaling the Tree of Knowledge was very heaven.

After the war, the Air Force, wanting an institution similar to Los Alamos to continue working for it, dreamed up RAND—a safe little collegial place where scientists and analysts could have fun designing Armageddon weapons and strategies. Anyone working in nuclear physics at the University of Chicago in the 1950s heard a lot about that shining establishment by the sea. To some of the graduate students—the hawkish on the one hand, the naive and sentimental on the other— RAND looked like the Lord's work. Vernon wasn't hawkish, but he was still a small-town Southern Baptist who'd been saved by the Bomb. In the summer of 1956, diploma in hand and wife and daughter in tow— he'd gotten married five years previously—he signed on with RAND and moved to Santa Monica.

THEY RENTED A bungalow on Dimmick Avenue, about a mile from the RAND offices. Vernon walked the twenty minutes to work every morning through miraculous California weather, past palm and eucalyptus trees, aloes, bougainvillea. Unless the Santa Ana was blowing, he could feel the cool breeze from the ocean a few blocks away. The RAND building was a low rectangle of pale pink. It had been designed, he was told, to facilitate interaction between the workers, with each office opening directly onto long corridors leading to common areas, so that scientists and analysts would always be walking past each other, depositing pollen on each other's pistils. There were eight internal courtyards where you could eat your lunch in the eternal sunshine and fecundate some more with your colleagues.

The work of the nuclear physicists was classified, but Vernon had had little difficulty obtaining his clearance. Unlike most of his colleagues,

who'd come from academic—or worse, European—families, sullied by
socialist flirtations on the part of siblings, parents, spouses, or even their
past selves, Vernon's and his wife Imogen's backgrounds (excepting one
loose-lipped homo from whom Vernon was convincingly estranged) was
a pristine phalanx of incurious dirt farmers, appliance salesmen, insurance agents, racists, mountain moonshiners, and a lone college graduate (Imogen's father, a civil engineer and deep-dyed Republican), most of
whom would have lynched any Commie of their acquaintance faster than
the House Un-American Activities Committee could say, "Are you now, or
have you ever been . . . ?"

The RAND offices were open around the clock, to allow self-styled
geniuses their 3:00 a.m. brainstorms, but Vernon kept regular hours.
Maybe that was the Navy Pier in him. Imogen had his breakfast ready
at 7:30; he left the house at 8:00 and reached his office half an hour
later. Taking an hour for lunch, he left at 5:30 and arrived home for dinner at 6:00. On weekends he relaxed at the house, listening to a record
or a ball game on the radio, fiddling with the antenna for the black-and-
white TV set he'd recently bought, watching *Dragnet* or *Playhouse 90*
with Imogen after she'd put stubborn, squally Susan to bed.

Every now and then his colleagues would get it into their heads to
stay in the offices late to finish some project. One enthusiast would rub
his hands and say, "We'll have to work through the night!" and another
would catch the bug and chirp, "Let's brew coffee and set up cots!"
RAND encouraged that sort of malarkey: fortifying whiskey in the bottom desk drawer, camaraderie around the urinal, cheek stubble glinting
in the morning light, pats all around, "We've done it, boys!" Maybe it
was from growing up in the swampy South, but Vernon felt in his bones
that slow and deliberate was the smarter way to go. He'd call Imogen,
give her the bad news, work through the night, at least maybe hear a
good joke or two, then walk home bleary-eyed in the leaden morning.

Once, half asleep, he stepped in front of a car and RAND nearly lost one of its geniuses.

For the first year or so, though, he believed in the work. In 1956, the hydrogen bomb was three years old. The original theoretical insights that made it possible were not something Vernon would ever have been able to figure out on his own, but now it was tinkerers' time. The first Atlas missiles were under development and would enter production within a year or two. Preliminary tests had indicated—surprise!—that their accuracy wasn't as good as the military had promised. It was therefore desirable to raise yield without increasing the size or weight of the physics package. And once you had your clearance and got a look at the basic design of a two-stage weapon, you saw it was a fiddler's dream come true. Scores of slightly different configurations of slightly different materials were possible, each requiring reams of calculations to produce semi-educated guesses about yields. Vernon chose to study the interstage, the part of the warhead that transmitted the radiation from the fission primary in a (one hoped) efficient way so as to implode and ignite the fusion-fission secondary. As with most dynamic processes, the physics was complicated, the engineering problems fantastically finicky, and Vernon spent a happy eight months immersed in the details.

Years later, people would occasionally ask him how he could have worked on the Bomb. Since those who had the simplicity of mind to ask essentially knew nothing, he didn't dignify them with an answer. But after he'd left RAND he pondered the question himself from time to time. The August 7, 1945, newspaper article telling him he would live a while longer had identified Hiroshima as an important army base. Later, it became a little clearer that it was an army base surrounded by 300,000 civilians. Still later, Vernon read Hersey's *Hiroshima*, and that account bothered him enough that he read others. Somewhere among all the horror he picked up a detail he couldn't get out of his head. On August

5, 1945, the city of Hiroshima had ordered schoolgirls to help raze houses in order to create firebreaks in case of an incendiary raid. So when Little Boy threw a tantrum at 1900 feet on August 6 there were more than eight thousand of these young girls working outside under the clear sky. Most were killed instantly, but survivors' accounts kept mentioning seeing girls tottering blindly, their faces burned featureless, holding their boiled arms out in front of them with their hands dangling down—like kangaroos, one witness said—the skin of their hands slipping off like rubber gloves.

Yes, the fire-bombing of Tokyo killed as many people as the Hiroshima bomb. But that was the result of a decision to use those bombs in a particular way, a decision a society could abjure, while retaining incendiary bombs for other uses. That is, you didn't have to "uninvent" the incendiary bomb. But atomic weapons were different. There was no conceivable use for them that did not involve the indiscriminate slaughter of populations. And now here was the H-bomb, which made Little Boy look like a firecracker. As a physicist, Vernon could appreciate more than most how admirable the H-bomb was as a product of the human intellect. It was a brilliantly designed, exquisitely engineered instrument for turning as many schoolgirls as you might want into kangaroos.

So how could he have worked on it (boo hoo)?

To the simple-minded, he would have said (had he dignified them, etc), It depends on your definition of the word "use." In fact, the H-bomb did have a use, though it involved not using it. It was the only thing ever invented that could keep the other guy from using his own H-bomb. Yes, deterrence. Yes, Mutually Assured Destruction. Go ahead, make mushheaded jokes about it. Anyone with an ounce of practical sense in 1945, anyone who paused for a moment to remember how human societies actually worked, as opposed to humane dreams about how they might work if humans weren't human, knew that world government was an impossibility. If you liked the idea of not dropping more nuclear bombs on more cities, there was only one hope. MAD, but true.

So you could say the robustness of deterrence was the reason he signed on with RAND. And he supposes you could say it was also the reason he quit.

It takes a lot to make Vernon change direction. He loves routine. He thinks of himself as a homebody. Imogen calls him a wet blanket. If Imogen could ever compromise on anything—a condition contrary to fact—maybe they could agree that he's merely a stick-in-the-mud. On his own, perhaps he would have reached the necessary point of anger and disgust with RAND within six or eight years. Gen helped him get there inside twenty-four months. Anger and disgust are her specialties.

IN SEPTEMBER 1950, there were seventy graduate students in physics at the University of Chicago, sixty-nine of whom were men. The seventieth was Imogen.

All of the men wanted to help her with her homework. In fact, she needed it. As an undergraduate, she'd taken more classes in chemistry than in physics, and at a women's college to boot. She freely admitted she was having difficulty. She was pretty, with wavy auburn hair, dark brown eyes, a good figure. Out of sixty-nine men jostling at her door, textbooks in hand, she eventually chose Vernon. Part of him has always wondered why. She was better-looking than he was, came from a better family. But she has never talked about her reasons.

At the university, before she chose him, she liked to go out with the men in a group, drink, smoke, argue; not physics, but everything else, especially religion and politics. She had a way of throwing back her head and snapping, "That's the most ridiculous thing I ever heard." She had another way of pointing her somewhat pointy nose down, pushing her glasses against the bridge, and snorting, "What a crock of shit!" The first time she swore in his presence, he objected, probably said something priggish about unladylike behavior, and she slapped him right down. "I'll speak as I like." She noticed he always ordered Coke, and when he explained he didn't drink alcohol, she averred that that was the most ridiculous thing she'd ever heard.

Vernon had a girlfriend back in North Carolina—his first and, he'd assumed, his last. She was a sweet hometown girl, recently become his fiancée. But she mailed the ring back to him along with a brief letter just before he went home for Christmas, no doubt to forestall an awkward scene on her doorstep. She was sorry, he was a great guy and would do great things, but she'd fallen for a sweet hometown boy. Vernon had already been helping Imogen with her homework—from entirely innocent motives—and the broken engagement upset him enough that he spoke of it to her. Which was the first time outside the drinking group that they discussed anything personal. So he supposed he had Margaret to thank for breaking the ice.

A few of the things that, individually, were the most ridiculous thing Imogen had ever heard were the various beliefs and customs of the Southern Baptist Church. Like Vernon, she'd grown up in it. Her mother's roots were in Alabama, where Gen was born. Her father had taken a job with the federal government in D.C. when she was two, and by the time she was twelve she was attending services, family be damned, in the basement chapel of the unfinished National Cathedral. High Church Episcopalianism was as far as she could get from Southern Baptism without turning Catholic—which was out of the question, as Catholicism unavoidably involved the Papacy, than which there was no larger crock of shit. "Episcopalian music is beautiful," she said, "and the ministers are less likely to be small-town ignorant assholes."

She got him out on the dance floor and she put a beer into his hand, later a scotch. She made wicked fun of their professors. His church became

St. Edmund's Episcopal, near the campus, and for special services, St. James Cathedral. The St. James choir sang Bach cantatas and Mendelssohn motets, which music was a revelation to this former jazzman. Clouds of incense rose into the ribbed vaults, carrying his sinful soul with them. Imogen hadn't bothered to argue him into any of this. It was simpler than that. Did he want to be with her, or didn't he? He did. His main worry was that he didn't deserve her. She was an only child, the apple of her parents' eyes. She'd won piano competitions as a teenager, horse-jumping competitions in college. Her father had an engineering degree from Cornell.

At least he could help her with her homework. As the end of the year approached, she needed it more and more. "It was a mistake to switch from chemistry," she said, and he silently agreed. They studied together every evening in the last month, and she squeaked through her exams. Then she wrote to her parents telling them she was engaged and would be leaving school. From her indignant reaction to the letter she received back from her father, Vernon knew they weren't pleased. "They think it's too sudden, that I'm too young." Vernon wondered if they also disapproved of him, his background. But he couldn't quite ask.

"My mother married late. But it's none of their business." She wrote back and slapped them down.

Vernon's parents and his sister Patty drove up from Durham to D.C. late in the summer, so that the two families could meet. They said they'd stay in a reasonably priced motel somewhere, have dinner with Imogen and her parents, and spend the following day seeing the capital sights, which they'd always promised themselves they'd do. Vernon's mother wrote him that she didn't know how they would ever make it, it was so far, what if a hurricane flooded the roads, or the old car gave up the ghost in the middle of nowhere, she was a silly woman, and wouldn't burden Vernon's father with her fears, and she knew J. V. was out of patience with her, so she'd say no more about it.

On the day, both the prevailing weather system and the Fuller family's

1942 Ford were kind, and they arrived unscathed at the house on Harrison Street NW. The car doors opened and out popped the homely, heavy faces. They were all overweight, as Vernon had been before the Navy (only Julian seemed naturally slender), and his mother and Patty in particular looked, he suddenly realized, an awful lot like W. C. Fields. When Imogen's father invited them in, Vernon could see that his mother and sister were discomfited by the comparative fineness of the furnishings, and he worried that his mother would declare she was afraid to sit on so good a chair, provoking his sister into opining that a chair was a chair and for her part she didn't understand why some people spent more than they had to. But his father must have given them a talking-to ahead of time.

Vernon was particularly anxious about Patty, who wasn't so easily quelled as his mother. She disapproved of people who were smarter or better than she was, and as that description fit just about everybody, she was perpetually aggrieved. He was afraid someone might offhandedly refer to something universally accepted as true—say, that objects expand when heated, or that ice floats—and Patty would retaliate against the chairs, the slimmer figures, the better education, and declare, with a tone of brooking no nonsense, "Well, I don't believe that." He was equally worried she would make some reference to Negroes—as shiftless, lazy, stupid, thieving, lying, violent, self-gratifying, childlike, improvident, impulsive, or some combination thereof—because Imogen was fierce about Negro rights.

But disaster failed to strike. It turned out that Gen herself was nervous because she had prepared the meal with her mother, who was acknowledged a fine cook. Over the tomato soup (Imogen wondered if she'd oversalted it; "Not at all," Vernon and his father said simultaneously) it was Imogen's own mother who introduced a story turning on recent activity by local blacks—in this case, thieving plus self-gratifying plus lying—and Imogen went after her hammer and tongs, while both fathers respectfully addressed their bowls and Patty visibly relaxed. The dessert was a peach pie made by Imogen—table-lore had it that her mother was famous for her pies—and Gen was so flustered she delivered a dollop of whipped cream straight into Vernon's mother's lap. Gen yelped, but Vernon's mother laughed with genuine good humor. After eight hours on the road wondering whether the catastrophe lying in wait for her was a hurricane or a spontaneously combusting automobile, discovering that it was only a spoonful of whipped cream on her ten-year-old Woolworth's dress was giddy relief.

The only other time the two sets of parents met was four months later, at the wedding. By then Vernon had figured out that Imogen's mother came from nearly as backwoods a background as his parents, having grown up on three Alabama acres of chickens, yams, corn, swamp, and clutter. She had a passel of loud, ignorant brothers, one of whom had climbed a grid pylon in drunken mischief when he was twenty and managed to electrocute himself, and a handful of slightly smarter sisters who tended toward cheerful circular chatter that, accelerating, gradually rose free of the ground of facts. One of the sisters insisted on being the photographer at the wedding, unaware that her camera was cracked. The photos all showed Imogen on the arm of an attention-seeking blob of light, or Vernon cutting the cake with help from the blob, or the blob flanked by proud parents. Vernon thought it unfortunate but hardly calamitous, whereas Imogen was—as she would have termed it—apeshit. She threw the photos away and didn't speak to her aunt for five years.

The newlyweds had neither time nor money for a honeymoon. Vernon had classes and Imogen had found a paid research position at a chemical company. They moved into an apartment in the attic of a Presbyterian parsonage three blocks from the University of Chicago campus. Vernon remembers those times as the happiest of his life. He'd survived his war, he'd won his freedom, he loved his work, and he'd found his girl. Occasionally now—decades later, in his study, listening to Beethoven with his headphones on—he glances through the notebook of household accounts he kept daily for the first three years of his marriage: 69¢ for lunch, 23¢ for cigarettes, 6¢ for a cup of coffee. He remembers the dim light of the physics department canteen, the cherry-tobacco smell of the corner store, the shade and sun of the walk to the laundromat. At the end of every day he totaled the expenses, subtracted them from cash on hand, added each week his stipend as a teaching assistant and Imogen's paycheck. Everything—savings, income, expenditures—such small amounts. He sees that on January 16, 1953, he calculated that at some point during the day he had lost a penny. *Weep for what little things could make them glad.*

The plan was to put off children until he had his PhD, but Murphy's Law decreed the appearance of Susan in 1954, when he still had two years to go. Life was more complicated after that. Imogen's mother came out to help for six weeks and the two women fought like cats. Then Vernon's father delivered Vernon's mother as a replacement, and for a while things were at least less noisy. Babies were one of the few things on God's green earth that did not frighten Vernon's mother, and as long as he and Gen didn't ask her to do anything else, such as step out of the apartment, they could count on her with Susan during the day while they each worked. On evenings and weekends she kept up a continual prattling, weaving mundane, not wholly ridiculous concerns—electric outlets, kitchen knives, heavy items of furniture that conceivably could topple on a baby if a large enough person blundered into them at sufficient speed—with outlandish scenarios—the fact, for example, that lightning did occasionally kill people indoors, or that airplanes did occasionally fall on houses.

"But not on parsonages," Vernon told her. "Not even Presbyterian ones."

Oddly enough, Imogen reproached him for mocking his mother. His principal method was to tune her out, which he'd decided long ago was merely respecting her wishes, since she interlarded her fanciful voyages to the continent of Catastrophia with statements like, "But I'm just a foolish old woman," or even (the key to the kingdom), "Just ignore me." Imogen seemed to think that was unfilial, so she allowed herself to be drawn in ("We're not even in the flight path to the airport, Mother"), then complained to Vernon when they were alone together that he left it all up to her.

"She'll talk you into the ground," he said.

"She's just lonely."

"She's been impossible all her life. She's like that woman in Flannery O'Connor. 'She'd be all right if somebody just shot her in the head once a day.'"

Imogen laughed. They'd discovered long ago that they shared a sense of humor.

AFTER VERNON'S MOTHER went home their expenses ballooned, because they had to pay the minister's wife to watch Susan during the day. They ate less meat and stopped going to the movies. During this time, Imogen felt overburdened with her job and the baby, just when Vernon was deep in his dissertation research on neutron transport in breeder reactors. "Eighteen more months," he promised her, when she complained.

"Only a year now."

"Almost there."

It didn't help that Susan was one of those caterwauling babies you read about in stories of tenement life. He and Imogen had about half an hour of peace and quiet after she'd woken up before she would start fussing. Nights were a torment. But they survived. Didn't they? He earned his PhD and they moved to California. Imogen no longer needed to work. They settled into the routine both of them had planned all along. Another year of happiness ensued.

That's his memory, anyway. Imogen said years later that maybe *he* was happy, but not her. Had he missed something? "Of course you didn't notice it, you were too wrapped up in yourself." Was that true? Or was she reinterpreting the past, to make it all black and white, the way she likes to look at things? He doesn't want her to take away that year, or the later years in Lexington, when she was raising the kids and he was working at Hanscom Field, and he came straight home every day, stayed home every weekend, fixed everything that needed fixing, paid the bills, always on time, not a late payment his entire life, and never a debt except the mortgage. He took care of them, as his father had done, only better—money for a second car, for summer camps, for college. He was what, he thought, every husband and father should be: a stable provider. He held up his end, she held up hers, and they still shared a bed, and of course they argued sometimes, but all couples did that.

"Tell me what I did wrong."

"There's no point."

"Why won't you just tell me?"

"You don't really want to know, you just want to win another argument."

Dark thoughts. (Sick, sitting in his study alone, Mark living in another state, Susan long gone.)

He and Imogen once shared a sense of humor, they shared a worldview. Sure, as far as the worldview went, it was a matter of him coming over to where she was already standing, but he felt at the time, and he's never thought differently, that she was standing in the place he wanted to be anyway: her dim view of religion, her distrust of authority, her leftist politics. She saw everything in black and white, and it often made her wrong about little things, but on the big things she was usually right. She took that small-town Baptist bumpkin and slapped him a few times. Maybe there was nothing wrong with him that getting slapped once a day wouldn't cure.

IN HIS SECOND YEAR at RAND he modeled atmospheric forces for the final designs of the Atlas missile. Looking back, he wonders if it was perhaps significant that he had already taken one step away from work on the bomb itself.

Looking back, he wonders a lot of things.

It is hard to untangle, this many years later, what he began to suspect then and what he became more sure of later. What he noticed, or would eventually have noticed, on his own, and what Imogen slapped him into seeing. And to what extent her own unhappiness with him (she would have him believe now) strengthened her jaundiced view of the RAND culture, which she then passed on to him, and which he misread as criticism of *them* and support for *him*, and so more readily adopted.

Stuck in the fucking house all day with Susan while he was off enjoying himself at work (it is not inconceivable that she uttered those words to him at some point), Imogen found a babysitter for six hours a week and signed up for German classes at a nearby community college. For the record, he supported her decision. She'd taken German at Mount Holyoke and wanted to brush up. He had also learned German at Chicago, since any good physicist needs to be able to read German scientific papers, so he proofread the essay she wrote for her class at the end of the semester. It could have been about anything; the assignment was merely to practice grammar and vocabulary. Imogen wrote about the shitty construction of their house on Dimmick Ave. This widened into a description of the cookie-cutter shitboxes on either side and in the surrounding streets. Then came an eloquent diatribe—her German was better than his—against California land speculation, despoliation of nature, corrupt profiteering, collusion of government, and the inherently predatory and destructive essence of capitalism. As usual, though her ferocity startled him, he agreed with her basic viewpoint.

From the distance of years, he thinks he can see now her essay's deeper theme: males building unlivable worlds, then leaving females to live in them. Presumably he sensed a smidgen of this at the time, and it must have had its influence. He doubts it's coincidental that his ultimate view of the typical RAND scientist was of an intelligent male (needless to say, they were all male) ingeniously building in his head a world he imagined was the real one, populated principally by phenomena that proved his own intelligence.

Ed Paxson and Edward Quade, for example, were very smart men. "Do you know about the Paxson-Quade fighter-bomber study?" Vernon would ask his lunchmates in one of the courtyards. Vernon had seen Ed Paxson at briefings, gleefully shooting down his colleagues' ideas. He was a systems analyst, so he liked constructing mathematical equations to determine the best way of doing anything, supposedly taking all the relevant factors into account. In 1949, he and Quade devised a mathematical model to evaluate optimum strategies in a fighter-bomber duel. Their math decreed that, in a certain determined best configuration, the fighter ought to be able to shoot down the bomber 60 percent of the time. When they compared that figure with actual data from World War II, they discovered that the real percentage of successful bomber kills in that configuration was 2 percent.

"Real fighter pilots pull away too early," Vernon would say at the lunch table. "They don't care about Paxson's calculations, they care about not dying."

Paxson was a mathematician. In Vernon's experience, it's the engineers who have the healthiest attitude toward numbers. They make the math just good enough to accomplish the task at hand. Physicists are more rigorous, but most of them would agree that beautiful mathematical constructs do not necessarily have manifestations in physical reality.

The two sorts of scientists who let numbers make them foolish are soft scientists, like sociologists, who dress their work in spurious equations to convince themselves their science is hard, and mathematicians, who think numbers are the deepest reality, and if the physical world doesn't live up to their equations, well then, too bad for the physical world. World War II fighter pilots *ought to* have shot down bombers 60 percent of the time, and that's what counts.

Thinking about Paxson's error fed Vernon's general unease about RAND. Could it be that this imposing modern building, these briefings so ostentatiously featuring "vigorous debate" and "a hard look," this blizzard of working papers stamped CONFIDENTIAL, the red-eye flights to Washington to brief Air Force chiefs—could it be that the subconscious intent of it all was to blind RAND men to the fact that they were doing nothing useful? The Copernican Principle, as applied to psychology: one should be skeptical of any theory that has the side effect of elevating the importance of the theorist.

Vernon remembered seeing something in a newspaper shortly after the war ended. A delicatessen owner in Manhattan had put photographs of the Hiroshima and Nagasaki moonscapes in his store window, to raise awareness among his customers about the need to avoid nuclear war. As he explained to the reporter, "If somebody starts dropping these bombs, there won't even *be* any delicatessens."

Vernon started saying to his lunchmates, "We have to work all night, because if there's an all-out nuclear exchange, there won't even *be* a RAND."

ONE OF THE watchwords at RAND was "vulnerability." Sure, we had enough bombs to destroy every city, midsized town, and lonely crossroad in the Soviet Union—but maybe our bombs were vulnerable to surprise attack, after which we might not retain enough to retaliate.

How could we address this problem? Should we disperse our bases, harden our bases, harden our communications, bury our missiles, increase our missiles' power, increase their accuracy, increase their number?

One of RAND's gurus of vulnerability was Albert Wohlstetter, a mathematical logician in the Economics division. He came from a wealthy New York family and favored suspenders and patent-leather shoes. His silvering hair was swept back from his forehead as though blown there by the force of his thoughts. Early in his tenure, he had made a name for himself by showing where Ed Paxson's analyses went wrong. (Make way for the new alpha dog.) He compiled a huge logistical study of overseas US nuclear bomber bases that supposedly showed how easy it would be for the Soviet Union to destroy up to 85 percent of American bombers in a surprise attack. In talks to generals and cabinet secretaries in the early 1950s, he'd argued that this was tantamount to *inviting* an attack. He was currently working on a RAND paper called "The Delicate Balance of Terror."

Wohlstetter and his wife, Roberta, lived in Laurel Canyon, in a house designed by a well-known modernist architect. When it was finished, Wohlstetter induced a Los Angeles paper to write an admiring article titled "The House in the Sky," with photographs of the heavenly abode and its enviable inhabitants. Maybe realizing that too few of his colleagues could be counted on to have seen it, Wohlstetter got into the habit of hosting large parties, where admiration could be performed mouth-to-mouth.

Vernon would happily never have attended another party between any particular present moment and the day of his death, but Imogen now and then liked to get out of the shitbox, so one evening early in the summer of '58 they hired a babysitter and drove in their recently acquired '52 Chevy toward Hollywood, then up the winding roads of the canyon. The sun was still well up, the weather (of course) beautiful, and as the car gained height, glimpses of the Pacific sparkled in the crooks of the golden hills.

There were already two or three dozen people in attendance when they arrived, which made it easy for Vernon to wander off on his own. He grabbed a martini off a passing tray and filled a plate with canapés from a buffet table. He had long ago perfected the art of moving through a crowd of acquaintances with a smile and a regretful gesture onward, signaling that he would love to chat if only he wasn't already committed somewhere else in the room. In this way he could just keep circulating, exploring every nook, leaving one plate here and picking up another there. Now and then someone he knew better might rope him into conversation, but that's what jokes are for. He would tell one, and laughter works like applause—you can exit on it.

The house certainly was beautiful, if you liked living in a yacht: rooms so long they made the standard ceilings seem low, polished steel window frames, tube-steel banisters. The walls consisted predominantly of sliding glass doors. On the second-floor balcony you could look out over the hillside and imagine you were in the captain's wheelhouse, with a commanding view of the calm seas of your prosperous voyage. Maybe that was the Navy man in Vernon. Whereas the engineer noted the cork walls, the acoustic-tile ceilings, and inferred that sounds carried all too well through the open floor plan. The weekend suburbanite judged the abstract lozenges of lawn to be awkward to mow, while the wet blanket rejected the built-in pool entirely as a nightmare of upkeep.

The only thing Vernon envied was Wohlstetter's classical record collection, some thirty times the size of his own. He lingered by Imogen now and then, in case she was in an argument for which she would otherwise later say she'd looked in vain for his agreement. She was drinking gin and tonics and each time he circled back she was pinker in the face and pointier in the nose. She knew to be on good behavior with his colleagues, but after ninety minutes had gone by, he judged that pretty soon she would tell someone—who would richly deserve it, but still— that he had his head up his ass. Fortunately it was not unreasonable to plead the time, given the likelihood that Susan with every passing minute was back-talking herself out of a repeat visit from the babysitter, so he managed to get Imogen out the door and down the drive toward the gate.

In the deepening darkness the house blazed, a parallelepiped of light. "The House That Terror Built," Imogen said. "No wonder he feels vulnerable. If the Big One gets dropped on LA, he'll have a front row seat."

"For a thousandth of a second."

"Before the x-ray flash chars his silver hair."

"I think the car's this way."

"I remember we drove *past* the gate."

"Yes, but we were coming from the other direction."

"Suit yourself," she said, as though that were the point at issue. They walked down the dark road to where he knew the car was with 100 percent certainty.

Vernon drove. Imogen smoked and stared out the windshield. "Your colleagues trail after Wohlstetter like high school girls with a crush on the queen bee."

"Some of them have started wearing suspenders."

They descended into West Hollywood. Vernon was thinking about Bertrand Russell. Whenever Russell climbed up on his hobby horse about world government, he complained that people were so illogical, and if they would only listen to the reasoning force of his titanic mind, all these unnecessary political problems would vanish. Russell somehow failed to understand that if people were illogical, only fools made logical appeals to them.

"We only ever see ourselves," Vernon mused.

"What?"

Vernon remembered a sketch he saw in *Life* magazine a few weeks after the end of the last war. It accompanied an article speculating about what the next war would be like. It showed men in radiation suits with Geiger counters on the steps of the New York Public Library. The lions were still there, but the building was rubble, the city beyond flattened, with only here and there a twisted steel structure half standing. It looked uncannily like photos of Hiroshima.

"Only seeing ourselves," Vernon repeated. "Like Walt Kelly says, 'We have met the enemy and he is us.' I've wondered lately if Americans, more than other nationalities, fear nuclear attack because we're the only ones to have dropped the bomb on anybody."

"I don't think Americans are capable of guilt."

"I'm talking about projection."

The neon lights of Santa Monica went by. So bright, this coastline in the dark, so clear the skies. The houses so lightly built. "Speaking of Japan," Vernon went on. "One of our bibles at work is a study called *Meeting the Threat of Surprise Attack*. Or course it's about the Soviets. But if you look at Russia's behavior in World War II, it was all defensive. The surprise attack that strategists like Wohlstetter fear most is the enemy managing to destroy our bombers on the ground. They're thinking of Pearl Harbor."

"So instead of worrying about Russia, maybe we should just nuke Japan for good. That would *really* be a surprise attack."

"The funny thing is, do you know what Wohlstetter's wife is famous for?"

"No."

"She wrote the definitive study of Pearl Harbor."

They laughed together until Vernon got wheezy.

Vernon turned onto their bungalow's concrete parking pad. Susan's bedroom window was dark. "Thank God," they said simultaneously.

What Vernon couldn't say to Imogen, because it was classified, was that even if Wohlstetter's unlikely scenario came true, and 85 percent of the US bomber fleet was taken out during a surprise Soviet attack, the United States could still respond by hitting them with *six hundred* nuclear weapons. He couldn't say, because it was classified, that the Navy was working on Polaris, which would enable the US to launch ICBMs from submarines, undetectable mobile platforms that were therefore invulnerable. If real Soviet leaders in the real world during a real crisis were likely to avoid behavior that might conceivably lead to just one H-bomb landing on Moscow—a hypothesis Vernon considered so plausible as to be axiomatic—then the US could put fifty Polaris missiles on five subs and everybody else—SAC, RAND, the bomber crews, the Atlas and Titan teams, the launch pad crews, the weapons labs—could collect their final paychecks and go home.

And maybe what bothered him most of all was just that—that he couldn't say these things to Imogen. *The secrecy shit*, she called it. He and she were scientists, for God's sake. Vernon had had a physics teacher at Wake Forest who one day plowed through a long string of calculations on the blackboard to arrive at one of Maxwell's equations. He turned toward the class and jabbed the chalk against the board behind him. "This is true." The students sat in a midafternoon doze. He tried to wake them: "Ninety-nine point nine nine percent of whatever any of you have ever said, or will ever say in your lives, is either unproven, unprovable, or false. This"—jab—"is"—jab—"*true*," and on the final word he broke the chalk against the board, fragments falling to the floor in arcs determined by their initial direction and velocity, the force of gravity, and air resistance. There had always been, would always be, too little knowledge in the world, and a scientist's role was to enlarge it. Which meant sharing it.

In his last weeks, Vernon couldn't stop saying to his RAND lunchmates, "Cheer up! We've got the keys to the candy store." Even though he is an introvert—or maybe because of it—he has never shied away from arguments. Sometimes a colleague got mad at him and he got mad back. He has never shied away from anger, either. Sitting in his study looking back, seventy years old, lonely as hell, surrounded by six and a half thousand classical music records, he can't remember what anyone else at the lunch table said. He sees that, in rejecting RAND, he became a true RANDoid: he was Wohlstetter and Paxson, obliterating his opponents with his rightness, leaving behind nothing of their idiocy but melted steel frames.

He submitted his resignation in August. For two months he'd been secretly casting about for other employment, and he'd found a job in Massachusetts. Imogen had always wanted to live in the Northeast, after her college days at Mount Holyoke. His paycheck would come from the Air Force, but he would be doing pure research on the absorption profile of ultraviolet light in the upper atmosphere. Unclassy and unclassified. Over the next thirty-five years, through a series of carefully designed balloon and rocket tests, he amassed the data set that became the accepted standard in his field. There are half a dozen solar physicists worldwide who know and value his work. To anyone else who asked him, during those years, what kind of physics he did, his pleasure was to begin and end with the disclaimer, "It has no conceivable application."

1953

Wednesdays after work at the Victor Chemical Company, instead of taking the train back into Chicago, she hops on a bus to Park Forest. She gets off near the clock tower and walks through the brand-new shopping plaza, where she stops to get a bite to eat, then continues north to the farmhouse at the edge of the open field. In good weather, as on this cloudless late April day, the walk gives her such a lift. The sun has just gone down and half the sky is orange.

She always arrives punctually at 7:50 for her 8:00–11:00 shift. Greets the funny old fart, "Sarge" Dannenfelser, who's often in the downstairs office fussing about the incomplete schedule and the unpredictable volunteers. He was an army sergeant in World War II—his real name is Hubert—who keeps his hair in a bristly flattop and sits as though he has an ironing board up his ass. But he likes Imogen, because he's got just enough brains to see she's reliable. He's somewhere in his forties, fit and trim. Occasionally as she comes downstairs from the lookout she can hear him doing push-ups in the office.

"Hi, Sarge."

"Mrs. Fuller! I heard your steps and knew it was you. Good viewing weather."

"The best. Still no one at eleven?"

"Not a blessed soul. Midweek is hard. But we're doing better than the other area posts. There are a lot of ex-military folks in Park Forest with a can-do, pitch-in attitude."

"That's what I hear." From you, in fact, once a week. Sweet old fool. She signs in, pins on her wings (this is hilarious, but Sarge likes them to be "in uniform" when they're manning the post), and heads up the stairs, out onto the roof, and up the three steps into the booth. "Hi, Viv."

"Hi, Gen."

"Anything interesting?"

"Well, the full moon just came up."

"Did you call it in?"

"Satellite flash! Satellite flash!"

They both laugh. Viv is wonderful. Smart and lively. She majored in astronomy at Northwestern but now has two little boys, comes out here twice a week to give her husband a little practice at helping out at home. She wishes she could take a midnight shift to enjoy the stars, but Warren won't have it. What if one of the boys is sick, or has a nightmare, Viv says he says. He has a full-time job.

Viv pulls the string to turn on the overhead lightbulb, gathers her things. "Did you hear about the Friday graveyard shift hullabaloo?" she asks.

"No."

"Turns out that high school boy who volunteered so eagerly was waiting until Sarge went home, then sneaking his girlfriend in."

"No!"

"Yes!"

"How funny! How'd they get caught?"

"You know Sarge. He came back last Friday about 2:00 a.m. all in a dither because he thought he'd left the office window open. He caught them in flagrante delicto."

"Oh my god, that's a scream. I'll bet his hair stood up."

"How would anyone tell?"

They laugh and laugh. Gen just loves Viv.

Viv heads down and Gen settles in. Signs in to the logbook, twitches the string to turn off the light, opens all the glass windows wide, buttons her wool coat, puts the binoculars around her neck. The little room was built on the backside of the farmhouse roof, high enough to give views in every direction. Even in cold weather one of the windows is always open so the spotters can hear as well as see. Winter coats advised. There's a space heater, but it's best to keep it off so the noise of the fan doesn't interfere.

Imogen saw the article last September in the *Chicago Heights Star*, which she often glances at during her lunch break at Victor Chemical. Park Forest needed more volunteers for its Operation Skywatch post, because it was planning to move to twenty-four-hour duty. Imogen snorted at some of the language. Volunteers would be those "who recognize their responsibility to the defense of their home, their community, and their nation." That kind of talk always sounded Hitlerite to her. She would have forgotten the whole thing except that there was an amusing quote from Sarge in the article, she still remembers it almost verbatim: "One weak point in Operation Skywatch could bring disaster on our nation. It seems unfair to run the risk of having to point a dead finger at yourself in the rubble of a bombed community when volunteering might have saved a life—your own!" The chirpy silliness of it just slayed her. She quoted it to Vernon that evening and it subsequently became a joke between them. If Vernon forgot to pick up milk on his way home from class or lab, Imogen would say, "Well you'll just have to point a dead finger at yourself." Or if an argument was getting testy, one of them would say, "Don't you dare point that dead finger at me!" and it would help them laugh the tension away.

In February another appeal went out. The post still didn't have round-the-clock coverage, and May to September was the time of year when atmospheric conditions were most propitious for Soviet bombers to, well, you know—do unto us. Maybe because the original article had stayed in her mind all through the winter as a pleasant joke, Imogen found herself tempted.

Just for fun. That's what she had to say over and over to Vernon, when he thought it was a stupid caprice. You get to learn new things every day, she said. I spend all my time doing tests on phosphorus compounds. I just want a break.

But that's not a break from work, he said, it's a break from home.

I just want something new.

Not that she needed his permission, she made that clear. But she didn't want her sweet big man mad at her. And he certainly was mad at first. But he came around.

She hears the growl of a plane to the north. Goes to the window with the binoculars. On clear nights like this, it's relatively easy to find the wing and taillights. Soviet bombers would be flying dark, so this aircraft right here and now is probably not the end of Chicago as we know it, but she follows the protocol. Which is awfully crude, but what the hell. They give you a transparent plastic sheet with different-size circles on it, and you fit the plane into one of the circles. If you've determined the type of aircraft and thus its size (there's a poster on the wall, useless in the dark, identifying twenty-five different silhouettes), the circle tells you how far away the plane is, or how high. The way to decide whether you're measuring distance or height is, if the plane is less than 45 degrees above the horizon, it's distance; if more than 45 degrees, it's height. No kidding, that's really what they teach you during your two hours of "training." (Trigonometry, anyone?) In any case, in the dark it's more or less impossible to identify the type of aircraft from its silhouette, so the distance or height measurement is also impossible. Nonetheless, you note the plane's direction, you pick up the phone, you say (ideally breathlessly), "Aircraft flash! Aircraft flash!" and you're connected to the Air

Defense Filter Center, where you tell them everything you know. Then you hang up, write every detail in the logbook, and go back to dreaming. During Imogen's training they showed her a peppy little film, so she knows that at the Filter Center a lot of women are standing around a big table map and pushing little airplanes around with croupier sticks as they receive the raw data. There's a group of self-important men sitting above them making calls to aviation authorities to check the identities of the aircraft. Unidentified aircraft are promptly blasted out of the sky. Ha! Not really, more inquiries are made, very occasionally fighter planes are sent to check them out, or so they claim, and everything always turns out to be innocent.

In other words, what a crock of shit! What a glorious boondoggle!

Of course most of the planes she calls in are approaching or departing O'Hare. High-altitude planes are commercial flights on the transcontinental flight corridor, or our own bombers or fighters, or military reconnaissance flights. Small planes are amateur pilots or business executives' charter flights out of one of the smaller airfields in the area. Imogen wonders if the real reason for the Ground Observer Corps is that the US military would love to know how well volunteer spotters can track US bombers, in case the Soviets have ginned up a similar corps of boobies with binoculars. Or maybe the objective is merely public relations, getting as many citizens as possible fired up about the Soviet threat so they'll support more money for the military. The one thing she knows for sure, it isn't for what they say it's for. But no matter. She just wanted one night a week on her own.

In between plane sightings, she gazes out at the darkness, at the ghostly streetlights of Park Forest, the yellow postage stamps of bedroom windows, the stacked blinking red lights of radio and television towers, the as-yet-nonradioactive glow of Chicago on the north horizon. She spends a lot of time looking at the stars, and after her first three

weeks of wondering why she had never taken the time to learn any constellations other than the Big Dipper and Orion, she bought a star chart.
Tonight's full moon doesn't make for good stargazing, but on other
nights she's found Hercules, Draco, Cassiopeia, Libra, Boötes, the Little
Dipper. She's seen lots of shooting stars, and gets a little thrill every
time. Meteor flash!

The cool air, the quiet night sounds of wind in the trees, rustling
nocturnal ground animals, flitting bats—it reminds her of camping out
in the Poconos with the dear trusting adolescent girls when she taught
them horseback riding during her college summers. And it reminds her,
way way back, of summer nights lying in the back field with her cousins
on the Alabama farm, telling jokes and having simple fun, when her
mother wanted her to come in and she wanted to stay out.

There's a percolator in the corner (Sarge has taped a sheet of paper
above it: "An alert spotter is a reliable spotter") and she fills a cup, sits
again, hugs her wool coat close. Eyes and ears of the Air Force—that's
what they call the gallant G.O.C. "Look to the sky!" the posters say. She
sips her coffee. Imogen is having a great Cold War.

She and Vernon never got a honeymoon. Three days after the wedding, Imogen was due to start work at Victor and Vernon had to prep
for his teaching.

She remembers sitting in the last row for the lectures in graduate
school. She wouldn't have admitted it, but she felt intimidated. All
those entitled men in front of her. And among them Vernon, whom she
first noticed because he had the broadest shoulders. He was so broken
up when his fiancée returned the ring. It touched her to see this big
man, so capable and confident, who'd come from a family of nincom-
poops and was making something of himself, it really touched her to see
him cry like a little boy. And she was realizing at the time that she
didn't much like physics. What had she been thinking? Her real love at

Mount Holyoke had been horses, but what kind of future was in that unless she snagged a man with a heap of money, the way Mac did? (Mac has her own horse farm now, the lucky duck.)

To be honest, she's having some trouble getting used to the idea that now she needs to be responsible. This is where her mother would make that tight little prim little mouth and say, I told you so. Imogen thinks sometimes with great longing of the carefree days when Mac and she used to take off for the National Horse Show in New York City. They'd stay in Madison Square Garden fifteen hours a day because they couldn't afford to leave and then have to pay another admission fee, and they'd eat nothing but hot dogs because they didn't have enough money to eat anything else. She tried talking about this once to Vernon, but he didn't understand. Having extricated himself from his hopeless family, he couldn't afford not to be sensible. She guesses she admires him for that.

Her mother gave her such a hard time when she got engaged. She knew it meant Imogen slipping out of her control. Typical for her, she dragooned Imogen's dad into mounting the assault, and typical for him, he went along like a mouse. Vernon seems a fine fellow, etc, he wrote to her, but why not wait a year to make certain the feelings will last, you're still young blather blather. They were always standing in her way, always second-guessing her. But she was almost twenty-two, and guess what, dear folks, she could do whatever she damned well pleased. She picked out for herself a new plaid dress to celebrate and brought her eighteen hands of blue-ribbon manhood to DC and for once *she* was the one who asked her father to get out his stupid camera. And in every photo she's beaming.

She hears another plane, approaching from the west. Locates it, makes a stab at identification, calls it in, logs it. Even if this is pointless, there's something satisfying about the orderliness. It's like filing things away, all in the right place, who gives a shit if you never look at it again.

Her mother really started to give her a hard time in her adolescence, criticizing her attitudes, her opinions. Especially her looks. Imogen understands now that when she was fifteen, her mother, who'd always been considered the beauty of her family, was fifty-two. Something going on there.

Half an hour of nothing goes by. Imogen identifies Cygnus and Lyra. Is that Corona Borealis, near the horizon? Thinking of when she was fifteen, she remembers her first civil defense gig, riding horses through Rock Creek Park. Was it Marx who said that history repeats itself? In her case, she gets two farces. Fifteen more minutes. Still nothing. The night air smells damp and earthy and good. A whiff of cigarette smoke rising from below. Smoke 'em if you got 'em, Sarge.

Sometimes on very quiet nights she puts on the light for a minute and has fun perusing the G.O.C.'s monthly magazine, *Aircraft Flash.* It turns out the biggest problem in more-rural areas is that whole weeks can go by without a single airplane. Of course the observers get bored, then disheartened, and then they quit. So the Air Force occasionally assigns planes to fly over outlying posts just to give the poor observers something to observe. You couldn't make this stuff up.

The opposite problem is all the flying saucers idiots are seeing. The Air Force has lately been trying to train G.O.C. personnel not to jump to fanciful conclusions. They've requested that any airborne device that cannot be positively identified as an airplane of some kind—most of the "saucers" are surely Skyhook meteorological balloons, which look like disks when they're overhead—should simply be designated an Unidentified Flying Object, or U.F.O. Good luck with that.

Schiller said it: Against stupidity, the gods themselves contend in vain.

Imogen logs in ten planes that evening. Chicago survives another shift. At eleven she signs the book, shelves the binoculars, goes downstairs. Sarge is still hanging around the office doing God knows what. Imogen doesn't know if he has a bad home life, or no home life at all.

"Good night, Sarge. You staying?"

"Good night, Mrs. Fuller. Yes, I thought I'd go up myself for a couple of hours, since there's no one else."

"You're like the little Dutch boy."

"Excuse me?"

"Putting your finger in the dike."

"Oh . . . Yes, I suppose you could call it that."

Better than your thumb up your ass! "Well you have a good night, Sarge. It's beautiful up there."

She goes outside. She notices Sarge has recently tacked a Skywatch recruitment poster next to the front door, where it can be seen from the road. His hope just keeps on springing. A majority of the Ground Observer Corps are women, but of course the poster shows a man. *Join Us in Skywatch!* He's pointing upward at a 45-degree angle, his straight arm looking like a— Ugh.

She walks through dark suburban streets toward the train station. They're still building large tracts of this town, dozens of houses at a time. It's all planned. It's like the country never left off war production, just changed the product. She catches the 11:25 to Chicago. During the forty-five-minute ride she often reads, but tonight she writes a letter to her German pen pal, Hildegard. When Imogen was at Mount Holyoke, a woman at the Episcopal church in Westfield was organizing food and clothing shipments to Germany, where so much of the postwar population was suffering such deprivation. "Many of these people were also victims of Hitler," this woman would say. Since Imogen was taking classes in German, she signed up to be a pen pal and also to contribute whatever goods she could afford.

Hildegard lives in a town in the eastern zone, where conditions are especially hard. She writes long letters about the bombed-out buildings, the food lines, the water shortages, her younger brothers, her ailing father, her depressed and listless mother. Her father is a pastor who opposed the Nazis and was interned during the war. Since marrying Vernon, Imogen has been able to send more goods, and Hildegard's letters are extravagantly grateful. She recently sent Imogen a photograph of herself. She has been urging Imogen to visit her someday, which Imogen would love to do. Imogen has always wanted to travel abroad. She would especially love someday to see Norway. There was a book she liked when she was a teenager, about Norwegian children during the war sneaking their country's gold reserves past Nazis by hiding it on sleds. She can't remember the title, but it was a true story about bravery that for once involved as many girls as boys.

Ihr fotograph ist sehr schön, she writes. *Ich möchte soviel gern, jedenzeit in der Zukunft Ihnen besuchen. Vielleicht kann ich das tun, wenn mein Mann sein Phd vollendet hat.*

She gets off at 63rd Street, walks the five blocks to the parsonage where she and Vernon are renting a crappy apartment with a nosy sanctimonious parson's wife for a landlady. (When they told her the fridge thermostat wasn't working right, she came to check and got huffy when she saw the beer.) It's half past midnight when she comes through the apartment door. All the lights are off and Vernon is asleep. Poor boy, he's been telling her how much he misses her on Wednesday evenings. It's very sweet of him, so she tries not to find it annoying.

1957

She slams the door on her way out, and of course Susan starts crying again.

How can he be like that? Yes, he works all week—but what does he think she's doing all day every day with Susan—he knows how Susan is. He's happy to let Imogen get up in the night while he sleeps like a log. He comes home, wants his dinner, eats cheese and crackers while she cooks—he's getting chubby—and he's a picky eater, he wants his food bland, meat and potatoes, doesn't even tolerate lamb, says it's too gamy, and after dinner, instead of engaging with his daughter he's tinkering with the stove light, or tightening a belt on the washing machine. If she makes the smallest innocuous complaint—*Why does it take so long for the water to get hot in the kitchen sink?*—boom! he's down in the crawlspace, mapping the configuration of the pipes and drawing a diagram and then going on about the plumber's puzzling choices or unintended consequences or counterintuitive reasons. "I'll bet I know why they did it that way . . ." he'll say after an hour of cogitation, and he's off in Discoveryland, while she's waiting for the water to get hot so she can wash the dishes and Susan is in the next room fussing.

She plops Susan in the stroller—"Shush, now, come on, just shush up"—and heads up Dimmick Avenue in the Saturday sunshine. It's beautiful weather and Susan's been a hellion all week and all Imogen said was, could Vernon maybe take her to the beach or the carousel on the pier for a couple of hours, so she could have a break. *I work hard all week,* huff huff—he was even a little angry. The hardworking man earns his weekend rest.

She turns right on Dewey Street. There's a little park up this way. Susan squirms, bleats. "We go to beat! We go to beat!"

"No, we're not going to the beach right now."

"I want go to beat!"

"We don't have the right clothes on."

"I want go!"

"That's just tough, missie, 'cause we're not going."

"Why can't we go?"

"Because I said so."

Imogen can feel her straining against the straps. She's doing that thing where she arches her back and balls her fists and twists her head half around. She looks like she's trying to turn herself inside out.

For some reason she's often more pliable with Vernon. Hasn't he noticed that? Of course he hasn't, he hardly notices her at all. "I'm not sure what to do with a girl," he said once. "Aren't daughters your job?" What the hell was that supposed to mean? She knows he doesn't like his sister or mother, but that's only because they're a pair of dolts—does he think all females are as stupid as they are? Does he think none of them could share his interests? Because with men it's always about sharing their interests, isn't it? Her father has his bridges and highways, his fishing trips. Everything else he just tolerates. When Imogen first met Vernon and he was so good about helping her with her physics homework, she thought it was about her, but really it was about the physics. He's never shown the tiniest interest in learning anything about horses, for example.

Oh, she knows he loves her, she knows that—

She and Susan reach the park, which is this funny little strip of grass between Dewey and Ozone, with a metal slide and swings and a splintery old roundabout shedding green paint. There are often one or two dogs here with their owners—as today, thank goodness. Susan likes dogs as much as Imogen does. She likes dogs more than she likes her mother.

"Look, honey! Look at the cute dog!" Imogen unstraps her, helps her out. "Hold my hand—no, you have to hold my hand—is he friendly? he is?—well hello there, sweet boy—you have to be more gentle, honey—"

Peace for a while. The sweet sleepy-eyed Lab, then a nervous ingratiating Miniature Schnauzer who takes their pats trembling, then a brainless Cocker Spaniel (overbred bug-eyed poor little things with their silly ears). Then Susan satisfies herself for a while on the slide—"Mommy, *watch*!"—then fusses and gripes, then eats the box of Sunkist raisins Imogen threw in the bag on her angry way out the door.

And yes, there's the wonderful weather. They've been here for close to a year now, and the weather is the one thing Imogen likes. The RAND men are impossible, the most self-satisfied horses' asses she's met in her life, and their wives are either gooses in awe of them or disenchanted drinkers. And she'd always heard about Californians and their cars, but really, it's ridiculous. On all the neighborhood streets there's parking up and down both sides, and there are also concrete pads between the houses where you might have a side yard instead, and then instead of any backyards—and these are small plots, you would think every square foot counted—there's another "avenue," more like a lane, that runs the length of the block, giving automobile access to sheds and garages. Thirty or forty blocks in any direction, it feels like one gigantic parking lot with sunstruck bungalows and potted trees set down on the pavement. Maybe no one likes to keep a yard or garden because it doesn't rain enough most of the year. In fact, all this sun can get monotonous.

She misses cloud formations. The play of shade and sun. The deep color green on a gray day.

And she misses her work. The Victor Chemical research was dull, but it got her out of the apartment, gave her a daily challenge. Her lab colleagues, mostly women doing the drudge work, could be funny. And making her own goddamn money.

Another dog arrives at the park, a Poodle mix, and Susan gets licked in the face and cries. Imogen picks her up to comfort her, but she struggles furiously in her arms, wailing as though she's being kidnapped, and Imogen plops her firmly back on her feet, "Have it your way." Susan throws herself on her stomach and performs the full tantrum: a blur of drumming Mary Janes, pounding fists, chin propped forward on the ground to give the scream maximum projection. Christ, can she pour it out. Other mothers and dog walkers look on—yes, she's my daughter, I'm the mother who can't handle her, gaze on us and feel superior.

She sits on a bench nearby and ignores it for half a minute, since she knows nothing will stop Susan except exhaustion. Then can't stand it anymore and pulls her daughter up, hisses furiously in her ear, "Pipe down!," and stuffs her into the stroller, pressing hard against her heaving chest while she forces the straps around the flailing limbs. "What's wrong with you?" She pushes the stroller away from the rapt audience. Instead of heading directly back to the house, she turns randomly left and right, keeping up a brisk pace down the narrow streets, letting the bumps and jostles distract Susan, or maybe comfort her the way Imogen can't, and the child subsides to whimpering and eventually falls asleep. It must have been time for her nap. Isn't that what parents always say? It's not me, it's fatigue. Now she keeps on randomly turning left and right in order to calm herself down.

From the moment Susan was born, Imogen couldn't comfort her. She tried everything. Her mother was there supposedly to help, but only criticized. And Vernon left her to it, goo-gahing at Susan with a finger or holding her warily for a minute before handing her back to Imogen the moment she started to fuss. And Imogen's father hung back with his camera for mask and shield. In the photos Imogen looks horribly like her mother, that exact tight smile and iron in her eyes, or no smile at all, in which case she looks like the Bitch of Buchenwald.

They need another child. Susan needs a little brother or sister to love and care for, they all need someone to break up this dynamic of mother vs. daughter. Imogen hopes dearly it's a boy. *Girls are the mother's job, aren't they?* What the *fuck* is that supposed to mean?

But Susan was an accident, and Vernon wants to hold off on another child until they have more money. He says ideally they would wait until they owned their own home. He implied that Susan is such a handful, maybe two would be—

"Stop right there, buster," Imogen said. "Don't you dare say another word."

He held up his hands, as though to signal innocently, Geez, why so angry? But she could tell *he* was angry. He was angry a lot.

"I am not raising an only child, and that's final," she said.

She arrives at a corner. Bentley Court and Marine Street. Not sure where that is. She can see a commercial street a block away, which, when she gets to it, turns out to be Lincoln Boulevard. From here she knows how to get back to Ozone. She passes the park again—can't tell if it's different people now, fuck them all anyway—and goes back down Dewey to Dimmick to the little stucco box. She parks the stroller with sleeping Susan in the shade just inside the front door.

Vernon is out on the side patio, stretching a screen across a window frame. The worktable there is the first thing he built when they moved in. He's secured the frame to the table with clamp screws and is manipulating a long dowel to which he's stapled the leading edge of the screen. She watches him for a few seconds. He's good with his hands. Imogen mentioned yesterday that insects were getting in through a tear.

"Thank you," she says.

He starts to talk about the frame, something about the inadequate way it was reinforced at the corners. She waits patiently. Really, what would her life be like without him? She certainly wouldn't want to be a single mother, would she? And face it, she would never fix anything, any house she lived in would fall apart around her, or she'd have to find the money to hire a handyman.

He leans far across the table and his stomach bulges out from his belt. She wishes he wouldn't snack so much. He was so lean and square-jawed when they married. The physical side has never been her favorite, and his increasing roundness isn't helping. "I don't understand how a person could let himself go like that," her mother said on her last visit. She deliberately said it in Vernon's hearing, which made Imogen feel angry at her and defensive of her husband, but also hopeful he might be embarrassed enough to start dieting.

He's still talking about the frame. He truly thinks she's interested.

He's a good man, trying to be kind.

When he got his PhD last year, Imogen thought they could finally go to Norway. Just three weeks, before he started work at RAND, a delayed honeymoon. Her mother had offered to take care of Susan. All the magazine photos and travel agency posters Imogen had looked at through the years—fjords, snowy glaciers, the midnight sun, little seaside villages of red and ocher houses on stilts above the kelp. She and Vernon could take the coastal steamer—didn't that sound romantic?— and stay in refurbished huts with sod roofs. Then for the last four or five days they could go down into Germany and she could finally meet Hildegard and her family. She'd looked forward for years and years. But Vernon didn't want to travel. He said they needed furniture. Most of what they had in Chicago belonged to the apartment, and the bungalow they'd agreed to rent in Santa Monica was unfurnished.

We can sleep on the floor, Imogen said.

That makes for a nice story, but have you ever tried it? Vernon said. And what do we eat on? And where does Susan sleep?

For everything Imogen said, he had a reasonable answer. She probably could have insisted—she'd earned about three-quarters of the money during the previous five years—but partly he wore her down with logic, and partly she saw that traveling with him after this disagreement would be no fun at all. So she caved. And the moment she did, he turned with the same tirelessness to the task of buying furniture. He contacted companies, requested brochures, had her pore with him over photos of tables, dressers, bed frames. He made lists of prices and wrote letters to store managers asking for more particulars. One day she came home from work and found him drawing a diagram. He'd contacted the owner of the bungalow and requested measurements of all the rooms, including the placement of the windows and doors. He was cross-checking that diagram with the dimensions of all the furniture candidates she and he had discussed. He was determining the optimal pieces to buy and the best way to arrange them.

She looked at that diagram with its neatly ruled lines and saw the bars of a cage. She saw that he would always be right.

And now when she sets his beef and potatoes down on the green Formica kitchen table, or does her sewing at the dining room table with the driftwood maple finish, or puts Susan in her Hollywood twin bed, or sits on the Naugahyde sofa with him to watch some silly program on TV, or joins his sleeping form late at night on the double extra-long Beautyrest mattress and box spring with the mocha maple headboard, it all reminds her of the trip he wouldn't let her take.

But also—lying next to him in bed, his oblivious (and therefore, she supposes, innocent) breathing, the dip of the mattress down toward his warm solid bulk—she thinks of the floor that she doesn't have to sleep on. She sees the dark little house he grew up in, and she remembers that even in his father's last years, his parents' money was so tight they couldn't afford the paint to spruce up one of their bedrooms. She remembers that he helped her find the Victor Chemical job by scouring ads and making lists of addresses and telephone numbers, scouting managers' names by writing to friends of friends. And years ago, when she mentioned that she occasionally sent care packages to Hildegard, he pitched in with his usual energy and his alarming focus and his sincere interest in the logistics of any project. He drew up more lists, researched nutritional needs and perishabilities, calculated mailing weights and costs. He improved every aspect of her system. Hell, she hadn't had a system at all, she'd merely shipped stuff to Hildegard.

Long years with any man would be a challenge, right? In many ways—in *most* ways—she's lucky.

But they will have another child. That is not negotiable.

1996

God's in his heaven, Vernon's in his study.

Vargas lies curled in the padded chair, enjoying the lingering warmth from Vernon's padded ass. Gen is out for the evening at her so-called Spanish lesson.

All his life he has hated watching other people handle vinyl records. They grip them like Frisbees, rotating them this way and that, their fingers slathering the surface in skin oil and dead cells. Vernon takes the record in its paper sleeve and holds the vinyl-edge against the base of his right palm, supporting the disk from below with middle and pinkie fingers. He pulls the sleeve off with his left hand, allowing it to slide beneath the fingers until—voilà!—he is holding the naked record via edge and label. His ring finger is perfectly positioned for its tip to find the spindle hole. Now, if Vernon wanted, he could throw the sleeve over his shoulder, feint toward the cat, and duck through the linemen's gap to the stereo, touchdown!, all with the record secure in his hand.

He brushes side A with a damp cotton cloth. (Wet the cloth, wring it out, roll it up inside a larger dry cloth, wring both. Special cleaning fluids and velvety wands sold by stereo stores are a waste of money.) He places the record on the turntable, lowers the needle, adjusts the volume. Sweeps cat from chair, sits, dons headphones, leans back. Beethoven Opus 127.

Vargas jumps into his lap.

Vernon's former colleague Eugene came back to the lab for a visit a couple of years ago and they took him out to lunch, but the poor son of a bitch was a doddering shell. "When I can't understand my old papers, show me the door," Vernon would say to Frances, and she would make that exasperated gesture. She was difficult. Sometimes when she saw him in the morning, she'd say, "Don't be depressed today, I can't handle it right now." It always surprised him. Was it that obvious?

Frances was the only reason he had published anything in the last decade. She arrived in the early eighties, the first woman in the lab—physicist, that is—and you had to be careful with her, she had a chip on her shoulder. She couldn't write grammatically. You young people and the English language, he would try to joke with her. But she was a good scientist. She noticed a collection of data he had left over from a series of balloon shots he'd done in the seventies. Along with his target range in the near-UV he'd amassed figures for solar irradiance between 2000 and 3100 angstroms at 40 kilometers.

"J. V.," she said, "why haven't you published these?"

He told her he'd checked them against Ackerman and Frimout and they didn't match very well, so he assumed he'd made a mistake somewhere.

She shot him that look. "Your figures are probably better. Nobody's measured that range as carefully as you have."

So they collaborated. She crunched the numbers, he introduced her to the subjunctive. They ended up publishing five papers in the *Journal of Geophysical Research*. On three of them, he insisted she put her name first.

But it was becoming clear he was just taking up space. He would fiddle around, forget what he was doing, go to lunch with Don and Mike, read articles in the afternoon, drift off. It was a disgrace to keep paying him. At his retirement party they gave him a pin and a citation suitable for keeping rolled in a drawer. Don and Mike told jokes, Frances hugged him tearily goodbye. He'd miss her, but he wouldn't miss her moods.

So now he's home all day, trying not to turn into Eugene.

Dead house, windowless room. Left and right walls are entirely covered in records, a glorious sight, except for a patch on the right where the ventilation blower is mounted. When Mark was little he would ask if he could rotate the steel crank, and Vernon would say go ahead. Mark would start turning, and after a second or two he'd begin to wail—he claimed like a fire engine, though he sounded coincidentally more like a civil defense siren. Vernon has thought about removing the blower for thirty years. Still thinking.

Not turning into Eugene means keeping busy, so he's been reorganizing his LPs. He built new shelves above his desk and along the floor to the left of the door, then lugged down the four hundred overflow vinyls he was keeping in a small room off the bedroom, mainly records bought in the last ten years from desperate mail-order outfits offering twenty LPs for the price of one. He's given pride of place to his string quartets, now arranged alphabetically by composer, from Arriaga to Wynne, in a big beautiful block on the left-hand wall. To paraphrase a line from C. P. Snow, "Excellent! Anyone with half an eye can see that that's a collection of string quartets."

The older he gets, the more he finds that string quartets speak to him like nothing else. He doesn't know why. He has never really understood music, never grasped why it moves him so deeply. He was a bad sax player. He never took music theory in school. He has trouble picking out on the piano the tunes he remembers in his head. (Interesting that he seems to be able to hear them clearly, yet can't sing them accurately enough to find the right keys on the piano.) He knows what the dominant of a key is, but can't hear a circle of fifths progression when it occurs in a Bach bass line. When a melody dips below the tonic to linger on the sixth of the scale, it sounds to him like unbearable longing: in the sixth measure of the *Méditation* from *Thaïs*, or at the word "stranger" in "My Days Are Gliding Swiftly By," or (who would believe him?) at the end of the first phrase in the title theme from *Star Trek: First Contact*, which he heard the other night while flipping channels after a ball game. Why on earth would this be true? Is it a quirk in him, or do others feel it?

While organizing his string quartets, he decided to listen to them all again. He's gotten to that point in his life where if he doesn't do things now, he'll never do them. Some of these recordings he's played only two or three times, in some cases more than twenty years ago. He made a back-of-the-envelope calculation on the back of an envelope, keeping in mind multiple recordings of some of his favorite quartets, the complete Beethovens and Shostakoviches, too many Mozarts, all those Haydns, and he came up with something like 900 performances. If he listens to two or three a day, it will take him about a year.

Listening to them in alphabetical rather than chronological order will prevent him from getting tired of a particular era. It might also offer interesting juxtapositions. He began ten days ago with Arriaga, of whose three quartets he has two, written in 1821, when Arriaga was fifteen. A decent recording, cheaply produced by the Musical Heritage Society, which inimitably managed to misspell Arriaga's name in the headline on the back cover. Then the mathematician-serialist Milton Babbitt, whose Quartet no. 2 (1952) Vernon has by the Composers Quartet, and no. 3 (1970) by the Fine Arts. This time around, no. 2 almost started to make a little sense, sounding here and there like a fugue based on tone-row fragments. Then Grażyna Bacewicz's Quartet no. 7, from sometime in the 1960s—almost tuneful (after Babbitt), occasionally toe-tapping. Why so few female composers? Vernon's an old fart, yes, an asshole male like all males, but even he noticed that the liner notes were all about the male Pipkov, whose Quartet no. 3 had been paired with Bacewicz's.

Following that, Bach—*Art of the Fugue*, by the Portland String Quartet, breaking off in the middle of a phrase where Bach put down his quill and died, which always moves this old man—and Barber's single quartet from 1936, which includes the original version of *Adagio for Strings*, by the Cleveland Quartet on Red Seal, paired with Ives for that Americana effect. Then five thorny days of Bartók, because Vernon has two complete sets of the six quartets, Tátrai and Végh, both excellent and sounding remarkably alike, maybe it's a Hungarian thing.

What does Vernon know? Nothing! But Bartók has always struck him as the greatest twentieth-century composer of string quartets. Something about those six—something unsystematic but compelling, something surprising yet inevitable, something nonBabbitty, disCartery, unSchoenbergisch—should Vernon punt, and call it genius?—reminds him of Beethoven. Whom he has now reached! And he's not cheating by starting with the late quartets, because this yearlong perusal is alphabetical, not chronological, and all of Beethoven's quartets are by Beethoven.

Plus, he can't wait, and he might die tomorrow. Thus, Opus 127. Performed by the Pascal Quartet, on the dear old Concert Hall Society label. These were the first Beethovens he ever owned. He bought the whole set when he was still a student in Chicago, and they arrived monthly, in allotments of two or three. Jesus, he feels such nostalgia looking at the covers, in varied hues with a uniform illustration, a scrabbly charcoal sketch of Beethoven's head, face down and scowling like an angry toddler. Susan was two; his unbearable mother; that broiling attic apartment in which it was so important to keep the LPs perfectly vertical.

This is a mono recording, the master from the late forties. To his spoiled ears of today it sounds tinny. The Pascals play Beethoven with that old-fashioned sweet sound, the vibratos fast and cloying. Too much first violin. There's tracing distortion toward the end of each side, some of which would be wear and tear. He didn't buy another set of the quartets until 1962, so it's likely he's played each of these Pascals more times than any other record he's ever owned.

Vargas is asleep on his chest. This always happens. Vernon will lean back to listen and Vargas will edge up his stomach. Vernon leans farther back and Vargas inches higher. The cat ends up with his head tucked under Vernon's chin, curled on the nearly level surface of Vernon's expanding girth. *Get your fat self out of my sight.*

The tone arm has swung back, the turntable has clicked off. Vernon contemplates getting up.

He never wanted cats. Like so many things, it was Gen's idea. She always said she preferred dogs (from 1958 on, they always had one or two); she couldn't understand how anyone could like cats, they were so aloof, cat people were annoying nutjobs. Then about twenty years ago a black cat started hanging around the back door during a cold December.

"She looks hungry," Imogen said.

"You feed that cat, you own that cat," Vernon said.

"She's shivering."

"Shivering is the body's way of generating heat. We ascribe emotion to it, but a cat doesn't."

Imogen set up a box with a blanket on a piece of basement roof that projected out below one of the dining room windows.

"She'll be living here in no time," Vernon said.

"Nonsense. She's too wary."

Imogen fed the cat. By knocking on nearby doors, she found the family who had owned her and lost interest. It turned out her name was Brandy. The vet pronounced her healthy and in no time she got less wary.

A dozen cats have followed. They tend to show up after Gen talks too much with her socially maladjusted vet friend at the shelter. They arrive in groups of two or three, like the Pascal recordings, based on the same sketch but in different colors. Several have been lost to cars, so the current trio—Vargas, Llosa, Yolanda—are strictly indoor cats. The dogs are long gone. Vernon doesn't miss their barking, their hair, their smell, their need for walks. He never wanted dogs, either.

Vargas breathes against his neck. The one thing Vernon is still good for: providing a warm platform for a cat.

She moved into Mark's old bedroom so suddenly. *No more of that!* she said. *You can just forget about that.* That was six years ago.

Get your fat self out of my sight.

You called Susan a whore. I'll never forgive you for that.

He sweeps Vargas to the floor, gets his fat self up. All his family was heavy, it was in their genes. There isn't anything *moral* about it. Doesn't it say something about her?

Wanting to get that tinny 127 out of his head, he returns the Pascal to the shelf, takes down Budapest's performance of the same quartet. Kicks Vargas out, closes the door. It's only a screen door, there's no other ventilation in the room, unless he wants to rotate the blower crank and wail. Vargas scratches at the screen. Vernon swivels away from him, puts on his headphones, takes the score into his lap.

The opening chords: more balanced, more "chordal." Mischa Schneider's wonderful cello sound. He never realized until he bought the Dover scores that half of these opening chords are off the beat. Is a listener supposed to be able to hear that? It was a revelation when he first heard the Budapest play on the radio while he was at RAND. Suddenly the late Beethovens sounded both righter and stranger. The innovative architecture was there. (Vernon is groping; he reminds himself that he knows nothing.) He bought their middle and late quartets as soon as they were issued in stereo by Columbia in 1962. By then, he had this room for listening.

Here comes the Adagio. One of those gorgeous melancholy slow movements in late Beethoven that seem to want never to end, and almost don't.

One false cadence after another, one more variation, one more doodle. A coda that goes on long enough to wag the dog. Vernon is probably reading in too much, but these lingering adagios sound to him like a dying man kicking against his mortality.

Irascible, lonely old wretch, unlucky in love all his life. He didn't even have a cat to sleep on his chest.

Vernon puts the LP back on the shelf. Opens the screen door. Vargas has disappeared. It's past eleven, and Gen is still not home. She and Carlos drink while they gab in Spanish. A couple of weeks ago, driving home, she was so drunk she was seeing double. No doubt she's sorry she admitted this to Vernon.

He stands for a moment in the narrow doorway, looking at the original basement.

He still wonders why the company contacted him. It was 1961. Sure, in his last months at RAND he'd helped out with an absurd civil defense study, but his new job at the Geophysics Lab was unrelated. The Berlin Crisis was all over the news that summer, so maybe the company assumed he'd get back into the Armageddon business. Anyway, the company president called him up and addressed him by his correct name, fed him some boilerplate claptrap and offered him a top-of-the-line home fallout shelter for free. This in exchange for the possibility—which of course would not be construed by the company to imply a commitment—that if Vernon were satisfied with the result, he might lend his name to the company's advertising, in conjunction, perhaps, with a testimonial that Vernon could craft himself if he so wished, or leave to the firm's top-notch team of copywriters. Vernon was still furious at the whole booming business—bombs, fear of bombs, more bombs to allay fear of bombs—and at every product, advertisement, and pusillanimous political utterance that fed off it, so he said, Sure, come build me a shelter. In addition to liking the idea of wasting the company's money, the engineer in him was curious to see how they'd spend it.

They told him they'd treat him well by building the most secure and convenient model, usually reserved for new home construction: a 7' by 11' belowground room opening off the basement. Space for six people plus storage.

Vernon asked if they could build him something larger. Say, 10' by 11'.

After a moment's hesitation, the company president said, "Of course."

"I'd rather invite in our closest neighbors than shoot them," Vernon explained.

"That's commendable," the president said. "But may I ask, what about your other neighbors?"

"I'm hoping that the neighbors I let in will shoot them."

Two seconds passed, after which the president decided to laugh.

One golden autumn day a backhoe and a small bulldozer showed up and proceeded to dig a far larger hole in the side yard than Vernon had anticipated. Subsequently he could see that its size was necessary to permit access and egress to the machines digging it, but Christ, was Imogen pissed. A team of three mixers set concrete footers in the ground and poured a 4" pad, after which a barrel-shaped mason named Hugh constructed the walls out of 12" concrete blocks. The mixers returned to cap it all with a 6" concrete roof. Since the basement floor was only 61" below ground level, the top of the roofing slab exceeded it by 27", and on top of the slab was going to go 15" of pit-run gravel and 3" of topsoil. To deal with the 45" discrepancy, Vernon was offered the choice of attractive peripheral brick planters or a soil slope. He chose the latter on grounds of needing less maintenance, and requested a 1:4 gradient so that he could cut the grass easily with his hand mower. Thus the mound tapered to the level of the rest of the yard over fifteen feet in three directions.

Vernon thanked the mixers, thanked Hugh, thanked the company president and bowed them all off his property, politely declining to lend his name to their ads. Then he inspected his new room. He estimated the job would have cost him roughly $2500, or one-eighth the price of his house. The increase in resale value was probably less than that, perhaps around $1000. The doorway was only 2' wide, to restrict radiation from that direction. To assist the blower in ventilation, there was no door, but since radiation, like Chinese demons, travels only in straight lines, Hugh had built a baffle wall just inside the doorway.

Curious about the room's effectiveness against radiation from an atomic blast, Vernon dug up some shielding data from his cache of unclassified RAND documents. The part of the shelter most exposed to direct radiation was the ceiling, which consisted of 6" of concrete, 15" of packed gravel, and 3" of topsoil. Radiation shielding was measured in halving thicknesses, that is, the thickness required of any material to reduce radiation by half. Approximately 4.5" of soil equaled one halving thickness. The density of a material was roughly proportional to its shielding strength. Soil had an average density of 1.25 g/cm^3, whereas concrete was 2.4 g/cm^3, and thus, 6" of concrete provided the same shielding as approximately 11.5" of soil. Gravel was around 1.68 g/cm^3, so 15" of gravel equaled about 20" of soil. Thus, the top of his shelter had the equivalent of 34.5" of soil, or 7.67 halving thicknesses, which would cut radiation by a factor of 200. Radiation through the buried walls would be virtually nonexistent. The open doorway was harder to calculate, but the baffle wall alone would reduce radiation by a factor of nearly 35, and the preexisting basement might do approximately the same. On the whole, then, the room provided significant protection. If one assumed Vernon had any interest in surviving a nuclear war.

He hired a contractor a few days later to remove the baffle wall. The rest he did himself, hanging a screen door, mounting electrical raceways with masonry screws, an antenna wire conduit near the ceiling, easing his disassembled desk through the narrow door and rebuilding it in situ, etc. Gradually over the years he has improved the radiation cladding by augmenting the walls with a 12"-thick layer of polyvinyl chloride, also known as his record collection. LP vinyl, at 1.3 g/cm³, is slightly denser than soil. Additionally, it offers higher protection against some forms of radiation because of its high hydrogen content. But ignoring this last factlet—electromagnetic shielding is pretty far outside of Vernon's wheelhouse—his LPs would still reduce radiation a further 85 percent. Thank you, Beethoven, Babbitt, Bacewicz, et al. Not to mention providing additional field insulation against the idiot ham radio operator four houses away, plus better sound insulation against barking neighborhood dogs, crying children, loitering teenagers, road traffic, ambulance sirens, top-40 crap played by other people's outdoor contractors, birdsong, Good Humor trucks. In other words, life.

Vernon heads up the stairs to the ground floor. 11:25 p.m., no sign of Imogen. Carlos's apartment is ten miles away, which is a pretty long drive if you're drunk as a skunk. Gen used to berate him for sleeping soundly when Susan was out late. She said it was proof he only cared for himself. Now he sits up and worries about Gen, and she sees it as trying to control her.

He leaves the back door unlocked, the porch light on. Checks to make sure the front door is locked. Heads upstairs to his bedroom, consciously lifting each foot high enough. Worries that she'll kill herself. Worries that she'll kill a family in the opposing lane. Wonders if she and Carlos do more than practice Spanish. She dotes on him, quotes him. He's an Old World man, with his dark shabby apartment full of books and his ascot, for God's sake. (Vernon's never been there, but on the fridge there's a photograph of the lion in his den.) He needs a señorita to take care of him and apparently none of his five ex-wives fit the bill. Imogen jokes about that. "He's terrible," she says, and seems to mean it.

Maybe what she feels is more sisterly. She was lonely, growing up.

He gets ready for bed, climbs in. Stares at the darkness, kicks against his mortality.

The first thing he noticed, maybe ten years ago, was that he was fre-quently catching his toe against the riser of a stairstep. Then he ob-served his handwriting getting smaller. Sometimes in the middle of writing a sentence his hand would stop and he'd stare at it, unsure how to make it move. It also seemed as though his gait had changed. He shambled. He made an appointment with a neurologist and read these and other symptoms from a list he'd drawn up the night before. The man was impressed at his observational powers. "You've given a text-book description of the onset of Parkinson's disease," he said.

Vernon was relieved. He'd thought he had Alzheimer's. He would sur-render his body before his brain any day. He didn't know then that many Parkinson's patients eventually develop something called Lewy body de-mentia. Well—he sure knows now. Sometimes he fades out. This inter-mittency is one of the things that distinguishes LBD from Alzheimer's. He'll fade out more as time goes by, until it will be more useful to speak of the times he fades in. His periods of clarity give him opportunities to stand back and really appreciate the inexorable ruin of his mind. Another co-incident condition of Parkinson's, his doctor tells him, is depression. By that is meant an organic condition, over and above the depression any-one would feel at having a progressive, incurable, terminal disease.

Imogen thinks his neurologist is an idiot. *I can't believe you're still seeing that incompetent fool.* Maybe that counts as caring for him. But it sounds like anger at his stubbornness. Maybe it's an excuse to blame him for his disease. Get your fat, diseased self out of here.

It's true that he slept soundly when Susan, during her wild teenage years, was out late with the car. Talk about stubborn. She was so bull-headed, he couldn't imagine anything as mundane as a car accident changing her trajectory.

You called Susan a whore.

Well, no, not technically. He remembers the evening perfectly well, probably a hell of a lot better than Imogen does. Susan was fourteen or fifteen, headed out with friends. She had only recently begun applying makeup, and like lots of inexperienced girls she had put on too much. He was only trying to shield her from embarrassment. He was her father. And since he knew she rarely listened to him, he wanted to say something that would catch her attention. A rhetorical ploy. He said, "With all that makeup, you know, you look like a streetwalker."

Yes of course, now he sees, he concedes, he surrenders, his hands are up, his throat is bared—he shouldn't have used that word.

It's called a mistake.

Gen twists things. She hated her mother. Maybe it's a compliment to him, maybe it indicates his importance to her, that she's furious with him most of the time.

He hears the car in the driveway. The back door opening, the cats converging in the kitchen, the affectionate voice she reserves for them. She will linger downstairs. She's hoping he's asleep. He tells himself he wants to oblige her. But he's waiting. He wants the tiniest bit of normal conversation between a man and his wife. How was your evening? Go to sleep, dear. To be honest, maybe he also wants to find out if she is too drunk to have driven safely, so he can score some points.

He struggles to stay awake while she waits downstairs for him to fall asleep.

As usual, she wins.

THERE'S AN EPISODE of *The Twilight Zone* in which Burgess Meredith plays a myopic milquetoast with an awful wife. He loves to read and she mocks him for it, tearing up his books in front of him. Each lunch hour at the bank where he works, he closes himself in the vault, so that he can read in peace. One day, while he's in there, a nuclear war occurs. He emerges to find himself alone. He wanders the city ruins, disconsolate, until he happens upon the grand stone steps of the library. (Vernon suspects that Rod Serling also saw the 1945 *Life* magazine sketch of the New York Public Library set amid Hiroshima-style desolation.) Books are spilled everywhere. Now our hero is happy. Maybe the world has been destroyed, but he can read all the Dickens, Tolstoy, Chekhov, and Shakespeare he wants. Plus, his wife has been vaporized. In his excitement, he drops his glasses on the stone steps and they shatter. Now he's blind. End of story.

Vernon sits looking at his Beethoven quartets.

The Pascal kept him satisfied for seven years, the Budapest for five. He doesn't have to remember the dates, he has a note inserted in every record stating when he acquired it. In 1967 he bought another box of the lates performed by the Hungarian Quartet, on Seraphim. They played squarer and sparer than the Budapest. Another step away from Pascal-style lyricism to something more "classical." The cellist, Gábor Magyar, tended to play too quietly. Vernon missed Budapest's Schneider. And the paper sleeves had no cutouts for the labels, which was intensely annoying. Like every other customer on Earth, Vernon had to write on the outside of each sleeve which quartet it contained.

For the Beethoven Bicentennial in 1970 new recordings sprang up like mushrooms. Vernon bought the Yale Quartet on Vanguard in 1971. Again, no label cutouts! What could they be thinking? (The trouble is, they *don't* think.) The acoustics were a tad cavernous, but Yale was technically the most proficient Vernon had heard. They were the first to get the crazily fast Presto in Opus 131 to hang together, and their pianoforte contrasts throughout were more pronounced. Vernon finds the correct Yale disk, slides it out against his palm—the A minor Opus 132. Runs his damp cloth over it. You can feel how, by 1971, the vinyl is getting thinner. By the mid-seventies, LPs were almost floppy. He places it on the turntable. Padded chair, headphones, score. God's in his heaven.

He's struck again by how similar the opening measures sound to the Grosse Fuge theme. Those rising and falling half-steps haunted Beethoven throughout the late quartets. Why? Does the chromaticism uncenter the key? Vernon should ask Mark.

He remembers years ago, looking out through the screen door at Mark playing in the basement. Mark used to sit at the wooden table— now holding laundry supplies—building model cars, planes, spaceships. Cheap plastic parts with translucent flash, which Vernon showed Mark how to shave off with a penknife. Sensitive, shy kid. Worrisomely girly when young, like his uncle Julian. Hopeless at touch football or catch. Susan was the talented one there. Vernon would engage the three of them in a ball game out in the yard, to get Mark out of the house and let Susan work off nervous energy. This was before Susan turned into a juvenile delinquent, so she'd have been thirteen or so. Since Mark was five years younger, and not naturally gifted, he'd usually end up crying. He had this way of collapsing into a damp heap. Vernon knew his son would get into endless trouble at school, so he urged him to butch it up a little. Later, in his twenties, he seems to have had a girlfriend or two. But he never married, so you have to wonder.

An image sticks in Vernon's mind. He was sitting right here, with his headphones on, listening to the Trout Quintet, looking through the doorway. The screen door was open. Mark was hunched over a model piece sitting on the spread-out newspaper, applying red enamel paint from one of those cubic jars the toy stores sell. For some reason, Susan was standing behind him, looking on. Maybe Vernon remembers this because it was rare for her to take an interest. He couldn't hear anything, but he could see that she asked Mark something, and Mark turned his head to answer. She leaned closer and gestured toward the plastic part. Then she said something that made Mark laugh and he turned away, as though abashed by his own delight, and the tacky tip of the brush he was holding snagged against the newspaper and started to pull it off the table. Susan put a hand down to hold it in place.

That's the whole memory. In the last year or two it has come to his mind with increasing frequency. It feels to Vernon like it represents everything he's lost—his wife, his children. Of course Susan is gone, something he thinks about as rarely as possible. In a more subtle but no less real way, Mark is also gone—*that* Mark. You have your children and you love them, and where do they go?

He wishes he knew what they'd been saying.

Some years ago he read in an essay a whimsical idea about a Museum of Lost Gestures. The writer was talking about habitual motions people used to make that have disappeared because of changing technology. An example he gave was shielding a candle flame with your hand as you walked down a dark hallway. The lost gesture that Vernon often thinks of is the position you take when a child is standing in front of you— watching a parade, a ball game—and you put your hands on his shoulders. He misses that like hell. It's probably this trio section of the Opus 132 that's carrying him out on a tide of wistfulness. It's a musette, meant to imitate a bagpipe, with a bass-line drone and a simple melody. Something about the static harmony—whatever the reason, it sounds like nostalgia to him, like stopped time.

End of side. Vernon rotates the disk between palms to the opposite side, holds the edge against his shirt-front, cleans the surface with his cloth. With CDs taking over the world, these will soon be lost gestures. On to the third movement.

Beethoven had recently recovered from a serious illness, and he labeled this movement "Holy Song of Thanksgiving of a Convalescent to the Deity, in the Lydian Mode." (He would be dead within the year.) According to *The Beethoven Companion*, Beethoven's recent study of Palestrina had piqued his interest in the old church modes. Vernon had no idea what those were, so he read up about them. Apparently, if he plays from C to C on Gen's old piano using only the white keys, he's playing the Ionian mode. If he begins at A, he's playing the Aeolian. A lot of English border ballads, as it turns out, are in the Dorian mode (D to D), which—if you stare stupidly at the piano keyboard long enough, you can figure out—is like a standard minor key with a raised sixth. The Locrian mode (B to B) has a diminished chord for a root triad, which means—for some reason that Vernon can't fathom—composers almost never use it. (He so wishes he had a natural aptitude for music. This room would not be his study, but his studio. He'd have widened the door to get his piano in. He would nod his head knowingly to Locrian impossibility, or he'd convert the heathen with his melting Locrian études. He would understand his own emotions.)

As for this movement's Lydian mode—here's the theory that Vernon has read: Lydian is like a major key with a raised fourth, which means it doesn't use the subdominant chord, since the raised fourth is a tritone, which is too remote from the tonic to sound right. So instead of the usual I-IV-V harmonies you get a lot of I-V alone, which in this case is F and C. Since F Lydian has the same key signature as C major, the melody seems to float between the two, making it sound ethereal. Additionally, whenever it sounds like C major, the F and C harmonies seem no longer to be I-V, but IV-I, which is the "amen" cadence at the end of Protestant hymns. Which is obviously appropriate to a song of thanksgiving.

Got that? If so, please explain it to Vernon.

Vernon sets the needle down.

Yale plays it extremely slowly. He approves. May this movement truly never end. It begins, indeed, sounding like a hymn. But even with the score in his lap, even after having laboriously picked out the chords on the piano, he can't convince himself that it sounds like anything other than C major. For example, the end of the second strain, a C major chord, sounds like home. The fourth strain, which in many hymns would be the final one, does end on an F triad, but it doesn't sound, to Vernon, like the final cadence, and in fact Beethoven continues into a fifth strain, which on the last chord modulates to A major and then leads in the next measure to a new melody—marked "Feeling New Strength"—which is in D major.

Well—who cares. It's one of the most beautiful passages in the world, and F Lydian to A major to D major doesn't explain a damn thing. Some musicians say C major sounds joyful, E-flat major heroic, F major pastoral. Vernon can't hear any of that. He feels like a purblind man who can glimpse just enough of outlines and shadows to wonder agonizingly what forms and colors are.

He listens. He has thought for years that he would like to hear this movement on his deathbed. *Note to self: leave a note.*

His father used to say, whenever you make a to-do list, begin it with *#1: Make a List.* That way, when you finish writing the list, you can cross off the first item.

God, he misses his father.

He closes the score, closes his eyes, keeps listening. The delicate dance of new strength—he sees Beethoven tottering on his pins around his squalid room—is followed by the hymn again, the voices weaving around each other in a more complicated way. Then another dance, and then the hymn again, with even more complication, but still so open, so guileless, so grateful. It gets to the long crescendo, where the first violin edges higher and higher, and the chords get more insistent, like hands reaching up, fingers stretched as far as they will go, and the chords repeat themselves, the fingers will stretch no farther, no matter how they try. And this always happens, right here—he is weeping. So fragile, so yearning, so mortal.

. . .

A STORY Vernon's dad used to tell:

A man is out on a bird hunt. Nothing is going his way. The water-fowl near his stand have disappeared. The field birds flush before he creeps close enough. Now it's evening, and he's walking home through the woods, tired and discouraged. His path takes him across a log bridg-ing a stream. When he reaches the midpoint he sees a catfish below him, just under the surface. The man doesn't have a fishing pole with him, but he has his bird gun. He raises the gun to his shoulder. Now, he likes to think he's a clever man, and it occurs to him that if he fires the gun, the recoil will knock him off the log. After pondering the problem, he realizes he can lean forward until he's off-balance, then shoot, and the recoil will push him back upright. He knows his gun; he's confident he'll be able to sense the right moment to fire. So, sight-ing on the fish, he leans forward and begins to fall. He pulls the trigger. The gun misfires and he topples into the stream.

One of the last things Vernon did at RAND, when he had more or less stopped work on his real project involving the aerodynamics of ICBMs, was to double-check the data from a civil defense study headed up by Herman Kahn. Vernon was drawn to Kahn's work because it seemed the epitome of what he had come to loathe about RAND. When engineers express contempt for aspects of a proposal, they talk about "hand-waving"—the moment when the idea guys get vague on the de-tails of how one might actually bring into working existence that winged pig they're dreaming of. Kahn, RAND's jovial clown peddling patter and pixie-dust magic at the generals' parties, was a hand-waver *par excel-lence.*

This must have been the spring of 1958, and the idea was that any American threat of escalation during a crisis would be more credible if the United States had in place a robust civil defense program—i.e., go ahead and nuke us, you Soviet savages, we'll ride it out in our shelters and then turn everything east of the Urals into a glass plain of trinitite. For rural areas, small towns, and suburbs, fallout shelters like the one Vernon is sitting in right now would be sufficient, but cities would need blast shelters. Kahn actually envisioned a future in which much of the US population would have to descend into shelters two or three times a decade. He talked about the strategic danger of a "mine gap"—whether the Soviets had more and deeper mines than we did, to hide their people in. So he hired an outside engineering firm to evaluate the feasibility of excavating shelter space for four million people in the bedrock under Manhattan. The plan called for a network of chambers 800 feet below the surface, providing 20 square feet per person, a 90-day supply of food and water, power generators, etc. There would be 91 entrances spaced regularly around the island, so that no residents would be farther than a ten-minute walk from the nearest entrance.

Since one aim of the study was to evaluate cost, Kahn postulated that humankind might find new uses for the crushed rock produced by the excavation. And since RAND really did let its employees pursue their private passions, Vernon spent a grimly hilarious two days calculating the volumes of Manhattan mica schist, Fordham gneiss, and Inwood marble likely to be brought to the surface, and then investigating what firms might be interested in buying it. It turns out that crushed mica schist— by far the bulk of the product, somewhere in the neighborhood of one billion cubic feet—is lousy for road construction, foundation work, landscaping, etc, because it cleaves in planes. For the same reason, it's rarely used as dimension stone in construction. On the other hand, it can be converted to vermiculite, which is that tuff-like stuff they mix into potting soil for water retention. So maybe the Great Manhattan Shelter could pay for itself by supplementing victory gardens across the country, after the Soviets bombed US agriculture back to the Stone Age.

The hand-waving here didn't involve technical details of construction,

which were well known and trivial, but pie-in-the-sky political and social expectations. The same realpolitikniks who had rightly scoffed at calls
for World Government somehow expected US politicians and the American public to act with long-range foresight, accepting immense expen-
diture, to defend against an emergency no one had ever experienced nor
could imagine. Part of Kahn's Manhattan study calculated how quickly
residents in high-rises could descend using preexisting elevators—but it
assumed that people would wait their turns. Evacuation plans to outlying areas proposed that families with even-numbered license plates wait
until all the odd-numbered people went first. They proposed that all
drivers have printed on their car registration their designated shelter,
which assumed that people would be willing to drive past a nearby
shelter in the hopes of reaching a farther one before the x-rays charred
them and their children. Someone working on Kahn's study worried that
Manhattanites might saunter to shelters *too slowly* and proposed that the
US detonate an atom bomb high over the city to get them moving.

Vernon knows all too well that logical people are prone to fantasies of
control. *Don't worry, dummies! I've got it all figured out!* Only experience
can show us what our logic has failed to anticipate. The gun misfires
and we fall into the stream. Conan Doyle didn't understand this. He had
Holmes say to Watson, "When you have eliminated the impossible, whatever remains, however improbable, must be the truth." Bullshit, Sherlock. It's more likely there's a possibility that hasn't occurred to you.
Charles Schultz knows better. Lucy spots a butterfly on the sidewalk
and enthuses to Linus about its long migration from Brazil. Linus looks
more closely and discovers it's a potato chip. Lucy responds like any scientist wedded to her paradigm: "Well, I'll be! I wonder how a potato
chip got all the way up here from Brazil."

No, no, the real world—human society, this moment, the cosmos—
will always be surprising to the human mind, our theories one step

behind. Our lifelong job is to find that one tiny island on whose beach we can spell out with driftwood *This is true*, and never turn our back on the unsoundable sea.

He contemplates his Beethovens. The opus numbers of the late quartets don't match chronology. Beethoven finished Opus 127 first, then 132. After that came 130, which ended with the Grosse Fuge, then 131 and 135. Friends advised Beethoven to detach from 130 the Grosse Fuge—too long, too strange, too unplayable—and he acceded. The Fuge was published separately as Opus 133, and Beethoven wrote a shorter, cheerier final movement for 130. Friends applauded. Beethoven died. Vernon will save 130 and the Grosse Fuge for last, which means it's time for Opus 131, the C-sharp minor. It's said that this was Beethoven's favorite, which shows once more what a dunderhead Vernon is. Yes, it's great, but he's always thought 132 and 130 were greater.

He bought the Végh Quartet recordings in 1973, on Telefunken, and their renditions are among his favorites. They play with a stolidity that at first seems somnolent, all their tempi slower than other quartets. But they win you over. Nothing is showy, but everything is there. He takes the box down from the shelf, looks at the photo on the cover. Four old men, padded asses in chairs, leading worthwhile lives. He slips side five out, handles it immaculately, cleans it meticulously, places it on the turntable.

After Beethoven received the sacraments, he uttered what he thought would be his last words to the admirers crowding the bed: *"Plaudite, amici, comedia finita est."* Pretty corny. He'd probably thought it up weeks before. But life is surprising. He didn't die that night, and the following morning a gift of wine arrived from his publisher. Gazing on all that delicious booze, delirious, he uttered his actual last words: "Pity! Too late!"

Vernon's father woke up in his own bed on an everyday morning and uttered his final words: "I feel funny."

According to Mark, Susan's last word was "Figures."

That sounds so much like her.

Vernon's? He hopes it will be, "Play that Holy Song of Thanksgiving again, Sam."

He sets the needle down, leans back in his chair. Glances warily around for Vargas, but the cat is nowhere to be seen. The first violin begins alone, playing yet another motif featuring a lingering leading tone. This time it's B-sharp, wanting more than anything to be C-sharp.

There's a poem he memorized years ago and now fervently wishes he could get out of his head:

> Jenny kiss'd me when we met,
> Jumping from the chair she sat in;
> Time, you thief, who love to get
> Sweets into your list, put that in!
> Say I'm weary, say I'm sad,
> Say that health and wealth have missed me,
> Say I'm growing old, but add
> Jenny kiss'd me.

WHEN THE PIECE is over, he throws Vargas off (goddamnit) and climbs the stairs, concentrating on his feet. Gen is at the kitchen table, smoking a cigarette, reading a mystery. "There you are," she says, cheerfully enough. "What have you been doing?"

"Paying bills."

"Should I make you something for lunch?"

"I can fend for myself."

"I'm about to go to the Stop and Shop, I'm almost out of cigarettes. If you want anything, put it on the list. I'll get milk for your cereal. Did you take your pills this morning?"

"Yes."

"Isn't it time to take them again?"

"I suppose it is."

"I'll get them." She springs up, darts into the dining room, returns with the pillbox. So spry. And as slender as when he met her. "You're going to fall down those basement steps one day."

"I hold on to the handrail."

"You should move your stereo and records up into the dining room. I'll help you."

"I like it down there."

"Suit yourself. But if you fall down those stairs, I'll be the one who has to take care of you." Get your fat, injured self out of my sight.

"I won't fall down the stairs."

"You're the one who's always said it's illogical to say an accident won't happen."

"I said that to children. I'm not a child."

"You certainly act like one sometimes."

And not a gray hair on her head. Truly, not one. Her mother always proudly claimed there was Cherokee blood in the family. The stupid old biddy's head would have exploded at the suggestion there might be black blood.

"Anyway, I'm off to do the shopping."

And she's gone.

She runs on cigarettes. And high-octane dudgeon. She's much smarter than her mother was, but otherwise a chip off the block.

Vernon gets out crackers and cheese, a bottle of beer. He finds a ball game on the portable on the kitchen table, watches a couple of innings, eats too much. Some writer said once about some woman, "She had a whim of iron." His and Gen's parents are all dead now. His sister Patty died of cancer nearly twenty years ago. Julian's still alive, living with his boyfriend somewhere in California, but he and Vernon haven't communicated in years. Long ago, Vernon was giving his brother a monthly check to help with his support while he attended a school for interior design. Then Julian dropped out, but didn't tell Vernon and kept taking the money. Vernon had to learn the truth from Patty. When confronted, Julian didn't seem to think he'd done anything wrong. The amount of money hadn't changed, so what did it matter to Vernon?

Patty, when she had cancer, wrote to Vernon, "I wish you and Julian could reconcile your differences. When I am gone, I'm afraid he'll end up all alone."

Yes, well, some people deserve to be alone.

He contemplates calling Mark, but doesn't have a good reason.

This surprising world. His old vacuum-tube radio upstairs has the CONELRAD logo stamped on the dial at 640 and 1240 kHz. If the Soviets had attacked, all broadcasting would have shut down except at those two frequencies, and the stations using them would have operated round-robin, so that enemy bombers wouldn't be able to home in on any one signal and target its host city. A smart plan, thought up by a team of smarties. The broadcasting stations would direct populations to shelters, engineered and constructed by more smarties. People would wait their turn, drive sensibly in their millions, written directions in hand, with a full tank of gas they'd stored in their garage ahead of time. In the back seat, Sally, Dick, and Jane would be troopers, despite the fact that Spot had been left behind. Civil defense volunteers in their thousands would be distributed sensibly all over the road network, to help the lame, hurry the halt, inform the lost. They would not spend one distracting second thinking about seeking shelter themselves.

Except the shelters were never built. All those blueprints, studies, salaries. How far did we get? At the top of basement stairs in public buildings, we put up signs and printed stencils—three triangles, Trinity squared, pointing down to the underworld. Nearly every school had a stencil, because our children are important. And like the civil defense logo on Vernon's radio, many of those stencils and metal signs are still there, faded or rusting, because who wants to spend money to get rid of them? They don't lead down to food or water, or dosimeters or Geiger counters, or baffle walls for keeping out Chinese demons. They never did. All that's ever been down there is basement.

And now idiots think Reagan's anti-missile system will work, when all it does is relocate that chimerical shelter in the sky. After thirty years of designing balloon and rocket flights with instrumentation that must remain directed toward the Sun, Vernon knows something about pointer systems. And after RAND, he knows something about the flight of ICBMs. In fact, these are pretty much his only two islets in the vast, mysterious sea. And he'll signal with driftwood to anyone who will pay attention, which includes precisely no one who matters: dependable in-flight interception of an ICBM is impossible.

"But, you know," idiots have said to him, "we thought it was impossible to put someone on the Moon."

"That was acknowledged to be difficult, not impossible."

"But surely, if we don't try, how can we—"

"Do you know anything about the flight characteristics of an ICBM?"

"No, but—"

"You're right. You don't know. So your opinion is worthless."

Yet here we go, obeying that doddering fool's whim of iron: more studies, more salaries. Because our children are still important to us. Almost as important as our illusions.

Vernon puts his plate in the dishwasher, his bottle in the recycling tub. Redescends the basement stairs, holding on to the handrail for dear life.

Patty got the news about her bone marrow cancer when she was forty-seven. Two boys still in school. "Pray for me," she wrote to Vernon. She'd always liked him more than he'd liked her. Life could be sad that way. Of course he would have prayed for her, if he'd believed in any of that nonsense. He hoped her religion comforted her. As for him, he'll have to lose a lot more of his marbles for any consolation to come to him from that quarter.

In 1953 and 1955, the Federal Civil Defense Agency ran Operations Doorstep and Cue, in conjunction with atomic bomb tests run by the AEC. In the first, they built two wood-frame houses at 3500 and 7500 feet respectively from the shot tower, placed mannequins in them and filmed what happened when the bomb went off. The nearer house collapsed, which was expected, and in fact desired, because the FCDA was testing whether people in a lean-to shelter in the basement might survive the destruction of the house above them. (They concluded there was a good chance.) In the more ambitious Operation Cue, the FCDA built a wood-frame house, a brick house, and a concrete-block house—why the test wasn't called Operation Big Bad Wolf, Vernon will never understand—plus power lines, a working electrical substation, a propane storage site, and two radio towers. They spread a few dozen cars around, put mannequins in the cars and in the houses, this time with canned food to test afterward for radioactivity, and lined up more mannequins outside, facing toward the blast wearing different types and colors of clothing. They called this bigger settlement Survival Town, and the newsreels featured can-do narration detailing the relatively modest preparations citizens could make to help them get through a holocaust in one piece.

But all anyone remembers from those films is two clips. The first is of the nearer wood-frame house in Operation Doorstep. It might be any suburban home of the northeast US, built in colonial style of white clapboard. It stands two-thirds of a mile away from a 16-kiloton explosion. At the instant of detonation, the house is bathed in a weirdly stark light that makes it look, frighteningly and appropriately, like a toy model. An instant later, the paint all across the front lifts off, burning blackly from the x-ray flash. Two seconds after that, the blast wave hits and the house dissolves, leaving nothing behind other than—well, its doorstep.

The second clip is filmed from inside one of the houses in Operation Cue. A mannequin of a boy maybe ten years old has been placed near a window. He's wearing what might be a dosimeter on a long chain around his neck. Farther from the window and partly out of the frame sits his mother, who is opening one hand toward him. The Venetian blinds have been closed to test whether they will effectively shield the boy from the x-ray flash. When the flash comes, the blinds start to smoke, and vaporized plastic billows into the room as the light darkens from the approaching dust cloud. But the boy appears to be unhurt. That is, his face isn't smoking. Then the blast wave hits and in an instant everything in the room—boy, mother, sofa, recording camera—is annihilated.

The films were propaganda designed to inspire in viewers the confidence and determination to protect themselves. Instead, they shocked everyone into hopelessness and inaction. No one, in the years afterward, has ever called that eerie settlement Survival Town. It's always referred to as Doom Town. See, Sherlock? Surprise.

In 1954, Susan was born with strontium-90 in her skeleton. Mark, in 1959, was born with more. Half-life, 29 years. Effect, increased incidence of bone cancer and leukemia. By 1963, children in the United States were being born with 50 times the level of strontium-90 in their bodies compared with those born before 1950. By 1960, the pasteurized milk in sterilized glass bottles delivered to the back door every third day by the immaculate dairyman dressed in white contained iodine-131. Half-life, eight days. Effect, increased incidence of thyroid cancer. This is to say nothing of the army troops deliberately and openly exposed, or the downwind civilian populations deliberately and secretly exposed. Not one becquerel of this was thanks to the Soviets. No, it was thanks to our own military, thanks to Buster-Jangle, Tumbler-Snapper, Upshot-Knothole, Teapot, Plumbbob, Hardtack. Scrappy names for our team of streetfighting little rascals.

In the fifties, newspaper ads for suburban housing developments touted the fact that they were outside the radiation zone. While the pasty and sedentary Herman Kahn indulged fantasies of the entire population living underground, others proposed redesigning our cities as donuts, with industry and residential areas in a ring around a hollow core, so that Soviets would either obliterate the worthless center or have to waste megatonnage dropping bombs ring-around-the-rosy style. As with all other theories of civil defense, no one except paid consultants gave this plan a second thought. Then white people in the sixties accomplished it magnificently, not in order to escape the bomb, but to escape the blacks. Maybe some cultural memory lingered, since suburbanites began referring to inner-city ghettos as "bombed-out areas." Surprise.

Now smarty-pants Vernon can't count his own pills. At night, instead of dreaming he can fly, he dreams of a new impossible thing: that he can run. He examines his Beethovens in the catacomb they built him for free.

After Végh, he bought a set by the Bartók Quartet, on Hungaroton. By then, Mark was in high school getting straight As and Susan was God knows where. She'd dropped out of Tufts after one semester, lived for a while in Somerville, maybe waitressing—she'd more or less stopped talking to either Vernon or Imogen—then hopped on a plane at twenty and flew to Sri Lanka. She called from the airport to say nothing beyond the fact that she was going. Mark probably knew more, but both Imogen and Vernon saw that the one mistake they could perhaps *not* make was to try to leverage Susan's lingering feelings for her brother. She would no doubt have sworn him to secrecy.

The Bartók Quartet was a return to old-school dominance by the first violin. Vernon went back to listening to the Végh and the Yale, and in 1977 bought a reissue on the Columbia label of historic EMI recordings done by the Budapest in the 1930s. By this point Vernon owned seven complete sets, and he was about to pay for Mark's college, so with a mixture of embarrassment and regret he decided he'd indulged himself enough. But then Mark graduated in 1981, so in 1983 Vernon bought the complete set by the Cleveland Quartet on RCA Red Seal.

He pulls it down, slips out Opus 135.

Where was Susan in 1983? In Copenhagen, in that squatters' settlement? Or that nutty organic Belgian farm run by that manipulative deviant? She'd been back in the US for a couple of years around 1980, mainly on the West Coast, but she did come home for one of the Christmases. She and her mother smoked and argued politics—Imogen left-wing, Susan left-fringe—and Susan radiated more than a tinge of superiority regarding her wide experience of the world, compared with the parochial shut-ins she called her parents. But she hugged them both when she left and from then on she sent a couple of letters a year. Maybe she was finally growing up, learning not to blame every last thing on her upbringing. Toward the end she even went back to college. She was in so many ways a stranger. And in other ways, the same stubbornly independent child and turbulent teenager he'd been so angry at so often, and now unaccountably missed.

Vernon cradles the disk, wipes it clean, places it gently on the turntable.

Her letters were terse, mostly information about where she was and the bald assertion that she was fine, but in one of the last ones she added a postscript, *hey dad, I'm often reminded here of that thing you always used to say, that not all the crazy people are locked up; this place would drive you up the wall*. Vernon was surprised how moved he was that she'd remembered anything he'd ever said. Or that she thought of him at all in her daily life.

He lowers the needle. Technically speaking, this set just might be his favorite. And artistically it's right up there. Cleveland plays gorgeous fortes, even when the first violin is sky-high. And they aren't slaves to virtuosity, i.e., they don't play the fast movements too fucking fast. The last of the lates, and almost the last thing Beethoven composed, Opus

135 is quieter than the others. To Vernon's ears it has always sounded like the start of a new cycle that was cut short, rather than the end of this one. The calm before a new and unimaginable storm. Christ, what the world lost when he died. Or maybe that's not the right way to think of it. Someone wrote somewhere—was it E. M. Forster?—"Great art doesn't fill a need, it creates one. No one needed Beethoven's Fifth until he wrote it. But once he wrote it, we couldn't live without it."

He listens. The insouciant Allegretto, built out of scraps. The playful Vivace, which is surely meant to sound like country fiddlers that never can quite get on the same beat. The Lento, simplest and most peaceful of all his slow movements. All this written by a tortured, dying man. Astonishing. And now the final movement, at the head of which Beethoven wrote what seemed to be a programmatic explanation: *The Difficult Decision*. Above the opening three-note phrase of the Grave, which rises anxiously, he wrote *Must it be?* And above the emphatic Allegro motif, which is the same phrase turned upside down, he wrote *It must be!* For years and years, Vernon took this as Beethoven's anguished questioning of his mortality, followed by a profound acceptance, leading—so touchingly, so heroically—to joy. Then he read in *The Beethoven Companion* that it was all a joke, that some rich dumbass named Dembscher wanted to have the Opus 130 played at his house, but hadn't subscribed to the piece's premiere, so Beethoven refused to loan him the parts. When he asked through a friend what he might do to be forgiven, Beethoven responded that he could start by paying the goddamn subscription fee, which was fifty florins. Dembscher replied with such a miserable and weaselly "Must it be?" that Beethoven gleefully wrote a canon to the words, "It must be! Yes, yes, yes! Fork over the bucks! It must be!"

The recording ends. He slips the disk back into the sleeve. Is Gen back? Maybe he could help her put the groceries away. He turns out the desklight, heads up the stairs. He again considers calling Mark, but he still can't think of a good reason. Maybe he could ask him about that second subject in the last movement, why it sounds so American. Mark always understood music better than Vernon. He tries not to regret that Mark became an astronomer rather than a concert pianist. Another contest Gen won, though he shouldn't think of it that way.

At the top of the stairs, Vernon listens. "Gen?"

Silence.

He finds himself thinking for some unaccountable reason—maybe it was RCA's red seal—of a naval rule he first learned in the service: Red, Right, Return. Meaning, when your ship is returning to port, keep the red buoy on your right. How clever, the person who devised that rule, with its alliterative mnemonic to help even the idiots. Vernon has always admired simple ingenuity more than he can ever get anybody else to understand.

ANOTHER EVENING. The autumn weather has turned cold. Vernon is going through the house closing storm windows. He can't handle the leaves in the yard anymore. He used to rake them to the roadside and burn them. Mark loved watching that when he was little, jumping up and down and flapping his arms. Then the town outlawed burning, and it took a week to bag it all. Now a lawn company does it. Three or four young men that look Latino will arrive unannounced on a November day and clear the whole property in five hours.

A wet and windy night. The old sashes rattle, scaring Yolanda, who's hiding under the living room couch. No idea where Llosa is, but Vargas is staying in Vernon's vicinity. Gen is at Carlos's apartment again. Seems the old rogue has a cold. She's gone to brew him tea with lemon and honey, make him comfy, warm his ascot.

Behold! I tell you a mystery. We shall not all sleep . . .

Vernon finds himself at the end of his circuit in the dining room they never use, where the old upright is. Mark used to practice for an hour before school, then another hour in the afternoon. What a diligent kid. Vernon sits at the piano. (She dotes on him—that ridiculous ascot.) He finally got around to learning a few weeks ago what a Neapolitan sixth was, so he picks out a C minor chord, then plays the N6, which is what steely-eyed music men call it. Beethoven inserted the Neapolitan sixth several times into the *Moonlight Sonata*, and when Vernon was listening to a performance by Claudio Arrau the other day, he actually managed to hear it. Which made him feel pretty good. Cat on his chest, Neapolitan sixth in his ear—the life!

Vernon depresses the keys of a C minor chord gently, so that the strings don't sound. Then he whoops. The sound floating from the piano is a C minor chord. Magic. "Everything we do is music," John Cage used to say. Now Vernon depresses the damper pedal, so that all the strings are free to vibrate, and barks, "Testing!" A recognizable ghost of his own particular vocal timbre rises from the casing. Is he just imagining it or, if he speaks a short word quickly enough, can he discern the actual word coming off the strings? "You!" he barks. "Me!" Nope, he's imagining it.

Charles Ives loved his father. Alone among the unimaginative members of their family, he and George Ives were kindred spirits. Ives's father was a Civil War trumpeter and afterward a town bandleader, and he lived Cage's idea a hundred years before Cage. He tried to imitate the clacking of a train's wheels on a violin. He knew that the sound of the church bells near his house was a mix of tones and overtones, so he searched for a combination of keys on the piano that would reproduce it. He owned a slide trumpet, made specially for him, so that he could follow a church congregation up or down in pitch, no matter how far off-key they sang. Years later, his son composed a psalm setting in which one chorus remains in the starting key while a second modulates upward. It's intended to recall the revival meetings of Ives's youth, where spiritual excitement caused people to sing sharp. Father and son. Toward the end of his composing life, Charles Ives said that whenever he wrote music he heard somewhere in the back of his mind a brass band with angelic wings. He was thinking of his father's band.

Vernon touches the keys again. He has wanted for years to find a combination of notes that sounds like a train whistle. Like Ives's father, he has never found it. He remembers when he was a boy lying in bed, listening to the Norfolk & Western coal train coming into town. Half a mile from his house, by the old colored cemetery, the belt line split off from the main line, and the engineer would sound the whistle before hitting the switch. Vernon will never forget that sleepy clatter and the squealing cry. Different engineers voiced it differently, depending on how they pulled the cord. Julian would be dead asleep in the other bed. He always went out like a light.

That little house with its trio of silly gooses and his poor, patient father. Everyone but Vernon hung on him like a clutch of drowning children. When his father died, Vernon was the only one left with a lick of sense, and he understands now, looking back, that his lifelong project has been to avoid letting them drag him under, too. He saw his sister Patty as little as possible. Julian handed him the gift of his betrayal over the school money, so Vernon could wash his hands of him. And when his mother lost her teaspoonful of wits and never said anything anymore but "Isn't that nice?" and "Have we met?," she was rolled into a nursing home near where Patty lived with her husband, Ray, and vegetated there for twenty years. In lieu of visiting, Vernon sent money. Patty also avoided her mother. After all, she'd grown up with her. It was son-in-law Ray who went twice a week, sat with her, consulted with the staff. Over the years he managed to keep writing letters to Vernon, despite never having anything to report. Everything we do is music.

Vernon checks the clock on the kitchen wall. Eight-thirty. Chattering and drinking. *Hola, Carlos!* His cold won't keep him away from the wine. If he even has a cold.

He heads down to the study, leaving the door at the top of the stairs ajar so that Vargas can pretend to remember some unrelated thing he needs to accomplish in the basement. And people say cats have no personality. Of course he went to his mother's funeral. He's not *that* bad. None of the older relatives were still around to object, so they cremated her. It was the last time he saw Julian, who was there with Peter, his boyfriend of many years. Vernon understands that homosexuals are just people, and he agrees they ought to have their rights. Peter, as far as Vernon can tell, has made Julian happy, which is no easy task. He only wished, at the funeral, that Peter hadn't been so goddamn poofy.

Here's a terrifying detail from the bombing of Nagasaki: years after the radiation victims were cremated, it was discovered that their ashes had turned pitch black.

He pulls down the Lindsay box. Time at last for Opus 130.

There's that thing Oppenheimer always claimed he thought at the moment the first bomb exploded at Trinity, a line from the Bhagavad Gita: "I am become Death, destroyer of worlds." What a dandified fancypants. What he really said at the time, according to witnesses, was, "It worked." Which reminds Vernon of something he read in an oral history book about Hiroshima. A Japanese man from an outlying area climbed a hill on the morning after the bombing and looked out over the plain where the city was supposed to be. He was so stunned, the only thing his mind could formulate, over and over, was, "It's gone."

It worked.

It's gone.

In the moments after the bomb went off at Trinity, while other scientists were gazing awestruck at the mushroom cloud and Oppenheimer was ransacking his mind for a pretentious quote, Fermi was dropping scraps of notebook paper and watching how far the wind from the blast carried them. From that, he made a rough calculation of the kilotonnage of the explosion, and came within a factor of two of the correct answer. Simple ingenuity. There won't even *be* any Hiroshimas.

Vernon opens the box. He bought the Lindsay Quartet recordings in 1984. Two years later he was diagnosed with Parkinson's, and he hasn't bought any Beethovens since. Maybe he realized, with nine sets, that he already had more than he could take with him. Typical Musical Heritage Society—the recording quality is good, the performances are great, the packaging is shit. Get this, they actually managed to put the wrong labels on the disks. Opus 130 is on the disk labeled as 132. 132 is labeled 131. 131 is labeled 130. Unbelievable. Vernon slips out the right fucking disk because he relabeled them, maintaining order and minimal standards in the universe.

There's something the physicist Freeman Dyson liked to quote, something from a children's book about an imaginary land: "There's a dreadful law here—it was made by mistake, but there it is—that if anyone asks for machinery they have to have it and keep on using it." Vernon was dragged into Star Wars in his final years at work. He'd thought he'd escaped all that, but the Air Force was still paying his salary. Tracking ICBMs by their infrared emissions is difficult because infrared saturates the Earth's atmosphere, but ICBMs also produce UV, about which Vernon is one of the world experts. His bosses at the lab told him that if we wanted to continue to get funding, he had to convince the brass that his research would help them shoot down missiles. So there he was, a fat old man with his obsolete Ivorite Keuffel and Esser slide rule, and his spotless research in his innocent filing cabinet, standing in front of a bar of blockheaded generals and lying to them like Herman Kahn. Our end is in our beginning.

He lowers the needle.

The more Vernon has listened to this piece—perhaps forty times so far—the more convinced he is that Beethoven was wrong to listen to his dumbass friends and divorce the Grosse Fuge from it. Apparently others think so, too, since many quartets, like the Lindsay, have reverted to the original version. Not that Vernon understands the Grosse Fuge. Far from it.

Jesus, he loves the way these four Brits play. The second movement, the Presto, is one of those driving pieces Beethoven conjures out of nothing, the tiniest shred of a motif. The third, the Andante, oh god . . . it's so beautiful. The first statement of the theme (is it a gavotte? an allemand?) is by the viola, and in the old days of first-violin tyranny you could never hear it properly. (Wait—could it be a bourrée?) There's a moment where the music halts on a chord in a new key and then executes these dropping fourths that sound like an annunciation, like the end of a recitative in *Messiah* just before the trumpet sounds (*We shall not all sleep, but we shall all be changed, in a moment, in the twinkling of an eye*) and then a couple of measures later, everyone stops playing except for the first violin, which hits an accented note that sounds completely out of the key, Vernon has always wondered if it's a tritone, but . . . Holy shit! He just now figured it out, just this moment—it's a Neapolitan 6th!

Mark, listen—!

Time rushes on, to the fourth movement, Alla danza tedesca, serene and lovely, and then the side is over. Vernon sweeps Vargas off his stomach—the cat pooled against the score, blocking the bottom stanza with his butt—gets up to flip the record. "No," he says to Vargas, walling off his lap with the sheet music. "I mean it."

Now the Cavatina. Beethoven told an acquaintance he had never written anything that moved him so much. In the middle there's an eerie passage he marked "Afflicted," in which the lower instruments keep time in glacial eighth-note triplets like the tick of a cosmic clock, while the violin, in conflicting sixteenths, plays a halting series of notes that sound uncannily like a human voice, wandering and crying, unable even to formulate a question, let alone find an answer. (No facile "It Must Be!" comforts here.) Of all the violinists of all the quartets, Lindsay's Peter Cropper best brings out a feeling of anguished incomprehension. He somehow can make a single note sound bereft. Then the opening song returns, and though it's mainly a song of mourning, toward the end it rises to the hopeful major third above the tonic, first in the violin, then the cello. The piece dies slowly into silence on this same major third.

The Cavatina is the last piece of music on the Golden Record that went into space with the two Voyager probes. (It occurs to Vernon that Mark might not know this, since he was only a teenager when the Voyagers lifted off. That might be a good reason to call . . .) The record was nothing but a public relations stunt by Carl Sagan, as there's essentially no chance that an intelligent extraterrestrial, even if the galaxy were crawling with them, would stumble across this microscopic mote in the vastness of space. But Sagan's a genius. Even Vernon, against his better judgment, kind of loves the idea of the Golden Record. That lonely, frightened voice of Beethoven's cavatina, deciding at the last moment to choose hope, sailing out of the solar system at 17 kilometers per second, having to wait 40,000 years before encountering another star system, Gliese 445—where maybe the unfathomable aliens are playing the Grosse Fuge.

Speak of the devil, here it comes, starting on that same hopeful G that ended the Cavatina, but twisting it immediately—up a half step, then jumping up a sixth and down a half step, repeating—into something serpentine and sinister. (Word through the grapevine is that Sagan is dying.) Vernon will never understand the Grosse Fuge. Sixteen minutes of cacophony. But maybe that's the point. Maybe here, only here, Beethoven deliberately stepped beyond the edge of the comprehensible. (He's only sixty-two. Some kind of cancer, they say. Maybe it was electromagnetic signals from outer space, kissing him back.)

Fugues are probably the most orderly form of composition that exists. Beethoven grew up playing Bach fugues. He wrote more and more of his own as he turned old and deaf, and failed in all his loves, and discovered his life was shit. So maybe this piece is about life's chaos, and the attempt of the mind—never succeeding, but forever trying—to grasp it. Look, the most chaotic part is the first 158 measures. They play like a gradual breakdown of order, beginning in unison, then launching into a double fugue that's jarring and complicated to begin with, then introducing polyrhythms with triplets, then adding a layer of sixteenths, and finally going completely off the rails with hammering triplets fighting against the fugue subject now racing along at four times its original speed and accented off the beat.

Then what happens? The four shouting voices come to a sudden halt, and starting in measure 159 they proceed, pianissimo, to play steady, soothing sixteenths, with much simpler harmonies, and it sounds—doesn't it?—like the voices are weaving together something, trying to patch up the hole in the space-time fabric. The fugue subject returns, but quiet, tamed, and now plays against itself with a one-measure delay, and suddenly it seems tuneful, the two voices cooperating. Then the four instruments slip into unison and die down into repeated notes murmuring and rocking, getting simpler and simpler. *There, there. Everything makes sense.*

Then—boom! The fugue returns, still strange, and as it did in the beginning of the movement, it insists on getting stranger. But—and here's the point—it never gets *as* strange. It sounds like a version of the fugue that's trying to accommodate, at least a little, the plea for order that preceded it. More weaving happens, and there's a dance-like bit that comes in a couple of times, but the basic idea is the same: unruliness contained, just barely, by order. And when the serpentine theme comes back fortissimo unison for the final time, something wonderful happens (*listen!*): it's the same chromatic tune, seemingly unmoored from any key, but it sails past its previous ending and somehow, still sounding like itself, it lands clearly in B-flat major, the key of trumpet fanfares, the home key of the whole quartet. And the coda takes the B-flat ball and runs for the end zone, dodging and weaving past weird arabesques and trills and ending on an exuberant succession of dominant and tonic chords like any normal nineteenth-century piece. Voilà!

Vernon leans back, eyes on the ceiling, exalted.

The tone arm swings, the turntable shuts off.

Silence.

He contemplates the ceiling for a long while.

And then Beethoven died.

And the Cavatina passed Neptune seven years ago.

Vernon levers himself up, aching in his lower back. Puts the record away, turns out the light. Climbs up from the underworld. "Vargas? Oh, there you are." He lets the cat brush past him, closes the basement door.

Past eleven, and no sign of Imogen. He hovers for a minute in the hallway off the kitchen. Then goes and opens the front door. Stands inside the screen door, listening. (Oops. He forgot to put on the storm door here.) The wind has died down. He hears water dripping from the gutters, the eaves, the silver maple tree. He hears the granular hiss of a passing car's tires on the wet pavement. He hears the hum of the transformer on the telephone pole across the street. He isolates the sound of one drip from the eaves and another drip from a tree branch and listens to their interference pattern. Six to five. If they were sound waves, they would make a minor third.

He wishes he could have prayed for his sister.

He remembers a discussion in the fifties among civil defense planners, about how to solve the problem of identifying dead schoolchildren after a nuclear attack. One suggestion was to tattoo serial numbers on them ahead of time, but that recalled the Holocaust, and anyway, no one would be able to read tattoos on charred skin. Another was to have mothers sew their names into school clothing. But the clothes would burn right off the bodies, everyone knew that. They eventually settled on metal tags that the kids would wear around their necks. Sure, some of them would turn white hot for a while, sizzle down through flesh, others would melt. But most would remain readable. They ran ads in magazines, picturing a boy holding his tag up to a soldier who might be his dad: "See? It's just like yours." All society an armed camp, like the Spartans.

There's a dreadful law here.

He listens for a while longer to water falling on everything.

All his life, Charles Ives dreamed about composing what he conceived as his most important piece. He envisioned immense orchestras and choirs arrayed on mountaintops and in valleys, thundering out something magical and ineffable that would somehow capture, or maybe reawaken, the music of the world, the music of the spheres. He planned to call it *The Universe Symphony*. When he was old and suffering from dementia, and knew he would never write it, he said to his wife, "It's all there—the mountains and the fields. If only I could have done it."

It's time to look away. For Ives's sake, Vernon is weeping.

2006

He called it *giving him the runaround*. Meaning what you were saying had no merit as an argument, but was merely pointless obstinacy.

She said to him once, "You can argue better than I can."

To which he replied, "No, I can *think* better than you can."

He always won. And when you tried to walk away, because you knew that no matter what you said, he'd win, he would follow you from room to room. When you screamed at him, he'd look shocked and he would retreat, he would wait, he might even apologize for making you angry, then he'd assume a mild tone and start up again. He didn't just want to win, he wanted you to acknowledge that he'd won. It wasn't enough to surrender, you had to join his side. And if you said, "You're right, you win," he'd say, "You're just saying that to shut me up," and if you said, "You're right again," he accused you of being frivolous. It wasn't enough to join his side, you had to do it sincerely. You had to *really* lose.

Susan couldn't bear him. The moment she realized a conversation had turned into an argument, and therefore all paths through the maze led to his victory, she'd say, "Fuck you, Dad." No matter how he responded, she would again say, "Fuck you, Dad." It was kind of beautiful. It was like the soldier under torture who keeps repeating name, rank, and serial number. It made him so apoplectic, he was the one who finally had to give up.

Imogen wonders if she got married just so that she could have children. She wonders if she got married because Mac got married.

She wonders if she got married because she was failing physics, and the only self-respecting way for an intelligent woman to drop out of school in 1951 was to get married.

She wonders if she got married because her mother didn't want her to.

She wonders if she chose Vernon because she got to know him during the brief window when he felt unconfident, his fiancée having dumped him, and the only way she would ever have seen *that* Vernon again was if she had also dumped him.

The only thing she knows for sure: she's glad she had children. Susan was so difficult, but Imogen loved her, and surely Susan knew that, and her death was the worst thing that could possibly have happened. Imogen would have traded her life for Susan's in a moment. Whereas she's not sure Vernon would have. And isn't that the most damning thing you could say about a parent?

And look at all those years his mother was in the nursing home in North Carolina, when he hardly ever visited. "I would go down there if it meant anything to her," he said. "But she doesn't recognize me."

Me, me, me. He was the most selfish man she'd ever met. His mother thought the sun shone out of his asshole. He thought he was smarter than everyone else, but he was stupid enough to think that she and Carlos were having an affair. (Me, me, me. Betraying *me*.) As though he hadn't had plenty of evidence for many years that she didn't like sex. (Me, me, me. Not attracted to *me*.)

She asked him that one time if he would take Susan to the beach so she could have a break, and he got so angry she was frightened. She knew never to ask again.

He never wanted to go anywhere. He clutched at his routines. And since his routines included her, he clutched at her. When Susan was getting her life back together and teaching in Madrid, Imogen wanted to visit her. Imogen had *still* never been abroad. She had taken up Spanish again, and all she wanted to do was go to Spain and spend time with her daughter and practice her Spanish. Vernon didn't tell her she couldn't go, he knew she would never put up with that, but he didn't want to be alone, so he came along. And was miserable. He worried about the plane schedules, the tickets, the Spanish taxis, the tipping rules, the hotels. He got obsessed one night with the way the light switches were wired in a bungalow they'd rented on the south coast. There they were for two days on the beach with nothing to do but swim and read and eat out and be with Susan, but the double-switched hallway light didn't operate in the expected way, or some such damn thing, if you think Imogen paid any fucking attention you've got another think coming, and he couldn't let it go, he started searching for a screwdriver because he wanted to take off the faceplates and look at the wires, he wanted to call the property manager, he wanted Susan or Imogen to interpret for him, which they refused to do. "I don't know the Spanish for fucking killjoy," Imogen told him.

So there were no trips after that. Imogen had never gotten the opportunity to meet Hildegard in Germany. She had never gotten to see Norway. When her father had his retirement party in 1958, his colleagues at the Bureau of Public Roads gave him a new camera, which he took, along with her mother, on a two-month holiday in Europe. They saw the Eiffel Tower and the tulips in Holland. And guess what? They spent a month in Norway. Imogen sat on the living-room couch Vernon had made her buy and imagined her mother sailing the fjords.

She couldn't divorce him, no matter how many times she threatened it. For one thing, he would fall apart. For another, marrying him had been her mistake to make, and she believed you lived with your mistakes.

But she's so thankful she had children, and at least Vernon was a better father to Mark than he ever was to Susan. (*Aren't daughters your job?*

Could anyone believe he really said that? And he once called Susan a whore.) Mark has always been easy to love. From the time he was a baby, he was always happy. He would lie in her arms, sweetly smiling. When he was a toddler Imogen would ask him if he wanted juice or milk, and he would cheerfully say, "Either is fine!" Did he want to go to the park or the woods? "Either is fine!" Even in adolescence he never gave her a moment's trouble. (Susan had five car accidents before she was twenty.) His teachers loved him. Imogen has never understood what happened with that woman. Mark would have made such a good husband. Imogen has never seen her granddaughter. The woman is obviously a monster. Good riddance to her and her spawn.

Would Susan have been less footloose if Vernon had bothered to connect with her more? Would she be alive today?

Imogen remembers when Mark was fourteen and there was a little girl three houses away who was always out alone in her backyard. Imogen knew the parents slightly. The girl had been a late pregnancy, a surprise. Her only brother was twenty years older. Her parents were busy. She would gaze through the backyard fence, gripping the chain links, watching other kids play if there were any out, or just looking at emptiness if not. "Why don't you play with her?" Imogen said to Mark.

He hesitated. She could tell he didn't much want to. But his kindness kicked in and he said, "OK." Several times a week that summer he'd climb over the fence and toss a ball back and forth with her, play hide and seek, and so on. He was so goodhearted, so conscientious. Years later, the girl came by the house selling cookies to raise money for a high school band trip. She played the flute. She was very shy, but seemed normal. Imogen was glad for her. "Do you remember my son?" she asked. The girl said she didn't, but maybe she was too shy.

When Mark entered college, Imogen went back to school and got a degree in library science. If she had had everything to do all over again, she would have studied astronomy, she had such fond memories of those nights watching the sky in Park Forest. (Dear, silly Sarge, where are you now?) But Imogen was fifty, it was too late for that. She started by volunteering at Harvard's medical library, then after she got her degree she worked in their interlibrary loan department for fifteen years. She loved it. A regular job! A paycheck. A pension. A commute. A parking permit. In a way, her work was similar to Skywatch, since it depended on orderliness and consistency. The library's filing system was a stack of contradictory layers dating from different periods going back more than a hundred years, and her job was to navigate them quickly, find that one obscure requested item, sometimes misfiled, among the millions of items, send it on its way, record the transaction correctly. They told her she was the best employee they'd ever had, and she believed it, because she saw every day the sloppy work that had preceded her. She became a supervisor. She loved her bosses and her coworkers and her underlings. Maybe libraries attract collegial people. Or maybe it was because nearly all of them were female.

Of course there were frustrations. But if she ever complained about work, or said she was tired, Vernon would wonder aloud why she bothered, since they didn't need the money. His cluelessness, as always, was stunning. No thought of the satisfaction she might get from doing a job well. No thought that perhaps the library and its patrons actually needed her, for fuck's sake. No, anything she did was merely to satisfy a whim, and therefore if it wasn't fun for her all the time, it wasn't worth doing.

Then he got sick. By the time he retired, it was clear she had better retire as well.

Of course Imogen pitied him, or had compassion, or whatever. But her resentment toward him was his fault. He had always wanted to keep her at home, and as an invalid he got his wish in spades.

Parkinson's is like a glacier. It nibbles away relentlessly over months and years. Vernon hung on for a decade after his retirement. The last five years were the most awful thing Imogen could have imagined. Each morning after her coffee and cigarette she would check to see if he was awake. He might have been lying in bed waiting for her, silent and motionless. He would apologize. She would remove the foam block from his left foot that kept his toes from pointing during the night and giving him a leg cramp. His toenails were thick and yellow, and she hated trimming them. They looked diseased. She would help him make the transition to his wheelchair, although she could only steady him, she wasn't strong enough to hold him up. She would wheel him into the bathroom, help him remove the night's diaper, help him shift to the toilet. Wipe him. Wheel him to the top of the stairs, help him transfer to the chair lift. Precede him down the stairs, help him into the downstairs wheelchair, wheel him into the kitchen, try to figure out what he wanted to eat. He was often too depressed to have an appetite. She would park him in the living room in front of the television and try to pretend he wasn't there. A woman from social services came three times a week to engage him in conversation, as the doctor had recommended. He would say he didn't need it, and that he didn't like the woman, but occasionally he would liven up in her presence. Imogen should have sat with him more, but she couldn't stand to. He would begin a sentence, stop. He would worry about things and want her to check on things and half the time she couldn't even tell what he was talking about. When she lost her patience he would look at her apologetically with his ghostly gray eyes. Sometimes he would say, "I know I'm a burden."

With every one of his apologies, she could feel the millstone around her neck get heavier. She wanted to say to him, *I don't want your goddamn apologies, I want you to not need me.* She was so furious at him, she was sometimes sick with rage, first for all those years of him being his fucking unchanging self, and then for changing, for coming down with this horrible disease. But of course she could never say this, no one would understand, everyone would rightly condemn her, she felt guilty even to be feeling it.

In other words, he had finally *really* won.

She told him never to try to get out of bed on his own, yet sometimes he did, and fell. He'd lost weight but he had a big frame, and when he fell the whole house shook. He lay there, eyes wide and puzzled, limbs floating up and down like a creature underwater. She couldn't lift him, so she would call Jim and Alice next door, and if Jim was home he could lift Vernon on his own, otherwise, Imogen and Alice would struggle to do it together. Three times she had to call an ambulance just to get the EMTs in the house so *they* could lift him. Each time cost $300.

She hadn't wanted to put him in a nursing home, but finally admitted to herself that it was too much. She found an open spot in a place five miles away. She felt terribly guilty. She visited him every day. His depression deepened. He sometimes seemed almost catatonic with grief. He asked her if she would bring in a gun so he could kill himself, and she was horrified. Where would she find a gun? How would that make her feel? What about the nursing staff? She asked him, "How can you be so selfish?"

After ten months he stopped eating and drinking and late last Friday night she called Mark and said, "They're saying it could be any time."

Mark caught a morning flight out of Ithaca, arrived at the house and went straight on to the nursing home. Imogen, exhausted, took a nap. Vernon died minutes later, in Mark's presence. Hard to know what he was aware of by then, but maybe he had been waiting for his son.

Mark has been helping with the funeral arrangements, and it's wonderful to have him here for a few days. Neither she nor he give a shit about caskets and all that crap, they made that clear to the smarmy funeral director. But even the bare-bones option included a viewing.

Mark asked, "Should we invite anyone?"

"He wasn't in touch with anyone for years."

Which was true. But more important, frankly, Imogen couldn't bear the thought of someone trying to say a single solitary word of consolation or understanding to her. Nobody knew, and they could all go fuck themselves.

She and Mark declined putting a notice in the local newspaper. Vernon was a private person, and so are they. So it's just the two of them in the viewing room at the funeral home. They sit in the middle of the front row of the folding chairs in the stark white space. An empty table and two easels are backed against the wall. Those would be for bouquets and wreaths.

Mark goes up and puts his hand on Vernon's and stands there silently for a minute. Then Imogen goes up, since that's what Mark did. But she has no sentimentality about the body. This isn't Vernon. The brow and nose are large and sharp. You can see the skull under the skin. Imogen returns to her chair and says, "He really looks dead, doesn't he?"

Mark says, "Since they didn't embalm him, gravity has pooled all the fluids at the back of his head."

"Well of course I know that."

They sit silently for a minute, then leave. They will return in three days to pick up the ashes. On the drive home, Mark says, "Now you can do some of that traveling you've always wanted to do."

The thought fills her with something like panic, which she buries under a derisory snort. "I have so much to take care of first," she says. Logistics related to his death. Nursing home and funeral home bills. Notifying the pension people. Life insurance policies, veteran's policies. God knows what else. Vernon always took care of all that.

PART
THREE

Friday, February 19, 2016

She stayed awake through last night and the following morning, then slept all afternoon between Billings and Missoula, when the bus was crowded. Woke up at 7:30 p.m. for the transfer. The bus leaving Missoula had fourteen passengers, of which six remained after the stop in Spokane at 1:30 a.m. (It's "Spoke-ann." Who knew?) Now it's 3:00 a.m. and the other five are asleep, all quiet except for the hum of the tires and that vertical undulation like breathing that buses often do on highways, something modular in the construction of the roadbed. Her cone of light reminds her of her gooseneck lamp back home. She can almost believe the rest of the world doesn't exist. So this is how to ride a long-distance bus—working the night shift. Maybe she could do it forever. In Seattle, buy a ticket for New York, repeat. Oscillate between the coasts like a cesium-133 atom in an atomic clock. From time dilation, she'd age slower than the rest of the population, gain maybe a millionth of a second over the course of her lifetime. Who needs love?

In Missoula she used the free Wi-Fi in the station to research tire hum. It turns out engineers use computers to randomize the size and placement of tread blocks on tires so that they (the tires, not the engineers) will generate, when rotating, a sound as close as possible to white noise. But as with light curves from stars, there will always exist a predominating

frequency, however slight. It intrigues her that, of the six buses she's been
on since New York, the hum at highway cruising speed has always been
somewhere between G and B-flat. As the tire model is probably standard throughout the Greyhound fleet, the differences in frequency could
be the result of different amounts of wear on the treads, or different road-
beds, or different speeds at which the different drivers cruise. It's true that
the pitch drops when the bus slows.

Still no one has sat next to her. However, the buses since Chicago have
been considerably less than full, so probably it doesn't mean anything.
How asymmetrical of her that she cares, since she loves pretending she's
the only person in the world. Asymmetry, thy name is human.

Remembering her gooseneck lamp, her nights of reading in her happier youth, she rummages in her pack and pulls out the first Newman
volume. She turns it over in her hand. Impossible to describe how much
comfort she gets from these books. The four volumes together weigh six
pounds, fourteen ounces, the mass of a newborn baby, more fulfilling,
less demanding. Slate-blue, full cloth, sewn bindings, a summation symbol stamped in copper on the front and spine, the title on the spine in
gold: *The World of Mathematics.* The volumes are sixty years old, but the
binding is tight, the pages seem new. Bravo, Simon and Schuster.

She still remembers opening the present. Her twelfth birthday. She
and her mother were still living in that apartment in Astoria she loved
so much. The present had been mailed from her father. He'd used Christmas paper—candy canes—at which her mother rolled her eyes. The
note said he'd found the books among his own father's things. "Thought
you might be interested. Love, Your Father." She opened the first volume and read the subtitle, *A small library of the literature of mathematics
from A'h-mosé the Scribe to Albert Einstein, presented with commentaries and
notes by James R. Newman,* and knew on the spot that a fine project for
the next few weeks of her life would be to read the series from cover to
cover to cover to cover to cover to cover to cover to cover.

She had never met her father's father, nor wondered about him. But now she wishes she could write him a letter of thanks. She wonders if he loved Newman as much as she does. Whoever he was, he took good care of his books. Bravo, Mr. Vernon Fuller.

At night, under her cone of silence, she breezed through Newman's first selection, "The Nature of Mathematics," by Philip E. B. Jourdain, in two days. Since this was an overview, she nodded at the math she understood and hopped over everything she didn't, trusting it would be elaborated on later. The second entry was "The Great Mathematicians," by Herbert Westren Turnbull, and here was where she realized that her plan to peruse the entire series in a mere few weeks would be unworkable. On the first page there was a reference to an Egyptian priest of around 1700 BC named Ahmes who—she turns right now to that very page—"was much concerned with the reduction of fractions such as $2/(2n + 1)$ to a sum of fractions each of whose numerators is unity. Even with our improved notation it is a complicated matter to work through such remarkable examples as: $2/29 = 1/24 + 1/58 + 1/174 + 1/232$."

Adding fractions was a cinch, of course, she'd been able to do it since she was five. But this notion of reducing them to sums of unit fractions had never occurred to her. Indeed, a good deal of her attraction to Ahmes derived from sheer puzzlement as to why he wanted to do it in the first place. Did the Egyptians have some idea that unit fractions were more fundamental? *Were* they? And what would "fundamental" mean in this context?

Starting with $2/3$, she assumed that reducing it to $1/3 + 1/3$ was not allowed. So instead she quickly came up with $1/2 + 1/6$. $2/5$ and $2/7$ were just as easy: $1/3 + 1/15$ and $1/4 + 1/28$, respectively. By the time she got to $2/9$ she could see that all of these fractions could be reduced simply by subtracting the largest possible unit fraction; the difference would always be another unit fraction. $2/9 = 1/5 + 1/45$. $2/11 = 1/6 + 1/66$. $2/13 = 1/7 + 1/91$. In each case, the quotient of the denominators of the two unit fractions was equal to the denominator of the original fraction. And if you generalized the math, you could easily see why this would always be the case. So there was a much better solution to 2/29 than what old Ahmes had come up with, namely 1/15 + 1/435. Discovering that she was smarter than the greatest of all the Egyptian mathematicians was highly gratifying. (Only later did it occur to her—maybe, for Ahmes, complexity was the point? Maybe the challenge was to string out as many unit fractions as you could? Was *that* more "fundamental"?)

By this time she had realized that to do Newman properly, it wouldn't be enough to read every page, she would need to reproduce every result. Next came Thales of Miletus, 640 to 550 BC, who proved (as Mette proved again) that a circle is bisected by any diameter and that the angle inscribed in a semicircle is always right. After Thales came the Pythagoreans, a large subject. Mette proved the Pythagorean theorem three different ways. She studied triangular numbers and square numbers. Everything Turnbull mentioned led her down branching paths beyond what he himself covered. For example, she figured out all by herself that, since every odd number could be expressed as the difference between two squares, then every odd number was also the lowest term in a unique Pythagorean triple, in which the two larger terms were consecutive integers: 3-4-5; 5-12-13; 7-24-25; 9-40-41; 11-60-61; 13-84-85; etc. In this kind of Pythagorean triple, not only would the sum of the squares of the two lower terms equal the square of the largest term, but the sum of the two larger terms, unsquared, would equal the square of the smallest term. It felt like magic.

She spent a week studying the five regular solids and their properties, getting lost in calculations of their internal angles. She spent another week trying to square the circle and trisect the angle, in case somebody had missed something. She spent hours with a compass and straightedge drawing nested pentagons and pentagrams, continuing their fractal recursions down to infinitesimal points—or anyway, points smaller than a sharpened pencil point. She proved once again that the legs of a regular pentagram are golden triangles. She drew a nested recursion of a golden triangle and marveled at its beauty, the way the successively smaller triangles and golden gnomons called one another into existence like divinely matched pairs, like "turtles all the way down." This led to the logarithmic spiral, to Robinson triangles and Sierpinski triangles, to Penrose tilings. She fooled around with Ruth-Aaron numbers, Smith numbers, Carmichael numbers. She spent several weeks filling page after page with numbers subjected to the $3n + 1$ rule, graphing the results. (Mathematician Jeffrey Lagarias: "This is an extraordinarily difficult problem, completely out of reach of present day mathematics.") She found something calming in repetitive calculations, something deeply satisfying in the slow emergence of an inexorable pattern.

She always eventually returned to Newman so that, while exploring alleyways and jungle paths, she wouldn't miss continents. Six months after her birthday she had reached Diophantine numbers (an extremely large subject), which at page 113 out of a four-volume tally of 2469 pages, not counting the index, represented only 4.58 percent of the whole. At this rate, it would take her 10.92 years to complete the project. And that was under the unlikely assumption that the material would not get more complicated as it went along. So maybe it would take her fifteen years, maybe twenty.

The thought of a twenty-year program of Newman study filled her with unutterable happiness.

Now (3:45 a.m., breathing with the bus) she misses that happiness. She misses youth. She misses the youthful idea that a subject really might be *conquered*, that all the gorgeous order lying hidden under disorder could be unearthed like sacred bones, laid out in neat rows on pristine sheets, labeled in a neat hand. She misses the youthful delusion that conquering a subject would validate her existence. She has the impression that her father still has it, this belief, this happiness. And though

she just now thought of it as a delusion, isn't it true that if you still have
it, then it *does* validate your existence, and therefore is not a delusion? An
Epimenides paradox. She has the impression that her father doesn't need
anyone else. He has remained pure. Whereas she opened her gates, she
welcomed disorder, she gave it a parade. She'll never get it back, will
she? Peace of mind. The thought fills her with a terrible fear.

   She'll be in Seattle in three hours and fifteen minutes. What then? A
ticket back to New York would be to make the futility of her situation
obvious. She could go on a random walk through the Seattle streets, let
a dark alley decide. She could check into a hotel, pay two weeks in ad-
vance, decline all room service, nail the door shut. A simple burrow. She
could go up and then come down from the Space Needle.

   She's been sitting on a text from her father that came in between Missoula and Spoke-ann. I guess I'm a little worried. Could you send
me a note? It made her feel bad. It's nearly 7:00 a.m. where he is, so
he's probably awake. She takes out her phone and forces herself: Please
don't worry. taking time to think. Life choices.

1984–2002

When she was a lonely and strange twelve-year-old, she wrote her auto-biography, whose sole purpose was to convince its sole reader that her life had meaning. During its composition she happened to make a friend, a plot development so astonishing she decided to end her story on it: "And thus it came to pass that Saskia White and Jane Singh lived happily for many years, until the Last Days and the destruction of the world." (Or something like that; she was enamored of Tolkienesque High Hokum.) The ink, as they say, wasn't even dry when a note arrived out of the blue from her long-absent father, inviting her on a summer camping trip in Norway. Jane came along and terrible things happened, not a few of them Saskia's fault, and the friendship was destroyed.

Saskia has thought about story endings ever since. There's that logical fallacy, *post hoc ergo propter hoc*, and she wishes her Latin were good enough (ha! she doesn't really know any Latin at all) to know how to express an analogous idea (well, mainly, to show off her Latin): the emotional fallacy that later occurrences in life have more meaning than earlier ones. If you read a story about a person with a sad childhood and a happy adulthood, you tend to think of it as a happy story, *n'est-ce pas?* Whereas a life that begins happily and ends sadly seems like a sad story. But why shouldn't all periods of a life have equally weighty—or for that matter, evanescent—meaning? If only the present moment exists, chronology is not important. (She has a feeling Epictetus talks about this somewhere, where's her copy? Or maybe it's Vonnegut.) However, people are addicted to narrative, and the last line of a story feels like a provisional title for all the blank pages that follow.

Starting when she was thirteen, she cultivated the habit of occasionally asking herself the question, What if my story ended here? It was a way of affirming that whatever was happening at that time, whatever she was feeling, no matter how brief or provisional, had its own validity, which subsequent events could not alter. She tried it for the first time when she returned home after having run away. (Long story short—her friendship with Jane destroyed, her revered father unmasked, her share of guilt undeniable, she jumped on a bus, clung for a few weeks to an ebb-tide reef in Brooklyn, discovered like so many others before her that she could not escape herself, floated back home on the flow tide like an unsinkable plastic bag, hey, jetsam, here comes flotsam.) She noticed, as her bus descended into Ithaca, that she was feeling kind of glad to be coming home. She was even glad to see her mother, Lauren, who had been more or less invisible to her during all the years she'd fabulated about the whereabouts of her heroic dad. So when she hugged Lauren in the cold winter kitchen, she thought, "The End." *This* story was about reconciliation. Of course she and Lauren went right back to fighting and playing dirty—but that was a different story.

Since she could choose when to step back and announce "The End," she preferred to wait for the rare good moments, so that her generally lonely, often miserable teenage years became a series of YA books with the kind of plot teenagers—hell, adults, too—prefer, beginning in angst and obstacles, sinking lower into destructive behavior and despair, then turning unexpectedly upward in the final pages, finishing on a quiet moment of connection, redemption, or awareness of wisdom gained. The quieter and more ambiguous that final moment, the more literary the

YA, correct?, so her imagined row of books—let's call it *A Series of Saskia Events*—were all Newbery Award winners.

And thus it came to pass that one tempestuous April night, far into the wee hours, both a little high, Lauren and Saskia listened together to the storm and talked about many personal things, and did not once, either of them, take advantage of a glimpsed chink in the other's armor to slip in a dirk. The End.

And thus it came to pass that Mr. Anderson, tenth-grade history teacher, who hated Saskia for despising his educational methods and basically ignoring everything he said all year, accused her of cribbing her final paper, "Intentional Communities in Seneca County, 1967–1978," from some other student or paid factotum, but was thoroughly told off, nay, publicly shamed by Ms. Schwartz (Pretty Good Teacher of English, MA, OBE), who assured him that Saskia could write a paper like that with one hand tied behind her back. The End.

And thus it came to pass, after two years of awful silence, that one January afternoon there arrived in the mail a letter from Jane's boarding school, with Jane's name on it, at the sight of which Saskia's face went numb with dread, but Jane said that she was doing all right, that Saskia shouldn't blame herself too much, that Jane's therapist had helped her see that Saskia had also been a victim of Thomas, and although Saskia didn't believe in her own innocence for a second, still, the fact that Jane was willing to write her a letter and offer such compassionately false reassurances filled her with indescribable relief. The End.

And thus it came to pass that, following months of skirmishing in which Saskia never knew exactly what was up, or even approximately what was up, she and Shelly Landis went to the Junior Prom together and laughingly stared down the stares of the homophobic hordes that crowded the hallowed halls in those benighted yesteryears, and subsequently spent a fair fraction of the night fooling around in Shelly's bedroom. The End.

Almost sounds like a happy childhood, doesn't it? Saskia would like to teach this trick to everyone, perhaps offer an online course: "Ringing Down the Curtain: How to Know When to End It All, *sans* Gun, Cliff, or Razor."

YA Newberry honorands (honorees?) yielded in the fullness of time to National Book Award nods. Or maybe by this point she was thinking in terms of film. For example, there was the low-budget sleeper about her ill-conceived affair with her professor (first act), followed by her ill-conceived conception (second act), with a third act of paralysis and fear— lots of staring out windows, beautifully shot by the DP in wintry rural whites and grays—but lightening in the final minutes with the birth of a beautiful baby, garnished with parsley-sprig adumbrations of a new and deeper mother-daughter bond.

She hates to say it (she really does), but that first year with Mette and Lauren on the shitty old property north of Ithaca was in some ways the happiest of her life. Just being a mother with a baby . . . For that brief season, the otherwise veiled meaning of her life became clear. If Mette hungry, then nurse. If Mette stink, then clean. Saskia's fear and self-doubt in the first week gave way to the realization that there were two things she could demonstrably do better than any other human being on the planet, namely, intuit what Mette wanted and supply same. An ego boost, for sure. But in the service of the sweetest human interaction imaginable. (Did she already say she hated to admit it? To be clear: she believes that men might also find it incomparably fulfilling, if they'd only try it, the fuckwads.)

Of course she sometimes felt stifled, bored. The space she was asked to occupy was so small. But it reminded her of an idea that had once thrilled her, when she was a teenager, but hadn't thought of in a long time—that fitting into a space that was defined for you, dwelling in it with acceptance, partook of the timeless and "right" actions of Homeric epic, in which formulaic language bodies forth a world of humans living by an unchanging code. *Pouring water from a splendid and golden pitcher into a silver basin, generous with her provisions, she put her hand to the dirty diaper that lay ready before her.*

Everything she had always disliked about her mother—her vagueness, her determined air of unreality—started to look, when helping with the baby, like gentleness, "present"ness. Saskia saw that Lauren *loved* babies, and since Saskia was discovering that she also loved them, it was the first time she could acknowledge that she and her mother had something positive in common. Lauren's boyfriend Bill, another cold-molasses dreamer, also turned out to be great with Mette. She would fall asleep on him while he read on the couch, and he'd happily lie there for hours, gingerly turning the pages above her head. When Lauren went out to work in the field—she sold produce at the Farmer's Market on weekends—she'd pop Mette in a sling around her waist. She never tired as she weeded or culled, expertly cradling Mette's head as she bent over, continually murmuring who-knew-what to her, adjusting her sun bonnet, passing her a fresh pea pod or string bean to nibble on.

By this period, the clutch of pseudo-siblings whom Saskia had helped raise had all decamped. Melanie's wolf in pastor's collar had carried her off to San Jose after the hurried nuptials, and at twenty-three she already had a two-year-old boy and a baby girl, glimpsed only in cherub-trumpeted birth announcements and doe-eyed-Christ Christmas cards that arrived with neither invitations to visit nor photos of the mother. Shannon and Austin had moved out the previous year, and were currently living farther up the lake in a decrepit farmhouse that seemed part group home, part 24/7 party house, part two-level garage for the ever-reformulating grunge band. Hopelessly slow Quentin was a sophomore at Yale. The brood mother, Jo, still lived in her trailer on Lauren's property and still shared dinner with the other adults, but back when Saskia was pregnant Jo had declared, with an air of nipping in the bud any selfish notions, that she had already done her share of raising children. To which Saskia longed to retort, "Whose names, by the way, are . . . ?"

So in effect it was just the four of them—Saskia, her mother, Bill, and the baby—and for fifteen months it formed enough of an idyll that no one would ever have made a movie out of it. The year of living somnolently.

But a gal has a brain. And too much timelessness starts to look like death. So once Mette was stumbling around upright and burbling in code, Saskia got a part-time job at a coffee roaster for the money and joined the Shakespeare Duffers for the grins. For the next three years she did the sort of thing wannabe actors do when they live near a little college town and can't go anywhere because they have a young child and no money. She showed up at every piddling audition she saw posted and got used to making a fool of herself. She looked at it this way: an actor, ideally, is an empty vessel filled with inspiration, or in other words, a holy fool. So she was a fool in training. There was a line from *Love's Labour's Lost* that she ritually said to herself before entering an audition, to summon luck. Berowne is speaking to his king after they've put on a courtly masque and failed spectacularly. They're about to present a second theatrical effort to the same women who mocked the first, and the king says, with endearing boyish pathos, "They will shame us." To which Berowne responds, "We are shame-proof, my lord."

For its size, Ithaca had a lot of theater and filmmaking going on—student films at Ithaca College and Cornell, one semi-professional theater of decent repute, one mostly amateur company of no fixed abode, plus, in the summer, Shakespeare alfresco in the Cornell Plantations and a more commercial enterprise (*Guys and Dolls, The Crucible,* etc) housed in a repurposed airplane hangar built back when airplanes had more than two wings. In addition, there were several small production companies doing documentaries, commercials, HR training films, and the occasional short narrative fledged with its creators' hopes of Robin Hooding some bull's-eye at Sundance, Berlin, New York, you name it.

She remembers her first audition, for a student film at Ithaca College, a pink basement room inhabited by two giggling nerds (director and writer), and a lifeless page of stoned dialogue about some betrayal. She couldn't summon up a thing except embarrassment, which the nerds, to their credit, figured out in under a minute. Other early auditions have gummed together in her memory. There were stages with dazzling lights in her eyes, offices with comfy chairs and a glass of water, long readings and brutally short ones, asshole directors and kind directors and clueless, insecure directors. Meanwhile, she did more Shakespeare—ironic that the only work she could get at first was with the immortal Bard—although the long-entrenched regulars of the company (speaking of immortal) continued to take most of the best parts. Still, she landed Hermia in *Midsummer Night's Dream*, probably because for once, here was an actress hilariously short enough for all the dwarf jokes to make sense.

She learned how to be a bigger and better fool. She took a Meisner workshop, which helped her to stay true in the moment. In one of the showcases she performed a twelve-minute playlet with her favorite fellow attendee—bald, big-browed Paul; the scene was a bitter marital argument about a dead son—and she felt it lift off in front of the audience, she could see that Paul felt it, too, and they mentally joined hands and flew out the window. Like Wendy and Peter, they could keep flying so long as the audience kept thinking, *You can fly*. All her life, she had worried that she was too self-absorbed (have you ever noticed, by the way, that no man ever worries about this?) but this felt like a profligate sharing. It felt shame-proof.

But you're only a good actor until your good scene ends. Then it's back to being a fool. She started to land a few parts. And she had to learn, as all actors must, how to keep searching for something true in the succession of false moments of a bad script. (Who knew that not every writer out there is as good as Shakespeare?) This was particularly true with regard to the student films. There was one about cutting, for example, in which—milestone!—she played the lead. That being said, her humble goal ever since has been never to recall a single second of it. In her last year in Ithaca she had small roles in five of the nine plays put on by the second-best non-university-affiliated theater in town, which she liked to refer to by the Marquez-y name MACONFA—Mostly Amateur Company Of No Fixed Abode—although its official name was The Other Shoe. They rented out different venues for different productions, depending on availability and cost. The artistic director, Jules, was a forty-five-year-old woman who'd done some theater in New York but disliked the city—she'd grown up in a Nebraska town whose only claim to fame was that in 1936 a tornado destroyed every standing structure in it—and had moved to Ithaca when her partner landed a job in the Cornell chemistry department. Eight months later she got dumped when said partner moved in with one of the professors on the hiring committee. Turned out the two women had been carrying on a torrid affair for years at conferences around the country. (A joke not to make to Jules: "Talk about chemistry!")

Jules figured that the way to compete with the more established theater in town was to be adventuresome and high-concept. The Other Shoe's much lower production costs made it practicable to throw a ton of shit at the wall and see what stuck. So in the one season that Saskia worked regularly with the company, the first two plays were Aristophanes' *The Birds* and Brook and Carrière's *The Conference of the Birds*, both performed with masks in the lecture hall at Cornell's Lab of Ornithology. The pitch was, Hey folks, how often do you get to see the hoopoe as a major character twice in one season? It actually worked pretty well, because the lab director got excited and did a fantastic job, for free, of putting together a soundtrack of the appropriate birdcalls. He also spread the word to Ithaca's legion of birders, who showed up in force. Another of Jules's strategies was to put on lesser-known plays by well-known playwrights. So for Stoppard, instead of *Arcadia* or *Rosencrantz* or *The Invention of Love*, they did *Hapgood*. (Yes, you've never heard of it.) And for Brecht, instead of *Mother Courage* or *Caucasian Chalk Circle*, they did *St. Joan of the Stockyards*. (Ugh.) The final show, in June, was made up of three one-acts, all involving The Power of Story (Saskia can't take credit for that original idea, it was on the poster): Sam Shepard's *Icarus's Mother*, followed by the two one-acts that make up Caryl Churchill's *Blue Heart*. Feminist Churchill blew macho Shepard out of the water, which maybe was Jules's sneaky idea all along.

Still, *Icarus's Mother* has good bits, and Saskia got to play Pat. She and the play's four other characters—Bill, Howard, Jill, and Frank—are in a park overlooking an ocean beach, waiting for fireworks to begin. Bill and Howard, who seem to be the boyfriends of Jill and Pat respectively, continually mock the women in a revolting conspiratorial bromantic way, and Howard occasionally manhandles Pat. Meanwhile, there's a jet circling in the sky, making everyone nervous. Each character at some point gets a monologue that indulges a fantasy, or attempts to delude the other characters (the Power of Story!), and these monologues gradually spin off into flights of crazed weirdness, à la Saint Sam the Badass in the wilderness dining on locusts and wild honey. Self-loving Howard gets the longest one, while his cowed girlfriend Pat gets the shortest, but hers is the best. She imagines an evening in which all the fireworks have failed, the crowd has gone home disappointed, the fireworks company departed in shame, while she alone remains behind in the darkness. Examining the launchers, she discovers there's one firework left and lights it. It rockets skyward and explodes in glorious light and color, and she is the only one who gets to see it.

They performed the play five times and then the season was over. Saskia was surprised at how bereft she felt. It was her first experience of the bond one can form with fellow actors when you work together as a company, reveling in the good plays and struggling against the bad, sometimes loving each other, sometimes hating. Like a family, yes! Ohmygod, trust falls on stage, yes! To Saskia, the coming summer looked desolate. But it turned out that four of the five actors in *Icarus's Mother* were going to be in town for the July 4 holiday, so Saskia, the dewy-eyed newbie, proposed that they mount a repeat performance somewhere outside, timing it so that the play's fireworks would coincide with Ithaca's real fireworks (which actually were always on July 2, when the city could get a discounted rate). The fifth actor was Jason, who played Howard, and though he was, one had to admit *sub rosa*, even if one loved him like family, a bit of a dick, he agreed to come up from New York City just for the one performance, for which hugs and kisses and trust falls forever. Allie, who played Jill, suggested they do it at Sunset Park, a quarter acre of lawn owned by the village of Cayuga Heights with a view over Ithaca and the lake. Judging from a certain previous experience she never fully explained, Allie doubted they could get a permit from the village police, and they didn't want to put up with the hassle anyway (they would probably be told they needed two porta-johns, a security guard, and a medic with a defibrillator), so Allie and Sean (who played Frank) spread the word rave-style, the details of which Saskia was already too old to understand. Something involving cell phones.

Whatever it was they did, about forty people had shown up by 8:45 p.m. on the day, just as the sun was setting. The city fireworks reliably started within a few minutes of 9:45, and the play took forty minutes to perform, so they crossed their fingers and began at 9:10. It was as beautiful an evening as they could have hoped for, clear and unseasonably cool, with three stage-managed clouds above the western ridge turning, as they spoke the first lines, from rose to maroon. The location was *perfect*. Saskia wondered if the other actors, like her, only gradually realized how perfect it was. All the lines in the play that referred to the setting fit the actual setting. People frequently picnicked in Sunset Park, so their props—blanket and empty plates, tipped-over wine glasses, disarranged hamper—without changing a molecule, became real. The actors found themselves spontaneously adjusting the blocking. When Frank enthused about the beach and urged everyone to go down there, Sean moved to the lip of the slope, and gestured toward the lake. When Bill referred to the moon, Hayden pointed upward and lo, there she was in the southeast, a good trouper come up specially from New York City along with Jason to help out. For Pat's monologue, Saskia lay down on the blanket, looked at the sky, and wished her bullying boyfriend would leave her alone. The only way she knew to protect herself was to retreat into childishness, to make her powerlessness more pitiable. "If none of them work except one, it will be worth it," she said. "I'll wait all night on my back." Did the others realize that she was also talking about sex with Howard, which repulsed her? That her only release was in lonely masturbation? "Even if I'm the only one left in the whole park and even if all the men who launch the firecrackers go home in despair and anguish and humiliation. I'll go down there myself and hook up the thing by myself and fire the thing without any help and run back up here and lie on my back and wait and listen and watch the goddamn thing explode all over the sky."

The play went on in its perfect way. Allie's friend Danielle stood in the putative wings with watch and script, raising her hand high when they needed to pick up the pace, lowering it when they needed to slow. Frank had gone for a walk along the beach and had seen something, either the crash of the jet into the water or an atomic bomb going off, or maybe they were the same thing, and he described it in a mounting frenzy, heading for the line "What a light!" at which point, in the stage directions, the first firework is supposed to go off, as if called into being by Frank's exclamation. (*Let there be*—, Genesis and Apocalypse rolled into one; like sex with Howard, it's over almost before it begins.) This was the tricky part. Thanks to Danielle, it was 9:45, but of course they couldn't know precisely when the first firework would be lit. Sean gestured and gibbered magnificently—*His flashing eyes! His floating hair!*—and came up to the line invoking the Light, then on a hunch veered off and improvised for a minute, a stoned word-salad that fit the script pretty well (go Sean!), then circled back around and hit his mark, "What a light!"

Well, nothing in this fallen world, after all, is perfect. Fortunately, Frank's words never directly refer to the detonations, so there's a bit of leeway, and eighty-two seconds later (by Danielle's stopwatch), just as Sean was saying, "—and to hear a sound so shrieking that it ain't even a sound at all but goes beyond that into the inside of the center of each ear," there was a whistle and a pencil-line of orange light ascending from the lakeshore below, followed by a crack and a bloom. Which in this fallen world is pretty fucking good. The rest of Frank's monologue is more and more frenzied, and through it all the City of Ithaca and the fireworks company did a fantastic job with the sound and light effects, Thanks guys, you're the best! The End!

There was a celebration afterward at a pizza bar, and they all agreed that the performance had been fucking awesome, indescribable, so-and-so should have been there, what a . . . ! wasn't it a . . . ? They drank and gorged and loved each other, and Saskia drove back to the old farm in a state of bliss like nothing she had ever experienced. She would do nearly anything to experience it again.

The next day, Quentin drove over from an internship in Boston to celebrate Saskia's birthday on the 4th. That evening, the 3rd, Lauren told both of them, with an air so serene it was like a blank wall, that she was dying of cancer.

.   .   .

SASKIA HATES TO think about this period. She's never been able to put her feelings about it in any order. She was fucking furious. (OK, she supposes if she *had* to order it, that would be the first.) Lauren had known for eighteen months. She was first diagnosed at stage II, which if treated, has a 93 percent survival rate after five years and a 75 percent survival rate after ten. You can bet your ass Saskia looked up the data on this. Lauren told Bill after six months, but swore him to secrecy, and this hapless feckless boob who couldn't keep from blurting out the ends of movies he'd already seen, or providing his bank account and social security number to robocalls with Russian accents, somehow managed to spend a year watching Lauren fail to beat it, and not say one single goddamn word to Saskia, with whom he sat down to break bread every day.

And how was Lauren trying to beat it? With herbal infusions, sesame oil massages, yoga, crystals, a gluten-free diet, low-temperature cooking, meditation, levitation, spontaneous combustion, vomiting pea soup, rotating her head completely around, etc. Saskia hadn't noticed anything because Lauren was always following some sort of regime that mixed and matched this crap. A woman has a right to make decisions about her own body, *of course.* So thank you, Mom! Saskia was fucking furious *and* felt guilty about it. (Can she be horrifically selfish just for a second? It made sense for Lauren to wait for an opportunity when Quentin was also around, since he and Saskia were the closest to her, but did she really have to break the news on the eve of Saskia's birthday? Really, after eighteen months, right then, thus ruining Saskia's birthday for the rest of her life?)

Lumpectomy, radiation, a little chemo, hormone therapy: that was the treatment recommended by the oncologist back when Lauren had every chance to save her life. But those were "Western." And everything

Western is evil, like nuclear weapons and double-blind medical trials. All her peacefulness and gentleness, without changing a molecule, turned back into passiveness and vagueness, a fastidious aversion to grappling with the real world, a refusal to be "impure"—yes! That was her word! Pure food, pure energy, pure thoughts. As if Saskia's father hadn't abundantly shown how far you could sink into selfish cruelty through this pursuit of "purity." Though, come to think of it, Lauren had never agreed with Saskia about the damage Thomas had done, and a woman is entitled to her own stupid opinions, so Saskia is a selfish bitch, we've already established that. Lauren even said that she wouldn't bring "poisons" into the house (dry-ice tendrils of chemo wafting off her sweater, dilatory high-energy photons, etc) because Mette was living there. Saskia was apoplectic. You're blaming *Mette* for your refusal to save yourself? How about how much Mette is attached to you? You're as important to her as I am! Maybe family ties are impure! Maybe accommodating what people close to you might need means occasionally taking your ass off the Throne of Purity and laying down the fucking Orb of Righteousness!

By the time Lauren told Quentin and Saskia, the cancer had spread to her lymph nodes and the long bones of her legs. Maybe she told them when she told them because the pain was soon to become too strong to hide. Or maybe she told them when she told them because it was too late for effective treatment, and she could glide burning down the Nile on her golden barge without having to listen to inconvenient arguments from other people. She was dying, and the one thing Saskia could do, should do, was comfort her, but Saskia was carried back to her awful childhood when Lauren, burying her head in clouds of incense, didn't see her, let alone love her, and so instead of comforting her dying mother, Saskia berated her, because she was a selfish bitch who maybe didn't deserve to be loved after all.

Saskia told Austin and Shannon, who came to the house a number of times over the next two months to help out, as Lauren weakened and spent more of each day in bed, at first refusing pain medication, opting for acupuncture instead, then accepting it when the full carpet-bombing power of the disease began to make itself felt. Melanie flew home for a week at the end of July and everything Saskia wanted to find out about her marriage was hidden behind a screen of Christian goodwifery, braced with two-by-fours of happy anticipation of the fourth (fifth?) blessed event in the offing, and subsumed anyway by Lauren's more pressing needs. For about five minutes Saskia considered trying to find out how to reach Thomas, then decided without a tremor of remorse that he didn't deserve to know.

Of course, shortly afterward, Lauren brought him up. She had clambered that morning out of bed and come downstairs, then immediately had lain on the living room couch. It was a hot day, but she pulled around herself the blanket that Saskia kept there for her, and accepted an offer of tea. When Saskia brought it, she gestured to have it placed on the coffee table by her hand, then didn't touch it, which was unusual. Her face was very pale.

"Are you in pain?" Saskia asked.

Lauren ignored this. "You've never forgiven your father," she said. Over the last few weeks her voice had lowered in pitch, become friable.

"That's right," Saskia said.

"I wish you would."

"Is that a dying wish?"

"If that's what it takes."

Saskia sat on the floor next to the couch and looked at her mother. What a beautiful woman she had always been. How tough it was, probably, to be such a beautiful woman. To have to deal continually with men who believed they had a claim on her merely because they desired her. Men like her father, who wanted to control women, mold them, encage them.

"It would be easy to lie to you, I guess," Saskia said. "And I probably would, if this weren't a dying wish. But Thomas doesn't deserve forgiveness."

"It's not for him, it's for you."

"Yeah, that's what people always say. I don't buy it. Forgiving him feels like abandoning any standards of decency. Those standards comfort me."

"But he—"

"He fucked Jane when she was thirteen, right? Remember? I knew about it when he did it in a tent in Norway, and you knew about it when he kept doing it here in the loft in the barn. And we did nothing. Yeah, yeah, we were all under his spell. We were three weak women, two of us still munchkins, one of us getting fucked by the Wizard of Oz. Well, no, I'm pretty sure he was fucking you, too, right? Jane in the afternoon, you at night, right? Though I've never directly asked you about it. Here's my chance, do I get a dying wish, too?"

Lauren closed her eyes. "I can't talk to you when you're like this."

"I'm always like this."

"Yes . . . well . . ."

"If I weren't his daughter he would have fucked me, too. And I'd have let him do it. What is that called, the hat trick, the triple crown?"

Forgiving Thomas would mean forgiving Lauren and herself, and yes, wasn't it a grotesque irony that one of Thomas's legacies was that she couldn't do that. But cult leaders were possible only because of their followers, and to absolve the latter of their gullibility was to invite the phenomenon to occur again and again. One has a moral responsibility to be a grownup. Lauren actually *was* a grownup at the time, so her culpability was greater. But Saskia restrained herself from saying this out loud. She was mean, but she wasn't *that* mean.

The next morning, when Lauren was still in bed, Saskia apologized. Sort of.

"I'm sorry for some of what I said. Any other wish you want to express, I'll do it, I promise. But not Thomas. I can't."

Lauren stared into space for a number of seconds. Then she said, "I understand."

Saskia burst into tears.

After that, Lauren's cancer progressed quickly, maybe aided (even the Western doctor said) by her acceptance of it, and in late August Bill and Saskia set up a bed in the living room and brought in a hospice nurse to teach them how to administer palliative care. During the last two weeks a friend of Lauren's named Amethyst showed up several times, usually bringing along three other women, and the coven would burn little bowls of greenery and chant, holding hands in a circle. They praised Lauren for the beautiful death she was having and cried what looked to Saskia like tears of joy. Meanwhile, Mette wouldn't get with the program. The different routine in the house upset her. She acted out, broke a dish.

When Lauren wasn't sleeping, she murmured softly, references to things in the past that Saskia didn't recognize—"No, you said that"; "The bicycle isn't there"; "Far, it's far, it's far." Sometimes she repeated a phrase over and over, in Hindi or maybe Sanskrit. Saskia asked Bill, who said he had no idea. She couldn't ask Jeeves, because Lauren didn't have dial-up internet at the house (Saskia should be grateful there was a phone), so she steeled herself and called Amethyst, who recognized it right away from fragments Saskia had been able to make out: "*Om asato ma sadgamaya*. It's a mantra."

"What does it mean?"

"Lead me from unreality to reality. Lead me from darkness to light. Lead me from death to immortality. It's so wonderful that she's saying that."

"Mm, thanks."

"How are you doing, sweetheart?"

"I'm managing, thanks."

The unreal days went on. Lauren's long auburn hair, which had never turned gray, lay spread out on the pillow to either side of her large, handsome head. Saskia gently brushed it every morning, struggling with emotions that clashed painfully. For one thing, the hair made her think about the treatments that Lauren had refused. Saskia knew it wasn't literally for the sake of her hair that Lauren had refused them, but hair was natural and healthy, while losing it was what happened to Hiroshima victims. Also, her hair was beautiful, and Saskia couldn't help thinking that Lauren's devotion to purity was rooted partly in vanity. At the same time, not having brushed Lauren's hair in many years, Saskia was carried back to when she was twelve years old, when she considered it the greatest privilege to be allowed to do so. She had envied her mother's hair—in truth, worshipped it—and it was only while brushing it, in the evening, in long meditative sessions, that she could occasionally get her mother to talk to her about anything personal. And here she was, all grown up, still envying the hair, still hoping that her mother might say something meaningful to her—about motherhood, about raising a daughter, about her own childhood, about dying, about anything. Anything except Thomas. Saskia had never called her "Mom." Lauren hadn't wanted it. She'd always said she wanted their relationship to be one of equals, which sounded supportive and wise when Saskia was ten, and like a self-deluding abdication of responsibility when Saskia was fifteen.

Every day, she looked more angelic. Her halo of brushed hair glowed in the sunlight coming through the living room windows. The September weather was heavenly. When Saskia sat next to her bed, she sometimes held her hand, which felt awkward, since they had hardly ever touched. Sometimes she talked to Lauren's closed eyes about any quotidian thing that came into her head, the temperature outside, the goldenrod just beginning to flower, the rice Saskia burned that morning, the rat they couldn't catch who was eating the soap at night. That felt awkward, too, but she persevered.

What does she remember now, these many years later? The last days blur together. At one point she said to Lauren, "I'm sorry I said all those angry things to you about the cancer treatments. It was none of my business." At which she felt another spurt of anger: *You never allowed yourself to be my business.* At another point she said, "I feel like I want to call you 'Mom' now. Unless you complain, that's what I'll do."

Bill, the goodhearted boob, though devastated, was helpful and attentive. He said to Saskia, "She always loved you."

"You forgot to add, 'in her own way.'"

"You know that, don't you?"

"She's dying. This isn't about me, is it?"

Examine every hard impression, and test it by this rule: whether the impression has to do with the things which are up to us, or those which are not; and, if it has to do with the things that are not up to us, be ready to reply, "It is nothing to me." (Saskia has found her Epictetus.)

She remembers one other thing. When Lauren wasn't sleeping or looking forward to reality, she occasionally opened her eyes and said simple things like, "Thank you" (adjusted blanket) or "That's nice" (damp hair stroked back from forehead). At rare intervals she seemed more lucid for a few seconds. Once she looked pointedly at various parts of the room, as if memorizing them. Then she looked at Saskia and held her gaze steadily, which she had done very seldom in her life. She said almost inaudibly, with a teaspoon of breath, "You're a good girl, Saskia." She used to say that when Saskia was twelve, helping care for the younger children, and Saskia would retort, "Woof." Now, she wondered if Lauren might be seeing the child.

"I'll take care of everything," Saskia said. "Don't worry." Lauren smiled and closed her eyes.

In the case of everything that is loved with fond affection, remember to tell yourself what sort of thing it is, beginning with the least of things. If you are fond of a jug, say, "It is a jug that I am fond of"; then if it is broken, you will not be disturbed. If you kiss your child, or your wife, say to yourself that it is a human being that you are kissing; and then you will not be disturbed if either of them dies.

At the end of the first week of September the hospice nurse checked Lauren's vitals and said they had better call in everyone who could make it. Melanie couldn't come because she had just given birth, and Jo was in San Jose helping out. Quentin flew in from Boston, Austin and Shannon drove down from the farmhouse. Then Lauren hung on through the next three days, breathing long and deeply, hour after hour. It seemed as though she was relaxing herself with a meditative technique. The nurse said she had never seen anything quite like it at this stage. Quentin had to return to his job. The twins drove back to their place. The following day, Saskia and Bill took turns by the bedside. Nothing changed.

Remember that you are an actor in a play, which is as the author wants it to be: short, if he wants it to be short; long, if he wants it to be long. If he wants you to act a poor man, a cripple, a public official, or a private person, see that you act it with skill. For it is your job to act well the part that is assigned to you; but to choose it is another's.

That night, the room began to smell of death from Lauren's breath (she, who had always smelled so good). At 3:00 a.m. her breathing became labored. Her head began to inscribe circles as her lungs heaved, and her eyes opened sightlessly. Sometimes her breathing would stop for several seconds, then begin again. At 7:17 a.m., her breath halted and Saskia, looking at her face, knew at once that she had died. The clear demarcation startled her. The minute tremors and blood-cell pulses of a living face that one normally doesn't notice, all ceased simultaneously. The effect was like a freeze frame.

It was September 12, 2001. Saskia called the nurse, who arrived at eight and made an offhand, appalled reference to New York City that neither Bill nor Saskia understood.

So LAUREN'S DEATH was the fall of a sparrow.

Bill arranged for a memorial service at the New Age retreat center Lauren often went to. Lauren's friends popped up, one after the other, and celebrated her triumph with wet shining faces. Unable to bear it after a certain point, Saskia escaped outside with Mette and kept her entertained by walking with her through a labyrinth, which had been constructed with lines of stones set in the grass. This kind of thing was right up Mette's alley—a demarcated path, a rule to follow. Saskia had the vague idea that New Agers believed that when you reached the center of the labyrinth you were supposed to have gained some insight, or attained peace or something. All she found was the Minotaur—thoughts of her father. She did feel guilty, after all, for not having tried to reach him regarding her mother's illness. But she told herself that her feelings were her concern, not his. He had banished them from his concern long ago.

It turned out the house and land didn't belong to Lauren, but to a trust owned by her brothers, from whom she'd been estranged for many years. Not that it mattered. Saskia had never expected to inherit anything from Lauren beyond an eating bowl and a pair of sandals. In fact, there was a little more than that. Lauren had left the contents of the house equally to Bill, Saskia, Jo, Melanie, Shannon, Austin, and Quentin. Saskia would have cleared maybe a thousand dollars, except that a crude pencil sketch of a naked hairy man graphically fucking a naked hairy woman that had hung in the dining room forever—a payment for a few weeks of macrobiotic food and a lively co-ed crash by a long-ago communard who was now a famous artist—sold for $82,000. Saskia's

share amounted to just enough money to make it conceivable, if somewhat reckless, to move to New York City. A number of people that fall
were going in the opposite direction. But Saskia felt passionately that
9/11 was an assault by purists on mongrelism, and she wanted to throw
her lot in with the mongrels.

Well—that, and also she had an acting career to pursue. It was January 2002. Mette was almost seven, Saskia was thirty. It was high time
to figure out what her actual life would look like.

2011

Dear Mette,

Happy 16th birthday. Please say hello to your mother for me.

I'm pleased that the Newman volumes continue to interest you. You've increasingly made me regret that I never looked into them myself, although I remember their position in my father's bedroom bookcase when I was growing up. I, too, thought the bindings were attractive. As for your comments about Laplace, if you want to have fun with probability problems in more depth, I could mail you the textbook I worked through when I was a little older than you are now. I have a feeling you would like the subject. Let me know.

Have you heard of the Monty Hall problem? If not, google it. It's an extremely simple veridical paradox. The solution has always made sense to me, but plenty of people, otherwise good with numbers, have been bothered by it, including my father. He had good company—none other than Paul Erdös refused to believe it until he saw it proved in a computer simulation.

Speaking of my father, I wrote one of those "data sets" the other day, the first I've written in a long while. You were probably hoping they had disappeared forever. I wondered why I was thinking about him more lately, then realized that he died five years ago this

January. I've always found it interesting how the human brain can subconsciously keep track of time passing with remarkable precision. Even more, that the subconscious seems to prefer round numbers. If we humans had twelve fingers, I probably wouldn't be thinking about my father until next year. In any case, here it is:

Data Set: Futility

My father hated parties.
But he did have one party trick.
He would imitate a defense satellite trying to destroy a wave of incoming ICBMs.
He would pump his arms like recoiling cannons and rotate from the waist, moving in jerks, with incremental backward corrections.
This was meant to evoke the recalculations of a feedback mechanism trying to track a fast-moving object.
He would give up one ICBM, jerkily try to target the next, give up on that, try the next.
It was a good imitation, and everyone would laugh.
Except for my father, whose face wore a wild and angry glare.
Years later, he developed Parkinson's disease.
Because Parkinson's induces both muscle tremors and muscle rigidity, it leads to a characteristic movement called "cogwheeling," in which the limbs move in incremental spurts.
The disease also rigidifies the face and suppresses the blink reflex, causing the sufferer to look wild-eyed and angry.
Finally, it often destroys the brain's ability to focus on a subject.
Now life in bits and pieces flew continually past my father.
Like some frightful episode of *The Twilight Zone*, he had been turned into his party trick.

Love,
Your Father

1:10 a.m., March 3, 2011

I looked up the Monty Hall problem. I agree with you, it only seems paradoxical at first. Speaking of twelve fingers, what are the next three terms in the following sequence: 84, 91, 100, 121, 144, 202, 244, 400, ___, ___, ___?

That thing with your dad sounds bad.

Please send me your probability textbook. Do you need it back?

1994

Mark landed in Zagreb, relieved to have survived another flight. He hated flying. All construction designed for public use was structurally overengineered except airplanes, which had to be light enough to get off the ground. In bad turbulence he could hear the cabin flex like a drinking straw, he could watch the wings flap. It was inarguably the safest form of travel, and normally he trusted statistics, but not in this case, not on some unreachable limbic level. He wished he could say to Saskia, *See? I can be irrational, too.*

After checking into his hotel, he found his way to UN headquarters. They were housed in a dingy white building, probably nineteenth century, but he didn't know enough about European architecture to be confident. Surrounding the building was a makeshift wall with a different person's name written on each brick, flowers laid along the bottom, candles lining the top, tattered photos, scribbled messages. Inside, he was told it was a memorial to Croats who had died or disappeared during the siege of Vukovar. "They blame us," said the young UN soldier at the intake desk, speaking with cheerful dislike. "They think we should fight their war for them."

Mark found the correct office, waited an hour, confirmed he had permission to be on the flight the next day, was handed a waiver indemnifying the UN, its agencies and personnel, including but not limited to etc—it was a long sentence—from any legal liability in the event of his injury or death. He was to affirm that he was acting under his own volition as an independent agent etc—another long sentence. He signed here and there, initialed there, there, and there. He was told to appear again at 0800 hours. It was the first time Mark had heard someone outside of a movie say "oh-eight-hundred hours." What a sheltered life he had led.

He returned to the city center on foot. He always walked in unfamiliar cities if he had the time. He liked to absorb details as they randomly presented themselves, the look of buildings and people, the sound of conversation, the amount and kinds of shops. He tried not to form opinions—that universal human delight and comfort—which would necessarily be ignorant. Simply hear and see. But today he didn't take in much, other than an impression of summery youth, old men in black hats that maybe were fedoras, fake-limestone stucco nearly black with soot, blue trolley cars, a plethora of Croatian flags in red and white. His thoughts were in what would probably be called "turmoil," and a fair fraction of that turmoil was a self-questioning about whether all his life he had insulated himself too much from mental turmoil. How cowardly of him that he had left that to Susan—the family and its unhappinesses, the world and its tragedies—freeing himself to focus on more-rewarding topics. Obliviousness often served selfish ends.

He ended up in the old central square, where restaurants had set out tables in the August sunshine. He sat and ordered a coffee. Then he realized it was 1:00 p.m., so when the waiter returned, he asked for a lunch menu. He had spent some of the last six months reading up on Yugoslavia, but had arrived only at the conclusion that local opinions were passionate and prejudiced, and that there was virtually no trustworthy data. The various peoples here did not seem to share the same reality. He was surprised at how deeply it unnerved him, this inability to find a factual foundation to stand on. Then again, he didn't often read about ethnic conflict, maybe it was always this vertiginous. If so, he wanted no part of it.

There he went again, retreating, with his hands up. Protect me, big sis.

He ordered. He'd learned a couple of phrases for politeness's sake, but assumed English would be widespread in the city. He had never been good at languages. Whereas Susan had become fluent in Spanish after a year in Madrid, had picked up Dutch while living in Belgium and the Netherlands, had acquired a working knowledge of Serbo-Croatian (or Bosnian, or whatever you were supposed to call it, what a load of nonsense over a label) before she came here. Yes, children in families differentiate assiduously, studies showed that. Competition for parental attention, need for a secure sense of self. Reverence for a sibling could be just as strong a motivation as resentment. How much of his personality had been formed in opposition to Susan? Susan disobedient, Mark obedient. Susan combative, Mark conflict averse. Susan impulsive, Mark strategic. In a strangely compelling way, he felt that, with her gone, he no longer had any justification for being the kind of person that he was. Illogically, he felt like a fraud.

If one feels like a fraud, one behaves fraudulently. He and Saskia had had their first coffee date on March 2, only five months ago, and their last dinner on June 21. So they were "together" for three months and nineteen days. In that interval, they were alone in each other's presence on nine separate occasions, yet he had never told her about Susan's recent death, nor about Susan at all. What did that say? Oh, he had fooled himself with reasons. First, he'd thought it was too big a subject to bring up early. It might be seen as a pity ploy. It might have *been* a pity ploy. Then, on the night of the Lyrids, she had told him that her childhood had been unhappy, and that made him worry on their next two dates that talking about Susan might appear to undermine the gravity of her complaint, or even seem like competition. After *that*, it felt increasingly awkward to bring up because he could imagine her expostulating, "Why haven't you told me this before?" By this time it had become clear that she considered him hyper-logical and hypo-"emotional," and to bring up Susan so late, and to explicate his reasons for doing so, might confirm for her all that she found lacking in him. He knew he would eventually have to tell her, but from moment to moment he kept avoiding it. Then she broke up with him, and obviated the problem.

The whole sordid affair—his unethical pursuit of her, his suspiciously quick emotional attachment—filled him with shame. He was grateful she had had the common sense to end it, as he doubted he would have been able to do it himself.

He ate his lunch and paid, walked a block and couldn't remember what he'd eaten. He was in a narrow street heading upward. Someone at the hotel had said there was a palace and church on top of a hill.

When Saskia dropped him he spent two weeks in such anguish that it disrupted all his work. It was fortunate the semester was over. He remembered the resolution he'd made in his twenties, after two relationships came and went in quick succession, to avoid entanglements. They were too unpredictable and painful. Smart people were supposed to learn from experience. He saw that he was in danger of continuing to repeat this folly if he didn't address the underlying cause. He had hidden from Susan's death the way he hid from everything uncomfortable. Bubble-boy had become bubble-man.

He had had the excuse, when she died, that the place where it happened was too dangerous to visit. (Her body was shipped home and his mother identified it. Mark saw nothing but the box, later the urn.) But the area had quieted down after some political agreement was signed in Washington this past March. You could be granted access, and even transport, provided you had a compelling reason, such as the death of a relative who had worked for the UN. So Saskia dumped him in June, and after he picked himself up off the floor he started calling people. And here he was.

At the top of the hill. He looked at the church. He looked at the palace. He went back to his hotel. He spent the rest of the afternoon catching up on colleagues' recent research, then dined in the hotel restaurant. Heavy curtains, silver-plated claptrap, Central European fare: wiener schnitzels and the like. He wasn't hungry, but he ate a cutlet in a brown sauce with those doughy wet white things whose name he couldn't remember. He usually didn't drink, but he had a glass of red wine.

His last conversation with Susan had been over dinner in New York City. That was March of last year. She'd just spent a number of months in the Netherlands. She'd originally gone for pleasure, a stay with old friends, but while she was there she got caught up with the plight of the Bosnian refugees who'd recently washed up in the country. There was as yet little structure in place to help them, so Susan, Susan-style, merely showed up where the refugees were being housed and volunteered to do whatever was needed. Within six weeks she was able to speak and understand elementary Bosnian, and since she also knew Dutch, she accompanied refugee families to welfare bureaus, rental agencies, school offices, and so on, serving as an interpreter. Some of that work brought her into contact with officials at UNHCR in The Hague, and eventually she decided she could be more helpful if she went to Bosnia. But first she returned briefly to the US.

"To put your affairs in order?" Mark remembered joking uneasily, during their dinner. She was in the city for only a day and a night. She had called him out of the blue all of six hours ago, expecting to catch up with him by phone, but by chance he was in Manhattan for a conference. They met at a cheap Indian place she knew in the East Village.

"Well, sure," she said (or something similar). She still had some stuff in storage in Cleveland, and wanted to pick up a few things, also visit friends. She might be gone for a while.

How long since he had seen her? He had to think for a moment. More than two years. She'd dropped by their parents' house briefly for Christmas in 1990. Seeing her now, he thought she looked great, but he always thought she looked great: capable, full of ideas and energy. She was tall like him, nearly six feet, broader-shouldered than he was. She had their father's build. Her hair, which she kept short, was ashy like Mark's, but thicker and wavier. Strong chin, strong nose. When she was still in her twenties, she would turn her face profile and say, "hatchet," then turn it back forward and say, "shovel." But that was just a joke.

Now she was thirty-eight. She'd spent her twenties bouncing around the world. She ended up in Cleveland—Mark didn't know why, there were a lot of things she kept to herself—doing some kind of work (gofer? researcher?) for a legal aid firm. After she'd established Ohio residency, she went to Kent State and majored in Peace and Conflict Studies. Turns out, she told him, the Kent State program was one of the oldest in the country. They'd started it after the Ohio National Guard came for a visit and shot those four students dead. She'd obtained her degree a year ago.

"I learned a few things in the program," she said over dinner, "but mainly I wanted the diploma. You remember Mom and Dad telling us ad nauseam—telling *me,* anyway—to ignore school stupidities, a B.A. was a ticket. Like so many things, I didn't believe them until I saw it myself." She was planning to fly to Zagreb. "That's where UNPROFOR HQ is. United Nations Protection Force. Protection for citizens. Because of all that ethnic cleansing shit. How much of a sad joke the UN efforts are, I don't know yet, but at least they're trying." She had some contacts in UNPROFOR, through her work with UNHCR in the Netherlands. "Nothing official yet, I'm too lowly. But if you have some skills, like language, and you're willing to do dangerous work for a meal and a floor to sleep on, it's amazing how many doors open." From Zagreb, she hoped to make it to Herzegovina. "The Spanish Battalion is headquartered there—they're called SPANBAT, you gotta love it—and since I speak Spanish and some Bosnian, that's a pretty obvious place for me. First the Serb militias did their thing and pounded the shit out of everyone else, then the Croats and Bosnian Muslims worked together to push them out. Now everyone's wondering when the Croats will make their move against their Muslim friends. Anyway, lots of displaced people, destroyed housing, food shortages, orphaned children. It's a fucking mess." She looked happy. That wasn't the right word. It was corny, but Mark would have said she looked alive.

After dinner, they made their goodbyes on the sidewalk. Since the March evening was warm, lots of people were out. "I'll call Mom and Dad before I leave the country," she said. "How are they?"

"His Parkinson's is worse. You can really see it now in his face. He talks a lot about how stupid he's getting. Mom's angry at him all the time."

"No place like home."

Mark didn't say anything.

After a moment, she said, "Thank you for being the one to support them all these years."

"Say what?"

"I just ran away."

"Oh, no . . . I mean . . . You had every right—"

"Speaking of which, I gotta go."

She had friends in Brooklyn she was spending the night with. All these friends she had, around the globe. Mark had never met any of them.

She hugged him. "I love you, baby brother."

"Me too. I mean—"

She laughed, shouldering her knapsack. "I know what you mean." She turned and walked away. Her goodbyes were always quick.

That's how he remembered it, anyway, sitting at his table in the

Zagreb hotel restaurant. He'd eaten everything, finished his glass of wine. Wine made him sleepy, which was why he rarely drank it. The restaurant was mostly empty. Tourism probably hadn't rebounded much since the war in this region had ended. And anyway, Mark had read somewhere that this might be only a lull. Rumor was, the Croatian government wanted to take back some areas that Serbs were holding. Christ, it was depressing.

He went up to his room and caught up on more reading. Then he wished there was a piano he could play. It might make him feel better. Instead, he went to bed early. Though still groggy from the wine, he lay awake for a long time. Eventually he was in a large white room. It had a high ceiling and decorative moldings and one of those European wooden parquet floors that rattle like a field of bones when you walk across them. The room was crowded with pianos, both grands and uprights, some in good shape, some wrecks. His job was to change all their positions, which was difficult logistically, because they were in one another's way. The work went on and on, monotonously. He heaved, the pianos resisted (their casters were rusty), and the parquet floor sounded like the xylophone in *Danse Macabre*.

AT THE AIRPORT the next day, there was a sign warning people not to deviate from the paved paths outside, lest someone step on a mine. A man had been badly injured two weeks ago. "Even here?" Mark asked the liaison from the UN press office who'd arranged the flight. "Aren't we nowhere near a front line?"

"The Yugoslav army mined their facilities when they withdrew in 1991, after Croatia declared independence. That included this airport." Her name was Samantha, from Maryland. She had reddish hair in a ponytail and a bright bar of teeth. She looked to be in her mid-twenties. Another idealistic young person.

"They haven't been cleared yet?"

"There are millions of mines sown across ex-Yugoslavia. De-mining is a slow business."

Mark met the others while they waited for the plane to be fueled. The flight hadn't been arranged for him, he was just tagging along on a UN junket for reporters. "They don't think there's been enough positive coverage of the job they're doing," said Jeff, a reporter for some US news outlet Mark had heard of, but never read. Also on the trip was John, a freelancer who'd written a book about the early phase of the war; and Roberta, a political columnist who was apparently well known, although Mark had never heard of her. He didn't often read about politics. The three of them, along with the UN liaison Samantha, had been on a flight into Sarajevo three days ago, but their pilot had had to turn around when the cargo plane in front of them was hit by .50 caliber machine gun fire.

"Serbs in the hills around the city, having some fun," Jeff said. "The bullets go right through the plane—"

"Yes," Mark said, "planes are built very light—"

"—and with all the engine noise they're usually not even noticed during flight unless someone gets hit. This time, a UN security guy caught one in the thigh. Poor bastard, those are big bullets. I heard it shattered his ball joint."

All this was said with what seemed flagrant insouciance. Mark hadn't met war reporters before, but it made sense they'd be a thrill-seeking bunch. There was a certain dopamine receptor in the brain that was responsible, increasing the pleasure reward for dangerous behavior, inducing restlessness and boredom when the stimulus was absent. It was gene-linked. Mark was pretty sure he didn't have the gene. He derived sufficient reward from discovering that his car hadn't developed a flat tire while he wasn't looking.

He learned another thing about war reporters: they liked to tease anyone who didn't have the gene. When Jeff caught sight of the plane they'd be getting on he said, "Christ, it's a Yak-40. You know the safety record of these things is abysmal."

John said, "We'll be fine as long as the crew isn't—"

"Ukrainian?"

"Oh man, are they fucking Ukrainian? Shit, we're screwed."

Roberta the columnist looked unhappy. Mark tried to be impervious, but he had to admit that the scruffy pilot, copilot, and mechanic all looked like hard-drinking muleteers. He could imagine one of them whacking a faulty altimeter with a wrench, then giving the others a grinning thumbs-up.

"UN-issue, right?" Jeff was pointing at the blue protective vest someone had handed Mark that morning at headquarters.

"Yes."

"Look, you should know, those UN vests suck. They won't stop a high-powered round. You need ceramic panels, like mine has." He unbuttoned the top of his shirt to show Mark a few inches of gleaming black armor. "A vest like this costs five hundred dollars. I forced my bosses to pay for it."

"Thank you for the advice," Mark said. The mechanic out on the tarmac was giving a grinning thumbs-up. The pilot popped the clutch and whipped the plane around, pointing it toward the runway. Mark tried to remember whatever he knew about aeronautics. The plane's low-mounted wings and rear engines would presumably give the plane good lift at low speeds. It was probably designed for small airfields.

John and Jeff were talking about high-powered sniper rounds. "I saw a girl reporter in Sarajevo get hit square in the chest. Her armor stopped the round, but she went flying. She hit the ground, like, a dozen feet from where she'd been standing."

The plane was accelerating. There had been no announcement about seat belts or lighted exits. "Hey man." Jeff tapped Mark on the shoulder.

"Once we're in the air, you should sit on your vest." He indicated his superior model, under his smug ass. "Any rounds would come from below, right?"

"That makes sense," Mark said. The nose jerked up, the pilot floored it, and the wings carved a hyperbolic slice out of the wall of air. The asymptote was at an angle Mark would have thought impossible. Roberta let out a frightened moan. Or maybe that was Mark.

AT AN AIRPORT NEAR a coastal city called Split, they transferred to a helicopter for the final leg to Mostar. Now they were in the hands of the British. One of the soldiers explained that Split was the headquarters for BRITBAT. A painful spasm went through Mark. "You gotta love it," he said.

While they were waiting for the helicopter to take off, the same soldier talked about a massacre the BRITBAT troops had uncovered the previous year. (Susan had been right: the Croats had turned on their Muslim allies right around the time she arrived in Mostar.) "The Croat militias decided to take over three districts in central Bosnia. The local Croat men stayed behind to help find and kill their neighbors. The militias had marksmen in place to shoot villagers as they fled across the fields. Everyone here is fucking crazy. We're supposed to keep them from doing what they want to do."

They lifted off and the coast disappeared behind them. Sitting on his tissue-paper vest, Mark looked out the open side door at limestone ridges denuded of trees and dusty dark-green valleys between. Small villages of white houses, terra-cotta roofs. His view was partly obstructed by a soldier manning a machine gun.

"I hate helicopters!" Jeff said, off to the side. Worryingly, he looked like he meant it. He was huddled against the wall, his arms between his knees.

"Why?" Mark asked. They had to yell because of the noise.

"A helicopter is like a cartoon safe with a rotor attached! If a single bullet knocks out a blade, the thing falls like a rock!"

"Or like a safe, I guess!" Mark yelled.

Talking was too difficult, so no one said anything for the rest of the flight. Mark kept his eye out the open door, watching the ground fall away into a valley, then rise again as they crossed another ridge. He thought about how certain words are almost always used for certain situations, and no one seems to think about it. When helicopters hit a mountainside, they're always said to have "slammed" into it. When they fall like a safe, they're said to have "plunged."

They crossed another ridge. The valley below them appeared to be empty of houses or roads. The soldier manning the machine gun sat up straight and did something that looked like flipping off a safety catch. Perhaps they'd entered an area known to have snipers. Mark leaned closer to the open door. He wondered if he would see a puff of smoke down there, whether he'd feel the bullet as it came out the top of his head. But nothing happened, because he'd always been the lucky one. After another twenty minutes they crested a round-topped mountain and suddenly Mostar lay below them.

The helicopter landed at an airport south of the city, where two UN jeeps picked them up. Mark sat with Roberta and Samantha as they drove to the city center. They were on the east side of the city, the Muslim side, which, as Mark understood it, had been pounded first by the Serbs, then pulverized by the Croats. He watched the concrete buildings go by, for the most part roofless, their walls perforated by artillery shells and pockmarked by bullets in a profuse stochastic pattern. On the sidewalks and roadbed he saw scarred dimples with radiating lines that showed where mortar shells had landed. They looked somewhat like lunar craters, since the physics were analogous, the shell's explosive charge contributing energy to mimic an asteroid's greater momentum. The whole city looked lunar, in fact: exposed gray stone and regolith. He reminded himself that this wasn't the city that Susan saw. She had died on May 7 last year, and the fighting between Croats and Muslims in Mostar began on May 9.

The jeeps disgorged the party near the place where a famous stone bridge had once stood. Now there was a temporary footbridge slung from steel cables that swayed and bounced as they crossed it. The opaque green river below boiled and seethed. Roberta said something about the tragedy of this destruction of a UNESCO world heritage cultural something or other, bridges being hopeful symbols of connection, etc. Everyone nodded except Mark, who surprised himself by saying, "It's only stone. It can be rebuilt." He felt himself blushing.

The reporters were being shepherded to a building on the west side, and Mark went along because he'd been told he would meet his interpreter there. It turned out that this young man, Goran, had a prior agreement to translate for the reporters' interview with the deputy mayor of West Mostar, so Mark sat with the rest of them in a low-ceilinged room and listened. The deputy mayor, whose name Mark never caught, was a small man with black thinning hair whose face glistened with sweat in the hot space. He gave long responses to the questions, in gradual crescendos. The one that really set him off was a request by Roberta that he explain why Croats and Muslims could not go back to peacefully cohabiting in the city, as they had done for many years. The man's answer, as interpreted by Goran, sounded to Mark like mush-brained nonsense about the Ottoman Empire and the clash of civilizations, that the thing to understand about the Turks and therefore the Bosnian Muslims was that they had never had an Enlightenment, while Croatia had been part of the Austrian empire, where there was rule of law, universities, Beethoven, table linen etc. Then he claimed that all Bosnian Muslims were really Croats, anyway, and that's why all of this region should be run by Croats, and the proof of their ethnic identity was that there was a certain dialect of Croatian that only Croats spoke, and the Muslims of Bosnia spoke that dialect.

Mark had been getting angry—the social metastasis of this lizard-brain idiocy had killed his sister—and now he shot up his hand and blurted out, "Wait a minute." The deputy mayor stopped babbling and everyone looked at him. Mark said to Goran, "That last thing he said—it's circular reasoning. Is he really so stupid that he doesn't understand that?" No one said anything, so Mark elaborated. "He said that Muslims are really Croats because Muslims speak a dialect that only Croats speak. But one can only claim that only Croats speak that dialect if one has previously assumed that Muslims are Croats."

More silence. Then Goran said, "Is that a question?"

"It's a refutation. Tell him that."

"Hey, man," Jeff interjected, "I don't think—"

"Just tell him. He shouldn't be allowed—"

"You're wasting your time, pal," Jeff was saying. "These people say twelve kinds of stupid before morning coffee."

"Just tell him! It's unbearable that he can sit there and spout such nonsense."

"Uh, sure," Goran said. He and the reporters were looking at Mark with frowns of sympathy. They all knew why he was here. "So . . ." Goran went on tentatively, "what was it again you wanted me to say?"

At this moment, Mark caught up with the rest of the room. Yes, he was wasting everyone's time. "I'm sorry," he said. "Forget it." He said to the room at large, "Ignore me," and made it easier for everyone to do that by leaving. Goran met up with him in the corridor twenty minutes later. "I'm sorry," Mark said again.

Goran held up his hand. "No need." Then he put his hand forward. "It is good to meet you, though of course very sad." They shook hands. "Your sister was a wonderful person. Everyone loved her."

Mark nodded. They left the building. Goran led him around a corner to where a battered dark green Zastava was parked. He reached through the open passenger window to unlatch the door from the inside and gestured, "Please." They drove south along damaged streets. After a few minutes, Goran stopped at a two-story concrete box surrounded by sandbags piled twelve feet high. "Spanish battalion local HQ," he said.

They walked through a gap in the sandbags and made a right angle turn to get around a baffle wall. A memory stirred in Mark concerning his father, something about Chinese demons. Inside the building were soldiers, desks, a conference table, a coffee machine. All the glass in all the windows had been removed, or maybe blown out, and replaced with plastic sheeting. Goran asked around, using what sounded like simple Spanish, until a man with some sort of insignia on his shoulders introduced himself as Major so-and-so, and took Mark's hand, putting his other hand on Mark's shoulder. He said in English, "Everyone loved your sister. She helped the people here very much. It is a terrible thing that happened."

Presumably, Mark replied. The major called out something and other soldiers converged. They spoke mainly in Spanish, fragments in English, and several of them put their hands on Mark's shoulders and arms. They all agreed: everyone had loved Susan, her death was a tragedy. There was nothing to say in response that wasn't so obvious as to be unnecessary, so Mark didn't say anything. He didn't know precisely when she had arrived in Mostar, but she couldn't have been here more than three weeks. He wondered how well any of these people really had known her. But she was dead, and therefore had been lovable.

One of the soldiers was handing him a three-by-five photograph, a shot of a sunny street, two figures standing next to an armored personnel carrier. One was Susan, with her knapsack, short hair windblown, looking to the left and beginning a gesture, perhaps saying to someone out of the frame, *Come on.* The other figure was the soldier standing in front of Mark. Mark nodded and tried to hand it back. He could hardly bear to look at it. The soldier gestured, *You keep it.*

Nothing occurred to Mark to say to any of these people. He allowed them to put their hands on him, he felt their goodwill and concern. He probably kept nodding, and probably said thank you. He stopped hearing whatever they were saying. A psychosomatic deafness had come over him. Then he and Goran were back on the sidewalk, back in the car, and Goran was heading southwest out of the city, toward the round-topped mountain the helicopter had flown over on the way in. Mark returned to watching ruined buildings go by.

Susan had never been much of a correspondent. Over the years Mark got a letter every four or five months. "Dashed off" was probably the way to describe them. He always imagined her borrowing someone else's back to write them on, out on some dusty tarmac, a chance courier waiting. She sent only two letters to the family from Yugoslavia, or "ex-Yugoslavia," as everyone seemed to call it now—one to his parents and one to him. His had been written in Mostar, eight days before she died.

Hey little brother—

This place! Wild! They need everything—the kids break your heart. Some adults can drive you crazy—but not all. I hate the attitude of reporters and some UN people here—"these Balkan savages." Ignorance hiding behind condescension. Turns out my Bosnian sucks—Mostar dialect is different, a lot of Turkish loanwords. But I don't think I'm wasting space. Mainly translating, but also doing anything that needs doing. Found ten typewriters in a building the Serbs bombed and spent all day yesterday cleaning them. Also helping a local engineer, a sweetheart of a guy, who's repairing waterlines on the east side (Serbs again). For example. Maybe you already read somewhere, fighting has broken out between Croats and Muslims in some villages in central Bosnia. People here are scared. I'm counting on

*the city being different from villages. Civilization, I tell people—
invented by cities! Hope your work's going well. If you want to
write, the return address on the envelope should work.*

Love Susan

"What's that?" Goran asked.

Mark folded the letter and put it back in his pocket. "Nothing."

The car was climbing the mountain. No houses now, just yellow
rocks and vegetation gray with dust. They swung around a hairpin
curve, and Mostar was spread out below them on the left. It looked like
Dresden, circa March 1945. "It's a letter Susan wrote to me," Mark admitted. "April thirtieth."

Goran clucked his tongue. They went around another hairpin and
passed a retaining wall black with graffiti. "What does 'ne, nikad, ni-
kako' mean?" Mark asked.

"Where did you hear that?"

"It was on the wall back there. The deputy mayor kept saying something similar."

"It means 'No, never, not in any way.'"

Mark thought for a few seconds about whether there was any comment worth making. "Many things are impossible with people like that,"
he finally came up with.

The car cleared the steep lip of the slope and entered a saddle between two rises. This was the landscape they'd flown over, where snipers
shot at helicopters.

"That population chart the deputy mayor showed," Goran said. "You
should not believe it."

"I didn't."

"The Croats love to show census figures, which they say prove most

Muslims came to Mostar after 1961. But the reason the Muslim numbers go up after 1961 is because that was the first year they were allowed to choose 'Muslim' as their ethnicity on the census."

Mark didn't say anything. He didn't want Goran to think he was judging all Yugoslavs. Instead, he said, "May I ask what your ethnic background is?"

"My father is Croat, my mother is Muslim. But here—" he gestured to the land going by—"this is West Herzegovina. Croats here are very strong Croats, very Catholic. So it is lucky for me that my name, Goran Galić, is a good Croatian name. I don't tell anyone here that my mother is Muslim."

"Mm."

"'Goran' means 'mountain man.' Maybe I'll go up into the mountains to escape all this stupid ethnic shit."

"The in-group/out-group obsession does seem particularly strong here," Mark ventured.

Goran winced. "The question is why. Even some Yugoslavs say we have this, what do you call it, a predisposition for ethnic hatred. But I reject this."

"I didn't mean to imply—"

"This war is the result of deliberate planning by certain political parties to enhance their power. Their use of propaganda—have you seen what the Croatian and Serbian media broadcast in this country?"

"No."

"Lies, every day. People watch these lies and believe them. There is a deliberate creation of fear. I am telling you, Mark, if people in the United States had this same kind of media propaganda, after five years you would have a civil war, too."

Mark was silent for a while. "National cultures differ," people liked to say, but what did that mean? Few things meant much at all when framed in such general terms. He forced himself to really look at Goran. He found this hard to do with new acquaintances. The man was quite handsome. Thick brown hair, regular features, olive skin, notably light gray eyes. Against his skin, the eyes seemed to glow. Susan had probably liked him, perhaps been attracted to him. "How did you learn such good English?"

"I majored in American literature," Goran said. "I wrote my thesis on Dos Passos."

Who? Mark thought, but didn't say. Since he was American, his ignorance of this writer might be interpreted by Goran as a judgment that he or she was not important. And for all Mark knew, Dos Passos was the most celebrated writer of . . . whatever time period he or she had written in.

By this time they were driving through a mostly level upland area. Low dry hills were visible here and there in the distance. They passed a crossroads where a few houses were clustered, then another. "There doesn't seem to be much damage here," Mark said.

"You are right," Goran said. "The Croats of Herzegovina have done very well for themselves." Neither spoke for a minute. The car rattled and made a continuous throaty sound. "The Virgin Mary visits them every day, that's how loved they are."

"In Medjugorje," Mark said. He'd read about the claims of visitations there.

"Mary wants peace. Medjugorje was getting rich on all the pilgrims, but the war stopped that. The main Spanish HQ is there, because they have so many comfortable new buildings, all completely undamaged. A miracle!"

The car came to a rise where the road turned to the right so as to ascend the slope laterally. They went around one switchback, and as they approached a second Goran slowed the car and steered it into an area of beaten dirt on the outside of the curve. Stopping by some low bushes, he switched the engine off. He turned to look at Mark with eyes that seemed strangely deep and bright. "This is where it happened."

Mark looked around. "Where are we, exactly?"

"Ten kilometers from Medjugorje. We're just about to get to a village called Sretnice."

Mark wrote down, "Sretnice." Then got out of the car. It was midafternoon, hot and dazzling. There was a light breeze, a smell of stone dust. Also of the pungent oils that vegetation produces in dry climates to impede respiration and provide a chemical shield against thirsty insects. Also, a sweetish carob-like smell that was some sort of feces, maybe goat. Mark turned slowly to take in more of the view in all directions.

"Don't step off the road," Goran said. "Mines are unlikely here, but you never know."

Unlikely, because this was the land that Mary loved, where Croats had done very well for themselves. "The sniper was probably a Croat, right?" Mark said.

Goran shrugged. "Probably. But it could have been a Muslim, trying to make the Croats look bad. The car had clear UN markings."

"The bullet came from where?"

Goran pointed away from the hairpin, up the hill. Bushes and boulders lined what appeared to be a distinct upper edge, but was probably just where the slope curved away from the sight line. "He was lying on the ground somewhere up there."

Mark turned to look back down the road. "Cars coming up the hill would slow down before entering the hairpin," he said. "He would have a good shot through the windshield."

"Yes," Goran said.

"You were driving?"

"Yes."

"And Susan was sitting next to you."

"Yes."

"And someone else was in the car, right? Some official?"

"There was a guy from the UN who'd been in Mostar looking for places to house some refugees. People were fleeing central Bosnia, the fighting hadn't started here yet. He didn't speak Spanish very well, and of course no Bosnian, so your sister was going around with him. He needed to go to Spanish HQ in Medjugorje and she came along to help. I was driving because I knew the route. Also, I had permission to drive the UN-leased vehicles."

"Where was he sitting?"

"In the back."

"You two were chauffeuring him."

"He might have preferred to sit in the front, but your sister had some things she wanted to talk to me about during the drive."

What? Mark wanted to know, but didn't ask. Perhaps it was private. Susan had always valued her privacy. "What kind of car was it?"

"You mean . . . ?"

"What make?"

"I don't remember for sure. A Fiat, maybe. You know, one of the boxy ones. It looked a lot like this car." Goran pointed at the Zastava.

"A Fiat 128."

"Maybe."

Mark returned to sit in the passenger seat and spoke to Goran through the open window. "Show me where the bullet hit the windshield."

"I don't know exactly, the whole windshield fractured."

"You didn't notice an impact hole afterward?"

"Well . . . I guess it was just about in the center of the right side."

"Point to the spot."

"Look, I don't really know—"

"Just point to the spot you think is most likely."

Goran did so. Mark sat in the seat and looked past Goran's finger toward the slope rising beyond the hairpin. The angle would be roughly the same back on the road. According to the autopsy, Susan had been hit on her right side just below the seventh rib. The bullet had gone through her liver and out her lower back. If the sniper was hidden approximately where the curving slope seemed to present a vantage point, then the trajectory Mark was looking at seemed conceivable.

He climbed out of the car and starting walking back down the road. Goran followed. "Could you show me the exact location of the car when it was hit?"

"I'll try." They continued down the slope for another ten meters, then Goran turned around and walked slowly back up, glancing left and right. "About here."

Mark joined him at the spot and examined the pavement for a number of yards in every direction. Nothing. Of course, it had happened fifteen months ago. "I need to picture it. Tell me exactly what happened."

"I was approaching the turn. There was a bang. The windshield went white, with all those little lines. I thought at first it was a rock."

"Just one shot?"

"I think so. Since it seemed to have hit the right side, I turned left. Whatever it was, rock or whatever, I was afraid of another, so I drove the car off the road and down into the bushes. Over here."

Mark followed him to the road edge and looked down the slope. There was a four-foot-wide band of gravel, then the ubiquitous cover of waist-high plants with gnarled branches and leathery leaves—he wondered if they called it "maquis" here, too. A few meters farther up the verge he could see a place where some of the bushes looked shorter. "Maybe there," he said.

"Maybe."

Mark climbed down, mines be damned, and looked closer. He could see scarring on some of the branches. Two bushes looked as though they'd been nearly uprooted. He sifted through the stones for a minute and found a dozen or so cubes of safety glass. "This must be the place," he said up to Goran, who'd remained on the roadbed. He lay down among the bushes, on his back.

Goran called down, "Are you okay?"

The sky was so clear and light-flooded, so blindingly blue. On the left there was a contrail from probably a military aircraft, and straight over-head a thin smudge of cloud, like an attempted erasure with one of those worthless latex nubs. Stargazing would be excellent in this dry and re-mote terrain. "What did Susan want to talk to you about?" Mark asked the sky. "During the drive."

Goran's voice floated down to him. "She thought the UN official was an idiot. In love with himself. She'd spent the last two days with him, and he'd been flirting with her."

"Doing what?"

"The usual stuff."

"I don't know what that means."

"Putting his hands on her when talking. Her arm, her hip. Telling her she was beautiful." Mark couldn't see Goran, but it sounded like he'd braved the mines as well and come partway down the slope. "He'd invited her back to his room the night before. Maybe you shouldn't tell anyone I said this."

God forbid I should embarrass the fellow, Mark thought.

"Since he could hardly speak Spanish, and I understand it pretty well, she told me these things in the front seat, while he sat in the back. Prob-ably the car noise made it hard for him to hear anything. And also maybe she thought if she sat in the back, he'd insist on sitting with her."

Mark could feel a number of sharp stones pressing into his back. On a discomfort scale of one to ten, it counted as a one. The bushes smelled like creosote and thyme. There was a tiny lavender flower with five pet-als at the end of one branch. Just one flower, out of all the branches in

Mark's view. "Do you remember what Susan was saying just before the shot?"

"Nothing. Her complaints about the guy were all in the first ten minutes. She laughed at him—I wanted to hit him—a lot of these UN people are stupid members of rich families, sent off to do something where if they fuck up no one cares much, or it never comes out. After that we just drove. The windows were open, it was noisy."

Then the shot, the fracturing safety glass, the car veering to the left and sliding down the slope. The autopsy specified the bullet. It was something called an M75 ball, fired from a Zastava M76 sniper rifle. It had a mass of thirteen grams and traveled at 760 meters per second. That translated into 3750 joules of kinetic energy, equivalent to a bowling ball dropped from a height of 180 feet. But the bullet expended some of its energy on the windshield and then, with its full metal jacket, and missing Susan's ribs, it went right through her, with enough energy left over to tear through her seat back and the lower part of the rear seat. It probably lodged somewhere in the metal chassis between the rear wheels. If it had gone through her lung, or through her neck without hitting a major artery, she might have survived. "And after?" Mark asked. "Did she say anything?" The intensity of human desire to know a loved one's last words. Mark wondered at it, but felt it nonetheless.

"I put the car down off the road, it was quiet, I think I said, 'Is everyone okay?' And the UN guy was down on the floor in the back and he said, 'Was that a shot?' And it's strange, but it was only then I realized it might have been a bullet. I looked at your sister and . . . Do you want to hear this?"

"Yes."

"She was leaning against the passenger door, with her head down. I said, 'Are you okay?' and she said, I think she said, 'Jesus, what was that?' and I said, 'I don't know,' and then she said, 'Something hit me really hard,' and I leaned over, and that's when I saw the blood." Goran stopped.

"Please keep going."

"I think I said something like, 'Oh my god, you've been shot!' and she said, 'Figures.' I think she was trying to make light of it. Then the pain must have kicked in. She didn't say anything after that. I took off my shirt and pressed it on the wound on her front. We stayed in the car because we didn't know where the sniper was, we were afraid of also being shot."

"Of course."

"So we didn't move her, and she was bleeding into the seat and I couldn't see it."

"She never said anything else?"

"No. She was in a lot of pain. She was making sounds of . . . of great pain, of . . . what's the word . . . agony. I am very sorry to tell you that. It was terrible to hear. After a few minutes, she got quieter. We had no radio phones with us, and it was another maybe ten minutes before another car came by, a local villager, and we decided the sniper had left, or wouldn't shoot anymore, or anyway we had to risk it, so we moved her into the other car, and that's when I saw how much blood there was on the seat cushions."

"And she died on the way to the hospital."

"No, we drove her to a hospital in Mostar. She was still alive when the people from the ER took her out of the car."

"The report said DOA."

"That's incorrect."

Some unmeasurable period of silence went by. Some ants, or some other sort of sociable insects, had found Mark. The smudge of cloud had dissipated, and the contrail had drifted south, widening and blurring. "I'm guessing that the UN guy was sitting behind you, rather than behind my sister," Mark said. "Before the shot."

"Yes, I think that's right."

He would have done this if he was still trying to flirt, so that he could see her profile, try to engage her in conversation. The windows open, the noise of the hot wind and the car. She was in the front seat because he had been pestering her for two days. The shot came through her seat and missed him entirely because he was sitting behind the driver so that he could continue to pester her.

She had told Mark once, years after it had happened: she was eighteen, bumming around in Florida, and saw an ad for a cook on a yacht that was going sailing in the Caribbean. She inquired, got the job. Two days out, it became clear the captain wanted sex more than he wanted cooking. And he got it. "I wasn't raped," Susan said. "Or at least, not violently. I finally went along just to stop the hassle. It seemed easier. I was disgusted with myself for being so naive about the job. We got to some island and I jumped ship. And ever since I've been disgusted with myself for giving in to him like that. But look at this sick shit: he forced himself on me, and I'm mad at *myself*."

"Are you okay?" Goran asked again.

"I just want to lie here a little longer, if that's okay," Mark said.

"Sure."

Mark could hear Goran going back up the slope. Every now and then a crawling insect bit him. On a scale of one to ten it was less than .01. Goran had wanted to hit the man from the UN. Perhaps he'd liked Susan. Maybe Susan sat in the front seat not only because she disliked the UN man, but because she liked Goran. He seemed a good man. She was older than him, taller. Maybe the sniper shot her instead of Goran because she was the biggest target in the car. Or maybe he shot her because, even with all the hatred he reserved for Muslims (if he was a Croat), or for Croats (if he was a Muslim), he had a little extra hatred to spare for the only woman in the car, this meddling foreign bitch.

Had it comforted Susan that Goran was with her? She was so far from home. But then, Mark wasn't sure if she thought of a "home," the way he did. Goran no doubt felt terrible about what happened. Being human, he probably irrationally felt responsible. Maybe that's why he wanted to remember that she was still alive when they reached the hospital. Maybe she *was* still alive, but moribund, and the hospital listed her as DOA to make the paperwork simpler. Or maybe someone in the hospital didn't like meddling foreign bitches, either.

Mark knew what a Fiat 128 looked like because when he was eleven years old it was one of the last Matchbox cars he bought. He'd never paid much attention to real cars. His Fiat 128 was painted a color he'd always thought of as raspberry chocolate. No other car in his collection had a color like it. By the time he bought it, he was too old to play the game in which he dropped a blanket and then drove his cars around the folds. But lying now among the bushes, enduring the absurdly small pain of the stones in his back and the insects biting him and the heat of the sun, he closed his eyes and saw his delicious Fiat 128 turning right to ascend laterally the slope of the hill, then left at the first switchback, and he could see the whole terrain below him, and the sniper's hiding place, and all the possible trajectories, and he couldn't help himself, he imagined taking hold of the Fiat and swerving it right and left, avoiding the shot, then scooting it safely down into the bushes made of modeler's moss, admiring how realistic it all was.

2013

7:16 p.m., July 8, 2013

Dear Mette,

I hope you're well. Please say hello to your mother for me. I wrote a "data set" about my sister, who died many years ago.

Data Set: Cabin Fever

For our two-week family vacation in the summer of 1971 my
   parents rented a cabin on a lake in New Hampshire.
It rained for two weeks.
I was eleven and my sister was sixteen.
My sister and I played as many card games as we could
   stand, then we got bored.
My sister fought with my parents.
My parents fought with each other.
My mother proposed we all go see a movie.
She had noticed that *Song of Norway* was playing in a
   nearby town.
My sister and I didn't want to see *Song of Norway*, we
   wanted to see the other movie playing at that theater,
   The Anderson Tapes.
That movie is too violent, my mother said.

Song of Norway is too stupid, my sister said.

It's about the composer Edvard Grieg, my mother said.

Jesus, who cares? my sister said.

It has beautiful photography of Norway, my mother said.

Man, I can't wait, my sister said.

I loved classical music, and even I didn't want to see *Song
    of Norway.*

But my mother wouldn't let it go.

Don't you want to see it, Mark? she kept asking me.

This was strange, because she usually didn't care about
    movies.

We went to see *Song of Norway.*

It was terrible.

Even my mother hated it.

She called the actor who played Grieg "a whiny little twerp
    with a weak chin."

She said every time his lower lip trembled she wanted to
    punch him in the face.

My sister was good at recognizing leverage when she had it.

Two days later we went to see *The Anderson Tapes.*

It was violent and sexy.

My sister and I loved it.

On the merits of the movie my mother made no comment.

She confined herself to expressing the hope that maybe
    now my sister would shut up.

And my sister did, in a way.

Going to see *The Anderson Tapes* was the last thing she
    ever did with our family.

I can't tell whether I'm burdening you with these things. Whenever
I write one, I don't know what to do with it.

Love,
Your Father

8:05 p.m., July 8, 2013

well they're kind of depressing

11:10 p.m., July 8, 2013

I'm sorry to hear that. I don't intend them to be. I'll stop.

11:14 p.m., July 8, 2013

don't do that
    probably it's just me
    when did your sister die?

11:19 p.m., July 8, 2013

May 1993. I was thinking about her a lot in the last few weeks and
then I realized it had been 20 years. I think it's interesting how the
subconscious mind can keep track of time passing, and even
seems to prefer round numbers. If we had twelve fingers, I
probably wouldn't be remembering her so vividly until 2017

11:22 p.m., July 8, 2013

old man! you made the exact same lame joke when you sent me
the thing about your dad a couple of years ago.

11:24 p.m., July 8, 2013

wow that's embarrassing

11:25 p.m., July 8, 2013

nah, it's natural. what are you, sixty now? you're getting stupid
right on schedule

11:27 p.m., July 8, 2013

this 54-year-old relic needs to go to bed
    "probably it's just me" you said. things ok with you?

12:23 a.m., July 9, 2013

up and down
    wondering about the meaning of life

12:26 a.m., July 9, 2013

whenever students of mine brought this up, I always used to say,
"of course there's no meaning, so what?" Strangely, this never
seemed to cheer them. Then I heard a colleague say, "Life may
have no meaning, but it can have *purpose*." I liked that. So that's
now what I tell my depressed students
    any more thoughts about college?

12:31 a.m., July 9, 2013

still don't see why I need it; I like this job I got a few weeks ago,
maybe I mentioned it? a startup in Vinegar Hill, developing code
for 3D imaging effects
    video games are huge, so it pays well
    I wanted to ask you, Newman has an article on Cantor and
set theory and it's gotten me interested in the Continuum
Hypothesis, this whole issue of using different models to
prove the unprovability of a theorem. I have some questions,
I'll write them up tonight while you're recharging your
old-brain batteries and you'll see them in the morning,
okay?

12:34 a.m., July 9, 2013

sure; some of this is hard stuff
    remember I'm an astronomer, not a mathematician. I'll do
my best
    good night

Friday, February 19, 2016

A man and a woman are arguing in an upscale apartment. The argument has something to do with an errand the man has just run that the woman thinks was foolish and probably dangerous. Your first choice is, do you want to be the man or the woman? If you choose to be the man, you have a number of ways of conducting the argument, and you might even get physical, and there might be consequences to these choices down the line, but the short-term result is the same. The woman locks you outside on the balcony. You see New York City below you. You are on the 86th floor of a residential tower in lower Manhattan. The streets below you are canals. If at any point during the previous argument you had looked at your implanted wrist terminal, you would have seen that the year is 2120. You might also have seen the latest news report that some government agency you've never heard of is looking for you. Your second major choice: Do you climb over the balcony railing and negotiate the narrow ledge to the adjoining apartment's balcony, or do you call your impetuous and untrustworthy contact in building security and tell him to come up and "talk sense" into the woman?

If you choose to be the woman, you also have a number of ways of conducting the argument, which might also have consequences later. But once again, the short-term result is the same. The man will try to kill you. Your second major choice is, do you kill the man in self-defense, or do you flee the apartment and—discovering that the stairway door is locked—heed the urgings of a mysterious woman who beckons to you to join her in the elevator?

The game, as Mette envisioned it back when she was interested in things (and still thought of gender as binary), would eventually require the player to make ten major choices—that is, ones leading to a branch in the narrative, with no possible return to the alternative choice. The player's game could be saved only on top of the previous save, so choice was permachoice. There would be scores of minor decisions to make—dialogue options, which door to go through, whether or not to pick up an object. The player would not know which choices were the major ones. One consequence of the minor choices was that they would affect the way in which the next major choice was presented, thus influencing the likelihood that the player would choose one option over the other. Since there were a total of ten bifurcations, there were 1024 possible endings to the game, occurring in 256 differentiated portions of 32 basic worlds. For example, in one ending the player might be drinking a mai tai on a sunstruck beach with a loved companion of chosen gender (sorry!) and species. In another, Earth suffers a worldwide nuclear apocalypse. In another, the player is condemned for life to labor on an asteroidal mining colony. Of the 1024 possible endings, 916 exist somewhere on the spectrum between unhappy and horrifically miserable; 96 are mixed (e.g., you're alive, but lonely; you're a heroine, but everyone hates you; you won the war, but lost your legs). Only 12 endings are happy. (Little secret: 10 of those 12 are reserved for the female.)

The name of the game: *Oops!*

Back when she cared about shit like that.

The question was always money. Ideally, the settings would be fully navigable in 3D and the text would be voiced. Mette, Andres, and Seoyeon in their spare time were scripting and programming a sample, then planning to crowdsource it and see how much they could raise. Branching narrative games have never been very popular, both among players and programmers. The latter's dissatisfaction is that so much programming and scripting never gets experienced by any one player. As for the former, as much as they might claim to value interactivity and verisimilitude, players don't really like choices in games that are both potentially disastrous and irrevocable. That's a little too much like reality.

Yeah, yeah, Mette and Seo-yeon said to Andres. But maybe the unpopularity is due to the fact that no one has yet produced a branching narrative game with great 3D graphics and a kick-ass story line. Game designers have shied away from spending enough, so the examples thus far have been visually weak, and plotted in an annoyingly deceptive way so that the alleged hundreds of choices converge on a mere half dozen possible endings. Let's make history!

Back when, etc.

Speaking of too much like reality, here she is in Seattle

without a fucking clue

what to do

The bus pulled in at 7:43 a.m., forty-three minutes late. 43 of course is prime, and 743 is a Sophie Germain prime, meaning when you double it and add one you get another prime, namely 1487. Sophie Germain was a brilliant nineteenth-century mathematician who was barred from a career because she lacked a cock and arguably therefore a brain, and who further disqualified herself by having two breasts, one of which turned cancerous and killed her at fifty-five. Sequences of Sophie Germain primes are called Cunningham chains, and it's obvious that for prime numbers larger than 5, only those whose last digit is 9 can generate a Cunningham chain longer than three. Mette walked north on 6th Avenue because she could see tall buildings in the distance, then couldn't resist a left on Weller, because *The Adventures of Buckaroo Banzai Across the 8th Dimension* is a great flick of long ago, then right on 5th, then left on Jackson because *The Lord of the Rings* (but not *The Hobbit*), then right on 3rd, then left on Main, because who can resist a Main Street in the good old U S of A, and this randomish route brought her to what in any video game would be a beckoning quest destination, i.e., a fenced-in space of artificial falling water and granite-tubbed trees called Waterfall Garden Park, complete with, according to the sign by the gate, an Easter egg— it was the birthplace of the United Parcel Service. So this parcel sat down on a cold composite bench under a leafless birch and is waiting for some service and now it's 9:19.

919 is a palindromic prime.

No one else is in the park. (It's cold for sitting.)

It would appear that parcel service is not forthcoming.

how to get a clue

re: what to do?

It occurs to her to wonder whether 743 and/or 919 are happy numbers. She spent a couple of days when she was eight or so identifying all the happy numbers up to 1000. Take a number, square each digit, add the squares to make a new number, repeat. If the original number eventually reduces to 1, it's happy. If it reduces to the repeating sequence 4, 16, 37, 58, 89, 145, 42, 20, 4, etc, then it's unhappy. The implication being, it's unhappy to be stuck in an endless loop with a bunch of other dead-end losers, whereas it's happy to be solitary forever.

She used to be able to identify happy numbers on sight, since there's a relatively small number of combinations of digits that work (obviously, the order of the digits is irrelevant). But her memory's gotten a bit hazy. She does remember that of the first 1000 natural numbers, 143 are happy. So for two randomly chosen numbers from that set, the chance that both are happy is about 2 percent, and the chance that at least one is happy is about 26.6 percent. She opens her notebook and starts figuring: 743, 74, 65, 61, 37—unhappy. 919, 163, 46, 52, 29, 85, 89—unhappy. So the message from the math gods is, she's stuck in an endless loop. Which maybe means she *should* get back on a bus and return to NYC, rinse and repeat.

Not that she believes any of this. Messages from beyond. It's a sign of how empty-headed she is that she's even pretending.

She gets up, shoulders her burden, exiles herself from the garden. West on Main, north through a park, west on Washington because Denzel, north on 1st, then soft right on Cherry because that's her favorite pie, which her mother makes every July 4 for her own birthday and then gets teary. Munch on cherry pie for four blocks, at which point on her right is a modern glass building, which turns out to be Seattle City Hall. She has a vague feeling the famous library is nearby (she loves google-street-view-walking in random cities), and heads up 4th, and after three blocks there it is, in all its Koolhaas coolness, like a magnified head of a Rock-'Em-Sock-'Em Robot. (Andres has a YouTube channel netting him about $300 a month on which he plays and reviews toys from the 1960s.)

Now it's 10:21 a.m. And—1021 is another prime. And—1021, 6, 36, 45, 41, 17, 50, 25, 29—it's also unhappy. Probability of three randomly generated numbers all being unhappy, 63 percent. If it happens twice more, the probability falls below 50 percent, at which point it becomes a message from the math gods.

She continues up 4th, takes a left on Seneca because there's a street in Ithaca with that name, then right on 3rd and left on Union because that's what she foolishly wanted with Alex, then right on 2nd and left on Pine, because she foolishly pined for a union with Alex, then right on 1st and she's sick of this game so she just keeps walking northwest on 1st, thinking of her father.

Her mother told Mette, when Mette was six, that she thought it wasn't healthy for her not to know her father. Her mother had not known her own father when she was growing up, which had led to all sorts of unhealthy fantasizing and false hero worship that she (her mother) thought sometimes still, after all these years, screwed up her relationships with men. (This latter part was told to Mette later, when she was maybe thirteen.) Also (when Mette was six), her grandmother Lauren was dying, and her mother realized (this was another part she said later) that if *she* (Mette's mother) were to die, Mette would have no one in the world who knew her and whom she knew, to take care of her.

So one day (when Mette was six) this guy showed up who was her father. This was at the old farmhouse. Now that she's almost twenty-one, Mette has an idea from novels and movies that this is supposed to be a big emotional moment, fraught with tension or alienation, or maybe should involve blaming, or whatever. But at the time she just thought, "Right, a father. I figured there had to be one somewhere." He didn't annoy her with a lot of presumptuous questions and fake adult attention and invasiveness, and they figured out that they shared some interests, so their relationship settled pretty quickly into mainly email correspondence, which Mette far preferred, and still does, to both the excruciating tedium of face-to-face interactions and the annoying tendency toward real-time expectations of texting and messaging. And he's been a good part of her life, and he's a decent guy, and maybe she's being conceited but she does have the impression that maybe she's his only friend outside of his work, so there's that to consider, anyway.

She's arrived at Broad Street. To her right, up the hill, the Space Needle looms behind an office building. It's 10:52. 1052 is 2 times 526, which Mette has a vague memory might be a centered pentagonal number, and also 4 times 263, which is a safe prime, meaning if you subtract one and divide by two you get a Sophie Germain prime, namely 131. But most importantly: 1052, 30, 9, 81, 65—unhappy. Probability of four randomly chosen numbers being unhappy, 53.9 percent.

She heads up Broad Street toward the Space Needle.

The fact that she used to daydream a lot about Wishner, Steward of Chipmunks, maybe suggests she did miss having a father more present in her life, who knows? Navel gazing is not her thing. This is a pretty boring area of wide streets, modern office buildings, banks. It's sunny, and the temperature has risen to probably about 50 degrees, so people are out walking, and she sees more ahead, where she can make out what she thinks is probably the old grounds of the 1962 World's Fair, now called, apparently, the Seattle Center. There's still a working monorail, the kind of thing her father would weirdly enthuse over.

She crosses Broad Street and now, with the Space Needle only a hundred yards ahead, the sidewalk is getting crowded. In Astoria, she used to lie in bed—at this juncture in a personal recollection people always say "for hours," but the activity she's remembering probably maxed out at twenty minutes—where no one could see her but the birds, which fact she liked (her near-invisibility), and she'd think of the birds with gratitude as she watched them cross her field of vision, or hover in view, etc. Some of the first graphic programming she ever did was encoding different parameters to see how convincingly she could model the flocking behavior of starlings. She knew someone else had already done this, but she wanted to figure it out for herself and who knows, maybe come up with something better. The assumption for all these types of behaviors is that each individual follows a small number of simple rules, and that the complexly ordered behavior of the whole is an emergent phenomenon. (She ended up merely reproducing the original study in a more cumbersome form. Hey, she was only fourteen.) Plausible rules for people on a crowded sidewalk: collision avoidance, obviously. Probably a cultural tendency everywhere except England and Japan to shift to the right in doing so. Probably more individual variation than among birds, for example a spectrum of favorite speeds whenever allowed. Might be fun to fool around with the modeling, if she were still interested in anything.

Around the time she was trying to program bird flight, she was in Astoria Park hoping to see a chipmunk, and she came across something someone had painted on the path. They'd used a stencil to create a flock of birds, so when you looked down at the pavement it was as if you were looking up into the sky. The flock crossed the path, spreading as it went. There was a break in the middle of the flock where the person had painted, also with stencils, "How do you decide where you belong?"

Avoiding collisions by shifting to the right, striving to maintain her preferred pace, she arrives at the traffic turnaround at the base of the Needle. She looks up. Sixties Futurism against a blue sky. Her father would gesticulate, exclaim, lecture. Why is he so happy all the time? What's wrong with her? It's now 10:59. 1059, 107, 50—unhappy. Probability of five randomly chosen numbers all being unhappy, 46.2 percent. Math gods' message received. Height of Space Needle Observation Deck, according to the sign: 520 feet. Divide by 16, take the square root: 5.7 seconds. She closes her eyes, counts out the seconds in her head. Opens her eyes again.

Oops.

She stands there for what seems a very long time—actually, twelve minutes—while people pass to either side, occasionally bump against her. Human Brownian motion. Voices in her ears. It makes her feel claustrophobic. When chipmunks are overcrowded, their bodies produce more androgen. The male offspring of females with excess androgen display bisexual tendencies, leading to less reproduction.

She looks up at the Needle again. Is she merely play-acting? The thought fills her with self-disgust.

She has never met three of her four grandparents. Her father's father, Vernon Fuller, now deceased, was *Tamias Newmanensis*, Steward of Newman. Of her father's mother (name forgotten, also deceased) she knows only that she wanted to be an astronomer but was thwarted, probably because she was a woman. Her mother's father, Thomas Hansen, ironically the only one of the four still living, seems to have made, long ago, according to her mother, a genuinely serious stab—so to speak!—at suicide. She wonders what drove him to it. She wonders how he mentally prepared himself. She wonders why it is, exactly, that she has never met him.

Sunday, February 21, 2016

Saskia wakes from a nightmare about Benigno Aquino.

She was twelve when he was assassinated in Manila. She didn't know anything about politics in the Philippines, but Bill sometimes watched news on a portable TV sequestered in a dark corner of the living room, and over his shoulder she saw the footage. The interior of a plane, soldiers swarming around a man. The news report explained that Aquino was returning to Manila from political exile, and had been aware that he might be killed. The moment that stuck in her head ever afterward occurred in his last moments on camera. Trying to smile, he took hold of a seat belt strap near the cabin door and pulled on it as the soldiers bustled him out. It was probably unconscious. Of course he was frightened. He held on to the strap for maybe one second while they propelled him forward, then he dropped it and disappeared through the door. Moments later, out on the tarmac, one of the soldiers shot him in the back of the head.

Her dream was of that one second, that strap between the seat and the scared man, lengthening out straight like a lifeline, then falling.

She gets up, showers, dresses.

How easy it is, how effective, to kill troublesome people. Joan of Arc was propelled to her death with the same speed. The law required that she be handed over to the secular arm for punishment, but instead she was hurried straight from the ecclesiastical tribunal down to the marketplace where the wood was heaped and waiting. How stunning it is that once you kill a person, that person never comes back.

She locks her apartment, goes downstairs to the street. Eight o'clock, the tops of the buildings in sunlight, close to 50 degrees already. Back to the kind of climate change she likes. May as well enjoy what you can. She walks to a deli on Manhattan Avenue, grabs an empty seat along the counter, asks for a cup of coffee. She needs some people around her for a few minutes. Bad night. Mark called her Friday morning to relay Mette's text message to him: Don't worry. Taking time to think. Life choices. It was typical of him, and it annoyed her, that he seemed to believe her message meant they shouldn't worry. It also annoyed her that Mette had texted him, while ignoring all but one of Saskia's messages. Okay, maybe "hurt her" is a more accurate characterization. But there she goes again, right? Focusing on her own feelings.

Silas is on shift this morning, wiping down tables. A good way into a role is to decide how the character inhabits her body, so Saskia often watches the way other people move, later imitating them in her apartment. Silas is great. He looks like he's maybe twelve, slender and small for his age, all his accessories conspiring to make him look even smaller—the thick black frames on his windshield glasses, his inflated Nikes, his attenuated Afro like a peacock spray. His never-changing facial expression might be called a) dreamy, b) spacy, or c) catatonic. Think Shelley Duvall in *Three Women*. He bobs up and down as he walks in those clodhopper shoes, taking longer strides than you would expect, all in slow motion, as though he's in a weaker gravitational field than everyone else. After two or three steps, the rhythm of his walk sets his right hand to undulating at the wrist, in toward the hip, then out. After a couple more steps, his fingers start to snap at the end of the outward swing, seemingly of their own accord.

Of course she's trying to distract herself. What else can she do, since Mette won't answer her? Did she say it annoyed her? She raised Mette more or less entirely on her own, yet the girl is so much like her father it drives her crazy, the two of them seem to understand each other in some spatiotemporal hyper-dimension to which ordinary humans have no access. And to make things worse, it feels like karmic payback for Saskia's ignoring of her own mother. At least it gives her some sympathetic insight into her mother's burden, though of course too late to do either of them any good. And at least Mark, unlike her own father, seems to be a decent enough human being, if of no help nor clue.

Mette has never told Saskia a thing about her life outside the apartment. Saskia doesn't know whether she's satisfied with her programming job, or her private projects, or whether she's ever dated anyone, ever had sex, what her orientation is. She assumes Mark doesn't know any of this either. *If she wants us to know, she'll tell us*, she can hear him saying with that tone of *If A = B, then B = A*. Saskia called Mette's workplace again yesterday, and no one who happened to be there—a lot of them seem to work remotely a lot of the time, and she's never met any of them, and doesn't know any of their names—could tell her a fucking thing. Okay, it's only been five days. And Mette has plenty of money (Saskia's fairly sure, though she doesn't exactly *know* this, either), so she could be holed up in a decent hotel somewhere if she wanted, and it's not like she's not used to being alone. And since she and Mark are alike, maybe Mark has been right all along and if she were in a bad emotional place and were contemplating something drastic she'd have texted I'm in a bad emotional place and am contemplating something drastic.

In any case, there's nothing Saskia can do about it at the moment, so she may as well drink her coffee and think about something else, like that woman by the window with the long face and sadly too much makeup and penciled circumflex eyebrows and low-set mouth crowded with corn-kernel teeth who's squeezing her steaming teabag—the steam billows and writhes evilly against the light from the street—over her cup with her spidery fingers dancing and this wonderfully vivid fastidious expression produced by drawn-back lips and tidy doubled chin. The five-inch golden hoop earrings and gold-threaded purple shawl are a bit much, who's the costume designer?

She finishes her coffee, buys bread and a banana, walks home. She has nothing on her schedule until a recording session Tuesday, so if she can just keep not thinking about Mette, she can get in some hours revising her play.

For a while after she moved to the city in 2002, it looked like she might have a semi-viable stage career. First off—what made everything else possible—she lucked out and found a woman who could stay with Mette when necessary in the evenings. Elaine was a retired accountant, never married, who took a shine to Mette because she reminded her of her much younger sister, who when little had been "strange in exactly the same way and no one understood her except me." Saskia weed-whacked her sense of affront, watered her gratitude. She took a waitressing job and fit in another acting workshop during Mette's school hours. She gained experience, made connections, got an agent, went to a zillion auditions of which a zillion minus five were fiascos, the remainder being minorish roles in off-off-Broadway productions that limped along for a few weeks, steadily deflating. Finally she landed a part she liked to think of as minor-major, though everyone else probably saw it as major-minor, in a play that got generally good reviews and had an extended run of six months. The *Times* idiot liked the production but declined to devote a word to her, whereas the *Daily News* genius, in the midst of pooh-poohing everything else, said that she "tapped unexpected depths in an underwritten role." Meanwhile—fortunately—it turned out she enjoyed waitressing: enjoyed the insane bustle, her volatile fellow waitresses, the backbiting, the shouted resignations in the midst of slammed lunch hours, the busy holiday weekend revenge no-shows, the heat-crazed irascible cooks, the fluttery zoetropic interaction with almost-real-seeming customers, among whom she especially loved the assholes, who in their baroque assholery were fecund sources of acting ideas. At the same time she was doing occasional small roles in TV shows filming in the NYC area: a single mother and waitress (nailed it!) who'd witnessed a crime, a school guidance counselor, a nurse, another nurse, *another* nurse (what the fuck? male directors' little buxom nurse fantasies?), one of six bank hostages, a few other spear carriers that have blurred together, with lines like, "He went that way!" and "Are you sure you're all right?" and "It was too dark to see his face."

After four or five years of this she got a film role she fantasized might be her big break. She preferred the stage—the protean communication with the audience, the emotional through line, the danger—but of course was aware that if she ever wanted to give up her first love (waitressing!), then film was more likely to be her white-clad Richard Gere. The writer and director was the same guy who directed the play in which Saskia tapped unexpected depths in an underwritten role. (May she pause for a moment to note that fifty fucking years downwind from the founding of NOW, only 8 percent of film and television directors are women? Back to our regularly scheduled program—) She and this guy—Dexter, DGA, WGA, XY—had gotten along well during the stage production, including a couple of times when he seemed genuinely to consider a suggestion of hers before rejecting it, so when he asked her to audition for his pet project she fell on that grenade like a ton of bricks. Of course it was a low-budget indie, a post-apocalypse chamber piece wherein 95 percent of the screen time was handled by two actors, a man and a woman (Saskia!), in a jury-rigged shelter-cum-science-lab plus a withy-and-polyethylene greenhouse in a clearing in the woods. The script was spare and enigmatic, going for Mythic or maybe Folkloric, Adam and Evey, Death and Rebirthy. On the page it didn't look like much, but the words were speakable, occasionally even beautiful, and Saskia and the other actor (Fawad) built up a rapport. They shot for three weeks in the Finger Lakes National Forest—Mette, now twelve, showing a feline indifference to whether it was Saskia or Elaine who occasionally tapped fruitlessly on her bedroom door back in New York City—and Saskia had good feelings about what they had accomplished. But in film, actors don't know squat until they see the finished product. When she did, she was excited. Dexter had caught something fresh and nuanced in the way Saskia and Fawad played off each other. Plus, the editing and the cinematography were good, the score was moody and perfect. She started fantasizing about festivals, acceptance speeches, what she'd wear on the red carpet, etc.

The critics hated it. The first one, a prominent male reviewer, approached it as though it were trying to be realistic sci-fi and pompously mansplained the scientific "errors," which, since these would have been obvious to an innumerate ten-year-old, might in a better world have clued in Mr. Swinging-Dick to the fact that the film wasn't trying to be realistic sci-fi. Then three or four reviews followed in which the words "boring" and "static" and "pretentious" kept recurring. After that, some herd-instinct tipping point was passed and everyone piled on with cathartic glee: self-indulgent, politically correct, mind-numbing, dead-horse-flogging, slow-motion-train-wrecking, jaws-on-the-flooring, can't-look-awaying. This was in 2007, so social media was building steam but still kind of new and startling to a person born in 1971, and she was thunderstruck at the torrent of cruel comments about her (ugly, slutty, shrewish, whiny, unfuckable), Fawad (ugly, smarmy, stalkery, towelheady), and Dexter (narcissistic, privileged, French-influenced, shit-for-brainsy). Having unwisely just now googled the movie, she sees that on Metacritic it boasts a score of 38, indicating "generally unfavorable reviews," while over on the Tomatometer there's that green asterisk-blob of a thrown-at-the-actor rotting love apple and a rating of 31 percent. The only chance left for the film would be a festival of mockery on *Mystery Science Theater 3000* so vicious it goes viral. (A slut can hope.) Netflix picked it up for pennies a while ago and Saskia streamed it out of wary curiosity, the first time she'd seen it since it bombed. And is she crazy? It still seems like a decent movie to her. Okay, maybe a tad self-serious, but with, come on, folks, a lot of heart and hard work on display.

Anyway, a turbocharged rocket boost to her career it proved not to be, and some more years went by during which she had a few stage roles and a few minor film roles, and once she was nominated for an award, but as she spelunked deeper into her forties and her face began to look fortyish and she failed to get any taller and her large boobs stopped being certified fresh on the Tomatometer, the gigs thinned out. Hey, it's what happens to 95 percent of working actors, she's not complaining.

(Beat.)

Of course she's complaining!

She makes herself tea. Thank god for voice work. Thank god for honey and lemon.

Life choices. What does Mette mean by that? Did she intend it to sound ominous? If Saskia had a partner at the moment, she'd distract herself with him or her, send a text, hop in the sack, have an argument. But the thing with Maggie became such a nightmare, she's been wary lately. Or maybe weary. Or both.

One guy she dated during her Ithaca acting years was younger, twenty-four to her twenty-eight, a graduate student in English literature, cumulo masses of dark hair, sunken cheeks and sexily alive eyebrows—eyebrows seem to be a theme today—and he told her in a post-coitum tristesse that he dreamed about quitting the program, ghosting his family and friends, and going to live in a stone hut with a peat fire at the top of a wave-shattered cliff in the Orkney Islands, there to do naught but read classics and play ancient airs on his wooden flute. Yes, he was full of shit in all three directions, and she dumped him after a short and lusty while, but his adolescent fantasy stuck with her, probably because it was so much like the reveries of travel she'd lost herself in before getting to know her father, and maybe she missed the . . . she doesn't want to call it innocence . . . the wide-horizoned immaturity, which meeting her father despoiled early. Anyway, now, years later, when her life seems in some ways inadequate or emptyish or whatever, there are times when that lonely hut at the top of the cliff beckons, and she stands out at the lip where the mist from the waves rejuvenates her, then goes in to the fire where the peaty smoke toughens and preserves her. Witchlike, she listens to the wind talk in the chimney. Over on the next promontory Mette dwells in her own hut—Saskia can see her light burning at night—with high-speed internet yet no earthly way to receive communications, happy as a clam.

Okay, speaking of her love life, here's the problem in a nutshell. When she dates a man, she longs for a relationship with a woman, and vice versa. She hates to generalize (honest, she really does) but it is simply true that women (in general! not every individual!) communicate better, are more attuned to social and emotional cues, play the game at a higher level. As the rhyme says, when a relationship with a woman is good, it is very, very good, but when it is bad, it is horrid. Men may be boring, but they won't try to eat your brains. (We're talking about the subset of men who won't kill you, which Saskia likes to believe she can recognize by the third date.) Maybe she's just feeling discouraged right now because her last male partner turned out to be a classic withholding monosyllabic stone-faced narcissistic manchild, and her last female partner was Maggie, who was wonderful and exciting and intuitive and passionate and giving and delightfully unpredictable and then watchful and manipulative and groundlessly jealous and crazily accusatory and creepily stalkerish, not only in the cyber sense but actually physically creeping behind Saskia on sidewalks and up stairwells, and Saskia at this point would reference Glenn Close except she fucking detests that movie.

Life choices, as the mystery girl said.

Yes, and regardless of whether Saskia's lover was an innie or an outie, their relationship with Mette was never good, which became for Saskia a source of mounting frustration. The men tended to offer unsolicited and clue-free advice about getting her out of her room more, or not giving in to her whims, whereas the women often got jealous and competitive, which could be worse. It didn't help that Mette hated having anyone sleep over in the apartment other than herself and her mother. Routine is important for people like Mette, everyone knows this, but maybe they choose not to remember when it's midnight on a rainy night. Once Mette was old enough that Saskia could spend evenings and the occasional night at her partner's place, there seemed to her (Saskia) to be no conceivable grounds of complaint, but it's simply astonishing how many people want to feel thwarted by other people's children. *What, I get a new girlfriend, but I don't get a second TV, a second bed, a second coffee machine, a second local bagel joint?*

Another factor, which Saskia will acknowledge for the sake of strict fairness, is that Mette took a strong dislike to all of her partners, acting out (okay, sometimes outrageously) when she was young, and then when she was older, stoically enduring with displays of dieback and root blight, then time-lapse blooming when a relationship ended. The worst thing about this latter was that Saskia was pretty sure Mette wasn't being passive-aggressive, she simply was honestly happier to be alone with her mother again, just two gals sharing a spotless and never-varying kitchen and bathroom. Which eloquent testimonial from Ms. Undemonstrative touched Saskia rather deeply, so maybe it wasn't the worst thing, but the best thing.

She composes a text message. I'm trying not to be hurt that you communicated with your father but not with me. Speaking of not being passive-aggressive, that is *not* passive-aggressive, it is merely the truest thing she can say about her feelings right at the moment. But it certainly sounds passive-aggressive, doesn't it? She deletes it.

> Can't you just tell me where
> you are?

Deletes.

> Can't you just tell me what
> happened?

Deletes.

> I love you.

Man, that *really* sounds passive-aggressive. Deletes.

> Thank you for communicating with
> your father. I appreciate it.

Sends.

She cleans the kitchen, vacuums the apartment, does a load of laundry, alphabetizes her spices—well, not the last, but otherwise putters around, not merely to distract herself from worrying about Mette but also to delay working on her Joan play. Eventually the rising tide of self-disgust crests the grand dike of avoidance and she turns toward her desk—but first she has to brew another cup of tea, honey, lemon, remember that woman in the deli, imitate her grimace, etc—she advances on her desk—but now she needs to take a dump, hot liquids do this to her—she marches to her desk, boots up, booties down, opens the file containing her latest batch of notes, reminders, admonitions, half-baked ideas.

Saskia wants to become a director. Go, 8 percent!

Okay, complaining is fun, but that figure applies only to television and film. Saskia wants to direct her own play, off- or off-off-Broadway, or really, anywhere short of the horizon in that famous *New Yorker* cover. Among off-Broadway plays during the last five years, 33 percent have been directed by women and 30 percent have been written by women. As for plays written and directed by the same woman, who knows? Saskia would bet it's rare, because directing your own play is sort of a big-swinging-dick thing to do. But why should she even think that? What socially conditioned, shrinking-violet, who-me instinct overcomes her at moments like this? Of course she wants to direct her own play! Take your stinking paws off it, you damned dirty ape! She's rewriting the latest draft and there's a woman who's directed her twice in the past who's just become Artistic Director of an off-off theater in SoHo, and this woman has expressed interest, and has not immediately nixed the idea of Saskia directing, so . . .

Anyway, she's had an interest in Joan of Arc ever since she was a lonely and strange thirteen-year-old. Maybe because Joan was a lonely and strange thirteen-year-old when the Archangel Michael first assured her, against all the available evidence, that she was an important person. Or maybe because Joan idolized a distant father figure, otherwise known as the Dauphin of France, who eventually betrayed her. So here's the thing, don't laugh—Saskia is writing it as a mystery play. Not as in *The Real Inspector Hound*, but as in the kind of play performed by English craft guilds on decorated wagons during religious festivals in the fifteenth century, the older actors doing Herod and the Almighty, the younger ones Jesus and Lazarus, boys cross-dressing for Mary, both Madonna and whore, Eve, etc. Saskia first tried writing her play in the same mix of clunky, homespun stanza styles that the original mysteries used, for example the Chester stanza, which might be her favorite for sheer galumphing balladry:

> All peace to you that be present,
> And hearken now with good intent,

How Joan away from home is went
With all her company.
Attendants few, of small renown,
Avoiding hostile field and town,
Asleep in woods, with stars their crown,
The Dauphin gone to see.

But no matter how much she tinkered, it came off sounding hokey, like one of those coastal-city Christmas revels with mummers and wassail and figgy pudding. She's currently rewriting the whole play in irregular four-beat couplets, the simplest of the medieval forms, with abundant use of half rhymes:

JEAN DE METZ:
Eleven nights on horse we rode
Through Lenten fields not yet plowed.
The frozen stubble made weary bed
For men and girl alike, but the Maid
Tired not, nor feared anything, not even
The soldiers with her who might be forgiven
For thoughts impure while lying by her,
But the wonder was, none sought to try her,
Nor ever felt a natural lust
Which alone seemed miraculous.

She first conceived the idea of a mystery play six or seven years ago when she briefly dated an older woman who'd been flatteringly pursuing her for months, an NYU professor and poet born and raised in Budapest. This woman took her one evening to the Hungarian House on the Upper East Side to see a Genesis mystery play that had been discovered a few years previously in some Transylvanian castle's closet, and had already been staged in Budapest to great acclaim (probably 98 percent on the *paradicsom*-meter). The thing was in Hungarian, mind you, so Saskia didn't understand a word, but it was the best night at the theater she'd had in ages. Much of the story could be followed from emblematic action and props: Adam and Eve wore fig leaves, God the Father looked like Dumbledore (or vice versa), the snake spoke with a hiss, the luscious apple was straight out of *Snow White* (or vice versa), and so on. The actors stood hieratically, facing the audience wide-eyed and without expression, sometimes raising one hand when they spoke, as if to say "Hear me," or adopting a strange pose and freezing, as if to signal, "This is my intention," or "This is my inner nature." It was charming in its simplicity, but also powerful. Can she say mythic? She can *definitely* say Adam and Evey. It was theater as incantation, as magic, theater the way it was for a thousand years, when it brought rain and induced frenzy. It reminded Saskia of the two bird plays performed in masks years ago in Ithaca, and her realization back then that stylization could be more expressive than realism because it forced the audience to use its own imagination. In other words, fuck Ibsen. Give this middle-aged maenad the Eleusinian mysteries any day of the week.

She'd already been struggling to find a way to represent Joan. She hates the Shaw play. His Joan, like most of his major characters, is largely a mouthpiece for his own smug opinions. And Brecht's version is even worse. Is it a coincidence that the two most egregious mansplainers in modern theatrical history both decided to appropriate Joan's story? Or does the unruly bitch make such men nervous? The problem with any realistic portrayal of Joan is that she was a lunatic in an age when lunatics were seen as vessels of God. To a modern audience, any accurate depiction of Joan makes her too strangely medieval to empathize with, so maybe the solution is to make the whole play strangely medieval.

When you think about it, what could be more "realistic" than telling Joan's story in the form that stories were told in her own lifetime, stories that maybe shaped the way she thought?

You can probably tell that Saskia has been practicing her pitch to producers. Anyway, as soon as you abandon fourth-wall realism, all sorts of possibilities open up. The title of her play is *Joan, Maid*, which she hopes someone will notice is homophonic with *Joan, Made*—i.e., Joan, constructed. Because her play isn't just about the girl from Domrémy, it's about images of Joan, the legend of Joan, the need for someone like Joan, the false Joans that cropped up in her wake, the other prophet-lunatics that the time demanded, who dutifully appeared, failed, and died. For example, poor Guillaume, the shepherd boy whom the Arch-bishop of Reims pulled out of his miter two months after he and all the other French churchmen insouciantly let the English burn Joan.

> ARCHBISHOP OF REIMS:
> It pains me, truly, to say the Maid
> Became inordinately proud,
> Loved too much her garments rich
> And put herself before the Church.
> But by God's grace I have found
> Another shepherd we can send
> Against the foe, he's good or better
> Than Joan, he's suffered the stigmata!
> I've never heard anyone claim
> That jumped-up hoyden enjoyed the same.

Maybe the boy was more pliable than Joan. Maybe he was more pal-atable because he had a dick. But the English snapped him up in his first battle, sewed him in a sack and drowned him in the Seine.

Was he even a shepherd? Because Joan wasn't a shepherdess, even though every single account has made her one, both now and back then. She actually had to deny this in court: "No, sir, to the best of my recollection I never tended no fucking sheep." This sort of thing fascinates Saskia. What is it with shepherds and shepherdesses? Is it because of the Christmas story? In order for the angel of the Lord to come upon you, must you be abiding in the field keeping watch over your flock by night? Yes, probably that, and also because everything in the Bible is sheepy and goaty: shepherd of souls, the Lamb of God, scapegoats, the ram in the thicket, etc. And since people tend to have mystical revelations in accordance with social expectations, other Christian visionaries *have* been shepherds. Like Mélanie, the girl at La Salette. Can we talk about her for a moment? Saskia recently added some verses on this, and they're a mess, half inert lumber and half notes. Mélanie Calvat was born to a poor family in the French Alps in 1831, the fourth of ten children. From the age of nine to fourteen, she was sent by her family to work for other farmers in the region, returning home only during the winter. The farmer she was working for at the time of her vision, when she was fourteen, reported that she was lazy, disobedient, and sullen, didn't answer when spoken to, and that instead of sleeping in his house at night, she hid in the fields.

Hello? Alarm bells, anyone? In 2016 have we at last reached the point where people whose heads are not up their own asses can look at these bare facts and conclude that Mélanie Calvat was likely being sexually abused? A feminazi can hope.

Let's imagine the thousands of other young shepherdesses, through the centuries, living in remote areas with non-relatives. How much below one hundred would be the percentage of raped girls? Who among Christians, historically, has tended to have visions of the divine? Powerless, under-supervised adolescent girls. Who comes to them, promising absolution and love? Virgins. And the poor, rustic, uneducated girls, the lowest of the low, become seers, elevated by the local clergy, revered by the mob. So the last shall be first.

At least Joan, as a girl, was apparently left "intact." She had to prove this twice, to two separate committees of women, presumably armed with specula. (There's a scene in Saskia's play with a nuns' chorus, clacking specula like castanets.) But Joan, of course, did have to contend with patriarchy. Her parents wanted her to marry, and picked out the dick-equipped stranger who would be her lord and master. She refused, and was sued for breach of contract. She argued successfully in court that she had never agreed to the match. Her father was enraged. He dreamed that she would run off with soldiers—in other words, become a camp follower, a whore, give away for free what he had wanted to sell—and declared he'd take her to the village pond and drown her first. At this point Joan's two virginal visitants, Saint Catherine and Saint Margaret, wisely ordered her to get the hell out of Dodge. Oh, and while she was at it, to save France.

At her desk, Saskia tinkers for a while with her Mélanie material, makes it worse, restores the dispiriting crap she already had. Gets up to brew more tea, stares out the window at fascinating India Street, flips through the most interesting Crate&Barrel catalog she's seen in years. Eventually sits back at her desk and ruminates on those scenes in movies where the writer-hero clickety-clacks and *ding*-zzzzziiiiings through the night, while a montage shows the ashtray filling with cigarette butts, and suddenly it's morning and our man rips the last page from the platen, squares the pile, and bounds off to the post.

Taking time to think.

Maybe it's this sentence that worries Saskia the most. Mette has always had all the time in the world to think. And she's exceptionally straightforward. This sentence sounds like bullshit, or anyway, strategically vague. Taking time to think about what? What decision is so momentous that she has to run away in order to contemplate it, when she could stay in her room for days on end, undisturbed by Saskia or anyone else?

More tea!

Another pee!

Anthropologie's winter catalog, yessirree!

Back in chair . . .

She'd been tinkering and writing notes about the play for more than a year before it occurred to her that her conception of Joan owed a lot to Mette. What clued her in was something Eileen Atkins said about playing Shaw's Joan: "I am very attracted to parts that are very direct, and say what they think. Joan is saying what she means." And there was also something Régine Pernoud wrote about Joan: "We can sense that her prophetic character came from her belief that she transmitted the message of her voices without adding or deleting. Throughout her trial, she indicates that she feared above all to exceed what her voices had dictated, to be an insufficiently faithful instrument."

Once Saskia made the connection, it helped her notice patterns in Joan's thinking, for example, the way her piety maybe came out of a need for regularity. The church warden at Domrémy said, "When I did not ring the bells punctually for Compline, Joan would catch me and scold me, saying that I had not done well." It made Saskia wonder if Joan's flouting of social conventions was so easy for her because she had never noticed them in the first place. And her literal-mindedness—she never wavered from an untenably simple idea, one that equated labels with logic: France is for French people. Or something she said at her trial: "I had a great will and desire that my king have his kingdom." Yes, kings rule kingdoms, Q. E. D. A place for everything, and everything in its place.

Must, then, the question be asked? Is Saskia writing *Joan, Maid* in part because she longs to better understand her daughter? She finds it easy to envision Mette alone and spotlit on a stage, wide-eyed and blank-faced, holding her right hand up to signal, "Hear me," or adopting an unearthly pose as though to say, "This is my inner nature." In Saskia's imagination, the theater audience is dead quiet. Or maybe the theater is empty. Mette holds her pose. This image frightens Saskia.

She gets up again, moves in agitation around the room. It's 3:25 p.m. The fifth day. Maybe she should call Mark, see if he has heard anything new. There's no point, he's good about letting her know as soon as he knows. Still, she grabs her phone. She hesitates, staring into space. Then she realizes that what she's really doing is looking at the closed door to Mette's room. It is unquestionably respectful of Mette's wishes that she has not searched her room for clues. But is it also negligent?

The phone vibrates in her hand.

She looks at the screen. Her agent. Shit. Usually she'd care, indulge a hope—there are such things as retroactive Oscars, who knew?—but not now. "Marisa, what's up?"

"Hi Saskia, I just heard a strange message on my voicemail left about an hour ago from a guy who said he's your father? But why would he be calling me? He said your daughter was with him and you'd better come as soon as you can, any idea what that's about?"

Sunday, February 21, 2016

He can pick Saskia out easily as he comes down the concourse toward the gate, the small head lower in the chair than all the other heads, the tangled mist of weightless hair, the large nose. When alone and unobserved, she's always looking down, it seems, reading or writing, her mouth tensed on one side as though frozen mid-chew. She can block out the whole world. He last saw her almost a year ago, when he came to the city to take Mette to lunch for her twentieth birthday. He walks up to her, close enough that his shoes are in her line of sight, and waits a few seconds during which she continues reading, then says, "Hello."

She glances up. "Hey." Takes her knapsack off the chair next to her, slips the large book inside.

He sits down. "Thanks for letting me come along."

She seems to interpret that as an aggressive comment. "I'm not the gatekeeper."

He didn't mean it that way, he's grateful. That she's willing to let this be a joint venture.

Seven hours ago, he was working at his computer at home when she called. "She's with my father in Denmark. I just heard."

"Is she okay?"

"I don't know. I'm going to fly out there, I'm checking flights right now."

"What did she say?"

"It wasn't her who called. My father left a message with my agent."

"Can't you call your father back?"

"He doesn't have a phone. Or email, either. And apparently he doesn't know my number, he must have looked up my professional contact info. He told my agent I'd better come, so I'm going. There's a flight at 11:00 p.m. out of JFK, nonstop to Copenhagen, Norwegian Air."

Mark began typing on his own computer. "Does it have two seats available?"

"Two?"

"I would like to come also."

There was a long pause. "Aren't you teaching?"

"My T.A.s can fill in for a couple of days."

"This might take longer—"

"Or the whole week. They'll be fine."

Another pause. "Okay."

He pressed on. "I see the flight you're talking about. It looks like it has . . . eight free seats. Two are even together, in the last row. Why don't I buy them?"

"Don't be ridiculous. You buy yours, I'll buy mine."

"Okay. Do you want 36B or 36C?"

"I don't care."

"I'll take 36B. It's 3:45 now, I can leave by 4:15, I'll be at the airport by nine."

"See you at the gate, I guess." She ended the call.

Yes, it had sounded like she was hesitant to sit next to him. But perhaps he was overinterpreting. They were on good terms, weren't they? Ten minutes later, in the middle of packing his bag, he went back online to check the seating map, saw that 36C was now taken, and noted that he felt relief. Which is why he thanked her here in the airport for letting him come along. But she thought he was being sarcastic. He wonders if he should try to explain his thinking. He hates misunderstandings. But it's likely she's way ahead of him. Best to drop it.

"How have you been?" he asks.

She gives him what he thinks might be an incredulous look. "Terrible, of course. How have *you* been?"

"I didn't mean—I mean, *this* part is obvious—or I mean, I understand about this part—I meant, other than this, how have you been? Your work, and so on?"

"Fine." She waves the word away to suggest that she doesn't mean fine, or not fine, or anything evaluative. "I don't have energy to talk about any of that." She shifts in her chair, pulls her scarf higher around her neck. Mark remembers that she's often cold in indoor public spaces. It's clear she's anxious, and now that he's in her presence Mark begins to feel anxiety as well. He often has to take this sort of cue from other people. Physical proximity helps, suggesting the mechanism is pheromonal. He casts about for something to say.

"I'm trying to remember what you've told me about your father."

"Probably not much. I try not to think about him."

"He's Danish."

"Yep."

"And, um . . . I think you told me he wasn't around much."

"Took off when I was four. I saw him briefly again when I was thirteen. He's never been part of my life."

Normally voluble, she has always been reticent on this subject. He has never wanted to pry, and he doesn't want to pry now. Still, this mystery man has unaccountably become important. "Does Mette know him?"

"Thomas? No, they've never met. I wouldn't have let him come within a mile of her." Mark has no idea what she might be referring to. He wasn't worried when Mette was off on her own, but everything Saskia is saying now, or not saying, is a little alarming. "Although of course maybe they've been communicating online. I'd be more worried about that except I'd be surprised if Thomas did any online stuff. On the other hand, he can be surprising. He loves to be surprising."

She stops. Several seconds go by. Mark has never been in the position of trying to tease out personal information from anyone. "Um . . ." he says, his mind racing, but at the same time a blank. Or maybe it's his heart that's racing. "Is he . . . dangerous?"

"Physically? I doubt it."

"Okay, that's good."

"He's manipulative."

Mark ponders that for a while. Obviously, he needs details, and just as obviously, Saskia doesn't want to give him any. "Um . . ." he realizes he's saying again. "Do you have any idea why—"

"Good evening ladies and gentlemen," the PA system breaks in, "this is the pre-boarding announcement for Norwegian Air, Flight 187, non-stop to Copenhagen. We are inviting those passengers with small children to pre-board at this time—" Mark can't organize his thoughts when he hears words being spoken, so he gives up for the moment. He's also distracted by the physical impossibility of any person "pre-boarding" a plane. The main cabin is loaded by zone, and people start getting up and standing in line before their zone is called. As seems to be common now, the flight crew are loading the cabin from front to back, which is the less efficient way to do it. Mark's theory is that airlines discovered if they load the cabin starting in the rear, as many of them rationally did ten or fifteen years ago, passengers will tend to fill the overhead compartments that they pass on the way to their seats. Mark and Saskia's zone is called last, and Mark waves everyone else into the line in front of them. Saskia looks at him questioningly. "They're loading the plane from front to back, and we're in the last row," he says.

She doesn't say anything. They show their boarding passes and inch down the jetway.

Mark tries again: "Do you have any idea why Mette would be visiting him, what she'd be looking for?"

"Not a clue."

They take a few more steps. The woman immediately in front of them is holding a baby. Mark wonders why she didn't "pre-board." He also wonders if the baby will be near them and how much it will cry during takeoff and landing, when the changing air pressure will make its ears hurt.

"It's kind of a nightmare that he's involved at all," Saskia suddenly says.

"Your father?"

"I mean, I'm glad we know where she is, I'm glad we're going to go there and find her. But there, of all places." They pass into the plane cabin. A steward smiles and individually greets Mark. "I can't get away from the feeling that he somehow orchestrated this, that he lured Mette to him in order to force me to come. Which is ridiculous, but thinking of him makes me paranoid."

Mark doesn't say anything. He wonders whether, if he doesn't press, she might eventually tell him more. It feels sneaky to operate under this assumption, but he swallows his reservations. They reach the last row. All of the overheard compartments are full, but neither he nor Saskia has brought much, so they fit their carry-ons under the seats in front of them. The mother and baby are three rows away.

"Is Copenhagen our last stop?" he asks.

"What?"

"Is that where Thomas and Mette are?"

"Oh, I'm sorry, I didn't tell you? He lives on an island off of Funen. Funen's the big central island. We'll take a train, then a ferry."

"I didn't try to reach Mette."

"Neither did I."

"I was worried if she knew we were coming—"

"Same here. I meant to tell you not to, I'm glad you figured it out on your own."

The plane is pushed back. Mark wishes he had a window seat. He prefers, during interminable descents, to have visual confirmation that there remains plenty of room between the plane and the ground. But he's on the aisle. Saskia insisted on taking the middle seat so that he would have more leg room. He leans forward to glimpse what he can through the window. "Will you just look at that parking lot," he says.

"Hm?" Saskia says.

"Something I saw in a movie."

"The Coen brothers. *A Serious Man.* It's their best movie."

"You remember that?"

"I'm an actor. I have a good memory for scenes."

The plane begins its long trundle toward the runway, occasionally thumping in a worrisome manner. "Ladies and gentlemen, welcome to Norwegian Air Flight 187—" Mark continues to look as well as he can out the window, consciously appreciating, in an attempt to allay his anxiety, the extraordinarily pretty geometry of the intersecting lines of different colored ground lights. It always reminds him of flights he was taken on out of Boston's Logan Airport when he was little, to visit his grandmother in Florida. He was with his mother and Susan, and felt completely safe. They always let him have the window seat. It feels very strange to be the only person from his family who is still alive.

Now they are turning onto the runway. The brilliant yellow lines seem to extend for miles. The plane pauses, contemplating for a moment—Mark always imagines—its mortality. Then the engine noise rises to a reckless moan, the acceleration begins. Mark breathes. He never can quite believe the Bernoulli effect will be strong enough to lift this huge hunk of metal off the ground. But the nose lifts, the vector of motion curves upward, the city lights fall away. By god, they seem to be cheating the laws of physics once again.

The baby is not crying. Since the ascent is so fast, maybe the crew is careful to keep the cabin pressure steady for the first few minutes. He and Saskia have not flown together before, so he thinks it better to admit it: "I don't like flying."

"No kidding."

"You can tell?"

"Something about the Lamaze breathing and the convulsive grip on the armrest."

"It's ridiculous, airplanes are statistically the safest form of travel."

"I'm aware of that."

"I get more nervous when there's turbulence, even though pilots say turbulence poses little risk."

"Maybe it's a control thing. I remember my driving made you nervous."

"Did it?"

"Come on. You tried to hide it."

Mark has to think for a moment. "It had nothing to do with your skill."

"Thank you, that's a given."

"I guess I don't like being a passenger in anyone's car."

"Like I said, a control thing. You should get a pilot's license, then you can fly wherever you want."

Mark has nothing intelligent to say to this.

"It could also be a conditioned response," she goes on. "When I walk alone down a dark street in the city, I think of similar scenes in movies. They don't bother to film those scenes unless some mugger is about to appear, so naturally I think of muggers. It's even more true for scenes on airplanes. They're a bitch to film, so pretty much 100 percent of the time, if there's turbulence, one character will get nervous and the other character will reassuringly say that turbulence is nothing to worry about, and right after that the plane falls out of the sky."

"That's an interesting point. I don't watch many movies anymore, though."

"Back to theory one, you're a control freak."

" . . . "

"I'm kidding."

"No, I *am* a control freak." A few seconds go by. He goes on, "I was walking around campus a few weeks ago, and I stopped to look at the construction some company was doing on the new computer sciences building. It was evening, all the workers had gone home. They'd been installing glass panels for the lobby, eight feet by four, each one must have weighed a hundred and fifty pounds. Flawless surfaces, edges true to probably less than half a millimeter, double paned, high insulation and reflectivity indices. In each corner were set these delicate mounts of brushed steel secured with steel cylinders in black rubber collars, and the mounts interlocked so that each glass panel could be attached directly to its neighbor. I thought of all the research in materials science, all the advances in precision engineering that went into creating those beautiful objects. Then I noticed the assembly directions in the lower right-hand corners of each pane, these little labels that hadn't been removed yet. They were on the outside, and each label said, 'Install this side in.' That's the sort of thing that comes to my mind whenever I fly."

He gazes down the length of the cabin. He can see over all the other heads. The baby is out of sight, maybe asleep in its mother's lap. "Or I think about the Mars Climate Orbiter. On any interplanetary trajectory, tiny disruptive forces such as solar wind need to be corrected for. Lockheed calculated the forces and reported them to JPL, which sent the correction commands. But Lockheed calculated the forces in English units, while JPL thought they were in metric units. So JPL was overcorrecting. After a trip of 670 million km, the orbiter was only about 100 km off course, but that was enough to cause total failure. It either burned up in the atmosphere or bounced off it and re-entered heliocentric space. Worse, it turned out later that two different JPL navigators had noticed earlier that something was off with the trajectory, but their warnings were ignored because they didn't fill out the right form to submit to the oversight committee."

"Maybe we should change the subject," she says.

"I'm going on too long, aren't I? I'm sorry."

"It's not that, I just think you're making yourself more nervous."

"Maybe." And there's the Genesis probe, whose chute failed to open because a gravity switch had been mounted upside down— "Um . . ." He racks his brain. He can see a dozen lit screens in the seat backs in front of him, movie scenes set along dark city streets or on bucking airplanes, hideous and hysterical music videos, the surprisingly crude graphics of their own plane crawling up the coast toward Nova Scotia. All he can think of to say is, "Airlines today offer quite a number of viewing choices."

She says, "Not too long ago airplanes were one of the last places you still saw people reading books. There, and on the subway. In New York City, anyway. But even there you don't see it much anymore, except for women reading Elena Ferrante."

"Who?"

She makes a sound. Not really a snort, what might one call it? "You're a straight male, you don't read fiction."

Mark vaguely remembers an argument they had about this once. Something painful. He says, "It's true I haven't read much fiction for a long time. But a few weeks ago I was clearing out my mother's house and I saw all the mysteries she read in her last years, and I saw also the novels my father left behind, Faulkner and C. P. Snow and Le Carré. I even found in the attic some old science fiction paperbacks I'd read when I was a teenager. I realized I did kind of miss reading fiction. I'm reading something right now, something Mette suggested, a very long novel called *Infinite Jest*. Have you heard of it?"

"Um, yeah."

"The author clearly has a background in math and science. He doesn't quite understand how the Brocken spectre phenomenon works, I used to be intolerant of mistakes like that, but really you can only know so much. For example, he knows much more about pharmacology than I do. I was thinking of writing to him about Brocken spectres and suggesting an emendation, in case there's another edition."

"He's dead."

"Oh. That's too bad."

"He committed suicide."

Mark thinks about that for a few seconds. "Mette said when she recommended the book to me that when she was depressed he was the only writer who seemed to understand her."

"Mette told you she was depressed?"

"Not exactly. She said she had been depressed."

"When was this?"

"Two, three months ago? She's mentioned being down a couple of times in the past couple of years."

"And you just let it go?"

". . . I don't know what you mean."

"You didn't pursue it?"

"It just sounds like something she feels now and then."

"Why didn't you tell me anything about this?"

"It didn't occur to me that you didn't already know. You talk to her all the time."

"Depression is serious!"

"You don't need to tell me that. My father was depressed for the last twenty years of his life. The way Mette refers to it, it sounds less severe than what my father had."

"And you never connected this with her running off?"

"Of course it occurred to me as one possibility, among several. As I said, I thought you already knew she was occasionally depressed. The world is full of depressed people. Half of my students are on antidepressants."

"Jesus Christ." She seems to be angry.

"I'm sorry. I really am. I assumed you would know more about this than I did. You never mentioned anything in our recent phone calls about depression or suicide."

"Oh my god, you're impossible!"

Mark has already apologized, and meant it, so he's not sure what else he can do. He remembers reading a compelling argument that penitence is genuine only when there is a sincere will to change, so after a moment he says, "I promise, next time something like this comes up, I won't assume you already know potentially relevant facts."

She is looking away from him. She is still angry. Mark feels bad. Now that she has pointed it out, it does seem foolish, perhaps even culpable, that he didn't spend more time determining what each of them knew. Three or four minutes go by, during which a steward announces they'll be coming down the cabin with their complimentary beverage service. Eventually, Saskia says, "Partly, I'm upset because it bugs the shit out of me that Mette tells you things she doesn't tell me."

"There must be many things she tells you that she doesn't tell me."

"I'm not so sure about that."

Mark ponders this for a while. Then he says, "Maybe it's easier to say things to the parent you don't know as well. Like what they say about people pouring out their problems to the bartender."

"So she pours out her problems to you?"

"Well, no. We have fun doing puzzles together. This occasional mention of being down in spirits is the only thing I can think of."

"She has fun with you."

"Sure."

There's a long silence. Since they are seated in the back row, the beverage cart is a long way off.

"I've never understood her," she says.

"That's too imprecise to mean anything."

She makes an exasperated sound. "The very fact you say that proves my point. It's what *she* would say. But I know exactly what I mean."

There's a server at both ends of the beverage cart, and the cart blocks one row. After thinking about it for a second, Mark sees that in order to serve everyone, the servers need to alternate between advancing one row and three rows.

"Did I ever tell you I ran away from home once?" she asks.

"No."

"I was thirteen. I knew I couldn't hurt my father, so I was trying to hurt my mother. This thing with Mette feels like karmic payback. Except I don't think my mother worried about me much."

Mark has an insight, which he tries to formulate. "And so . . . perhaps . . . I haven't seemed to you in these past few days to be worried enough, either. Like your mother, maybe?"

"Well of course, I told you as much. Although you're nothing like my mother, believe me."

"But I have been worried. I sent Mette that text."

"I know, I know. You're the way you are, Mette's the way she is."

Mark can't argue with that. He doesn't want to accidentally make things worse, so he doesn't say this, or anything else, he just watches the beverage cart inch closer. He always gets tomato juice, since the potassium helps to calm his nerves.

"I've been working on this Joan of Arc play," she says.

"You mentioned that a couple of years ago. You're still working on it?"

"Writing takes a long time."

"I wasn't implying—"

"Or it does me, anyway."

"I didn't—"

"Sometimes I wonder if I'm writing it just to understand Mette better."

"I still don't quite know what you're referring to."

"She doesn't speak to me! Hardly ever!"

"You mean, she's mad at you?"

"No. Or . . . I don't know. That's the problem—I don't know what the problem is. I don't even know if there *is* a problem. I just get this idea that you and she are buddies and I'm excluded, and it . . . it's embarrassing to put it into words, it sounds like middle school . . . but I'm her mother, she's spent all her life with me and yet . . . You know, in a way, she's all I really have. Jesus, that sounds so melodramatic . . . Shit! Never mind, never mind."

Is she upset? Her face is turned away. Mark is dumbfounded. "I . . . She . . . I'm sure she . . ." All sorts of platitudes come to mind, but no one ever wants platitudes, do they? Mark hates it when people say *I'm sure everything will be fine*, when they have no way of knowing. It's insulting to a person's intelligence to think they will be comforted by empty words. The fact is, he doesn't really know anything about Saskia's relationship with Mette.

The beverage cart is still five rows away. Looking past it, Mark sees again all those lit screens and thinks about his students, how he and his colleagues have been forced to reduce class workload because students resolutely refuse to do more than a certain piddling amount, which

shrinks annually. He sometimes wonders if, along with resource depletion and environmental degradation, another reason intelligent civilizations never spread to other star systems is that, as the fruits of technology
proliferate, intelligent creatures prefer comfort and entertainment to the
hard challenge of scientific advancement or the risk of exploration. Maybe
intelligent civilizations are common in the Milky Way, but we never
hear from any of them because everyone's home watching movies. And
who's to say that's unfortunate? Adopting a cosmic perspective is all about
shedding privileged points of view. He's a scientist, so of course he values
the advancement of science. Maybe creatures that sit in recliners and
watch movies are less likely to kill one another and blow up their planet.

"His ways are not our ways," she says.

She has turned back toward him. Her face is blank. Or rather, he
can't read it. "What's that?"

"It's something Joan of Arc said at her trial. Referring to God, of
course."

"Ah."

"I say that to myself sometimes when I realize I'm inflating balloons
and hanging streamers for a pity party."

"Ah."

"Shaw fucked it up in his play, he changed it to 'His ways are not *your*
ways'—Joan talking to her judges. Shaw turned it into typical Shavian
lecturing and self-righteousness, when the original is more about Joan
accepting her fate."

"So . . . is that a little like saying, 'You're the way you are'?"

"Yeah, I guess. You know those mugs that say 'It is what it is'? I kind
of hate them because the phrase has been adopted as corporate-seminar-
speak, but like a lot of facile clichés there's a profound truth hidden
there if you can just see it fresh. You know, pretend you've never thought
of it before."

"There's a quote I've always liked," Mark says, "I think it's from Confucius. 'Wherever you go, go there with all your heart.'"

"Yeah, that's a good example. It actually means *everything*, if you can just hear it like a new idea."

"It's a good principle for scientists."

"It's similar to that Coen brothers line you mentioned, 'Just look at that parking lot.' Holding on to an idea of wonder."

"Which is what science is all about."

"I didn't know you believed in the heart, though."

"It's just an expression. It could easily be 'go there with all your attention.'"

"Don't you think 'heart' means more than that?"

"Well . . . maybe. Attention plus moral engagement. Plus intuition, which is probably related to empathy. All of that makes good science."

"Moral engagement?"

"Of course. All decent scientists struggle with the implications of their discoveries, whether it involves human biology or the military, or whatever. My father uprooted my mother and sister and left a secure position at RAND, he crossed the country to get away from nuclear weapons. Even though he loved the science. He never found atmospheric research to be as interesting. I think it's one of the things that made him depressed in his later years. What people don't understand is that, even if scientists dread the misuse of what they discover, they know that what is discoverable *will* be discovered, by someone. The whole nature of science—its openness, its explicable structure—means there's a strong likelihood that if you can see a way forward in a certain area of knowledge, other scientists can see it also."

"Yeah, that makes sense."

"While we're talking about quotes, there's one my father liked, he used to say it to me all the time, it's actually from some fantasy novel, I think, about some society on another planet. One of the characters ex-plains to a visitor, 'There's a dreadful law here, that if anyone asks for machinery they have to have it and keep on using it.' Of course my fa-ther was thinking of nuclear weapons. I guess anyone would. I always remember the quote when I'm on airplanes."

"It makes me think of automobiles. Maybe because I'm a New Yorker."

"And robocalls. And smartphones."

"And paperless voting machines."

"And traffic lights. Half of the intersections in Ithaca would work more efficiently with four-way stop signs."

The beverage cart has arrived. Mark gets his tomato juice, Saskia asks for hot water. "I've never seen that before," he says.

She sips. "Well, now you have."

He munches on his peanuts. The oil, like potassium, helps to calm him. Saskia gives him hers.

"I'm going to try to sleep," she says. She pulls a neck pillow out of her carry-on bag, arranges her blanket, closes her eyes. After a minute she opens them again. "You don't have any idea why Mette took off?"

"No."

"She didn't mention anything to you in the days or weeks right be-fore? Frustrations with work?"

"Nothing."

"Did she ever . . . Has she ever said anything about a boyfriend or girlfriend? Having one, wanting one, breaking up with one? Anything?"

"Not a thing."

"And you never thought to ask?"

Once again, she sounds irritated. "No. It sounds like you didn't, either."

"But I *thought* about it."

"As you irrefutably remarked a few minutes ago, I'm the way I am."

"You're right, my bad. I just thought . . . I don't know, thinking of you two as buddies, again. That you'd have had more opportunity than me."

"Perhaps I did. But unfortunately I wasn't aware of it." He ponders for a little while. "I'm getting the idea that we both thought the other knew more."

"Yeah."

"Maybe we should communicate more."

"Maybe."

She closes her eyes. After a minute or two it sounds like she's asleep. He remembers this about her, from all those years ago, her ease at falling asleep in chairs and other cramped spaces. Presumably her small size is an advantage. He's seen big men sleeping in chairs, too, but he can never do it. He would rather not even try, so he gets up and sticks his head in the rear galley and asks the two stewardesses chatting there if he could have a cup of coffee. One of them complies with that gratifying enthusiasm that fools foolish men such as himself into imagining she might be willing to be his girlfriend.

He returns to his seat with his coffee and tries to read more of that extremely long novel, but brief bouts of turbulence keep distracting him with jolts of adrenaline. Eventually he gives up. He avoids looking at Saskia for a while, then looks at her. She seems deep asleep. He had a dream several years ago about two women he dated for a brief while in his twenties, first Stephanie, then Janice. In both cases they initiated the relationship, for which he was surprised and grateful, and also ended it, by which he was pained and puzzled. In reality they were fellow graduate students in astronomy, but in his dream they were musicians. Obviously, he had conflated them with all those girls he'd had crushes on during his adolescent summers at music camp. In his dream, Stephanie and Janice were performing the Kodály duo in a recital, Stephanie on violin, Janice on cello. Mark was in the audience listening, and he knew, in the dream, that both of them had been anxious beforehand about not doing well, but they played beautifully, and when he met them afterward they were happy. They were also tired, so he took them home to his apartment, where he kept a bed for each. He put on fresh sheets while the two women lolled sleepily in chairs. Then he carried each to her bed. Their eyes were half closed. He tucked them in and kissed them good night. Each had just enough energy to murmur thanks before falling asleep. Then he sat in one of the chairs and watched them both sleep and felt terribly alone.

Saskia told him once, during the years after their relationship when they occasionally communicated regarding Mette, that he often struck her as an extraterrestrial, examining human life with a curiosity that seemed benevolent, but also creepy. She joked that he'd become an astronomer because he was searching for his home planet. Far from being offended, he found the idea flattering. One strives as a scientist to be clear-eyed, not to be enmired in distorting human emotions. (That's the word that always comes to him regarding emotions: "enmired.") It depresses him when he observes teams of scientists competing with each other to be the first to make a discovery, prejudicially denigrating the work of the other team. It depresses him when he observes prominent scientists motivated by personal ambition, fame, awards—paltry things in comparison with establishing a single true fact about the nature of reality. Most of the more famous scientists, even today, are male, and it depresses him to contemplate how much human male achievement is sublimated sexual display, fanning the peacock tail, lining the nest with bright objects, gaining access to more females.

When he was still a graduate student he was part of a team that came to suspect it had discovered the first brown dwarf, causing the team leader to dance with visions of sugarplums. Suddenly there was paranoia about what the team at the University of California was doing, and eventually there was a media circus, and then scientists who were peripheral observers criticized the findings with points that were partly valid and partly envious, and Mark had a revelatory vision of this mysterious low-temperature gaseous body, indubitably out there, with no awareness that it needed a designation, simply itself, a marvelous fact, and on a rocky planet 103 light-years away a bunch of chimpanzees were jumping up and down and hitting one another on the head for the right to call it an M dwarf or an L dwarf so that they could get more bananas in the form of a bigger chair in one of the congresses of learned chimps, or five minutes on TV with an ooh-ooh-ah-ah-ing host who thought light-years were units of time.

He's always been temperamentally attracted to unsexy subjects. He thought, in fact, that brown dwarfs were sufficiently unsexy, but he was wrong. He turned instead to astrometry, than which nothing could be unsexier. From there, it was natural to branch out into theories of galaxy formation, which depend on reams of accurate measurements of stellar mass and motion. The latter subject might, at rare intervals, generate a small public fuss, but except in cases where he has a responsibility to aid the professional prospects of a graduate student—ape behavior, but they are his trustful little chimps—he shares his data and his ideas freely. It may not have helped his professional standing, but it has certainly left more time for teaching.

Saskia sleeps on. It bothers him that he is attracted to small women. It's probably a control thing. Not that he could control her. In fact, what he seems to miss most about the brief time they were together is the way she ran circles around him. A scientist needs his paradigms jostled. Of course she's right that he likes to be an observer, to feel removed from the fray. When he played with his model train neighborhoods as a kid, gazing through the windows of a house, imagining the inhabitants washing dishes or reading in a chair, he found it gratifying that they were merely living their lives, while he was forming hypotheses about their lives. But the fact that smokers like cigarettes doesn't mean it's good for them.

He realized some time ago that he may be kind and patient with people, but that's pretty much all he is. He realized that the reason he tends to give people what they want is not because he's generous, but because he likes predictability. If you offer people what they want, they're likely to take it. It's a way of getting them out of your hair, so you can go back to eating at home alone and playing the piano for nobody. He and Saskia were trading favorite quotes a few minutes ago, and he would never admit it to her, but there's a quote that for years has occasionally come "unbidden" (as they say) to his mind, and every time it does so he's overcome with the feeling that it's the most important advice anyone has ever offered about human relations. The reasons he wouldn't admit it to her are, first, that it seems so sentimental, and second, that it's so comically, or maybe sadly, at odds with the way he's lived his life, or anyway with the outward appearance of the way he's lived his life. He doesn't know the origin of the quote, and of course he could google it, but he doesn't want to know, because it's probably from a Coke commercial, or some Disney cartoon song sung by simpering forest animals. The quote is, "Shower the people you love with love."

Saskia sleeps on.

He wonders if he's ever made it clear to Mette how much she means to him. He wonders if Saskia had any idea how upset he was when she left him. (Is "left" the right word? It was so brief.) On the other hand, who would want a person to stay with them solely because the person knew they would be miserable otherwise? That's manipulation. Saskia said her father was manipulative. In the past couple of hours Mark has been feeling more and more anxious. It's partly the flight, but also, suddenly, he's afraid for Mette. It's maddening that he has no way to assess the validity of his fear, since he knows nothing. He wonders if it's his own fault that he knows nothing.

He breathes deeply for several minutes, then takes refuge in the book again. Dawn comes early, but no one raises the shades on their windows because many passengers are still sleeping. He returns to the galley to ask about another cup of coffee and is assured it's no trouble by the same woman as before, who he could swear is on the verge of giving him her telephone number. Returns to his seat, reads. The book makes him think of Saskia's claim, or charge, that he and Mette are alike. He wonders whether Mette, like himself, might benefit from someone attempting to coax her out of a predilection for solitude that serves her well in some ways but badly in others. He wonders whether, during all these years in which he has been pleasing himself in his email exchanges with her, he has been failing her.

Daylight glows around the shades, which remain lowered, while Saskia and most of the other passengers sleep on. Some dozen young people watch their first movie of the day. Eventually stewards and stewardesses begin to move along the aisles, then one of them gets on the PA system and announces the imminence of breakfast. A few shades are raised, which brightens the cabin, which wakes more people who raise their shades, and suddenly it's a bright new day, in fact dazzling, thanks to the wondrously reliable 4.6-billion-year-old G-type main-sequence star rising in the southeast of the nitrogen-blue sky and the brilliant carpet of greenhouse-worsening but—on the plus side—albedo-enhancing white clouds below. Mark's wristwatch says 4:00 a.m. Local time is nine. They will land in two hours, or crash in approximately one hundred minutes. (Most airplane accidents occur on approach.)

Saskia wakes and stretches.

"Did you sleep well?" he asks.

"Mm," she murmurs drowsily. Another thing he remembers about her—her difficulty waking. On each of the five mornings she woke in his house he brought her coffee in bed, then worked downstairs for an hour before she appeared. She apologizes for making him get up, goes to the lavatory. When she returns to her seat she still seems stunned.

"They've just started serving breakfast," he says.

"Mm." She yawns. Then she says, "Thomas had a nervous breakdown. When I was four. Tried to kill himself. Part of me thinks I should be compassionate, but another part thinks the whole thing was a performance. He's one of these charismatic types who's been able to seduce people easily all his life. Where'd you get that coffee?"

"From the galley. Do you want me to get you a cup?"

"Nah, they're busy with breakfast, I'll wait. Anyway, when I spent a summer with him when I was thirteen, I saw how destructive he was. I haven't seen him for thirty years. I get a note from him every now and then, and I answer because I don't want there to be any mystery or drama, I send him these brief replies, I'm fine, etc. I've felt ever since I was thirteen that every moment I think about him is a moment that he wins. He certainly doesn't waste any time thinking about me."

As usual, Mark can think of nothing helpful to say. He wishes she would go on. After a few seconds he says, "Since he's Danish, how did he end up in America?"

"Long story. He grew up in some sandy wasteland in North Jutland, an only child, his father and grandfather were both ministers in this little parish. Or anyway, that's what he told me once, but a charming thing about him is that he loves to make shit up. It's part of the power thing—the less you know about him. He said he met my mother in India and that's probably true, my mother always said the same thing, then they came to upstate New York and he enthroned himself as guru on that old property I was living on when you and I met. Then he got restless and pretended he wanted to depart this mortal realm but probably he just wanted to run away from humdrum obligations. So when he got out of the hospital he left the US, seems to have traveled for a while, he might have done some eco-activism, when I met him again at thirteen he was trying to prevent a river in Norway from being dammed. When everyone else wouldn't do exactly what he wanted he took his bat and ball and left that game, too. Anyway, as far as I know he's been back in Denmark now for the last twenty years. His address is some island that's so small you only have to put his name and the island on the envelope. He wrote a few years ago that he was living in an old windmill he was repairing, which sounds so exactly like him, or like the image he's always liked to project, I've wondered if it's bullshit. He probably wants everyone to picture him sitting on top of it like a bearded holy man in a *New Yorker* cartoon. I think he wishes he were a trickster god, like Loki or Coyote. You know, God the Liar—what would that be, *Deus Mendax, Deus Mentiens?* Anyway, I'd bet anything he's got a Border Collie named Lila. All his life he's had a succession of dogs, all Border Collies, all named Lila. It's a way of making the dog timeless, making himself timeless. Narcissists live forever because they're convinced the whole cosmos ends when they die. He's probably about seventy by now, but he'll look fifty, max, you heard it here first. I'm kind of mad at myself that I gave Mette a Danish name, but I've always known the language a little, I can read simple stuff, I've always liked the sound of it. I should have given her the middle name Fuckthomas just so there'd be no misunderstanding. If you sound it out, it's actually got a pretty nice rhythm to it, Mette Fuckthomas White. Anyway, guess what? He's winning."

Mark's head is swimming. She has always done this to him.

The breakfast cart is approaching. "Earlier they said we had a choice of mushroom and cheese omelet, or pancakes and blueberries."

"Anything, as long as I get coffee. I'm not hungry. What are you getting?"

"The omelet."

"If I don't eat mine, which would you rather have?"

"Another omelet."

"I'll get that. I don't know how men eat so much."

"Of course you do, we're bigger."

"You're right, I was being rhetorical. Busted!"

The stewardess is by his elbow, holding breakfast boxes as neat and aseptic as astronaut food. "Sir?"

"Two omelets, please."

"I'm sorry, I can only give you one, as we have limited supplies."

"He means one for me and one for him," Saskia says. "Coffee?"

"Coming in a minute." The cart lurches into the rear galley.

Mark opens his plastic box, removes the plastic utensils from their plastic bag. Pulls back the plastic film covering the pat of butter, pries the plastic lid off the plastic tub of strawberry jam. Such impressive amounts of trash. Maybe the plane should just drop its quota directly into the ocean while they're flying over it. Save on fossil fuels powering the barges.

Coffee arrives at last. Mark eats, Saskia sips. Mark eats most of Saskia's food.

"Don't forget to drink all your buttermilk," she says.

"They have buttermilk?"

"Sorry, dumb joke. Never mind."

In the quiet minutes after eating, it occurs to Mark that Saskia "shared" with him, and maybe this is the time for him to "share" back. He remembers regretting, years ago, that there were certain personal things he'd never told her during the brief time they were together. He thinks about having, maybe, failed Mette. He looks down at the archeological ruins of his breakfast and says, "When my mother became demented after my father died, there were a few set phrases she would say repeatedly. For example, when she first came downstairs each morning she would say, 'Mark, I'm afraid the TV isn't working.' I never could figure out whether she was actually feeling anxiety, or even thinking about the TV, or whether the sentence was just a verbal tic elicited by her arrival in the living room. She'd always been an angry person. She became sweeter as she lost cognitive ability, but there were some things that would set her off. She wanted to watch the same movies over and over. One of them was a TV adaptation of a Dick Francis mystery called *Blood Sport*. A valuable racehorse is stolen, and the detective hero teams up with an insurance investigator who I think is supposed to be a comic character—he's heavy-set, slow-moving, talkative at the wrong moments, always sloppily eating something. Anyway, there's a scene toward the end where the detective and the insurance guy are racing down the road in a car, tailing some bad guys. The detective is driving, and the clock is running out before something bad happens, and the insurance guy starts into one of his longwinded objections to the hero's plan, and right at this moment, every time, my mother would pop forward on the couch and yell, 'Why don't you shut up, you fat shit!' Then she'd settle back and watch the rest of the scene with perfect equanimity."

Mark shifts his gaze to the ceiling. "Of course she was really yelling at my father, who by that point had been dead for years. Both my mother and my father had these rigidities, these . . . you could call them I guess frozen attitudes toward each other. Or maybe frozen emotions. In later years when either one of them complained to me about the other, they would always bring up the same anecdote to justify their indignation. My mother complained about some Saturday an eon ago when Susan was little and my mother wanted some free time and she asked my father if he'd look after her for the afternoon and he got angry and said he worked hard all week and she never asked him again because he was so angry it almost frightened her. She always told it the same way, in the

same words. For his part, my father would talk about the time when my
mother said he was a terrible father because he called Susan a whore,
when all he meant to say was that she was wearing too much makeup,
etcetera etcetera. They repeated these grievances over and over to *me*, but
as far as I could tell they never said them to each other. They seemed
incapable of listening to each other, of reformulating the tiniest detail of
their outraged memories."

"Trash?" The stewardess is passing with her bag. Mark throws it
all in.

"I can't remember when I finally told you that my sister was killed in
Yugoslavia," he says.

"Me neither."

"I might have said at some point that I went to Yugoslavia to see the
place where she died. Do you want more coffee? I see a pot coming."

"Yes." To the steward she says, "Cream, no sugar."

"I'll have one, too," Mark says. "Also with the nondairy creamer."

"No, you didn't tell me," Saskia says.

"I'd never paid much attention to politics. Most of it seems impervious to help, so why waste time on it? But my sister did try to help, and
even though it killed her, or maybe because it killed her, I respected her
desire to do that more than my own desire to be left alone. When I went
there I talked to people she worked with, including some government
officials. The hatred between the ethnic groups reminded me of my parents' fights, only with guns. No one was listening to anyone else, and as
a consequence good people like my sister died. I met the man who'd
been my sister's interpreter, and he said that the ethnic divisions in Yugoslavia had been deliberately exacerbated by the various state medias,
and that if we supposedly superior Americans had a propaganda outlet
working to foment discord, then in five years we, too, would have a civil
war. Well, look where we are today. My desire is still to ignore it, but for

my sister's sake, or in her memory, or whatever, I force myself to watch Fox News. It's hard to sit through, but I think of it as doing science. These are observations I need to make if I'm going to understand why the United States might self-destruct. Just yesterday Trump won the South Carolina primary."

"Yes, I know."

"A scientific paper last year presented results of a study of the human Y chromosome. It offered strong evidence of a bottleneck in male diversity occurring about 7000 years ago. The most convincing theory to account for this is that, with the spread of agriculture, which enabled larger population concentrations and an increase in social stratification, more-powerful patrilineal groups killed off all the males of less-powerful groups and took their females for mating purposes. Ninety-five percent of all human males during this period appear to have been wiped out. Human in-group/out-group murderousness goes far deeper than culture or economics, it's a biological consequence of the fact that genes good at crowding out competing genes survive to pass on to their descendants their proficiency at crowding out competing genes. It's such a robust argument that altruism among humans is much harder to explain."

"That's interesting. I wonder, though—"

"Of course we humans have enormous brains. We are able to become aware of these genetic tendencies and can choose not to follow them. But most humans don't seem to enjoy using their brains, or value its use in others."

"Mark?"

"On the other hand, you could argue that human intelligence is destroying the world more efficiently than human stupidity. Advances in agriculture and medicine lead to billions of people, resource depletion, and climate change. It's like forest management. The US Forest Service suppressed small fires for decades until the forests were unnaturally full of brush and deadwood, after which the fires became devastating and unstoppable. For 40,000 years, human intelligence has repeatedly figured its way out of the small fires, so now here comes the big one."

"Mark?"

"So is it people like Trump who are bringing on the end of the world as we know it, or is it people like me?"

"Mark?"

"Hm?"

"Why are you talking about all this?"

He can feel himself blush. "I'm rattling on. I'm sorry. I must be boring you."

"I didn't say you were boring me. What I asked was, 'Why are you talking about this?'"

He looks at her. He knows how maladroit he is at conversation. She has finished her second coffee and seems more awake now.

"I really am asking about your motivation," she says. "Use that brain nobody values. Why?"

In fact, it's a good question. He remembers there were times in the past when she helped him to see something, often right under his nose. He looks around the cabin. He's still embarrassed, despite her assurances. He looks some more. He tries merely to *see*. A bunch of fun-loving primates traveling to see other primates in their in-group. So they can go together to watch sublimated in-group/out-group warfare on a field, or spend time enjoying virtual worlds with endings manipulated in order to give them an illusory but pleasing sense of justice and order. He looks out the window at the beautiful bright world, the only world for life. He looks out at apocalyptic climate change. The Mediocrity Principle dictates that it's highly unlikely, given the span of time humans have existed on the planet, that he would just happen to live during the years when humans trigger a mass extinction event. Yet it seems increasingly probable.

His motivation? An actor's term. He remembers Saskia told him once about an acting workshop that involved repeating a phrase over and over until you lulled yourself out of rational thought and opened yourself up to instinctive feeling. "The teacher," she reported, "was always saying to the students, 'Get out of your head,' and I thought of you. You would be terrible at it."

Maybe he says it because he's sleep-deprived. He says it to his knees, which he only now notices are uncomfortable, jammed against the back of the seat in front of him. "I guess . . . I guess I've wondered a little bit, all these years, why you ended our relationship."

She doesn't say anything.

"I'm not blaming you. I've just wondered from time to time what the reasons were."

More silence. He doesn't look at her.

He plows on. "I wonder sometimes whether it was a mistake that we didn't try harder to understand each other. Something my parents never did." Now he gives her a longer time to respond. But she still says nothing. "I realize it's ridiculous that I feel this way, since we were hardly together in the first place. But you asked."

Finally, she says, "I'm sorry, I need to go to the bathroom again."

"Right." He lets her up. He waits for her in the aisle, but then the cart comes back through, this time collecting Styrofoam cups, so he returns to his seat. He shouldn't have spoken. Another social occasion mishandled.

She returns. They perform the awkward shuffle so that she can sit. "I know you don't watch a lot of movies," she says, "but by any chance have you seen *Serendipity*?"

"No."

"It's your standard rom-com. The male lead, played by John Cusack, has the usual rom-com bro, who he can go drink beer with and trade funny or rueful lines about women and life. But the unusual thing about

Serendipity is that the bro, played by Jeremy Piven, majored in Stoic philosophy in college, so he's always quoting Epictetus to Cusack. It's actually a brilliant idea, because a rom-com, until the end, is mainly about disappointment and longing and obstacles so severe they seem like malign Fate. You know, 'the course of true love never did run smooth,' and so on. What I'm saying is," and here she puts her hand on Mark's, "you need a friend like that. Not just anyone to talk to, but someone versed in the Stoics. It's actually occurred to me before that you might like Epictetus. He's not doing that head-banging epistemological stuff, he's concerned with ethics and happiness, very down-to-earth and usable."

"I could just read Epictetus," Mark says. "I don't need a friend to quote him to me."

"No, you need a friend."

Mark doesn't say anything.

"And you also need Epictetus. There's even a scene in *Serendipity* that takes place on a plane, I can't remember where it is in the plot, but Cusack is quixotically flying somewhere to search for his fated mate, and he's having doubts, so the quote Piven gives him is, 'If you want to improve, be content to be thought foolish and stupid.'"

Mark finally looks at her. She took her hand away a while ago. "How do you remember that?"

"Like I said, I'm an actor. I've also been rereading Epictetus lately. You can read the whole *Handbook* in an hour, it's like twenty-five pages."

"Okay." Mark feels deflated. What did he expect? He also feels a welter of things he can't process right now. He also can't think of anything to say. Which is probably best. This is why he hates talking to people. (He's dimly aware that it's not a good sign that he hates talking to people.) He remembers something his mother used to say, when his father tried to explain himself: "You've already done enough damage." He retrieves his book from the seat pocket in front of him. "I think I'll read this for a while," he says.

Saskia gets out her own book. It's almost as unwieldy as his. "*Lucky Per*," she says, showing it to him. "Great Danish novel, terrible translation. We'll be a couple of weirdos, reading in the last row."

Mark doesn't answer. He tries to concentrate, can't, pretends. Half an hour later, the plane begins its descent toward Copenhagen. The baby, which he still can't see, starts to cry.

Sunday, February 21, 2016

She didn't know ferries came this small. There would be just enough room for one car, if she and the other passenger jumped overboard. Thirty-five seconds after the scheduled time of 3:00 p.m. it pulls away from the quaint half-timbered town and throbs down the channel toward open water. The motor hums an 80-herz E. Temperature in the upper 30s, a cloudy sky with a crawling blob of blue far to the south. She'll reach the island by four. The Danish flag on the halyard snaps and flutters in totally convincing fashion.

She remembers a few years ago walking around the Greenpoint neighborhood to dezombify after a night-long bout at the screen and seeing on top of one of the houses an old Yagi television antenna getting buffeted by the wind. She's always liked Yagis, their rectilinear insect-feeler shapes. She filmed it as it described chaotic motion, twitching and flexing, occasionally erupting into wild gyrations. It looked alive, signaling with its arms for help, every now and then totally freaking out. Mette downloaded the film to her computer and spent a day creating a model, building the object, experimenting with different tensile strengths, resistance, restrictions of freedom of motion at the joints, wind forces and so on, until she had designed an algorithm that imitated it pretty well. She made a video that began with the original film of the antenna, then morphed into her animation, which she colored in hysterical reds and oranges, and added another algorithm that occasionally shot off nested waves of yellow lines that looked like psychic stress, or maybe sweat propagating in particle-wave duality. She posted it on her channel to join the few dozen other animations she'd done over the years and forgot about it. Six months later the film was bought by a South Korean production company for the opening clip of a K-drama about five young men sharing a house in Seoul, just barely managing to keep their shit together while they fucked up in quirky ways, disappointing and/or disgracing their parents. (She watched the first episode.) The company paid her a flat fee, but the drama was a hit, and suddenly thousands of people were viewing her original clip and saluting each other with messages like "Who else came here because of *Moonlight and Sunshine Boys*?" Seventeen percent were going on to look at some of her other clips, and within three months the ad revenue of her channel septupled.

As a programmer, she's never had trouble making money. She likes to chipmunk it away. Wishner mentions a guy named Lang Elliott who studied chipmunks in the Adirondacks. Elliott excavated a few burrows in the spring and found that most of the chipmunks still had plenty of winter food stored. One chipmunk had enough nuts for at least two more winters. And why not? You never know when the next asteroid will strike and block out sunlight for a few years, or when humans will find an opportunity to use all those missiles chipmunked underground. Or when you might need to buy at short notice an insanely expensive plane ticket involving multiple airlines from Seattle to Dublin to London to Denmark. Since she was digging into her stores anyway, she splurged on a suite at a fancy hotel last night in Copenhagen. (Home of the Copenhagen Interpretation! One of her first YouTube postings, when she was thirteen, was an animated whiteboard explication of the double-slit experiment.) This morning she treated herself to a sumptuous breakfast, then caught the train to the cutesy town, with the ferry leaving forty minutes (plus thirty-five seconds) later.

When she was fifteen, sixteen, she was often angry at her mother for being irresponsible about money, chasing her stupid actor's dream while the two of them barely got by. Why didn't she learn some programming, do it part time? Mette was willing to teach her. But she gradually became more tolerant. It must suck to want to do something you're not very good at, or that the world has little need for, or both. When her mother started doing voice work for video games Mette thought, Dreamer, shake hands with reality. She started contributing a quarter of basic expenses such as rent and food when she was seventeen, upped it to a third last year. Now that she thinks about it, it's kind of inexcusable that she hasn't been contributing half. It's also maybe a little embarrassing that she hasn't considered what the loss of her income might mean to her mother.

Still, in the final analysis, not her problem.

The ferry is rounding a low headland at the end of the channel and she can see from the GPS on her phone that the island should be coming into view. That beige-gray line on the horizon must be it. According to the Danish Ministry of Tourism site, the island's highest point is less than two meters above sea level. Meaning, So long soon. They've already built dikes, which have been breached twice in the past decade. (Dreamers, shake hands . . .) All that work, plus this toy ferry running twice a day, for only twelve inhabitants, including the nutjob in the windmill.

Her mother always said she never knew where her father was when she was a kid. Mette finds it hard to imagine that information Dark Age. When she decided in Seattle to locate him, she knew only his first name and that he lived in a windmill on a Danish island. It took her seventeen minutes: database of old mills in Denmark narrowed to ones on islands, modern photos of same (Google Maps, plus mill-loving Instagrammers, who, it turns out, are thick as thieves), assessment rolls for owners of renovated ones. It helped a little that Thomas seems to be an uncommon name for Danes of his generation.

She watches the island creep closer.

Her mother has never liked to admit it, but she, too, often gets depressed. Mette wonders if the struggle to make money or to succeed in her career helped keep her going. Or maybe the struggle of being a mother to Mette. From Mette's perspective, it's been hard to see the point. Mette has always had the impression that her mother, unlike herself, doesn't enjoy being alone. For evidence, there's that parade of partners. Mette was always rooting for her. Maybe her mother only wants short-term fixes. But Mette doubts it. There were one or two relationships that, when they ended, really broke her mom up.

The ferry sounds its horn, a low B with a rumbly G-sharp underneath that starts and ends a second after the first tone. Either two apertures, or the metal casing of the horn vibrates at a separate pitch. They've entered an area of ice on either side of the dredged channel. The water under the ice appears to be only a foot or two deep.

A hundred years ago there was an amateur mathematician named Paul Wolfskehl who got rejected by the woman he loved and decided to commit suicide. Since he was a mathematician, his plan had to be both precise and conceptually satisfying, so he decided to shoot himself in the old noggin at the stroke of midnight. That meant he had a few hours to kill. He read a paper by a mathematician named Kummer, who was trying to disprove a mathematician named Cauchy, who had been trying to prove Fermat's Last Theorem. Wolfskehl thought he saw a way he could disprove Kummer's disproof of Cauchy, so he worked on his idea all night and missed his appointment. He was wrong about Kummer, but now he was in love with Fermat's Last Theorem—which, it occurs to Mette, you might say had never yet abandoned a suitor. So instead of killing himself, he founded the Wolfskehl Prize.

Fifty years ago, another mathematician, named Yutaka Taniyama, did manage to off himself. He had tried and failed for years to prove a conjecture involving L-functions of elliptic curves. He left a suicide note that has haunted Mette over the past few days, so much so that she knows parts of it by heart. *Until yesterday I had no definite intention of killing myself . . . As to the cause of my suicide, I don't quite understand it myself . . . Merely may I say, I am in the frame of mind that I lost confidence in my future.*

Today, an unimportant computer programmer and hack mathematician, rejected in love and without confidence in her future, either does a Wolfskehl or a Taniyama. Is she still near enough to Copenhagen that, so long as no one looks, she can do both? Neither Fermat's Last Theorem nor the Taniyama-Shimura conjecture can save her, because the former was proved in 1995 and the latter in 1999.

Well, there's always the $3n + 1$ problem. Ha ha.

They've arrived at the island. The ferry honks again, turns around, backs into the slip. She and the other passenger, a woman, walk off. There's an empty expanse of gravel and two prefab buildings with red metal roofs, both locked and empty. A one-lane road heads off between brown fields patched with snow. She lets the other woman pull ahead, so there'll be no danger she'll be spoken to. All the blue in the sky has disappeared, the stiff wind is cold. After five minutes she comes to the one cluster of houses on the island. (None of this is a surprise, she previously google-viewed everything.) There are eleven, seven of them large, looking like manor houses with flanking outbuildings. Since there are only twelve permanent inhabitants, some of these must be summer residences, unless the island is filled with loners who like to rattle around in a dozen rooms like marbles in a maze. Anyway, rich people.

The other woman peeled off somewhere. No one else is out. Mette walks out the far side of the settlement and continues between more brown and snowy fields. There are almost no trees, even along the road, so the wind has free rein. She has an image of herself flailing her arms in chaotic motion, fucking up in a quirky way. There's no other ferry today, so if the nutjob isn't home she'll have to retrace her steps and throw herself on the mercy of a rich misanthrope. Or just freeze to death. She comes to a path heading left that she has already examined from the Google empyrean. Two more empty fields to left and right, more cold wind smacking her face. Now a frozen marsh. Who would want to live here. She can see the mill ahead, looking of course like its photos: pepperpotty and small, clad in brown shingles, perched on a stone foundation. The sails have been rebuilt, a nutjob job. It stands immediately in front of the beach, which is invisible from this vantage point. Expanse of gray ice and gray sea beyond. The sails are turning. Satisfying riposte to the stiff sea breeze she's begun to hate.

She hears a dog bark. A Border Collie pops into view over the verge of dead grass and races toward her. A man sticks his head out the mill door and yells, "Lila!," then says something in Danish. Mette doesn't know the language, but she's been told gramps speaks English, so she calls, "It's all right, I like dogs." The dog circles at close quarters, sniffing, wagging her tail. Mette continues up to the door, Lila following.

"Can I help you?" the man asks from the doorway in unaccented English. Like his mill, he's recognizable from an old photo Mette has seen, from the commune days. He's short like her mother, with pale blue eyes. Trim gray hair and beard, fit body. Wiry, you could say. An escape artist, her mother says.

"Maybe," she says. "I'm Saskia's daughter, Mette."

"Of course you are." He stands back from the door. "Welcome."

She mounts the stone steps. "Lila, you stay out for now," he says. Inside is an octagonal room, brighter than Mette expected, owing to three large windows in the west, south, and east walls. The northwest, southwest, southeast, and northeast walls are each filled floor to ceiling with books. The door she came through is in the north wall. In the middle of the room, descending from the ceiling and sinking into the floor, is the beveled wooden beam of the mill shaft, rotating. A circular table has been built around the shaft.

"Take off your shoes." He points to a vinyl mat. "Choose a pair of slippers." To the left of the door is a wooden case holding eight pairs in different sizes and colors. "Hang your pack there." To the right of the door is a row of six wrought-iron hooks. "Have a seat." He gestures toward one of the two chairs at the table. "Coffee or tea? Your mother was always a coffee drinker."

"Me, too."

"Sit."

She does so. He busies himself at a stove and countertop beneath the east window, taking a kettle, coffee tin, steel bowl, and whisk from shelves on either side of the window frame. From a shelf above the window he grabs flour and baking soda and fetches milk and eggs out of a mini-fridge below the south window. He works fast.

She finds it unpleasant to speak to anyone she doesn't know, so instead she examines the room. Everything is made out of wood. The floor, ceiling, and walls are old and darkly gleaming, the bookshelves, table, chairs, and counters are of a newer blond material, maybe birch, designed simply and built with precision. Surfaces are immaculate. The window frames and muntins are weathered wood, freshly painted white. Each window is square, divided into twenty-five small square panes. For some reason it looks nautical. Maybe old galleons had windows like these in the captain's quarters. Or maybe it's the view of the sea outside the south window. The walls slope inward so that the individually anchored shelves give the impression of bookcases that ought to fall over, but somehow don't. The books seem to float around her head. Below the west window is a wooden storage chest, built with the same neatness. Two shelves on each side of the south and west windows, making eight in all, are hinged, so that they can be lowered when needed, then raised again and hooked to eye bolts to keep them out of the way. A wooden ship's ladder next to the coat hooks to the right of the door leads to the upper floor. Efficient use of a small space. Maybe it's that Danish predilection for "coziness" Mette's mother has told her about. Whatever it is, Mette loves it. Get rid of the old man, move this excellent room to Brooklyn.

He hands her a cup of coffee, saying something that sounds like *vairssko.*

"Thank you."

"Milk, cream, sugar?"

"No, thank you."

"Biscuits will be ready in seven minutes. I love biscuits. So American! Fast food before McDonald's."

"Mm."

"I noticed you were examining my little place. You like it?"

"Yes."

He gestures to the shaft, rotating next to them. "My apologies for the creaking. You get used to it."

"It's okay, it sounds like a ship in a storm." Or to be precise, like a video-game sound effect for a ship in a storm.

"Exactly." He sits down, leaning toward her.

She leans back.

He says, "This mill was built a hundred and fifty years ago, to pump seawater out of the marsh. After that it was turned into a grist mill. These old mills, once they go out of service, the vanes, or the arms— what do you call them in English?"

"Sails."

"Perfect! In Danish we call them 'wings.' I like sails better. The sails don't last long, the canvas rots, the frames fall apart. I rebuilt all that."

"Nice job." It's what he seems to want.

"Thank you. The grindstones were still in the cellar when I bought the place. I grind my own wheat and barley. I ran a horizontal shaft through a culvert to pump seawater out of my garden, so I grow most of my own food. I also have batteries under the mill cap, so I make my own electricity and sell part of it to the grid."

"You're like Thoreau."

"Please. Thoreau was a lazy tourist." He pops up. "Biscuits are ready. Can you smell them?"

He brings them to the table wrapped in a cloth in a wicker basket, sets out two plates, forks, butter, and knife. "What do you Americans say? 'Dig in.' I love it." He forks open a biscuit, starts buttering. "When Danish housewives had guests for tea in the old days, they always served rolls and butter first. The hope was that the guests would fill up on the cheap stuff, before they brought out the cake. I don't have any cake, so eat up."

She tries a biscuit. It's very good.

"No butter?" He pushes the dish toward her. For the first time she notices that his right hand is missing the ring finger and pinkie. "Danish butter is the best in the world."

"No thanks."

"Biscuits without butter?" He looks skeptical.

"I prefer it that way."

"Suit yourself." He pauses for a second. "I'm trying to remember an American phrase I always liked. Oh, yes—'It's your funeral.'"

"What happened to your hand?" she asks. Her mother never mentioned anything about that.

He holds the hand palm up in front of himself, traces the scar line from the middle finger to the medial edge of the palm with the first two fingers of his other hand. "I lost an argument with a bomb I was making." He's turned on an eye-twinkle, like a battery-powered Santa Claus.

"Why were you making a bomb?"

He waves that aside. "Good liberal reasons. Wasn't supposed to hurt anyone. Like a good little liberal I ended up hurting only myself."

"Did you get in trouble? You must have been caught."

"You're imagining this happened in a well-regulated country."

She waits for him to go on, but it seems to be all he's going to say. She wonders if he's doing what her mother says he likes to do, i.e., make shit up. The scar forming the diagonal edge of his reduced palm is dramatic, but neat. Would a bomb leave no peripheral scarring?

"Have another biscuit," he says, holding the basket toward her.

She takes one. They really are exceptionally good.

"I briefly considered attaching what you Americans call a lazy Susan to the mill shaft just above the table," he says. "But the shaft turns too fast most of the time. Did you know that the lazy Susan was invented by the Oneida Community? You must know about them."

"No."

"Shame on you. They were in upstate New York, not far from the old commune. A hundred years before us hippies and our newfangled ideas, the Oneidans believed in eating each other's food and fucking each other's partners. Land of the free, home of the depraved."

It occurs to her that he hasn't asked her why she's here. Nor does he appear to be politely concealing curiosity. She wonders if he'd be happy to sit here all day and keep slinging bullshit in her direction. "I'm thinking about killing myself," she says.

"Of course you are. And you came to see me because I attempted suicide when your mother was young. That's a real gripe of hers, I'm sure she's mentioned it more than once."

She has to hand it to the old man, he's quick on his feet.

He gestures toward her. "All done?"

It takes her a moment to realize he's asking if she's done eating. "Yes."

He carries plates, cups, and cutlery to a small sink next to his cooking counter, squirts soap, turns on water. He says over his shoulder, "If you want me to talk you out of it, you've come to the wrong place."

"I don't want you to talk me out of it."

He rinses, dries, and stores the dishes away behind a door under the counter in a matter of seconds, sits back down at the table. "So what then?"

"I want to know why you did it. And whether you failed on purpose."

He gives her a small smile, and himself a little scratch on the beard. "I could say it's none of your business." The bottom lids of his eyes rise slightly, making his gaze look more intense, maybe "piercing," owing to his light blue irises. Mette dimly imagines that some people would find this mesmerizing. "But I'm not sure that I would mean it. I like the way you talk openly about suicide. I don't share the Christian attitude that it's a shameful thing. On the contrary, it's the greatest freedom we humans possess, our only god-like power. It's no surprise that a wannabe omnipotent bully like Yahweh would proscribe it. And capitalist societies happily go along with the taboo. Underpaid workers must stay at their posts. Finally, most people *want* to believe that suicide is shameful, or a betrayal of loved ones, or an act of cowardice, because the real cowardice is that they don't want that freedom. Their terror of it shows what a profound freedom it is."

He pauses. Mette doesn't say anything.

"To answer your second question first, I didn't fail on purpose. I didn't fail at all, and if your mother says I did, she either doesn't know what she's talking about or she's being malicious. Seppuku is supposed to be completed by an attendant, who has taken a vow to perform that duty. My attendant was your grandmother, Lauren, and she broke her vow."

He pauses again. He seems to be waiting for an objection. Mette has no interest in making one.

"I will say, however, that I'm glad she did—I mean, break her vow. Because my decision to kill myself was a mistake."

"Obviously," Mette says.

"Why do you say that?"

She shrugs. "You're still here. Despite plenty of opportunities to kill yourself later. You've clearly decided it's better to live."

"That's right. For me."

"Of course for you. It says nothing about me."

"That's right. But maybe you're confused in the same way that I was, so let me continue."

"Please."

"I was confusing the desire to suffer with the desire to die. Many people make this mistake. They want to suffer, and death looks like the biggest dose of suffering available. But it's nothing of the sort. Suffering has to be experienced, whereas death ends experience. Cutting is a far more rational response to this desire, and I applaud the kids who thought it up. Cutting is a modern phenomenon because modern life inflicts far less physical pain on the individual than many people want. On the other hand, there are people even in modern life who are unwillingly suffering, either physically or mentally, and they want to end that suffering. For them, suicide is rational."

"Why did you want to suffer?"

"Why does anyone? I thought I deserved it. I had let people down. I'd tried to lead them to a better way of life, and I'd failed." He glances out the west window. "The sun's about to go down, let's take a walk."

The old man likes to give orders. But Mette came to him for help, so it's reasonable to accommodate him. She puts on her jacket and shoes and follows him out the door. Circling around the mill, he steps down to the stony beach and calls for the dog, who comes racing along the waterline. The old man fondles her ears and turns west. Lila heads in the same general direction, dipping in close to sniff a hand or back of knee, then swinging wide to explore tufts and hollows, tail high and happy. The sun is a bleary smudge behind thin clouds, hovering just above the sea line. The ice, Mette now sees, stretches away from the shore for only about fifty yards, even though the water in the Baltic is of low salinity and here quite shallow. It has been a mild winter, on the whole.

"Any suicide that's painful or disfiguring is likely an expression of self-hatred or shame, rather than a true desire to die," he says. "People with terminal illnesses who decide to kill themselves don't blow their brains out or slit their wrists, they take an excess of painkiller and tie a bag around their heads. Your mother has always been angry at her mother for not fighting the cancer. But Lauren made the decision to end her suffering. That's a healthy attitude. When people tell you that you should continue to suffer so that they won't be 'abandoned,' or 'heart-broken,' or whatever manipulative formulation they choose, they're being selfish. That this isn't obvious to everyone is a tribute to how effective the propaganda against suicide has been."

A small hole has opened in the cloud cover right at the horizon, and as the sun's full diameter passes it, an edge of the photosphere is revealed as a blinding spark. They both stop, bringing their hands to their foreheads and gazing at the light past the edges of their palms. The gorgeous gleam lasts five seconds, then is gone. Now Mette has a spot of retinal gray in the center of her vision.

He walks on. She follows. It's his rodeo. "I won't ask you why you're considering suicide, because that's none of my business. But tell me, what methods have you considered?"

"I haven't figured out the logistics yet."

He makes a dismissive gesture. "Logistics are trivial. What I mean is, when you consider suicide, what image comes to mind?"

"Well, for one, I've thought about jumping off a high place."

"Yeah, you see, that's suspect. Maybe your imagined fall is inspired by the capital-f Fall. You feel like a sinner."

"I don't think so."

"Why not?"

"Your theory's too clever."

"Clever means smart."

"Unless it means too clever."

"The disfigurement from a fall is horrific. And the pain might be indescribable. No one really knows how long consciousness continues after the body is wrecked. There are stories about guillotined people's heads looking around in the basket for a number of seconds. Besides, you might land on someone and kill him. Or fall in view of a child and traumatize him."

"Or her. Or them."

"It's self-punishing and antisocial. It says, 'Look at me.' None of these motivations are pure. Lila, come away from there!"

"My mother always said you had a thing about purity."

"Did she also ever tell you that ad hominem remarks indicate the weakness of an argument? Lila!"

A good point, actually. She's starting to both like and detest this man in equal measure. A funny feeling.

He stops abruptly and turns to gesture at the shore ice and the open water beyond. "Right there is the truest method of suicide there is. Hypothermia, followed by drowning. Those who've experienced it accidentally and survived report that they felt a comforting sleepiness, followed by a powerful euphoria. In the moment, they *wanted* to die. It's how I'll kill myself when the time comes. Just walk out my door one winter day."

"When the time comes?"

"I have no intention of becoming decrepit."

"Sure. If you're otherwise content, though, the bitch is deciding when."

"It won't be for me."

"Okay."

"Let's head back," he says.

"Sure thing." She really wants to add "boss," but restrains herself.

Lila's now far up the shore, so he does that wide-mouthed whistle with the tucked upper lip she's always wished she could do. Lila bounds back and they turn around. There's still a lot of light in the sky. At this high latitude it will get dark much more slowly than in New York.

"I did think about walking into the Pacific Ocean," she says.

"Not the Atlantic?"

"I was in Seattle."

"But you didn't do it."

"I decided to come see you first."

"This visit seems like evidence of uncertainty. Which of course is an argument for holding off."

"Maybe."

"Look." He sounds impatient. "The test is right in front of you. There it is." He gestures again across the ice. "No logistics necessary, you could do it right now. The cold will relax you and your clothes will weigh you down. I won't stop you."

She looks across the ice.

"Having said that," he goes on, "I'd suggest you wait until morning. The majority of suicides happen in the evening or during the night, because people unconsciously associate the end of day with the end of life, loss of light with loss of hope, and so on. It's the same mistake that makes old people think the world around them—culture, values, common decency—is dying. It's because *they* are dying. What's it called in English? The pathetic fallacy, I think. It doesn't help that poetry and novels and television and every other form of human narrative traffic in exactly this confusion. The radio says that tomorrow will be a beautiful day. First thing in the morning, with the sun rising into a blue sky, go down to the beach. If you keep going then, maybe you mean it."

"Radio?"

"Hard to believe, I know, but I don't have internet."

"Not hard to believe at all. I was surprised you have a radio."

He smiles. "You're a witty one."

They walk in silence for a minute. It's getting to be that time in a cloudy evening when most of the light seems to be generated by the snow and the ice. Thomas veers off toward a stretch of sandy ground to pluck a stem of tall grass. He returns to her, displaying it. "*Ammophila arenaria*. Lila, it's not for you. The genus name means 'sand-lover.' In Danish we call it marram. There's not much of it on this island because it grows in sand dunes and the beaches here are mostly stony. Its beard looks like wheat, though of course the seeds are smaller. Look, can you see how the stalk curls around itself, almost forming a tube? That helps it retain moisture in windy conditions."

It is true that all facts are interesting in themselves, but this one is only mildly so to Mette. Why is he telling her this?

"In North Jutland this grass helped anchor the sand dunes, which are extensive there. Farmers used to cut it for fodder and thatch, and with the loss of the root systems, the dunes started migrating. They buried whole villages, leaving only the marram-grass thatched roofs visible. Ecological disaster in the comic mode."

This is more interesting, but still. They walk on. She can see the mill in the dusk not far ahead.

"I've been learning to identify every species of vegetation, insect, rodent, and bird on the island. I've lived here for eight years, and I figure the island is just small enough that I could accomplish it all before I die. The grasses are the hardest. Second are the beetles. This is like what Candide, after all his travels, called cultivating his garden."

"Or what Dorothy meant after Oz, when she said, 'There's no place like home.'"

She is trying to poke fun at him, but he says, "Exactly."

They leave the beach and walk around to the mill door. He pauses at the bottom of the stairs. Lila sticks her nose between his legs and he pats her flank vigorously. "It's deeply satisfying, conquering a subject. I think you, more than most people, understand what I'm talking about."

"You're telling me to find myself a project so that I won't drown myself."

"I'm not telling you anything. Drown yourself tomorrow morning if you want to. The question is, do you want to?"

"Look, it's great that naming the grasses and beetles makes you happy. I like knowing things, too. But no matter how much I learn, when I die it will all be snuffed out along with my brain, so what's the point?"

He says something in Danish.

"That's very helpful."

"It's from a novel that every schoolchild in Denmark used to read, about a schoolteacher living on a small island. In English, it's something like, 'This island is so small—a molehill in a field of blue. Dear God, what is that, set against the questions of the big world? Nothing! But how big are the big world's questions, seen from Orion's Belt?'"

Mette is not sure that he's trying to help her so much as showing off, playing the guru. "Sure. Which is an equally good argument for you to drown yourself tomorrow morning, too." For once she doesn't wait for him to take the lead, she wants to deny him the pleasure, so she goes up the stairs and through the door. He follows without a word. It's getting dark, so he switches on a shaded lamp attached to one of the bookshelves, above a reading chair. "I expected kerosene," Mette says.

"Or maybe whale oil? Both would be environmentally idiotic, considering I make my own electricity."

"I was trying to be witty again."

"Repetition is the soul of stupidity." He takes a can off one of the shelves, opens it with a Swiss Army knife, spoons glistening chunks into a bowl, and sets it down for the dog. "I want to pick up some coffee at a depot next to the ferry landing. Sanne closes at eight-thirty, so I'm going to head over there. I'll be back in an hour or so. If you need to piss or shit, there's a composting toilet ten meters away near the garden, you can see it from the window. The hut is insulated, paper's in there, another astonishing electric light, and even an electric heater if your ass gets too cold."

The dog is already done eating. "Lila, come." He disappears out the door, the dog crowding his heels. By the time she looks from the top of the steps a couple of seconds later, they're both out of sight. Escape artist. And your little dog, too!

She's momentarily at a loss for what to do. Then she realizes that she does need to piss so she goes out to the toilet. She flips a switch to the right of the door and an overhead bulb comes on. The small room, as by now she would expect, is well made and immaculate. It smells of fresh dirt and peat. She pisses and returns to the mill.

She spends some time idly looking at his books, most of which are in Danish or German. He has the complete works of Kierkegaard, whom Mette has vaguely heard of, but otherwise knows nothing about. She examines the way he anchored the shelves. She also looks at the collars he built to enclose the mill shaft where it comes out of the ceiling and goes into the floor. He fashioned single blocks of wood with beveled square cutouts and circular flanged rims that rotate smoothly within rings attached to the floor and ceiling. He is quite an impressive woodworker.

She climbs the ship's ladder to the second floor, which she rightly guessed was his bedroom. A smaller room, of course, owing to the sloping walls. There are four square windows identical to the ones below, which let in so much dusk-light she doesn't need to switch on the lamp. The dusk here really does last forever. His bed is single, placed lengthwise along the south wall, but somewhat separated from it because the bed is too long and has to accommodate a few inches of the adjacent walls. On the bed's far side is a set of built-in shelves holding books, an old-fashioned clock, a water glass, a small atlas. The bed's nearer side is only about two feet away from the mill shaft in the center of the room. She wonders if at night when he's sleepy he ever stumbles into the shaft and gets thrown to the floor by its rotation. The image amuses her. She's aware that her motive in coming up here is malicious, as she would hate the thought of anyone examining her own room. She looks out each of the four windows at the darkness of land and the glimmer of ice. What a view this man has during the day. She will admit, she admires the skill and energy he brings to creating exactly the world he wants to inhabit. His willpower. There's something ever-so-slightly wizardly about it.

She returns to the bottom floor, fishes Newman out of her pack, sits back at the table. She's almost done with volume three, and has just come across a figure Newman calls a parhexagon: a hexagon whose three pairs of opposite sides are equal and parallel but don't necessarily equal each other. Newman proposes a theorem that you can take any irregular hexagon and if you draw diagonals to the adjacent sides and connect as vertices the centroids of the resulting triangles, the figure thus created will always be a parhexagon. Which is kind of interesting. She'd like to prove it to her own satisfaction, so she takes out her notebook and ruler and starts drawing. After a while she hears a hand on the doorlatch and the old man and his familiar come in.

"Hungry?" he asks.

"No."

"It's almost nine, all you had was a couple of biscuits when you first arrived."

"Yet, strangely, I'm not hungry."

"I'm making American-style home fries in your honor. Potatoes, onions, and garlic I grew myself. You can eat or abstain, as you wish."

"Sounds good."

"Lila, lie down." She does exactly as he says, curling up on a rag rug under the ladder. He starts fetching, chopping, juggling, whistling, all-around bustling, while she continues to work on her diagram. The figure involves a lot of lines and she is just now realizing she should make it bigger. She sets the sheet aside, gets tape from her pack and connects four new sheets so that they form a 17" by 22" rectangle. Returns to work. A few minutes go by during which an ignorant observer who likes nothing better than to jump to conclusions might think, Here's a happy family.

"Food's ready," the old man announces.

"Dig in," she says, not looking up.

"Could you move that while we eat?"

As before, he doesn't seem interested in what she's doing. Which is fine with her. But it's kind of strange that he never asks anything.

She sees that she needs to move the large sheet to make enough room, even if he eats alone, and besides, the thought of him getting grease on her diagram is intolerable, so she folds it and places it on top of her pack by the door. Lila gives her a look and the last half inch of her tail wriggles. When Mette returns to the table she sees that he's put a plate down for her. "Just in case. You want a beer?"

"No thanks."

"It's home-brewed."

"No thanks."

"It's your funeral." He starts eating.

She realizes that, in part, she is just trying to bother him. This makes her feel petty and foolish. Worse, maybe he can tell. In fact, she is somewhat hungry and the home fries smell good. "I guess I'll try some," she says.

He swivels the handle of the serving spoon toward her. He also pours beer into her glass.

His home fries are excellent. The beer probably is as well, but she has this crazy feeling that if she drinks it, he will have captured her soul.

He eats and drinks while she nibbles, and that same ignorant observer would see a kindly old miller and his socially normal granddaughter sharing silent rapport of a winter evening.

"So you've never felt that you don't belong anywhere?" Mette asks.

"Belonging is for ungulates."

"And you're a leopard."

"I'm a man."

"Humans are gregarious."

"Human gregariousness is a holdover from chimpanzees, whose idea of socializing is to form tribes and kill outsiders. Predators like leopards are solitary by nature. The glory of humans is that they can choose to leave the herd."

"This sounds Ayn Rand-ish."

"Please. Have you read any Ayn Rand? She was a neurotic nitwit. She wanted to feel superior to other people, which is just gregariousness for megalomaniacs."

In fact, she hasn't read any Ayn Rand. Of course, maybe he hasn't, either. "Yet you were a guru in a commune."

"Which was a mistake. I wanted to inspire people, and I only made them weaker. Which made me feel like I deserved punishment, which made me stick a sword in my stomach, which was also a mistake, and now we've come full circle and proved to your satisfaction that I'm fallible."

He clears the table and washes up. He's so efficient, it doesn't occur to her to offer help, and he seems neither to expect nor want it. She brings her parhexagon diagram back to the table and finishes constructing it. She starts labeling equal line segments, congruent and supplementary angles. Drying his hands on a dish towel, he stands over her. "The only meaning your life will ever have is the one you give it. So you're all alone. Boo hoo! Everyone is alone. Most people don't figure that out until they're on their deathbeds, but you've been having fun making up your bed ahead of time, so if you don't go swimming tomorrow morning maybe you'll come out of this with a chance of leading a full and free life." He hangs the dish towel on a rack on the side of the countertop cupboard. "It's ten-thirty. I'm going to bed. If you get hungry, eat anything you see." Lila lifts her head, half rises. He puts out a palm and she lies back down. He lifts the lid of the storage chest beneath the west window and pulls out a bedroll and a pillow. "Pad, clean sheets, blanket. Roll it out when you want." He goes out to the toilet, returns, brushes his teeth at the sink. "Stay up as long as you want. One last piece of advice, though. A decision to kill yourself when you're tired is no proper decision at all."

"Pathetic fallacy, got it."

He turns to Lila and she jumps into his arms. He starts up the ladder one-handed. "She used to be able to manage this on her own, but she's getting old. Good night." He disappears through the ceiling.

She spends a while staring at her diagram. Either it's a harder problem than she thought, or she's tired. As he suggested. Fuck, once again he put an idea in her head that squats and propagates. She works for another half an hour just to spite him, but really, she's getting nowhere. She couldn't get to sleep in the Copenhagen hotel last night until four, because she was still on Seattle time. Now it's all crashing down on her, the three-day bus ride, the chain of flights, the bad night, the train, the ferry, the old man's symposium. She doesn't bother to brush her teeth.

Unrolls the pad on the floor near the south window and turns out the light. Crawls between the sheets with her clothes on. Stares at the ceiling.

She listens to the creaking of the mill shaft, the sighing of the wind. Silence from the ice, silence from upstairs. From her position on the floor, all she can see out the window are the dark clouds, occulted every four seconds by the tip of a sail sweeping past. It reminds her of her old room in Astoria, where she had her nest below the window from which she could observe the sky and the birds and feel safe and invisible. She loved being alone then. She wonders if the parhexagon theorem is easy and she's just being stupid. She wonders if her muddle-headedness is Alex's fault, or her own besotted idiocy's fault, or the long trip's fault, or if she's past her mental prime and it's all downhill from here. *I am in the frame of mind that I lost confidence in my future.*

When she opens her eyes again, it's still dark, but the first bit of dawnlight is creeping in. She checks her phone. 6:13 a.m. (613, 46— unhappy.) She rises, rolls up her bed, stores it away in the cupboard. Folds up her diagram and inserts it in her pack along with her Newman. No sound from upstairs. She steps onto the bottom slat of the ladder and listens. Nothing. (Creak of mill shaft.) She gingerly mounts two more slats and stretches to raise her eyes above the level of the upper floor. Nothing. The bed might be empty, but she can't be sure from this angle. Maybe he's in a hidden room, hanging upside down from a rafter.

She quietly descends, pulls on her boots, shrugs on her pack. Standing by the door, she scans the achingly beautiful space. She has left nothing behind. She steps out, latches the door, descends the stone steps. Circles around to the beach. There's an orange glow in the east. The sky is enormous, tessellated across its entire expanse with gray and silver clouds, breaking up. It's that time of dawn when the light makes everything shimmer, as though you can see individual water molecules jostling in the saturated air.

No fucking way is she going to remain within sight of those upper-floor windows. She walks west along the beach for half a mile, until the curve of the shore and some intervening bushes whose Linnaean names the old man surely knows put the mill out of sight. She steps across seaweed and driftwood onto the ice and walks straight out toward the open water.

Long ago in Astoria at bedtime when Mette wanted to read Wishner to her mother but her mother annoyingly wasn't in the mood, she (her mother) would annoyingly say that it was her turn, and she would describe some interminable lucid dream she'd had when she was a girl. Mette mostly tuned her out, but there was a set of recurring dreams about an island far in the north that were vivid enough, maybe "magical," that they stuck in Mette's head. There was a castle on the island, and a mage, and snow and sleds and dogs. In one of the dreams her mother rode with the mage down to the edge of the island and continued out across the frozen sea. At the edge of the ice she climbed out of the sled and looked out over the water, where a pod of whales was passing. One of the whales nudged up against the ice and her mother hugged it. That's the kind of romantic fluff her mother liked. It's deflating to think that she resolutely left her life behind and crossed the United States and then the Atlantic Ocean and somehow ended up in one of her mother's dreams.

She stands at the edge of the ice. If this piece under her cracked off, it would tilt and slide her in, like a burial at sea. If she couldn't climb back up, her decision would be made for her. She'd get colder and sleepier and happier, then she'd turn on her back and look up at the morning sky and her backpack would pull her under, trapping her arms, holding her against the bottom. Wishner and Newman would help. *Pumpkinseed excavated a simple burrow and failed to reappear from it in the spring.*

But the ice doesn't crack. And even though she's some seventy yards from shore, the water looks to be only about five feet deep. Of course she could just continue out another hundred or two hundred yards, getting colder, sleepier, happier, etc. Call to the old man, "Come on in, the water's fine!"

All her life she's assumed her personality came entirely from her father. But she recognizes something of herself in the old man. She and he share what one might call mental rigor. Or maybe one might call it a cold cast of mind. It occurs to Mette for the first time to have some sympathy for her mother, who has none of that coldness. It must be tough to be sandwiched between a father and a daughter both of whom are unfathomable.

The clouds have continued to break up and the light has strengthened so that the stars are now invisible and the clear parts of the sky are turning a bluish white. She looks across the bright mirror-plane of water, the moiré-like pattern of grays and mauves and pinks on the liquid surface fractally receding toward the molten horizon. As a programmer of visual effects for computer games, she is often struck by the beautifully designed and rendered detail of the world. She stands there for fifteen minutes, her mind more or less a blank, or maybe crammed so full of half-formed thoughts jostling each other that the cumulative result is white noise. Maybe this is her life passing in front of her eyes.

She stands some more.

In *Oops!*, this would be the moment when two options would appear on the screen, waiting for a mouse-click: (JUMP IN) (DON'T JUMP IN)

She stands some more.

She doesn't jump in.

She turns around. She had an inkling last night, when she regretted that she would never finish Newman. Goddamnit, the old man's idea about having a project. She walks back toward the shore. She has a feeling, though, that the real decision happened earlier, sometime during the bus or the plane rides. She gave up the idea without acknowledging it to herself. The blow to her trivial ego grew older and less interesting each day, while the great world kept renewing itself.

She picks her way back across the band of seaweed and driftwood, regains the beach. She turns to look back across the ice. In Seattle, when she wondered if she was play-acting, she felt self-disgust. But maybe she needed to play-act in order to discover how she really felt. Her mother would understand. She's also reminded of something her father once told her about his own father, this Vernon fellow. Vernon liked to say (her father said) that if you're ever unsure about a choice, the smart thing to do is flip a coin, because the moment the coin is in the air you know which way you want it to fall.

She walks back east along the shore. The sun is about to rise. She's hungry. Maybe the old man forgot to tell her to eat first, maybe she's confusing hunger for life with hunger for a french fry. As she approaches the mill, there's a moment when a sail catches sunlight on its tip at the top of its sweep, then thirty seconds later the whole face of the building is lit and across the ice and water the top edge of the sun blazes in her eye. She doesn't really want to talk to the old man, but she should at least say goodbye.

As she comes around the side of the mill he sticks his head out the door. "Breakfast is ready." He waves her triumphantly up the steps. Inside, there's fresh coffee, eggs, oatmeal, yogurt, biscuits, butter, cheese. The table is set for two.

Of course he would win either way. If she came back, she'd be amazed at his foreknowledge, and if she didn't, who would know? Lila would never tell.

He stands beside her, beaming as though he gives a shit whether she lives or dies, as though by "predicting" her survival he somehow conjured it, and now her life is his. She turns on her heel. "Goodbye, old man." She goes back down the stairs and keeps on along the path through the marsh.

He calls after her, "I called from the depot last night when I went to buy coffee. I left a message for your mother. She's probably on her way here. You don't want her to travel all this way for nothing, do you?" Mette keeps walking. He calls again, "Don't prove all the people right who say that those who contemplate suicide are selfish!" But his voice is already fainter.

New cloudbanks move in as she crosses the island, and by the time she arrives at the landing, the sun is gone. So is the morning ferry, which is fifty yards from the slip and chugging in the wrong direction. The afternoon ferry doesn't leave for seven hours. The little depot, which Mette would call a convenience store, opens at 9:00 a.m. In addition to basic supplies and a wide array of candy, it serves simple hot-food items, including french fries. Mette polishes off a greasy basketful, then tries the soft-serve ice cream. Reads Newman and Wishner at one of the two Formica-topped tables. She keeps expecting to look up and see the old man coming down the road waving a wand at her. But presumably he's the type who rejects you so fast after you reject him that later nobody can remember the order.

If her mother's on the way, she probably sent a text, but Mette hasn't bothered to download the app that would let her access it. Or maybe she's trying to sneak up on her, worried she'll move farther off if she sees the butterfly net. There always has to be so much drama.

She gets on the 3:30 ferry with the one other passenger—could it be the same woman?—and stands in the back and watches the island recede. She would like to put the old man out of her thoughts, but is finding it difficult. It annoys her that for all his cheap tricks to impress her, he actually did impress her. Still, he will fade, since she has no intention of ever seeing him again. Alex will be harder.

The ferry arrives at the quaint half-timbered town at 4:30. The train station is a fifteen-minute walk away, and there's a train back to Copenhagen at 5:02. Mette buys a ticket at the kiosk. There are only two platforms.

Mette stands on one of them, and at 4:55, a train from Copenhagen stops along the other. After a few moments of humming and hissing, it slides to the left like a piece of stage scenery, and behind it she sees, among the crowd of dispersing passengers, a tall thin man and a short curvy woman standing together, the man looking lost, the woman getting her bearings. Her parents.

July 4, 2016

Data Set: Echo

To S. W. on her birthday—left off the margin
of a yearbook twenty-two years ago

My father used to go out into the yard at night to watch Echo
    cross the sky.
The year was 1960.
I was a baby inside the house, with my mother.
My mother was the one who had wanted to be an astronomer.

. . .

Echo was the world's first communications satellite.
It was a balloon of aluminum-coated Mylar, 100 feet in
    diameter.
It was beautiful, looking like a perfect sphere of solid silver.
On August 12, 1960, a microwave transmission from the Jet
    Propulsion Laboratory in Pasadena, California, was bounced

off Echo and successfully received at the Bell Labs horn
   antenna in Holmdel, New Jersey.
The United States wanted to change international law to allow
   satellites, unlike airplanes, to fly over foreign countries.
Highlighting a non-military purpose for satellites would help
   establish this new legal right.
Echo transmitted the first ever live voice communication by
   satellite, a message from President Eisenhower: "This is one
   more significant step in the United States' program of space
   research and exploration being carried forward for peaceful
   purposes."
Echo provided the United States with more-accurate
   astronomical reference points.
This improved our military's ability to target Moscow with
   ICBMs.
My father hated the military.

.   .   .

The next-generation communications satellite, Telstar 1, was
   put in orbit in 1962.
Because the Telstar satellites required larger ground antennae,
   the Holmdel Horn Antenna was out of a job.
In 1964, two Bell Labs scientists began to use it as a radio
   telescope.
Arno Penzias studied intergalactic radio sources and Robert
   Wilson studied radio sources from within the Milky Way.
Since Penzias and Wilson were trying to analyze extremely
   weak signals, they were bothered by background noise.
Their tests showed that the noise did not come from New
   York City.

Nor was it thermal radiation from the ground.

Because it didn't vary with the seasons, and appeared to be
    uniform in all directions, Penzias and Wilson thought it
    must be generated by the telescope itself.

A pair of pigeons was nesting in the telescope.

Pigeon shit is dielectric.

Penzias and Wilson captured the pigeons, relocated them
    thirty miles away, and scraped the shit out of the telescope.

Pigeons are pigeons: they have a homing instinct.

The mating pair came back and nested in the telescope again.

Penzias and Wilson took a shotgun and killed the pigeons.

Years later, Penzias remembered that it was Wilson's decision
    to shoot the pigeons.

Wilson remembered that it was Penzias's decision.

Scientists are human.

. . .

Getting rid of the pigeons failed to get rid of the background
    radio noise.

This noise had an equivalent temperature of approximately
    three degrees above absolute zero.

It was driving Penzias and Wilson crazy.

Penzias related his troubles to a friend.

This friend had read a preprint paper from a Big Bang theorist
    named Jim Peebles.

The Big Bang theory had not yet been widely accepted, partly
    because no one knew how to test for it.

Peebles suggested in his paper that one way to test for it would
    be to look for the radiation remaining from the original
    explosion.

This radiation would emanate from all directions and, after
13.7 billion years of redshifting, it would have an equivalent
temperature of approximately three degrees above absolute
zero.

Peebles and his colleagues were planning to set up an
experiment to test this theory.

Penzias called Peebles and said, "Don't bother."

In 1978, Penzias and Wilson were awarded the Nobel Prize in
Physics for their discovery of the Cosmic Microwave
Background Radiation.

. . .

Pigeons mate for life, and so, alas, did my parents.

I am my parents' son.

But echoes can rebound in unexpected ways.

At this moment, every cubic centimeter of space in the
universe has approximately three hundred photons passing
through it that are a remnant of the Big Bang.

A poet might call this the leftover cry of the universe being
born.

In 1965, when my mother was stuck in the house with me,
and my father was out in the yard hoping to see Telstar 2
fly over, I sometimes looked at the static on the TV screen
when it was tuned to a dead channel.

Approximately 1 percent of that static was the echo of the
birth of the universe, dancing in front of my eyes in the
form of tiny silver spheres.

If only I had known.

Instead, I turned the dial to watch *Lost in Space*.

August 21, 2017

On the interstate out of St. Louis, Saskia reads laughing the electronic message board set up on the verge. "Solar Eclipse Today. No Photographing While Driving."

"You'd think that would be obvious," he says.

"That's why it's funny." Her mission, should she choose to accept it: train him to get a joke faster. They're heading for the town of St. Clair. They had a number of choices, but the forecast called for clouds around the time of the eclipse and St. Clair promised luck. "You don't believe in luck," she said, when he suggested it.

"I don't, but there's a great story about Niels Bohr, or maybe it was Freeman Dyson—"

"The horseshoe. You've already told me that one."

"It's a great story."

"It is." She could tell he was dying to tell it again, but he's getting better about that. Now she's looking up the eponymous saint on her phone. (He's driving. Being a passenger still makes him nervous. Her mission, should she choose . . .) "Saint Clare of Assisi," she announces. "Hm, different spelling. Maybe a French-English thing." She skims. "Yeah, this is the right gal . . . Looks like she first had the idea of devoting herself to Christ right around the time her parents wanted her to marry."

"A familiar theme."

"Another fun fact, she's the patron saint of television."

He's silent for several seconds. Then he says, "We can change the focus to a soft blur, or sharpen it to crystal clarity."

The Outer Limits."

"Saint Clare, clarity—get it?"

"I got it."

"That show scared the crap out of me when I was a kid."

"You're kidding."

"Nope."

In St. Clair, the service station next to the interstate is packed. A farmer is hawking watermelons for five dollars apiece off a flatbed truck. It's 10:30 a.m., ninety degrees. In the town center locals have set up booths in their front yards and are selling lemonade, baked goods, balloons, ice cream, eclipse glasses. The streets are packed with heat-stunned pedestrians trying to figure out how to have fun. "This is great," Saskia says. "Let's stop for a few minutes."

A church is charging $25 for ECLIPSE PARKING in its lot. He makes a puzzled comment, then parks on the other side of the street for free. Saskia wanders around soaking up the atmosphere. "Eclipse cookies!"

"Aren't those just half moon cookies?"

"Read the sign, dummy."

Saskia talks to a couple of people and finds out that the town council voted to hold a three-day music festival to take advantage of their position in the path of totality. Now they're hoping to repeat the festival every year. "Good luck with that," Mark says to them.

"Oh, I don't know," Saskia says, as they walk away, "traditions have to start somehow."

"This town is in the middle of nowhere."

"Says the man who lives in Ithaca, New York."

"From the vantage point of New York City I guess all towns look alike."

"From those giddy heights, yes."

They get back in the car and head east out of town. Mark wants to be in a place where they won't be distracted by other people. "Eclipse chasers like to cluster together and compare telescopes and boast about how many eclipses they've seen. They hoot and holler at the moment of totality as though it's a show staged solely for their enjoyment."

"Like the money shot in a porno film," she says.

He blushes. "I guess so."

"Oh man! It barely fits!"

"Please, stop. Eclipses are wonderful."

"Sorry."

He google-viewed the area ahead of time and found a fire station along a county road eight miles east of St. Clair that had a paved open area on the off-road side. Saskia is back on her phone. "The media is calling this The Great American Eclipse."

He makes an unhappy sound. "That's the kind of appropriation I'm talking about."

"We could sell hats. Make the Eclipse Great Again. It would be a MEGA-eclipse."

A silence follows. References to Trump's election still tend to kill conversation. Then he says, "I'm taking the long view. In a million years, the continents will barely have budged and life will have started diversifying again."

"One generation passes away and another generation comes, but the earth abides forever."

"Isn't that George R. Stewart?"

"It might be, if he was one of the kings of Israel. It's from Ecclesiastes."

"Another thing I've never read."

"You should. It's Epictetus before Epictetus."

"My next assignment."

"You liked Epictetus."

"I didn't say I didn't. I like assignments. Here we are." He turns into the access area alongside the station and gets out to ask permission from the volunteer firefighters on duty. Climbs back in. "They say no problem, we should park in the gravel lot on the other side."

They leave the windows wide open so the seats won't melt, carry knapsacks with water and lunch toward the back of the concrete-block building. As they round the corner, three young people setting up a telescope come into view. Mark hesitates for a fraction of a second, then continues toward them. It turns out the two men were college roommates six years ago, while the woman is a girlfriend of one of them. They rendezvoused in Chicago last night and got up at five this morning to drive down. One roommate majored in economics, the other in communications. The woman is a photographer. The men do most of the talking, about their roomie days, their corporate jobs, their ideas, their ambitions, while Saskia teases out from the woman that an exhibit of her photography just opened at a prestigious gallery in New York City. "Wow," she says, "what's your name?" She googles it. The woman's a young star.

The sky is mostly clear, but Mark must have mentioned the possibility of clouds, because one of the young men says, "I've heard the sky often clears right before an eclipse."

"Why would it do that?" Mark asks.

"Something to do with the air cooling."

"If anything, that would have the opposite effect."

"That's right," the other young man chimes in, "cool air can't hold as much moisture as warm air."

"It's not a question of holding moisture," Mark says, "it has to do with the kinetic energy of the water molecules—"

Saskia wanders off before the two young men decide to beat Mark to death. The eclipse doesn't begin for another twenty minutes, and then it takes ninety minutes to reach totality, so she's got plenty of time. She walks to the edge of the paved area and continues across a grassy field until she comes to a line of trees. Turns to look back. She's standing at the higher end of a long rise in the terrain, so she can see two or three miles westward. Bright green fields and darker woods, low hills. Ferociously hot haze. Hurry up, Moon, and show this fucking sun a thing or two.

Her eye lingers on Mark a hundred yards away, talking to the men. Yes, he's twelve years older, and there's still a part of her that's slightly embarrassed by that. But it's a free fucking country, right? It works well for her that they live 230 miles apart. They've been seeing each other every second weekend for about a year now, alternating between Ithaca and New York. He still works all the time, but let's face it, she does, too. And Mette doesn't seem to mind his occasional intrusions. Saskia was surprised at first, but probably shouldn't have been. They invited Mette to come with them to see the eclipse, but she declined. "I'd just be in the way of the two lovebirds," she hooted. That word is a source of never-failing mirth to her.

The glare out here is ridiculous. Saskia wanders back to hunker down in the narrow strip of shade at the bottom of the fire station's rear wall. The young men announce that the eclipse has begun. The three young people are taking turns looking through the telescope and Mark is holding a rectangle of welder's glass in front of his eyes. He gave Saskia a piece to call her own, so she leaves the shade to look up. Sure enough, in the ghostly pale image in the midnight window, there's a neat round bite in the sun's side. What perfect teeth the Moon has! Eat everything on your plate, little Moon!

She sits back in the shade and after a few minutes Mark joins her. "It's good of you to come with me for this," he says.

"Not at all. I've always wanted to see a solar eclipse."

"Still, aren't rehearsals starting tomorrow?"

"I'll be there in time." She's flying back to New York City tonight. He's taking a train to Syracuse. She takes hold of his hand. (She has always loved his hands.) "We're coming up on our first-year anniversary."

"Unless it's our twenty-third," he says.

"Hm. Let me think about that. I have to decide which is less depressing."

He looks pained. "Why depressing?"

"I don't mean that. I mean—" She has no idea what she means. After a moment she says, "It's a strange path, is all. But it's not like I value conventional paths."

He waits for her to go on. One advantage of his halting conversational style is this ability to wait. She often gets the sense he would wait for her forever.

What she is thinking: it is her nature to be ambivalent, and it is his to be ardently attached. This worries her. She fears she will hurt him. Of course she can't say that. (If *he* were thinking it, he would ineptly say it. But he wouldn't think it.) She wonders if her comment sprang from a regret for lost time. If so, it's mainly regret that she's getting older. Maybe regret that their twelve-year age difference doesn't mean anything, now that she's no spring chicken. Regret that no fellow old codger will look at them in a restaurant and grossly give Mark the thumbs-up for scoring such a young hottie.

She considers the possibility that, as she's getting older, she values sexiness less. Sexiness always has an element of mystery, and there's nothing mysterious about him. Maybe what she values now is crystal clarity, rather than the soft blur of romance. She's grown impatient with mating games. *Spit it out! Time's a wastin'!* She trusts completely that he will always tell her whatever he's thinking, that he will never lie to her. It makes her feel safe. Someone might say—maybe she would say it herself—that that's what a father figure does. But she would like to think that that's also what a partner should do. There's something so unsexy about it, it's kind of kinky.

She says, "I've wondered if Mette, when she took off like that, had an ulterior motive without being aware of it. You know, the heart has its reasons, which Reason knows not."

"Isn't that Pascal?"

"Yeah, you know him because he was a mathematician."

"You're probably right."

"Anyway, speaking of Mette's reasons, you can pick your movie version. Would you rather be Brian Keith or Dennis Quaid?"

"I have no idea what you're talking about."

"ILYGTFY."

"Still lost."

"I'll Let You Google That For Yourself."

"Hey, Professor," one of the young men calls. "How long did you say totality will be?"

"Two minutes, thirty-seven seconds."

"Why does it vary?"

He gets up and goes to them, happy as a clam. She stays where she is. The heat seems slightly less intense, but not enough yet. She thinks ahead to the rehearsals for *Joan, Maid*, which (egad! fuck!) she is indeed directing at the SoHo theater whose artistic director she calmly convinced, or maybe cajoled, stalked, and overwhelmed. In the movies, long-gestating artistic endeavors by the protagonist are always rewarded. The excruciatingly squeezed-out first novel becomes a best seller, the edgy smartphone movie made on a shoestring conquers Sundance. Whereas in this sublunary world she's still not sure whether her play is any good, and even if it's good, critics may dislike it for capricious or malicious reasons, and even if critics like it, it will probably not run long, nor make any money, as few plays do. The fact is, artistic careers are an uncertain trudge, with no discernible narrative arc.

. . .

THE BRIGHT LIGHT is fractionally lessening. One of the young men says, "Listen, you can hear crickets. They're getting fooled by the eclipse."

"Those are cicadas," Mark says. For the umpteenth time he marvels at all the simple things people don't notice. Cicadas sound nothing like crickets. These fellows remind him of many of his students nowadays: polite, breezy, uncaringly ignorant of their ignorance. But that's yet another old-fart thought, so he banishes it and peers again through the welder's glass. The sun now looks like a crescent moon. Approximately twenty minutes to go.

He adores solar eclipses. He spoke unkindly of eclipse chasers to Saskia this morning, but he's one, too. He has unblushingly finagled half a dozen free rides on ocean eclipse cruises as the eminent lecturer. His only difference from most other chasers is his desire to be alone when the event happens. To hoard it all to himself, he supposes. He glances briefly at Saskia, then returns to the crescent. Well, no, now he's being unfair to himself. His desire to be alone at important phenomenological moments arises, he's pretty sure, from the fact that he can't concentrate properly on external events when he's in close proximity with another person. This is especially true when the person in question is someone he cares about. He hopes Saskia understands that. When he's near her, most of his thoughts revolve around her.

It pains him that his mother died with a bad opinion of Saskia. "I'll never understand what's wrong with that woman," was the way she invariably phrased it. How could anyone not love her Marky-lark? He's thankful that his mother loved him, but her doting locked out Susan, and it might have also locked out Saskia, even if she and Mark had become a couple twenty-three years ago. How could anyone be good enough for her Marky-lark? His mother tended to see everything as absolutes of light and dark.

As far as he knows, she never got to witness a total eclipse. He remembers being ten, standing on the back porch of the Massachusetts house with a pinhole camera made out of two sheets of paper. It was the eclipse of March 7, 1970, and his family could have experienced totality if they had only driven the ninety miles to Woods Hole and taken the ferry to Nantucket. But he can easily imagine his father expressing horror at the thought of all those cars backed up at the Sagamore Bridge, with another traffic jam waiting outside the gates of the Steamship Authority. "It'll be the biggest mess you ever saw," he would have said, and that would have ended discussion. So they stayed in Lexington and he and his parents—who knows where Susan was—stood on the back porch with their punctured papers, and although the eclipse at that location was 96.5 percent of totality, Mark was astonished, and crushingly disappointed, at how little difference it made in the general light level. Equivalent to a storm cloud passing. Looking back, he wonders whether, or how much, his mother shared his disappointment. Whenever anything related to astronomy came up, she always said she was glad she had chosen motherhood over a career. As a kid, he swallowed that hook, line, and sinker.

By viewing eclipses, one can, in a way, travel back in time, since nearly identical eclipses happen every eighteen years, eleven days, and eight hours. He'll have a chance to view the 1970 eclipse properly on April 8, 2024. The path of totality, looking virtually the same in the shape it will inscribe on the Earth's surface, will have shifted slightly to the west, so instead of driving to Nantucket, he and Saskia will be able to see it in western New York. He doesn't want to curse the luck that he doesn't believe in, but he can't help imagining that they will still be together. He wishes his mother could be there, partly to see the eclipse that she missed, and partly to give her a chance to change her opinion about Saskia. As an adult he became his family's failed peacemaker, and he realizes he's still trying to carry out that mission, even though everyone else in his family is dead.

Ten more minutes. There was a contrail in the sky that was worrying him, but it has drifted south. The sky around the sun is completely clear. This eclipse is going to be a beauty. Saskia's first! Humans are so fortunate to have such a large moon. As is all life on Earth, probably— such an unusually massive satellite has prevented the Earth from under- going occasional chaotic motion in the tilt of its axis. A plausible theory proposes that complex life might not have arisen if the seasons had been as unstable as they would have been without the Moon. And for hu- mans, who love to look skyward and dream—and surely their dreaming gave birth to astronomy—there's the sheer coincidence that, while the Sun's diameter is 400 times that of the Moon, the Moon is 400 times closer to Earth. Thus this nearly perfect alignment. What are the chances? The Mediocrity Principle goes out the window again.

It won't last very long, cosmically speaking. The Moon is moving away from Earth about four centimeters each year, so in 600 million years, there will be no more total eclipses. Solar radiation will have increased by 5 percent, leading to an increase in global mean temperature of ten de- grees Celsius. There's no way to predict greenhouse warming from this remove, but there's a good chance life will have retreated to the oceans by then. If not, then probably during the next 200 or 300 million years. Complex life on Earth is about halfway through its allotted span. What, too, are the chances that his life would occur at this halfway point?

At that thought, all of a sudden, just as it happened to him last year when he was driving to the recycling center, his awareness suddenly blooms. An elation, an inflation—something firing ecstatically in the brain. He feels, really *feels*, that he is alive on this Earth, that he is standing at a fulcrum. This place is important, this moment is precious, something momentous is about to happen. One order will collapse and another, pos- sibly a better, will arise. He feels as if he can actually sense the stretch of billions of years. Life on Earth has a new chance every few million years. It has dozens more chances to get it right. His nanosecond life means nothing, yet he feels incredibly lucky to be alive.

He looks at Saskia, sitting in the shade. She stands up and comes to him. She kisses him. "I know you want to be by yourself for totality. There's a great view from the far end of the field. You should go there." She points.

"Do you want to come with me?"

"No, it's fine. Go on."

He gives her a grateful glance and squeezes her hand. "Remember not to look with the naked eye until—"

"I remember."

SHE WATCHES HIM execute his little-boy wave in the direction of the young people and start off, periodically walking backward with his head up and the slot-shaped welder's glass glued to his eyes. He looks like Gort, in *The Day the Earth Stood Still.*

She waits a few seconds, then also moves away from the young people, to the point where the pavement ends and the field begins. The darkness is rising faster. She looks through the glass and sees that the Moon is now covering almost all of the sun. She thinks of the Fenris Wolf and Ragnarok.

"Here it comes!" one of the young men calls out.

Saskia looks to east and west, north and south, to the ground at her feet. The light is failing uncannily, like a rheostat being turned down. It's nothing like a sunset. The Moon's shadow is approaching at 1500 miles per hour. Mark told her that if you stand at a high enough vantage point you can see the edge of the darkness racing toward you. It's thrilling to feel how huge the Moon is, how fast she moves. You can almost imagine a roar.

Through the welder's rectangle she sees the thinnest sliver, then a single strand of hair, then nothing. She takes away the dark glass and looks face to face. The total eclipse is a furiously glaring eyeball of deepest black, something sinister and evil. Or maybe it's a wondrous black hole, shining at the edges with Hawking radiation.

She has two minutes. She gazes at the crystalized ebony vegetation all around, at the weird sky of glistening iron, at the black hole she has journeyed millions of miles to see. She is standing on an alien world, where the native intelligent life form is not self-destructive, where an insignificant creature such as herself has the luxury to worry only about her art and her loved ones.

Acknowledgments

My thanks to Sarah Chalfant and Paul Slovak, for their support through the dry years. Presumably it's a cognitive bias, but I'm convinced I have the best agent and the best editor in this solar system. Also thanks to Elizabeth Kim and Madeleine Moss, for multiple readings of the manuscript and invaluable advice. And to two old friends, Paul Cody and J. Robert Lennon, for additional feedback, plus a shout-out to the latter for wisely suggesting a different chapter order.